THE LEGEND OF LUKE

A Tale of Redwall

Click onto the Redwall website – and
discover more about the legendary world of
Redwall and it's creator, Brian Jacques!
http://www.redwall.org

BRIAN JACQUES

❖

THE LEGEND
OF LUKE

A Tale of Redwall

Illustrated by Fangorn

**RED
FOX**

To the memory of Tony Jacques

The Legend of Luke

A RED FOX BOOK 1 86230331 2

First published in Great Britain by Hutchinson,
an imprint of Random House Children's Books

Hutchinson edition published 1999
Red Fox edition published 2000

Text © The Redwall Abbey Company Ltd 1999
Illustrations © Fangorn 1999
Map Illustrations © Andrew Warrington 1999

The right of The Redwall Abbey Company Ltd and Fangorn
to be identified as the author and illustrator of this work
has been asserted in accordance with
the Copyright, Designs and Patents Act 1988.

Papers used by Random House Children's Books are natural,
recyclable products made from wood grown in sustainable forests.
The manufacturing processes conform to the
environmental regulations of the country of origin.

Red Fox Books are published by Random House Children's Books,
61–63 Uxbridge Road, London W5 5SA,
a division of The Random House Group Ltd,
in Australia by Random House Australia (Pty) Ltd,
20 Alfred Street, Milsons Point, Sydney, NSW 2061, Australia,
in New Zealand by Random House New Zealand Ltd,
18 Poland Road, Glenfield, Auckland 10, New Zealand,
and in South Africa by Random House (Pty) Ltd,
Endulini, 5A Jubilee Road, Parktown 2193, South Africa

THE RANDOM HOUSE GROUP Limited Reg. No. 954009
www.randomhouse.co.uk

A CIP catalogue record for this book is available from the British Library.

Printed and bound in Great Britain by
Bookmarque Ltd, Croydon, Surrey

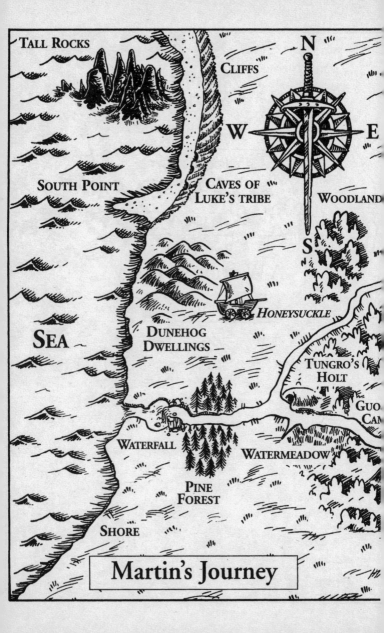

TALL ROCKS

CLIFFS

SOUTH POINT

CAVES OF
LUKE'S TRIBE

WOODLAND

Honeysuckle

SEA

DUNEHOG
DWELLINGS

TUNGRO'S
HOLT

GUO
CAM

WATERFALL

WATERMEADOW

PINE
FOREST

SHORE

Martin's Journey

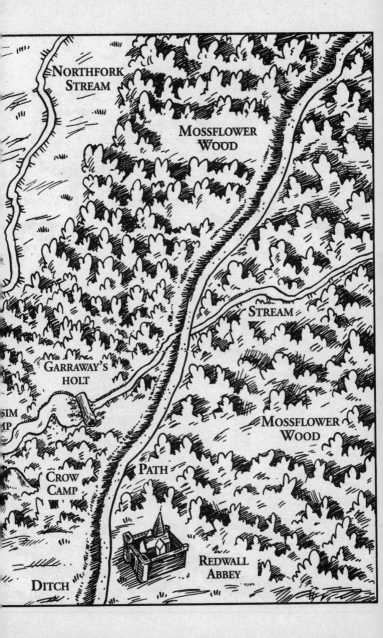

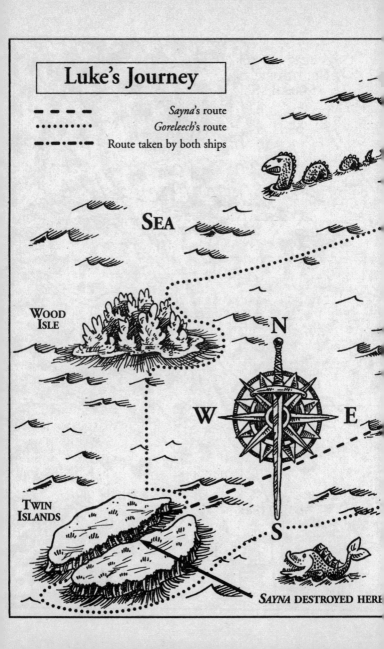

Luke's Journey

- – – – – *Sayna*'s route
- ·············· *Goreleech*'s route
- –·–·–·–·– Route taken by both ships

SEA

WOOD
ISLE

N

W E

S

TWIN
ISLANDS

SAYNA DESTROYED HERE

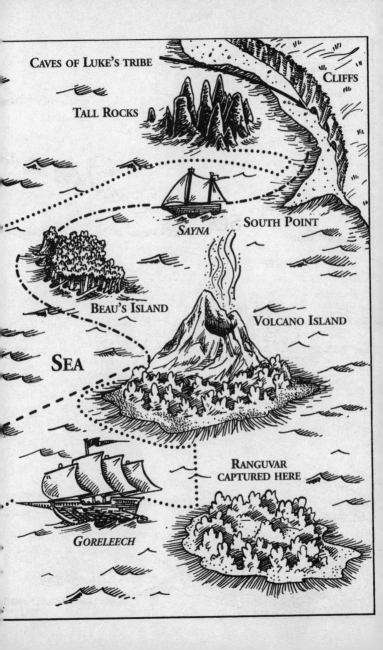

The young must grow old,
Whilst old ones grow older,
And cowards will shrink,
As the bold grow bolder.
Courage may blossom in quiet hearts,
For who can tell where bravery starts?
Truth is a song, oft lying unsung,
Some mother bird, protecting her young,
Those who lay down their lives for friends,
The echo rolls onward, it seldom ends.
Who never turned and ran, but stayed?
This is a warrior born, not made!
Living in peace, aye many a season,
Calm in life and sound in reason,
'Til evil arrives, a wicked horde,
Driving a warrior to pick up his sword,
The challenger rings then, straight and fair,
Justice is with us, beware. Beware!

BOOK ONE

Martin

1

Summer's first morn was like no other!

Trimp the roving hedgehog wandered through the woodlands like one in a dream, drinking in the beauty of Mossflower Country, so different from the cold north-land coast whence she had travelled. Dew was still upon each leaf, delicate mist tendrils wreathed into greengold sun shafts 'twixt mighty oak, slender rowan and stately elm. Birds trilled sweetly, butterflies fluttered silently, bees hummed busily over flowers, ferns and lichen-clad rocks. Trimp's heart felt as light as the haversack on her back. She ignored hunger, feasting her senses on the glory of her surroundings and the delight of the new season. Swinging her ash stave jauntily, she skipped a little jig and broke out into song.

'You lark on high,
O minstrel of the sky,
Sing out! Sing out!
Now sing you joyously,
To Mother Nature and her earth,
This is the golden summer's birth,
A wondrous sight to see!
Hail, fine tall trees,

Your leaves dance on the breeze,
Rejoice! Rejoice!
And sway so gracefully,
You'll feel your blossom soon give way,
To ripened fruit some sunny day,
Oh please save some for me!
Sing out! Rejoice!
Let all who have a voice,
Call out so sweet and happily,
O'er woodland vale and grassy lea,
Good day my friend to thee!'

As Trimp ended her song a voice hailed her.

'An' good day to thee too, pretty one!'

She halted at the edge of a ditch. Two sturdy old hedge-hogs stood on a path at the other edge, grinning cheerfully. They were alike as peas in a pod. One of them called to her, 'We'll 'elp you across yon ditch, missie. Stay there!'

Taking a few paces back, Trimp winked cheekily at the pair. 'Nay, you stay there. I'll help myself!'

With a short run and a hop she dug the long ash stave in the bank and pole-vaulted neatly across. Both hedge-hogs wriggled furiously until their backspikes rattled, an ancient hog form of applause. Trimp immediately took a liking to the jolly pair. She stood directly in front of them and lowered her head formally, and they did likewise until all three creatures' headspikes touched in the traditional greeting of their species. Introductions were made.

'Good sirs, I'm called Trimp the Rover.'

'Marm, I'm called Ferdy an' that fat 'un's my brother Coggs, both of Redwall Abbey.'

Coggs snorted, pointing to Ferdy's ample stomach. 'I ain't as fat as ole Ferdy, am I, miz Trimp?'

She giggled. 'You're as tubby as one another.'

Ferdy and Coggs exchanged wry glances.

'She's pretty all right, pretty impudent!'

'Aye, truthful an' pitiless, jus' like all the pretty 'uns!'

'She's thin, though. D'ye think she could 'elp pull a log?'

'Miz Trimp ain't thin, she's slender – but strong, I'll wager, the way she leaped yon ditch. She can pull logs.'

Trimp pursed her lips shrewdly. 'Of course I can pull logs. I could tow a log with both of you sitting atop of it, if I'd a mind to. But I'm feeling very slender today, owing to the fact that I've an empty haversack on my back. So, towing logs means payment in food.'

Ferdy and Coggs exchanged more wry glances.

'Miz Trimp knows wot she wants, don't she!'

'Ho, she certainly does, mate. That 'og ain't soft as moss nor green as the grass. We'll 'ave to feed 'er.'

'Only when we gets back to Redwall, though. Then she can tuck into vittles 'til she's like two of us'n's put t'gether. So, is it a bargain, marm?'

Trimp banged her stave butt down on the path decisively. 'Done! Lead me to your log, friends.'

It was not a very big log, more like a heavy sycamore limb. They attached ropes and pulled, and the wood slid easily along the dewy grass of the pathside. Trimp was full of questions for Ferdy and Coggs.

'What is this Redwall place and how far off is it?'

'Hah, missie, you won't say that someday. Anybeast'll be able to see it from a good league off. Right, Coggs?'

'Right, Ferdy. When we gets round this bend in the path, beyond that big grove of oaks, then you'll see it, Trimp. 'Tis goin' to be a great Abbey, but it ain't properly built yet. Martin reckons three more seasons should see the main Abbey buildin' showin' its spire top.'

Trimp suddenly stopped pulling and smote her forehead with an open paw, as if she had just remembered something. 'Of course! I've heard other travellers mention the great redstone building in Mossflower. You say there's a Martin there. Is he a mouse, son of Luke the Warrior?'

Ferdy shrugged and beckoned her to keep pulling. 'Oh, he's a warrior sure enough, missie. As to his father, I think somebeast mentioned his name was Luke, eh, Coggs?'

Coggs switched the rope to his other shoulder. 'Could be, mate. Nobeast knows much about our Martin – he keeps his past fairly quiet. Mark my words, though, Trimp, the noblest fighter that ever wielded a sword is Martin the Warrior – he fears nothin' an' battles like tenbeasts. Hoho, lookee there, marm, that's Redwall Abbey. See!'

Trimp's eyes grew wide with wonder. Never had she seen anything built on such a grand scale, even though it was still incomplete. The Abbey reared out of the forest on the path's east side, fashioned from mighty blocks of red sandstone. There was a high perimeter wall with battlements and a broad walkway behind them, and visible above this outer wall the main building stood two-thirds finished. Buttresses, arches and columns could be seen between the wooden scaffolding. Mice, moles, squirrels, otters, hedgehogs and voles laboured busily, hauling, laying, chipping, carving and carrying, all over the structure. Ferdy and Coggs chuckled at Trimp's astonishment.

'Hohoho. Shows wot honest 'ardworkin' woodlanders can do when they puts their paws t'work, eh, miss?'

'Aye, buildin' Redwall Abbey, a place o' safety an' cheer for goodbeasts to live in, with walls that'd stand the worst any vermin foes could think of!'

Trimp enjoyed the pride in her friends' faces as they spoke of their home. She cocked her head as a hollow booming sound echoed out.

'What's that noise? Are they doing something special?'

Coggs winked at her and patted his stomach. 'That's the call for lunch. We're just in time!'

8

The three hedgehogs pulled their log through the impressively solid wallgates, which were opened for them by a mole. He tugged his snout, saying in quaint molespeech, 'Hurr, gudd day to ee. Boi okey, mates, ee likkle 'ogmaid be purtier'n both of you 'uns. 'Ow be you'm called, miz?'

Trimp shook the formidable digging claw of the twinkle-eyed mole heartily. 'I'm Trimp, sir, ten times hungrier than I'm pretty.'

A deep smile crinkled the mole's velvety face. 'Gurtly pleasured to meet ee, miz Trimp. Oi'm ee Foremole yurrabouts. If'n ee be 'ungered then fear not, us'n's can vittle ee up to yore spoikeytips. Hurrhurrhurr!'

Leaving the log by the gatehouse wall, the three hedgehogs followed the Foremole across broad lawns to the pond, where scores of Redwallers were washing their paws before lunch. Trimp joined them, while Ferdy pointed out various individuals.

'That 'un swimmin' about is Skipper of Otters, a chieftain. Pretty mousewife by the reeds is Columbine, jolly-lookin' beast with 'er is Gonff, Prince of Mousethieves, an' the liddle 'un is their son Baby Gonflet. Dinny Foremole you already know.'

The hollow booming sounded out again, and this time Trimp saw that it was made by a squirrel beating on a hollowed section of tree trunk with two wooden batons. Ferdy nudged her. 'That's Lady Amber, our Squirrelqueen. Come on, young 'un, off to the Council afore you sit down to eat.'

Trimp followed Ferdy and Coggs to the orchard, where tables and benches were laid in an open square. Ferdy bade her stand back until all were seated. The travelling hogmaid could not wrench her eyes from the food – it was like being at the centre of a delicious dream. Cauldrons of fresh vegetable soup steamed savoury aromas around new oven-baked bread shaped into farls, batches and loaves. Cheeses, ranging from deep yellow to

9

pale cream and studded with nuts, celery and herbs, were placed between heaped trays of woodland salads. Small tarts showed the rich hues of damson, apple, blackberry and greengage through their pastry-latticed tops. Jugs and pitchers of ale, fruit cordial and cold mint tea were being brought to the tables by servers. Trimp held her kerchief politely to her mouth, lest anybeast see it watering. Ferdy tugged her tunic hem and whispered, 'Come on, missie, don't be afeared. Nobody will eat ye!' He led her round to the table nearest to the Abbey.

A huge, ancient badger, bent with the weight of many seasons, gazed at her with kind brown eyes and nodded. 'Welcome to Redwall Abbey, little one. I am Bella of Brockhall. You look as if you have travelled far.'

Trimp curtsied deeply. She liked Bella on first sight.

'Marm, I am Trimp the Rover, so travelling is my business. Since late winter I have been walking from the northlands.'

'Fourth clans? Did she say fourth clans?'

Next to Bella, the tiniest, oldest, frailest mouse Trimp had ever seen was sitting in a small cushioned chair, wrapped in a thick warm shawl. The mouse sitting on the old one's other side leaned close to her and spoke loudly.

'Northlands, Abbess Germaine. Our guest has walked all the way here from the northlands!'

He turned, smiling, to Trimp. The hogmaid warmed immediately to the sturdy beast, his strong features and friendly tone.

''Tis fitting to have one so pretty to grace our table as guest on summer's first day. I'm called Martin.'

The mouse named Gonff, seated close by with his wife and babe, winked at Trimp and called out, 'Aye, matey, an' he's never called late to table!'

Martin smiled at his friend and closest ally. 'Hah! Look who's talking. The greatest grubsnatcher ever to lift a ladle!'

Gonff pointed at himself innocently. 'Who me? I hardly

10

ever touch food, matey. A crust an' a beaker o' water's good enough for me!'

His wife Columbine adopted an expression of mock surprise. 'Lackaday, it must be the birds eating all those pies an' pasties I'm forever baking. What d'you think, Gonflet?'

Baby Gonflet chuckled uproariously. 'It's me'n'daddy, we pincha pies'n'pattees offa windersill when they be's gudd'n'ot, us eatem all up, yumyum!'

Gonff covered his baby son's mouth amid general laughter. 'It was his idea, Columbine. He's been leadin' me astray!'

Trimp took her seat amid the happy Redwallers. Old Abbess Germaine waited until Bella brought order to the assembly by tapping a spoon on the tabletop. Heads bowed whilst the ancient mouse recited grace in a quavery voice.

'May good fortune never cease,
Where we build and till the soil,
Mother Nature grant us peace,
And reward us for our toil.

Summer's come now life is sweet,
Food is here for one and all,
In good friendship let us eat,
As one family at Redwall.'

Bella served Trimp with soup, Martin passed the bread and cheese, Columbine piled a platter with salad for her and the charming squirrel called Lady Amber topped up her beaker with fruit cordial. Trimp went at it with the best. Dinny the Foremole shielded his mouth with a paw, whispering to the Skipper of Otters.

'Hurr hurr, dearie me, oi never afore see'd nobeast tuck into ee vittles loik miz Trimp. Zurr Gonff be eatin' loik ee buttyfly alongsoid o' that young 'un!'

11

Gonff the Mousethief wrinkled his nose at the mole. 'I heard that, matey. Shove that cheese this way an' I'll show ye what a dainty eater I am. Hoi, Gonflet, get yore spoon out o' my soup, you liddle bandit!'

Columbine smiled sweetly at Trimp. 'Like father, like son, I always say.'

After lunch Trimp volunteered to help Martin and his friends hoist a roofbeam. Skipper and his crew were atop the half-timbered dormitory with mallets and pegs, awaiting the heavy oaken beam. The jovial otter jiggled the rope in its pulley block and called down, 'Ahoy, mates, if'n we wait round much longer up 'ere we'll sprout wings'n'feathers an' fly off!'

Gonff secured the rope to the beam, and spat on his paws. 'Right, mateys, let's send 'er up with a will. Anybeast got a good haulin' river song t'help out?'

Bella held up a paw in response. 'I'll do "Grumbledum Tugg" if you like!'

A groan arose from the hauling party. Baby Gonflet clapped both paws over his tiny ears.

'Not dat one agin, miz Bell, you allus singin' Grungledun Tuggs. Ferdy say miz Trimpy be a good singer.'

Bella sighed, bowing slightly to the hedgehog maid. 'Trimp, nobeast is forcing you to sing, but it'd be nice if you'd oblige. D'you know any good hauling shanty songs?'

Trimp did, and she immediately sang out in a fine clear voice.

'Away O! Away O!
Haul hard an' take her out,
I'll tell ye of the *Greenhawk*,
An' her cap'n, ole Chopsnout.
Away O! Away O! Now bend yore backs an' heave ho!

Ole Reynard Chopsnout was a fox,
A bad corsair to boot,
Who ran his vessel on some rocks,
While searchin' round for loot.
Away O! Away O! Now bend yore backs an' heave ho!

So to the northlands he did steer,
The *Greenhawk* to repair,
A warrior who knew no fear,
Named Luke was livin' there.
Away O! Away O! Now bend yore backs an' heave ho!

That corsair came with all his horde,
I'll tell ye mates 'tis true,
Brave Luke took up his battlesword,
An' that bad fox he slew.
Away O! Away O! Now bend yore backs an' heave ho!

Then Luke called up his gallant crew,
And *Greenhawk* did repair,
He changed her name to *Sayna* too,
Which sounded good and fair.
Away O! Away O! Now bend yore backs an' heave ho!

So Luke the Warrior sailed away,
He left the northland shore,
He swore an oath that one fine day,
He'd come back home once more.
Away O! Away O! Now bend yore backs an' heave ho!'

The beam was halfway up when Trimp stopped
singing. Martin had his footpaws dug in firmly, holding
the swaying oaken baulk steady with the rest of his
friends. He stared at the roving hedgehog, gritting from
between clenched jaws: 'What've you stopped singing
for, missie? Keep on!'

Trimp returned his stare, shaking her head. 'But that's

all I know. I never learned the rest!'

Gonff slid forward a fraction as the beam began losing height. Urgently, he muttered, 'Then start from the beginnin' an' sing it again, matey, afore we're all wearin' an oakbeam for a hat!'

Trimp sang the hauling shanty, as far as she knew the verses, twice before the beam was safe in the otters' strong paws on the dormitory top.

When the others went off to new chores Martin called Trimp to him. Walking on either side of her, he and Gonff escorted her across to the gatehouse and showed her in. The Mousethief took flagon and beakers from a cupboard where he had hidden them, and poured drinks for all three.

'Ninian's cider, I calls this. Comes from the ole place down south on the path, where I live from time to time.'

They sipped the cold sweet cider appreciatively, in silence. It was cool and shady in the gatehouse after the bright noon sun outside. Martin leaned forward. 'Trimp, where did you hear that song?'

'My grandmum Welff Tiptip used to sing it. She told me that she once knew a little mouse named Martin, too. Was that you?'

Gazing into his beaker, he slowly swirled the cider. 'That was me. I am Martin of Redwall, son of Luke the Warrior. My mother's name was Sayna. Strange, I had almost forgotten it, until you sang your shanty. *Sayna* was the name my father gave to his ship as well. Being little more than a babe at the time I don't remember much. But it comes back to me a little now. Tell me, miss, what else did your grandmum say? Anything at all?'

Holding her beaker with both paws, Trimp sipped and pondered. 'There were names . . . Coll, Denno, Cordle, and others I can't recall. Is that any help to you, Martin?'

'I'm afraid not. But carry on, please.'

'Hmm, now let me see. She used to talk of old Twoola, er, Drunn Tunneller and Windred—'

'Windred! She was my grandmother!' Martin grabbed the hedgehog maid's paws. 'Think! Did I have brothers or sisters? A grandsire? What was my father really like? Tell me about Sayna, my mother!'

Even though her paws were hurting in the vicelike grip, Trimp's heart went out to the Warrior. 'I can only tell you what I know, sir. Grandmum died when I was very young. She told me that I was born on the northland coast, but we fled when the slavers attacked your tribe's settlement. Our family moved to the midnorth hills. When I became old enough I left to go roving, and first place I set out to see was my birthplace on northland shore. Alas, there was nothing left there of our old home, so I carried on roving until I met Ferdy and Coggs, and they brought me to Redwall.'

Gonff placed a paw on his friend's shoulder. 'Steady on there, mate. You'll crush miss Trimp's paw!'

Martin released her, and went to stand in the doorway, blinking to hold back welling tears. 'I used to know things, I'm sure of it. But after the injuries I suffered battling the wildcat Tsarmina, I've hardly been able to recall a single thing. D'you remember Timballisto?'

Gonff nodded. 'He was yore friend from the northlands, who was released from slavery and came here. A good mouse.'

Martin struck his paw hard against the doorpost. 'We must have been crazy, both of us. He lived here, yet for some unknown reason we never discussed our past. Poor Timbal – he died the winter following the great Moss-flower war.'

Gonff poured more cider for his friend. 'Mayhap 'twas too painful for either of you to mention, what you went through when you were young 'uns?'

Martin stood staring out across the sunlit lawns. 'You're probably right, Gonff. Perhaps it was. Trimp, can't you remember any more names at all?'

The hedgehog maid smiled pensively. 'Only that

grandmum used to say if we didn't stop our noise and go to sleep, Vilu Daskar would get us. Aye, Vilu Daskar. Does that name ring a bell, Martin?'

'No, not a thing. 'Tis all too hazy, too long ago now.'

The Warrior walked off towards the Abbey. Gonff watched him, sad for his friend and the forgotten past. 'I ain't seen Martin like that afore, miss.'

Trimp put aside her drink and stood up. 'Only since I came to Redwall and sang that song. This Abbey's a beautiful place, Gonff, but I wish I'd never come here and caused Martin such unhappiness. I'd best leave.'

Gonff barred her path to the door, chuckling. 'Sorry, me young beauty, but I can't allow it, and neither would Martin, or anybeast calls themselves a Redwaller. Come on now, cheer up, earn yore afternoon tea. I'll show ye how I collect honey from our bees – you can lend a paw.'

They strolled from the gatehouse towards the northeast wall corner, where the hives were situated.

'But I've never tried taking honey from bees, Gonff. Don't they have a nasty habit of stinging you?'

'What? Sting me, the Prince of Mousethieves? Never! Not as long as I can pretend I'm a bumblebee an' sing whilst I steal the honey from under their noses, missie.'

Trimp giggled. 'Oh really, Gonff? What do you sing to a bee?'

'Oh, this'n'that, y'know. I usually start like this.

'Ho fuzz buzz buzz, look who's a-buzzin',
Good day sir bee, I'm Gonff yore cuzzin . . .'

Trimp's laughter mingled with the Mousethief's song on the sunkissed noon air as they skipped paw in paw across the lawns of Redwall Abbey.

2

In the days following Trimp's arrival at Redwall Abbey it became obvious to everybeast that something was wrong with their Warrior. Martin was no longer his customary jovial and helpful self. Often he was missing at mealtimes, and he spent more and more time outside the Abbey. It was a worrisome situation: Martin, the very backbone of Redwall, silent and pensive, with a faraway look clouding his eyes. Skipper and Dinny Foremole wandered up on to the east walltop, which was an ideal place to view the beauty of Mossflower Wood in summer. Lady Amber and Coggs were also up on the ramparts. Foremole greeted them with a wave.

'Gudd day to ee. You'm bain't seen Marthen, 'ave ee?'

Lady Amber placed a paw to her lips, cautioning silence. Pointing downwards over a battlement, she said in a low voice, 'Martin's sittin' down there alone!'

Skipper crouched below the walltop, shaking his head. 'So that's where our Warrior goes when he leaves the Abbey. Still, y'can't blame him. 'Tis a good place for anybeast seekin' solitude from others.'

Coggs peeped over at the lonely figure sitting below. 'I tell ye, friends, 'tain't like Martin to act this way. He's just

17

sittin' there with his back agin the wall, starin' out at the trees. What'll we do?'

Ever the sensible otter, Skipper began descending the wallsteps, down to the lawn behind the orchard.

'Come away, mates. I'd hate t'think Martin would know we're up 'ere a-spyin' on him. Whilst he's outside we could 'old a quick meetin' with the Abbess to sort the problem out.'

All concerned gathered in the gatehouse. Ferdy and Coggs served them elderflower cordial and slices of plum cake. Old Abbess Germaine held a trumpet, made from a spiral seashell with its end cut off, to her ear. Though her body was frail and her hearing none too good, the ancient mouse's other senses were still sharp and her eyes twinkled and shone keenly. She let them rove over the assembly, Bella, Columbine, Skipper, Dinny Foremole and Lady Amber, finally coming to rest on Trimp and Gonff.

'Hmm. My intuition tells me that our guest Trimp and the Mousethief know more of this affair than we do, friends. So I want you to speak up clearly, one at a time please. Start at the beginning, always the best place to begin. Pray keep silent, the rest of you – I'll hear from everybeast in due course. When the story is complete I'll give you my decision as Mother Abbess, based of course on your facts.'

There were smiles and nods of agreement all round. Even as a young mouse, Abbess Germaine had possessed great sense and wisdom. Now, with the experience of countless seasons upon her old head, every Redwaller trusted her judgement without question. They were certain that their beloved Abbess could solve any problem.

It was late afternoon when Martin entered the Abbey by the main gate. He was immediately set on by a group of Dibbuns, the infant creatures of Redwall. Baby Gonflet was clearly the ringleader, wrestling fiercely with Martin's footpaw, until the Warrior allowed himself to be laid flat on his back. Martin was immensely fond of the abbeybabes, always managing to make time for them and their odd little games. He gasped as they sat on his paws and held his ears. Baby Gonflet knelt on Martin's chest, shaking a paw under the Warrior's nose.

'You be still, naughtymouse, or we choppa you whiskers off!'

Two baby moles hanging on to Martin's belt giggled uproariously at the idea, adding their own threats.

'Heeheehee, urr, an' us'n's bite ee paws offen!'

'Yurr, an' chuck ee inna pond, hurrhurrhurr!'

Martin looked with mock pleading at his captors. 'Oh, lackaday, will no kind creature help me? I'm captured by wild ruffians. Have mercy on me, you savage beasts!'

Baby Gonflet grinned triumphantly at his prisoner. 'On'y if'n you comes wiv us!'

Keeping up a pretence of fear, Martin was led protesting to the Abbey by a veritable swarm of mouse, squirrel, mole and hogbabes.

Cavern Hole was a comfortable room inside the Abbey, slightly below ground level. Abbess Germaine sat propped by cushions in her enormous ceremonial chair, surrounded by her Redwallers. Ferdy ran up the stairs and back down again, his spikes quivering excitedly.

'He's comin'! The Dibbuns are bringin' Martin!'

Agile squirrels scampered about with tapers, lighting the coloured lanterns which supplemented the customary tallow candles, lending the chamber a festive atmosphere. In front of the Abbess's chair stood a long solid elmwood table, unadorned and bare. Martin was marched up to it by the Dibbuns, and Gonflet raised a chubby paw in salute to Bella.

'Us catchered 'im an' brought 'im 'ere, miz Bell!'

The big badger nodded solemnly. 'Thank you, my

friends, good work. Sit down now, and we'll deal with him right away!'

Martin held silent, only moving one eyelid to return a wink from his friend Gonff. He was, however, mystified.

Abbess Germaine opened the proceedings by pointing an accusing paw at the Warrior. 'What does this creature stand charged with?'

Answers came rattling back like hailstones.

'Always helping others!'

'Defending our creatures with his life!'

'Never considering himself!'

'Being good and kind to all about him!'

'Assisting Abbess Germaine to design the Abbey!'

'Bein' the best friend a mousethief ever had, matey!'

'Hurr, an' keepin' gurt troubles to 'isself!'

Bella restored order by banging once on the table. She appealed to the Abbess. 'This could go on all season. Pass sentence on him!'

Germaine's eyes twinkled as she tapped her cane on the chair. 'Bring in the instruments of punishment!'

Two trolleys were borne downstairs from the kitchens. One had a big barrel of strawberry fizz and beakers on it, the other a magnificent three-tiered cake, surmounted by a marchpane figure of the Warrior himself. The Abbess looked sternly from the trolleys to Martin and announced in a no-nonsense voice, 'I order that you either eat all of this cake and drink the contents of that barrel . . . or share it with us before you embark upon your journey!'

Martin was plainly bewildered. 'Er, I'll share it with you all, of course, but, er, what journey is this I'm supposed to be embarking upon?'

Gonff stepped forward, carrying Martin's great sword. It was a plain warrior's weapon, nothing fancy. The hilt was the one that had belonged to his father's old sword: blackbound, with a red pommel stone at its top. But its blade was like no other, fashioned by a Badger Lord from a chunk of metal fallen from the stars. Martin took it from

Gonff, his face reflecting in the burnished steel as he said, 'This has been used for a lot of things, but never for anything as delicate as a cake.'

Gonff indicated a spot on the butter-coloured meadow-cream, between a candied chestnut and a honey-preserved rose petal. 'Cut the cackle an' slice the cake, matey!'

A loud cheer went up as the keen blade slid into the massive confection.

'Martin the Warrior! Redwaaaaaaaalllllll!'

Columbine took over the slicing and Coggs served drinks, whilst Martin sat in a corner with some of his friends, eating and sipping happily. He nudged the Mousethief.

'Gonff, you tubby rascal, I've a feeling you're at the back of all this. Come on, tell me, where's this journey going to take me?'

The Prince of Mousethieves blew out his cheeks airily. 'Huh! You, matey? What makes y'think yore goin' anyplace without me? I'll be with you every step o' the way!'

'Hurr, zurr, an' oi too. You'm bain't a-goin' an' leavin' Dinny Foremole ahind of ee!'

Martin wrinkled his brow in frustration, and put aside his slice of cake, which Baby Gonflet promptly stole.

'Look, will you all stop talking in circles and tell me where I'm supposed to be going?'

Trimp could hold the secret no longer. She blurted out, 'To the place you've been dreaming of, where your father Luke the Warrior swore to return someday. The north-land shore, where you were born!'

Martin looked this way and that, blinking. His paws took on a life of their own, fidgeting distractedly.

'But . . . but . . . what about the Abbey? I haven't made any arrangements, then there's provisions, directions, a thousand things that would have to be done . . .'

Columbine came over. Wiping cream and cake from

the great battle blade with her apron corner, she gave the sword to Martin and sat down beside him.

'No excuses, sir Warrior, 'tis all arranged and taken care of since this afternoon. Provisions are packed for you all, and you've got the entire summer ahead of you. Skipper and Bella will take charge of the building work, I'll look after the Abbess. There's absolutely nothing for you to do or worry about. After all you've done for Redwall and its creatures, the least we can do in return is to allow you a trip to the place of your birth, which 'tis clear you long to see.'

Martin squeezed Columbine's paw gratefully. 'Thank you – thank you all. What can I say?'

The irrepressible Gonff pounded him on the back. 'That's easy, matey, you can either say no, an' sit around with a face like thunder until the flippin' Abbey falls down on us, or you can say yes, when do we leave?'

For the first time in days Martin the Warrior laughed. He backpawed Gonff in the stomach, knocking the wind from him. 'Yes, when do we leave?'

Dinny did not notice Baby Gonflet purloining his slice of cake as he shook Martin's paw with a hefty digging claw.

'Boi dawn on ee morrow at furst loight, zurr matey!'

3

Stars paled into the receding night, cloudless sky turned
from aquamarine to soft pastel bands of a new day. Out
in the vast leagues of Mossflower, birds began singing
among still foliage of trees which stood like ancient
giants. The sun rose in the east, an immense golden ball,
ready to preside over the morning and noon.

Skipper and Bella opened the main gate wide, and all
the inhabitants of Redwall crowded out on to the path,
surrounding the four travellers. Trimp was sorry to be
leaving the beautiful Abbey and its friendly creatures.
Words of advice and farewells fell thick as leaves in
autumn.

'Fates an' fortunes be with ye!'

'Bringa me back lotsa seashells, daddy Gonff!'

'Go careful now. Watch yore step, Trimp!'

'Aye, an' don't let that Gonff scoff all the supplies.'

'Stay away from deep water, Dinny!'

'An' don't climb any tall trees, mate!'

'Keep that sword close t'paw, Martin. You never
know!'

'Have you got a clean kerchief, Gonff? I've packed
some extra for you. Oh, don't forget your flute!'

Martin kissed Abbess Germaine's wrinkled brow.

'Goodbye, Mother Abbess. Watch out for us near autumn.'

The ancient mouse sniffed as she straightened his swordbelt over one shoulder. 'Come back safe to Redwall Abbey, Martin the Warrior!'

Redwallers stopped out on the path, cheering and waving, until the four figures travelling north were lost in the shimmering dust.

Gonff strode out cheerfully, calling back to Dinny, who was lagging behind at a slower gait, 'Come on, Din, keep up, you old wobblechops!'

Shambling along at his own pace, the good mole was not about to be rushed. 'More 'aste less speed, zurr. We'm gotten all ee summer afore us'n's. You'm on'y get all 'ot an' wearied boi rushen along loik ee fussy rabbert!'

Martin slowed the pace slightly, allowing Dinny to catch up.

'Always take a mole's advice, Gonff. Remember, Dinny didn't get to be Foremole by being hasty and foolish.'

Their friend's homely face crinkled into a deep smile. 'Oi thankee furr ee koind wurds, Marthen. Moi ole granfer used t'say oi was wise, even when oi was but a h'infant!'

Gonff could not suppress a giggle. 'Hah! Yore ole granfer'd say anything for two pieces of pie, as I remember!'

Dinny nodded sagely at this remark. 'Aye, an' loik as not ee'd say more furr three pieces o' pie, if'n you'm 'adn't stolen 'em furst, zurr Mouseythief!'

Gonff pulled a sad face at Martin. 'Our Dinny can be very cruel at times!'

Martin tweaked his friend's ear playfully. 'Oh, I wouldn't say cruel as much as truthful!'

By midday the Abbey was well lost to sight. The four travellers crossed the ditch, leaving behind the path and entering the cool green woodlands. Trimp scouted ahead a bit and found a beautiful site for their early noontide meal. Dabbling their footpaws in a small streamlet, they sat beneath a willow, lunching on apples, cheese and honeyscones, which they washed down with cold clear water. Trimp watched Martin unbuckle the great sword from his shoulderbelt and lay it down within easy paw-reach. Admiringly, the hedgehog maid watched reflections of water patterns playing along the blade.

'What a wondrous thing your sword is, Martin.'

The Warrior picked it up and held it lightly, testing its flawless balance. 'Wondrous indeed, Trimp, but you must always remember what a sword is really made for. It has only one purpose, to slay. In the paws of the wrong beast it could become an awful thing, if 'twere used for evil purposes. As the Warrior who is privileged to carry the sword, I am honour bound to uphold two things: the safety of Redwall, and the memory of my father. The blade was made for me, but the hilt was always his.'

Trimp felt slightly sorry for Martin. 'This is a long trip we're undertaking and we have only the words of an old ballad to go on. Maybe your father never really said that he would return, or then again, he may have returned long seasons ago and sailed off once more. What I'm tryin' to say, Martin, is this. Don't be surprised or disappointed if there is no trace of him on the northland shores when we finally get there.'

The Warrior patted his companion's paw fondly. 'I've thought of all that, missie, don't worry about me. I've decided to treat the whole thing as a summer journey with three good friends along for the walk. Right at this moment I feel lighter of heart and happier than I've been for quite some time. So hush now and don't fret over me.'

Babbling streamwater, combined with distant bird-song and insects' lazy droning, soon had the four creatures taking a short nap in the shade and serenity offered by surrounding trees. They had not been dozing long when Martin became alert. Sitting bolt upright, he reached for his blade.

Trimp opened one eye enquiringly. 'What is it, Martin, what's the m—'

The Warrior touched her lips lightly. 'Quiet, miss, listen. Gonff, can you hear?'

The Mousethief had drawn his dagger and crawled forward. Crouching against the willow trunk, he strained to hear. 'Gourds knockin' together – sounds like little drums. Chantin', too. Bit far off t'make it out proper, mate.' He sniffed the air as if hoping for a breeze. 'No smell, though, matey, mayhap just as well too.'

Martin crouched alongside him and said one word.

'Flitchaye?'

Gonff nodded, still keeping his ears alerted for more sounds. 'That's what I was thinkin', but what are Flitchaye doin' this far south?'

Martin shrugged. 'Raiding party maybe?'

Trimp looked from one to the other anxiously. 'What's a Flitchaye? Do we need to fear them?'

Martin explained.

'Flitchaye are a tribe of runty weasels. We don't fear them, but they're within a day's journey of Redwall, so we'd best go and see what they're up to.'

As they tracked their way through silent woodlands towards the distant sound, Gonff whispered, 'Flitchayes are a bad lot, missie. They use powerful herb smoke to stun their captives. You wouldn't see a Flitchaye 'til he's right on top of ye, 'cos they disguise themselves with weeds an' shrubs an' live underground mostly. Though if this lot are Flitchaye raiders, they'll stay above ground, not bein' on their own territory. Keep your head down an' stay back with Dinny, behind me'n'Martin.'

Trimp's heart beat faster. She was very excited, but not afraid with Martin and Gonff leading the way. Skirting a fern bed they crept up behind a fallen sycamore, and as they stooped in its shelter the sounds grew more distinct. Voices were chanting in unison with the thokking noise of gourds being struck rhythmically together.

'We d'Flitchaye Flitchaye Flitchaye,
Worraworra gonnawinna lorralorra wars!'

Thockthockathockthock, thockathockathockthock!

Bushes rustled and a few twigs snapped. Peeping over the fungus-ridden trunk, Trimp blinked in surprise when she distinguished the shapes moving against the leafy terrain.

Close on twoscore Flitchaye came marching past, brandishing stoneheaded axes and carrying bundles of slender throwing spears. Smeared with plant dye and clad in a disguise of trailing weeds, the vermin were almost as one with their surroundings. It was a barbaric scene, heightened by the sight of a very young squirrel, paws bound and hobbled, being dragged along on a rope of vine thongs attached to his neck. Trimp's eyes began watering as four rearguard passed close to the sycamore trunk, for they carried big earthenware pots on hangers between them, averting their heads from the smoke which wreathed from the vessels. The hedgehog maid rubbed at her eyes, swaying as the smoke fogged her senses. Dinny slapped a glob of mud in her paws, murmuring low, 'Yurr, missie, stick this on ee nose an' breathe through ee mouth!'

Trimp did as the mole advised and immediately felt better. She noticed that Martin and Gonff were doing the same thing to counteract the effect of the drugged smoke. When the column of Flitchayes had passed, the four friends sat down in the lee of the fallen trunk, and after a safe wait Gonff indicated that they clean off their noses.

Martin nodded grimly at Trimp. 'Well, now you know what Flitchaye are like, the filthy villains. Did you see the little squirrel they'd taken?'

Trimp shuddered. 'Poor little fellow. What'll they do to him?'

Martin clasped his swordhilt resolutely. 'Nothing if we can help it, miss. Dinny, see if you can gather some ramsons.'

The industrious mole was no sooner gone than he was back, carrying two of the broad-leafed plants, still with their tiny starlike flowers in bloom. Trimp took a step back from the pungent garlic-smelling things.

'Whew! Keep away from me with that lot, Din. I can't abide the smell of ramsons!'

Dinny chuckled as he stripped the leaves and rolled them into small solid plugs. 'You'm bain't goin' to loik thiz, marm, but et could save ee loif. Yurr, take these.'

Trimp's face was a mask of disgust as she accepted a pawful of the reeking wild garlic pellets from Dinny.

'Gurgh! We'll defeat the Flitchaye easily by throwing these at them. What a dreadful stink!'

Dinny passed the pellets around. Gonff chuckled gleefully.

'We don't chuck them at the foebeast, missie, we stuff two up our noses an' chew the rest.'

The hedgehog maid looked horrified at the idea. 'Stuff them up our noses and chew them? You're joking!'

Martin was already plugging his nose with ramsons. 'No joke, Trimp. The garlic odour will overpower the smell of any drugged herb that the Flitchaye have. Come on, miss, get on with it, we're losing time!'

With Martin in the lead they set off trailing the Flitchayes. Both Dinny and Gonff were unaffected by the malodorous aroma of ramsons – in fact, they seemed to be enjoying it. Martin endured his in stoic silence, but Trimp felt close to vomiting at the overpowering smell. Travelling silent and fast, they soon heard the foebeast up ahead. Dropping flat amid some bushes, Martin, Dinny and Trimp waited whilst Gonff scouted ahead. Trimp sat miserably in the deep loam, her entire being swamped by ramsons. Gonff rejoined them, quiet as a shadow drifting over grass. The Mousethief made his report swiftly.

'They're camped in a clearin' up ahead – some must've been already there. I counted fifty-one all told, all Flitchaye savages. Saw the liddle squirrel, too, they got him bound to a post in the middle o' their camp. Fifty's too many for us, mateys. 'Tis goin' t'be hard gettin' the young 'un out o' there. Any ideas, pals?'

Martin looked from one to the other before speaking. 'Right, here's the plan. Listen carefully, because it all depends on pure bluff. If it works then we get out of there fast. Gonff, here's what you'll do, mate . . .'

4

A mess of bird bones and feathers mixed with squashed half-eaten fruit and vegetables littered the Flitchaye camp. Around the fire undersized weasels squabbled and fought tooth and claw over any morsel of food roasting in the flames. One, larger than the rest, his face daubed blue beneath a helmet of ivy and bugloss, grabbed a half-burnt wren carcass from a smaller Flitchaye. Snarling, the owner tried to retrieve his food from the big weasel, who booted him backward into the fire contemptuously. It was an act of wanton cruelty that caused great hilarity among the other vermin, who sniggered evilly as their scorched companion scrambled shrieking from the blaze and rolled about, trying to extinguish his smouldering fur.

The young squirrel, who was little more than a Dibbun, was trying to shake off the effects of the drugged smoke. He shrank back fearfully against the post he was bound to. Flitchayes with sharp sticks prodded him and licked their lips meaningfully. One weasel took out a blade and was about to start cutting the squirrel's bonds when the big Flitchaye spotted him and knocked him senseless with a well-aimed rock. He stood over the fallen weasel, baring his stained fangs at the rest and speaking in his high-pitched growl. 'Norra yet! Feed de swiggle, fatty 'im uppa plenny!' He thrust the remains of the dead bird at the helpless youngster, snarling into the squirrel's terrified face: 'You eat. Commona, eaty allup!'

Martin strode nonchalantly into the camp, as if he was quite used to this sort of thing. A puzzled silence settled over the Flitchaye at the sight of the bold unarmed stranger in their midst. Pushing them out of his way he went across to the two earthenware pots, still wreathing smoke from the drugged herbs which smouldered inside them. Leaning over, Martin appeared to sniff them both and gave a hard, scornful laugh.

'Hah! Don't think much o' yore cookin', ragbags!'

A gasp of surprise rose from the vermin. The stranger had suffered no ill effects from the fearful fumes! Still shouldering weasels aside, Martin pushed his way forcefully over to the little prisoner. Picking up the knife from the fallen weasel, he made as if to cut the squirrel free.

'Stoppima mousebeast!'

At the shout from their leader the Flitchaye surrounded Martin, hemming in on all sides. Swaggering forward, the big weasel thrust his ugly face close to that of Martin and sneered, 'We d'Flitchaye, Flitchaye, Flitchaye!'

The crowd took up the chant, moving around the Warrior in a shuffling stamping dance. Martin waited patiently awhile, an expression of bored indifference on his face. Then he pointed a paw at his own chest and shouted, 'I Martin the Warrior!'

Quiet fell over the vermin, and they stood still. The leader pointed a stoneheaded axe at the lone mouse, repeating Martin's words as best he could. 'Ma'tarn de Horrya!' He spat challengingly at the floor in front of the Warrior. Martin coolly returned the gesture, looking the weasel up and down insultingly as he spoke.

'Fish eye, you d'Fish eye?'

The Warrior had anticipated the Flitchaye leader's next move, and he took a pace smartly backward as the weasel swung his axe. The blow was delivered with such force that the Flitchaye could not stop it. He struck himself hard on the shin, cracking his bone audibly. Martin stretched both paws wide. Keeping his eyes on a double-topped oak at the camp's edge, he roared, 'Redwaaaaaalllll!'

Hidden by the foliage, Gonff held the sword like a spear and cast it accurately. To the Flitchaye it was magic! Seemingly zipping down out of the sky, the great blade thudded point first into the ground at Martin's side.

Wrenching it from the earth, the Warrior swung it skilfully, chopping a nearby vermin's bunch of throwing spears in half with a single swipe. It had the desired effect. Flitchaye scattered to get out of Martin's sword range, leaving him alone by the prisoner. Turning his back on the enemy, Martin gave the little squirrel a quick reassuring smile and whispered, 'Don't move 'til I say, matey. Soon have y'out of here.' The captive blinked with fright as Martin's sword hissed within a whisker of him, severing the ropes.

Whirring bright in the late afternoon sunlight, the sword weaved a deadly pattern as its owner wielded it. Martin narrowed his eyes to a fierce intensity, glaring slowly this way and that at the vermin.

'I Martin the Warrior, we go now!'

Gently lifting the dazed little squirrel on his shoulders, he turned and began walking from the camp. The leader, his face a mask of agony, limped forward, shouting, 'Stoppa mousebeast, sto—'

His cry was cut short when a slingstone smashed his jaw and laid him flat. A female, obviously the leader's mate, dashed forward, but she too was felled by a sling-stone which whacked her between the eyes. She fell like a log.

Martin muttered out the side of his mouth to the little

one, 'Good old Dinny, never known him to miss yet!' Then he turned sternly to the cowering Flitchaye. 'I go, you stay, Fish eye, hah!'

At a nod from him, slingstones poured in from Gonff, Dinny and Trimp, causing confusion among the stunned Flitchaye.

Back among the shelter of some big trees, Martin passed his sword to Gonff.

'Good work, mates, but if I know Flitchaye they won't stay still for long. We've got to get out of here, fast!'

Trimp just had time to spit and blow, ridding herself of the hated ramsons, then she was running, paw in paw with Dinny, Martin leading and Gonff behind her, guarding the rear. Trees and bushes sped by in a green blur as the rescuers hurtled through the woodlands, with the first streaks of evening marking the sky. Breathless and quivering they paused at a wide shallow stream. Trimp stooped and sucked up mouthfuls gratefully. Gonff struck her on the back, causing her to cough out the water.

'Don't drink now, matey, 'twill slow you up. Martin, listen!'

'Flitchayeeeeeeeeee! Flitchayeeeeeeeeee!'

The blood-curdling shouts of vermin crying for revenge rang out through the trees. Tapping the back of Martin's head, the little squirrel, who now seemed completely recovered from the evil smoke, spoke for the first time.

'Chugger not wanna get eated, quick, run!'

And run they did. Martin chose the streambed, to make tracking difficult, though it slowed their pace slightly. Pebbles clacked underpaw, water splashed noisily around the runners, and sometimes trailing crowfoot weeds tried to tangle them up. Gonff turned at the sound of rapidly advancing vermin, as the Flitchaye dashed screaming into the waters upstream.

'Flitchayeeeeee! Flitchayeeeeee!'

The Mousethief held a stone ready in his sling. 'They've seen us, mates. I'll say this for the rascals, they're good fast runners. Should we make for the bank and head into the woods, Martin?'

Martin pressed on doggedly with Chugger clinging to his back. 'No good, mate, they'd track wet pawprints easily. This water's getting deeper and they can only travel the same speed as us in a stream. Keep going!'

Further downstream the watercourse took a bend, getting deeper. It was now well above waist height and flowing fast. Dinny grunted to Trimp, 'Oi doan't loik water, oi'm gurtly afeared of ee wet!'

The Flitchaye, who were still in the shallower water, seemed to be gaining apace on their quarry. Gonff turned and brought one of the front runners down with a well-placed slingstone, and reloaded his sling immediately.

'They're too close for comfort now, mates. I reckon we'll have t'stand an' fight it out!'

'Gurr, no uz won't. Lookit, we'm be saved!'

In the curve of the streambend a big old crack willow, which had collapsed into the water from the crumbling bank, lay half in, half out of the flow, swaying gently.

Tripping and stumbling wildly, Dinny and Trimp waded through the eddying swirls, coughing and gasping, the foodpacks they were carrying hampering them greatly. However, they made it over to the tree and hauled themselves on to its bushy top. Their added weight did the trick. There was a tearing of the last few roots as the willow upended and slid off into the stream.

Martin and Gonff were both slinging stones now, dodging the long thin throwing spears which the Flitchaye flung at them. The little squirrel Chugger clung to Martin's back, yelling hoarsely, 'Fro' lotsa stones, don't lerra Fish eyes eat Chugga!'

The Warrior looked to Gonff for his sword. It was evident that ere long they would be battling paw to paw with the vermin in a life or death struggle.

'Hurr, 'urry an' jump on ee boat naow, mates!'

Dinny and Trimp had paddled the tree close up behind them, using long leafy branches they had broken from the willow. Martin pushed Gonff on to the makeshift vessel, and was about to pull himself aboard when a snarling Flitchaye grabbed his paw. For a moment the Warrior was helpless, clinging with one paw to the tree whilst being held by the vermin. Chugger scrambled up on to Martin's shoulder. Leaning over, he bit deep into the vermin's paw. An agonised scream ripped from the weasel's mouth as he let go of Martin's paw. Without a backward glance Martin heaved both himself and Chugger on to the willow trunk.

'Trimp, look after the little 'un. Gonff, you and I'll paddle. Dinny, get your sling and give those scum what for!'

Trimp felt the current pull strongly at the tree, then they were whipped away downstream, with Martin and Gonff paddling non-stop. Wedging little Chugger in the sprouting branches up front, she went to assist Dinny. The mole was roaring gruffly as he whirled his sling and flung rocks with deadly accuracy.

'Goo burr, oi'll give ee billoh, you'm choild-eatin' villyuns. Yurr be a gurt supper o' stones for ee!'

So fierce were the volleys of rock and round pebble with which Dinny and Trimp peppered the Flitchaye that the vermin waded for the banks, unable to keep balance and throw their spears in the deepening water. Martin chanced a backward glance at their molefriend, and winked at Gonff.

'Look at old Din there, slinging away like a good 'un!'

Watching admiringly, the Mousethief saw one of Dinny's rocks take a Flitchaye squarely between both ears, toppling him from the bank into the water.

'Aye, matey, that mole's enjoyin' himself all right!'

*

Dusk fell whilst the travellers made their way downstream, still harassed by Flitchaye foes running along both sides of the bank. Martin peered ahead into the darkness and bit his lip grimly at what he saw.

'Bad luck for us ahead. The stream is dammed right across!'

Trimp gave a cry of dismay. 'Look, some Flitchaye must've run ahead. I can see the shapes of 'em, waiting on the damtop for us!'

Sure enough, there were several creatures moving about on the dam, shrouded by the enclosing gloom. Dinny groaned.

'Hurr, us'n's be en real trouble naow!'

A hearty voice, quite unlike the Flitchaye, rang out from the dam as shadowy shapes dashed back and forth.

'Whupperyhoooo, cullies, I see Flitchayes. Whupperyhooooo!'

Gonff began jumping up and down with joy. Cupping both paws around his mouth he yelled to the creatures on the dam.

'Garraway Bullow, ye ole dogswamper, 'tis me, the Mousethief!'

A figure hurled itself from the damtop, cut the water neatly and came swimming at them with the speed of an attacking pike. Chugger nearly fell from his perch with surprise as a large powerful otter bounded on to the willow as if she had been propelled from the water on a giant spring. Gonff threw himself upon the otter and wrestled her the length of the trunk, both of them laughing and shouting.

'Well frazzle a frog, you ole Majesty, good to see yer!'

'Haharr, Gonffo me ole tatercake, you got a belly on ye like a poisoned plant louse! What brings ye to my neck o' the country, cullie?'

'Yah, we didn't wanna come, 'cept that there's more'n twoscore Flitchaye tryin' to slay an' eat us, mate!'

Garraway Bullow tossed Gonff aside like a leaf and

stood up. She looked Martin up and down, shaking his paw firmly.

''Strewth, I wager you'd account for a few vermin before they brought ye down, with a sword like that. No matter, cullie, you leave the filthy Flitchaye to my fighters!' Placing a paw to her mouth she gave a loud ear-piercing whistle, then called to the otters on the dam.

'Whupperyhoooo! 'Tis Flitchayes all right. Go an' get 'em afore they run off. Nought like a Flitchaye hide t'make cloaks for our liddle 'uns, an' winter's on'y two seasons off!'

Otters materialised from everywhere, big warlike beasts, tattooed from ear to tail and armed with double-tipped javelins. Whooping and bellowing they took off after the weasels, who turned and fled in terror. The tree nosed gently into the dam as Gonff was making introductions.

'That there's Dinny Foremole, the pretty hogmaid's called Trimp, an' the serious-lookin' sword carrier, who ain't nearly so pretty as me, is Martin the Warrior, my matey. Friends, I want ye to meet Garraway Bullow, Queen of all the Nort – the Northern Otter River Tribes!'

Garraway helped them on to the dam, then she hauled the willow in sideways and lashed it to the timber and mud structure, remarking, 'No sense in wastin' good wood – 'twill strengthen our dam. Come on, Gonffo, an' bring yore mateys too. Seein' as you ain't been ate by Flitchayes, you must be 'ungry, right?'

Gonff laughed impudently at the Otterqueen. 'D'ye ever recall a day when I wasn't hungry? I could eat a boiled otter right now, but I ain't got the time to cook ye, burly Bullow, so lead us t'the vittles!'

'Hoi, worra you fink, I'm a likkle flower growin' on dis tree? Worrabout Chugger?'

Trimp rescued the tiny squirrel from the branches, where he had been taking a short nap. He waved at Garraway Bullow.

''Lo, my name be Chugger, I 'ungry too!'

The Otterqueen swung him up on to her brawny shoulder. 'Haharrharr, you ain't back'ard in comin' forward, are ye, master Chugg? Well, I reckon you don't eat much, so we'll find a smidgen o' vittles for ye. Though I don't know rightly where yore from, or if'n our vittles'd suit ye, matey. How'd you get caught by the Flitchaye?'

The little fellow shrugged. 'I live inna woods wiv granny. One day she go 'sleep. Chugger shake'n'shake granny, but she not wake up. So I on me own, 'til Fish eyes catcher me. But Martin, Trimp'n'Gonffo be's Chugger's friends now. You be my friend too?'

Garraway Bullow wiped something from her eye with the back of a paw. 'I'd like t'meet the beast who says I ain't yore friend, Chugger mate!'

5

The otter den, or holt, consisted of a spacious cavern, dug into the bank, directly under where a massive ancient beech tree grew. Thick gnarled beech roots, criss-crossing in all directions, formed a ceiling, wallbeams, and in places long stout seats. It was lit by a great fire in a stonebuilt hearth and mantel, with ovens on both sides and cauldrons suspended over the flames by iron trivets. Otters were everywhere, though mainly babes and oldbeasts, since the mature males and females were out chasing Flitchayes. One wrinkled old male twitched his nose at Garraway, putting aside a wooden spoon he was carving.

'Why didn't ye tell me there was Flitchayes abroad? I'd 'ave gotten me javelins an' gone out with the crew. Young snipfur, y'are, never tell me nothin'!'

The Otterqueen inspected his work approvingly. 'That's a fine spoon, Daddo. You put paid to more vermin than anybeast in yore young seasons. Better f'you to take things easy an' whittle nice spoons. We need more spoons.'

The oldster sighed and resumed his carving. 'Yore tellin' me, daughter. 'Tis those Kitts. They think spoons is boats, go out a-sailin' 'em an' lose 'em, they do.'

The little otters, known as Kitts, were anxiously watching an old otterwife putting out spoons on the table for supper. She waggled a paw at them.

'I'll be countin' these spoons after, an' woe betide you Kitts if'n there's a single one gone astray!'

Gonff sniffed at one of the cauldrons appreciatively. 'Mmm, Bubblin' Bobbs if I ain't mistaken!'

Trimp allowed the delicious aroma to wreath her face. 'Smells marvellous, Gonff. What are Bubblin' Bobbs?'

The Mousethief managed to hook a sip on his knife edge before dodging a swipe from the big fat cook. 'Well, first you put on a soup of chopped leeks, parsley an' shredded white turnips, with loads o' secret otter herbs in. Then you get a paste made from cornflour, rolled oats an' carrot juice, roll it into dumplin's an' press a good fat watershrimp into the middle of each one. Fry 'em crispy in corn oil, then chuck 'em in the soup. At first they sink, but when the soup starts a-bubblin', the dumplin's bob to the top. That's why otters call it Bubblin' Bobbs. Come on, let's find a seat, Trimp. Supper looks about ready!'

Before the meal started, Daddo laid aside his carving and plucked a few chords with his tail on a flat round instrument, which made a banjo-like sound. He called to Garraway.

'C'mon, daughter, give us yore song afore the rest gits back.'

Queen Garraway fluttered her eyelashes demurely and launched into a ballad with a voice that shook the very rafters.

'I'm bound to sing this song,
Though I shouldn't really ought,
I'm Queen of all these otters yet,
They call me Queen of Nort?
Yes Queen of Nort!
My goodness who'd have thought,
One day I'd be a Majesty,

40

Or something of that sort,
But all the otters that I see,
Must bow and wave their tails to me,
Whilst I just nod back graciously,
I'm Queen of Nort!
Good Queen of Nort,
My northern otter tribe,
Live all along the riverbanks,
And beat their foes with tails like planks,
I rule them wisely and give thanks,
I'm Queen of Nort!
There's nought I'd rather be,
I say to myself constantly,
Your Majesty is really me,
And don't I look like royalty,
I'm Quee-ee-ee-ee-heeeeen of Nort!
N . . . O . . . R . . . T, may I rule long and graciously!'

Queen Garraway Bullow bowed modestly as the listeners applauded, clipping the ear of a Kitt who was stuffing a spoon in his apron pocket and rapping the paw of another who was making rude gestures at her elders. Suddenly the pre-supper calm was disrupted, as bounding and hooting the fighting otters returned, hungry as hunters and flushed with victory. Trimp found herself sandwiched between two husky females, who jostled and joked.

'Ahoy there, mate, budge over a bit, will ye!'

'Yah, go an' budge yoreself, barrelbeam!'

Eventually, after much shoving and hustling, everybeast was seated, and a big rough-looking one-eared male bellowed, 'Whupperyhoo! Wheel in the vittles hard'n'fast there!'

Queen Garraway threw him a frosty glance. 'Not afore you've made yore report, Cap'n Barrool!'

Barrool flicked his powerful tail and winked at her. 'Oh, that! Well, there ain't no more babe-eatin' wicked

Flitchayes plunderin' the land no more, we slew 'em all!'

Daddo eyed him doubtfully. 'How d'y'know they're all slain?'

One of the big females called out, ''Cos we asked 'em real nice, an' any who said they wasn't got fixed up good'n'quick!'

This brought roars of laughter from the fighters. Trimp shook her head sadly, remarking to the female next to her, 'How can you joke about killing other creatures?'

The otter's face became severe as she replied, 'If you'd seen wot Flitchayes have done to old 'uns an' Kitts when they raided here in bygone seasons, you'd unnerstand, missie. Besides, the crew's only jestin' 'cos they all came back alive an' un'urt. This time we were lucky. Those scum didn't 'ave time to sneak up on us with their smoulderin' herbs an' knock us out, so they 'ad t'fight paw to paw, see.'

The Bubbling Bobbs soup was delicious, as was the riverbank salad, arrowroot scones with honey, hotroot celery cream dip and dandelion cordial. Martin sat next to the Queen, explaining where the four were travelling to. Garraway was very helpful.

'Northern shores, eh? You'd be best to go by water, Martin.'

'Hmm, maybe so, but you've dammed the stream and we've lost our willow – it's reinforcing your dam, remember?'

Garraway brushed aside his objections cheerfully. 'We only dammed the stream to make a liddle waterfall an' a good slide for the Kitts. Another stream cuts in below the falls. We'll lend you a raft. It'll be easy, matey. The river runs straight west t'the sea shores, an' from there you only have t'head north along the coastline, right, Gonff?'

The Mousethief slurped the soup from his bowl. 'Right, marm, an' thankee kindly for yore 'elp'n'hospitality!'

Garraway whacked him playfully with her tail. 'Lissen, Gonff, you don't get off with it that easy. Come on, out with that flute of yours an' give us a jig. Er, "Tails in the stream"? Aye, that's wot it was called!'

Gonff pulled out his flute and returned the whack, grinning. 'Yore a wicked ole Queen, forcin' pore travellers t'sing for their supper. Right, here goes. "Tails in the stream"!'

At the first merry trills of the flute every otter in the holt was up and jigging wildly. Martin, Trimp and Dinny had to climb to a high root perch to avoid the flailing tails and whirling limbs. They sat clapping their paws in time to the furious pace. Chugger was down on the floor with a gang of Kitts, linking tails as they whooped and kicked up footpaws, speeding round in a milling circle. Even the oldsters danced vigorously. Every now and then the floor would reverberate as otters thumped their tails on it in unison as they sang.

'Tails in the stream mates, tails in the stream,
No time t'sit around the bank an' dream,
Is it a pike perch roach or a bream?
No, 'tis an otter with his tail in the stream!
Whupperyhoo mates whupperyhoo,
Clouds are white an' the sky is blue,
Rap with y'tail an' stamp that paw,
Bow to y'partner an' around once more!
Bread'n'honey'n'cakes'n'cream,
Supper's in the oven an' tails in the stream!'

Gonff tootled faster and faster, and the dance speeded up until the entire place was a blur of whirling fur and thumping tails, finishing finally in a glorious collapse of giggling, bellowing otters. Gonff danced nimbly around them, waving his flute and chuckling.

'Hahaha, c'mon now, you idle lot, up on y'paws. I'm goin' to play "Riverdogs ramble round"!'

Panting and blowing, Queen Garraway extricated herself from the jumble, waving her paws. 'Mercy,

Gonffo, ye picklenosed rogue, you'll have us danced out of our skins!'

Gonff helped her to a seat. 'Right then, ole Majesty, sit an' rest those ancient paws. Everybeast sit now, but leave a space in the centre. Hi there, Martin, get down here an' show 'em the Battleblade Dance. C'mon, matey, don't be shy!'

Reluctantly Martin clambered down and unsheathed his sword. 'Gonff, I'm sure nobeast wants to see that old thing!'

The Mousethief appealed to the otters. 'Course you do, mates, don't you?'

Martin sighed. By the furious applause that followed his friend's remark, it was obvious they wanted to see him perform. Trimp sat Chugger on her lap, settling down to watch Redwall's Champion, whilst Gonff and Dinny set the stage. A big red apple was placed on an oaken stump stool, and Dinny sat on the floor, an upturned cooking pot in front of him. When he began tapping it with his digging claws, it gave out a sound like raindrops hitting a thin slate roof. Tock tokkatokka tock tokka tokka!

The Mousethief sat beside his molefriend. Taking two mushrooms he stood one on Dinny's head and the other on his own, then he held his paws straight in front of him, a dandelion held firmly in either one. Gonff signalled Martin with a wink. What Trimp witnessed then she could scarce believe, but it convinced the hogmaid that nobeast living could wield a sword like Martin the Warrior.

Martin began moving slowly at first to Dinny's beat, whirling his blade in all directions. Underpaw and overpaw, round both shoulders and overhead, the sword moved in a slow flashing pattern, humming and whirring, with fireglow playing along its blade. Everybeast stared in silent fascination at the wonderful display. Martin skiphopped, his keen blade tip missing both footpaws by a fraction, then he gave a piercing yell.

'Redwaaaaaaall!'

Dinny speeded up his rhythm, with Martin keeping perfect time, eyes half closed in concentration. Redwall's great sword became a blur of liquid light, travelling so fast that it left patterns upon the air, figures of eight, circles, crescents, even shapes like flowers.

Tocktokkatokkatocktokkatokkatocktokkatokka . . .

Faster and faster the mole's digging claws rapped on the upturned copper pot. Otters held their breath as the perilous blade sang within a whisker of their faces. Trimp nearly bit through her lip at what happened next. Martin gave a wild animal roar, and whirled upon his two friends, the blade striking down on their heads. Once! Twice! Both mushrooms fell apart sliced from cap to base. Like a living thing the sword hummed and flicked round Gonff's paws, lopping off the dandelion heads so that they curled lazily up in twin arcs, landing neatly 'twixt the cut mushrooms on Gonff and Dinny's heads. With a leap and a bound, Martin was at the big red apple, his lethal blade appearing to be six swords at once, chopping like lightning at the apple. Never once was the blade edge heard to strike the oaken stump, on which twelve perfect apple slices lay. Sweeping the flat blade to and fro, the Warrior sent the slices spinning into the watchers' laps. Tossing the sword in the air so that it turned on its own length, Martin took a half-pace backward. With an audible thud the sword came down point first to stand quivering in the floor. Martin clasped both paws on the pommel-stoned hilt and bowed.

The Nort otters went wild. They cheered and danced around Martin and his two friends, lifting them shoulder high and carrying them round the cave. Chugger was already up with his pals, the Kitts, stuffing apple slices in their mouths as they cast about for dandelions, mushrooms and swordlike sticks to repeat the Warrior's feat. Queen Garraway Bullow gripped Martin's paw tight, pumping it up and down fiercely.

'Never seen aught like that on land or water, matey. Hoho! Thought you was goin' to make two moles out o' Dinny an' leave ole Gonffo pawless for a moment back there. You'll have t'show me how t'do it, Martin. Great thunder, matey, wot I wouldn't give for a sword like that'n o' yours!'

When the Warrior could get a word in edgeways, he shook his head ruefully at the crowd of admiring otters.

'Please, 'twas only a fancy exercise in sword control I thought up to relieve the boredom of training. Normally I wouldn't let anybeast see me do it, but I made the mistake of performing it once at a Redwall feast and Gonff's been trying to talk me into doing it again ever since.'

Gonff patted his friend's back, obviously proud of his skill. 'Fiddley dee, mate, shows yore a real Warrior. Huh, if'n I could do that I'd be at it ten times a day for sure!'

Late that night Martin sat alone on the dam. Inside the holt of Queen Garraway it was snug and warm, and he could hear the snores and murmurs of sleep talkers drifting forth into the soft summer darkness. Martin smiled, recalling how Gonff had grabbed the sword and told a disobedient gang of Kitts about a tail-chopping trick he knew, for naughty little otters who would not go to sleep. It worked like a treat – they fled to their beds instantly. The Warrior stared into the night, wondering what sort of a father Luke was. He wrestled with fogged memories, confusing the images of his mother Sayna and his grandmother Windred as they merged together in his mind's eye. He tossed a stone into the water, watching the moon-rimmed ripples. What sort of place had the far north shores been? Had Luke his father ever kept his word and returned there? It was all too puzzling, so he turned his mind to thoughts of the Abbey. What would Redwall look like, one day when it was finally completed? That turned out to be a puzzle too.

Next morning Queen Garraway took the travellers

beyond her dam. There had once been a broad waterfall further down the stream, but the damming had cut it down to half its original size, allowing the otters to build a steep mudslide. Squeaking Kitts, covered from ears to tails in wet brown clay, shot down it like stones from a sling, splashing into the pool below and emerging clean of mud. The friends laughed uproariously at their antics. Trimp pointed out one, zooming down backwards.

'Heeheehee, look at that liddle scamp. Bet he'd catch it off his mother if she saw him doing that!'

With a resounding splash the little one hit the water, vanished and came up again, washed recognisable. Trimp hid a smile as Dinny roared gruffly at the culprit: 'Yurr, git out'n thurr, maister Chugg. You'm bain't no h'otter – you'm apposed t'be ee squiggle, ee likkle rip!'

Chugger wrinkled his nose at the mole. 'I norra swiggle no more. Chugger a notter now!'

Crafty Gonff waved to the squirrelbabe. 'Righto then, otter matey, you stay there. We're goin' now.'

Chugger scrambled up the bank and clung to Trimp. 'Norra notter no more. Chugger go wiv you to da norfen seashores. 'Urry up, Martin, we go now!'

Below the falls the pool narrowed again into the stream. Queen Garraway lifted the fringe of bushes growing on its bank, showing them their transport.

'Here 'tis, mates, a stout liddle raft. C'mon, Gonffo, lend a paw to pull it out here.'

It had a collapsible mast and a sail which would double as a tent, plus four long ash poles, paddle-shaped at one end. They heaved it into the water and leaped aboard. Martin shook the Otterqueen's paw heartily.

'Thank you for everything, Majesty. May your tribe live in peace and plenty here always!'

The brawny otter grinned cheerfully at them. 'Thankee, an' may yore journey be a safe 'un. Go now, find what ye seek, an' don't let ole Gonffo git his nose into the grub supplies too often!'

6

By mid-morning the stream had widened out considerably, small white clouds decorated the sunny skies and a
gentle breeze convinced the friends they should erect the
mastpole and spread sail. Dinny was never fond of water,
and had to be dug out of the jumble of sail canvas where
he had hidden himself. Gonff, however, took on a
decidedly nautical mood, calling out orders.

'Ahoy, mateys, rig up that mastpole amidships, will ye?
Set yon sail an' unfurl 'er smartlike to catch the breeze!'

Martin and Trimp chuckled as Dinny threw a derisory
salute.

'Aye aye, Cap'n Gonff zurr. Do ee got any more
h'orders furr uz common waterbeasties?'

Hiding a grin, Gonff called back haughtily, 'I say,
Martin, tie a rock t'that fat ole mole's tail an' chuck him in
the river, will you? He's slowin' us up!'

Bushy-edged banks slipped by, casting lacy patterns of
sunshadow on the translucent waters. Trimp munched
on a damson scone and sipped raspberry cordial.

'Ah, this is the life, pals . . . Ouch!'

A muddy stick came spinning out of the northbank
bushes, striking her on the cheek, followed by a mocking
imitation of the hogmaid's voice.

'This's the life, pals, heeheehee!'

Martin grabbed a pole and punted the raft towards the south bank. Gonff's sharp eyes picked out the culprit.

'There he is, see, runnin' along behind the bushes!'

They followed the direction of Gonff's outstretched paw. A young grey-brown rat was barely visible amid the foliage. Then it emerged on to the bank, pointing back at the Mousethief and mimicking his voice in a nasty manner.

'Runnin' along be'ind the bushes, be'ind the bushes, heehee!'

Martin's grip relaxed on his swordhilt. 'Ignore the little villain. He's only trying to annoy us.'

The rat flung another stick, but the raft was now too far away from the north bank to be hit. He stuck out his tongue at Martin. 'Ignore the liddle villain, liddle villain, heeheehee!'

Chugger looked stern, and shook a tiny paw at the rat. 'Go 'way, naughty mouse, or I biff ya!'

Martin took hold of the little squirrel, who was about to jump from the raft, and held him wriggling in the air. 'Now now, I told you, ignore the naughty mouse!'

But something unlikeable in the creature's swaggering attitude caught Gonff's attention. He stood up. 'I thought that was a mouse at first, but he's a sneaky young water rat. Look at that thick tail, mates!'

The rat stuck his claws in both ears and waggled them impudently at the Mousethief, dancing up and down provokingly. 'Oh, look at 'is tail, mates, look at 'is tail. Heehee!'

Gonff whipped out his sling, fitted a small pebble to it and lobbed it expertly off. The stone, which Gonff had not cast with any great force, caught the rat a stinging blow on the tail. It leaped up and down, clinging to its tail and howling tearfully.

'Owowowowow, the mouse nearly slayed me, owowowowow!'

Gonff returned his impression of the whining vermin. 'Owowow, naughty mouse nearly slayed me, owow!'

The rat stopped wailing, his face a picture of fury. 'You shut ya face. Think ya funny, don't ya?'

Trimp came to stand beside Gonff. 'What's the matter, rat, don't you like a taste of your own medicine? Be off with you, go and boil your ugly head!'

The rat kept running along the bank to keep up with the raft, throwing twigs, mud and anything he could lay paws upon. But they fell far short of the travellers. He was livid with rage, shrieking out at them, 'Oh, you done it now, wait'n'see! Nearly slayed Riddig, son of mighty Girfang, Boss of alla streamrats!'

Gonff fitted another stone to his sling, a proper-sized rock this time. 'Ah, stop whingin' an' run off home to yore daddy. Quick now, or I'll show ye what a real slingstone can do. I'll give ye t'the count o' three, rat. One, two . . .'

Riddig stopped running and ducked off hastily into the bushes, still calling out threats to his enemies.

'Don't go 'sleep t'night – better not turn yer back. Youse lot are all deadbeasts, wait'n'see!'

Martin sighed, shaking his head at Gonff. 'That's all we need, more trouble. First the Flitchaye, now streamrats. Didn't I tell you to ignore him?'

Gonff shrugged apologetically. 'Nasty liddle vermin. Couldn't 'elp myself, mate.'

Trimp was about to agree when Dinny interrupted.

'Burr, nor could oi, Marthen, tho' oi'd 'a' gotten ee vurmint a gudd crack furst toim wi' moi slinger!'

Chugger thrust out his little jaw truculently. 'An' I woulda swimmed over an' bited 'is tail off too!'

Martin tickled Chugger behind the ear fondly. 'I wager that would've made him jump, eh, Chugg? Personally I felt a desire to kick that young horror's tail up and down the bank a bit, just to teach him a lesson in manners. But keep your eyes peeled, mates. I've a feeling we haven't heard the last of this little incident.'

The remainder of a pleasant day was spoiled for Trimp. She watched every rustle of bush or reed along the banks, expecting at any moment to see a mob of rats come springing out at them. However, the situation did not seem to bother her companions a bit. Chugger curled up amid the food packs and snored like a holtful of otters, whilst Martin, Dinny and Gonff chatted amiably, lying back and trailing their paws in the water. Had Trimp observed them more closely she would have noticed that the three Redwallers were alert as hunting hawks, keeping their weapons close by at all times.

Evening fell, and still there was no sign of rats. Martin took precautions by nosing the raft on to a rock which jutted up in centre stream and making a rope fast to it. Dinny fished about until he located a broad flat stone close to the rock. Hauling it aboard, the clever mole built a small fire on it. Martin chopped vegetables with his sword, whilst Trimp dug out dried watershrimp and herbs from a haversack. Gonff filled their small cauldron with fresh streamwater, and Chugger sat warming his paws by the fire. Martin tossed the vegetables into the pot and wiped his sword clean.

'A fire at night isn't the best idea in these parts, Din.'

The mole watched his soup carefully as he stirred it. 'May'ap 'tain't, zurr, but if'n anybeast be a-goin' to attack us'n's, they'd do et, foire or not. Breezes on ee water be a bit chill. Nought loik a gudd drop o' soup, noice an' 'ot, to keep ee warm an' 'appy!'

Gonff cut a loaf of ryebread into chunks. 'Can't argue with mole logic, mate, ole Din's right.'

Dinny's soup was good, and they sat around the cauldron, each with a wooden spoon and a chunk of bread, sharing the meal in true traveller fashion. Martin set up two oarpoles and brought the sail forward, draping it over them as a precaution against rain during the night. Trimp found a narrow flagon of elderberry wine and they passed it round, each taking a few sips.

The hogmaid smiled. 'There, that should keep the chills away. What now, mates?'

Gonff smiled back at her. 'Now you give us a song, missie.'

'No no, my voice would carry over water. Let Dinny sing.'

A look passed between Martin and Gonff, and they both sighed.

'Never heard a mole sing before, have you, Trimp?'

'No, I can't say I have. Why?'

'Oh, nothin', mate. You're sure you want t'hear molesong?'

'Of course I do, that's if Dinny would be kind enough to oblige us with one of his songs.'

The mole's homely face creased deeply with pleasure. 'Hurr, 'ow cudd oi refuse a pretty maid loik ee, miz!' Then he placed a paw over one ear in traditional molesinger's manner and launched into a mole ballad.

'*Ho doodlum roodlum wurdilum day,*
All on ee broight zummer mornin'!
Bold Doogul mole were gurtly brave,
As oi wurr told boi moi muther,
Furr maidens boi the score ee'd save,
Loik chesknutts wun arfter anuther,
Each morn ee rode owt frum 'is abode,
A-mounted on a milky whoit toad,
Surchin' ee danjeruss forest road,
A-lukkin' furr ee maidens.

Ho doodlum roodlum wurdilum day,
All on ee broight zummer mornin'!
Ee spied a gurt fat molewoif thurr,
An' doffed 'is 'at to 'er proudly,
Which froikkened ee molewoif out'n 'er wits,

She'm started to wail roight loudly,
Ee shuvved 'er up onna back of 'is toad,
An' troid t'ride off down ee road,
But two fat moles was an 'evvy load,
An' ee toad wurr crushed loik a beekle.

Ho doodlum roodlum wurdilum day,
All on ee broight zummer mornin'!
Then oop cumm ee gudd an' stoutly mole,
Ee croid, "Woe thurr bless moi loif,
Thurr be two villyuns tryin' to steal,
Moi dear ole fatty gurt woif!"
So pullin' owt a knotty ash club,
Bowth toad an' Doogul ee did drub,
Ee gave 'em black'n'bloo lumps t'rub,
An' 'is woif gave 'im cabbage furr supper.'

Trimp and little Chugger were laughing so hard that they had trouble trying to join in on the chorus. Gonff shook his head at them sadly.

'Don't encourage him, mates. I've heard that song – there's still another forty-seven verses t'go yet!'

Martin leaped on Dinny suddenly, stifling the mole's mouth with both paws. Trimp sniffed at the Warrior severely.

'Don't be so bad-mannered, sir. Let poor Dinny finish his song. Chugger and I were enjoying it!'

Martin shot her a warning glance, his voice an urgent whisper. 'Don't make another sound, Trimp. Gonff, throw some water on that fire, and let's get in the stream, quick!'

They obeyed Martin without question. Gonff flung water on the flames, which sizzled and hissed in clouds of white steam. Trimp found herself breathless in the cold stream, pulled there by Dinny. Keeping their heads low the travellers clung to the raft. A hail of arrows hit the sailcloth shelter, some zipping through, others bouncing off to stick in the deck timbers. These were followed by a volley of slingstones and a couple of throwing spears, both of which buried their points in the food haversacks. Then there was silence.

Chugger clung to Martin's neck, shivering. 'I cold an' wet, not nice inna water!'

Another lot of arrows hit the raft. Martin stroked the little squirrel's head, whispering softly, 'Ssshhh now, Chugg. Right, let's swim over to the far bank. Try not to make any splashes, go easy.'

As they swam off, a harsh voice called from the opposite bank, 'Give 'em some more just t'make sure, then we'll board the raft an' have fun with any still breathin'!'

The travellers made it safely to the far bank. Trimp found some dry grass and rolled Chugger in it, then she joined her friends, watching in the thick bushes by the stream's edge. Swaying under the impact, the raft took several more salvos of missiles. Gonff nudged Dinny. 'D'you reckon we're slain by now, Din?'

'Hurr, they'm ratters given ee raft 'nuff to finish off ee troib o' badgerfolk, oi be thinken!'

Martin began gathering pawfuls of pebbles from the shallows. 'Let's see how they like a spot of sniping. Wait for my word.'

Launching crude logboats, the rats made it clumsily across to the raft. There were so many of them that the raft began to tilt crazily. Boss Girfang, their leader, caught hold of his son Riddig, who was trying to undo one of the haversacks, and snarled at the young rat, 'Well, where are they, these creatures that tried t'slay yer? I don't see 'em anywheres.'

Riddig cowered under his father's angry glare. 'I dunno where they went, but there was five o' them, two ole mice, a fat mole, a young 'og an' a liddle squirrel. They all battered me wid slingstones fer no reason at all. I was jus' layin' on the bank, takin' a nap!'

Girfang tweaked his son's ear sharply. 'An' you jus' lay

there an' let 'em do it, you, a Boss's son? Stinkin' liddle coward, y'make me sick!'

Riddig squealed as Girfang stamped on his tail, protesting, 'I never jus' lay there. I got the 'og wid a stick an' the two mice wid big round stones. They can't 'ave got far!'

A dull thud sounded in the night, and one of the rats toppled into the water. Girfang turned on the rest.

'Be still an' leave them 'aversacks alone or you'll 'ave us all in the stream. Stop rockin' the raft, willyer!'

Thonk! A rat screeched and clapped both paws to his jaw. Girfang grabbed the nearest rat, using him as a shield.

'Somebeast's slingin' at us. Get 'em!'

Splat! Thwack! Crack! Thunk!

Vermin let out agonised yells, two fell in the stream, and the raft rocked wildly as big round river pebbles whizzed out of the darkness, causing injury and chaos.

Girfang leaped with the others into the water. Seizing their logboats' sides, they swam madly back to their own bank, peppered relentlessly with stones. No sooner was Girfang on dry land than the slinging ceased. He grabbed Riddig roughly by the scruff and hauled him ashore, then snapped a willow switch from a young sapling.

'Two ole mice, a fat mole, a young 'og an' a liddle squirrel, eh? Yew rotten barefaced liar!'

Riddig danced in an agonised circle, his father holding him tight by the neck scruff and whaling away mercilessly with the willow switch.

'Yeeeee! Oohooh! I wuz tellin' the truth, sir, 'onest I was! Aaaaagh! Yeekyeek! Owowowow!'

'Truth? Yew wouldn't know truth if'n it fell on yer 'ead out of a tree, yer mealy-mouthed fork-tongued worm!' Girfang laid on heavily with the switch, punctuating each word to drive home his message. 'There was more'n five beasts stonin' us there, yew forty-faced toad. Must've been at least a dozen, all trained warriors by the way they could aim an' hit so good! Own up, now. There was twelve of 'em, mostly otters from upstream, wasn't there, ye wretch? Tell the truth or I'll flay yer!'

Gonff twirled his sling idly, winking at Trimp as they crouched in the bushes on the far bank. 'Does yore heart good lissenin' t'justice bein' done, missie.'

The hedgehog maid listened with satisfaction as she heard Riddig's wails echoing into the night.

'Wahaaar, there was twelve otters beside the others. Don't 'it me no more, Boss, please! Twelve otters, you was right. Wahaaahaaahaaa!'

Following this revelation, Girfang could be heard calling to the rest of his tribe as they deserted him. 'Where are you lot off to? Git back 'ere!'

Derisive shouts followed his command. 'Yah, we ain't scrappin' wid no twelve otters. Go an' fight yer brat's battles yerself. Yore Riddig started it!'

Gonff grinned, stowing his sling about his waist. 'Y'know what they say, truth never hurt anybeast!'

Martin unbuckled his sword and borrowed Gonff's dagger. 'So they say, mate, but you try telling that to Riddig. I wager he's sorry he ever threw that stick at Trimp. Wait here, I'll swim out to our raft and cut it loose.'

Next morning, dry and well breakfasted, the friends sailed onward, staying close to the far bank. Summer warmth raised their spirits, with Gonff confiding aloud to Martin and Trimp, 'I reckon it wasn't Riddig caused all that fuss, y'know.'

Trimp looked up from the dough she was kneading for lunch. 'Was it not? Who do you think was responsible, then?'

'Dinny's singin', of course. It drove the rats wild an' they attacked us just to stop the 'orrible noise, missie.'

'Hurr, you'm turrible crool, zurr Gonffen. Moi ole granmum allus said oi 'ad a voice loik ee lark at furst loight.'

'Haha, that's 'cos yore ole grandmum was deaf as a post, Din.'

Dinny continued chopping candied fruit, not raising his eyes. 'Aye, an' thy ole grandad allus said you'm wurr ee most gurtly 'andsome creature. Noice ole beast ee wurr. Oi used to take 'im furr walks lest ee bump into trees. Bloind ee wurr, pore creetur!'

High noon found them pulled in to a shady inlet out of the hot midday sun. Trimp wanted to bake a candied fruit turnover, but she had no oven. With mole ingenuity, Dinny solved the problem. He cemented flat pieces of shale together with stiff brown clay and water, making a neat little box, which, with the turnover inside, was placed on the fire. Martin and Gonff repaired the torn sail, rent by rat weapons. Nobeast paid much attention to little Chugger. Trimp warned him to stay close to camp, and he did for a while, but whilst Trimp was busy with her cooking and Dinny was digging for fresh roots and vegetables, Chugger wandered off.

Trimp called to her friends. 'Come on, lunch is ready. Bring your appetite with you!'

Hastily washing their paws in the stream, they strolled into camp, sniffing the air appreciatively.

'Boi okey, sumthin' smells noice, marm!'

'Mmm, candied fruit turnover, just the thing!'

'Aye, 'tis ages since I tasted fruit turnover!'

The hedgehog maid had discovered a big flagon of new cider at the bottom of Martin's pack. She poured out beakers for all and laid out chunks of hot turnover on a piece of birch bark she had found before saying, 'Where's that rascal Chugger got to?'

Dinny shrugged as he helped himself to lunch. 'Ho, ee'm abowt yurr someplace, oi 'spect. You see'd 'im?'

Martin took a gulp of the crisp-tasting apple cider. 'Me? No, I thought he was with you, Din. Me an' Gonff were busy fixing up the raft. Did you notice Chugg around, Gonff?'

The Mousethief shook his head. 'No, sorry, I ain't seen him.' Seating himself, he began blowing on his turnover to cool it. 'Hah, ole Chugg'll soon come runnin' when he smells yore cookin', miss Trimp, you'll see!'

But Chugger didn't come. They sat and ate lunch, glancing about and giving an occasional shout of the little squirrel's name. Still nothing.

Trimp was worried. 'Martin, will you go and take a good look around? I'm sure Chugger can't have gone far.'

The Warrior put aside his food. 'Let's all take a look!'

Spreading out in different directions they began combing the area. Martin and Gonff went east and west along the bank, whilst Dinny searched in and around the camp area, in case Chugger was having a game with them. Trimp ventured alone into the woodland, knowing that Martin and Gonff would circle inward and meet up with her when they had searched the bank both ways. Tree shelter became thick and gloomy, blocking out most of the sunlight and leaving the depths cloaked in a murky green twilight. The hedgehog maid went cautiously, calling out in a subdued voice, 'Chugger, are you there, mate? Come out, my little Chugg!'

Her voice fell dead upon her ears, with no echo. She felt very small amid the tall columns of oak, elm and beech. Then her sharp ears began to pick up the odd noise, and she smiled to herself. That would be Chugger, playing one of his little tricks, stalking her mischievously. She decided to hide and turn the tables on him. Swiftly Trimp ran behind a broad bump-gnarled black poplar, and was knocked flat by the creature that had been following her. She squeaked in fright at the sight of it.

7

The gigantic goshawk took a pace backward, allowing Trimp to rise unsteadily. From its black hooked talons and bright yellow legs up the mighty body, feathered in brown-tipped white plumage, to the mottled headcap it was the most impressive bird Trimp had ever seen. Twin gleaming gold eyes with savage black pupils stared down at her over a lethally curved beak. The goshawk's voice was rasping, harsh. 'What doest thou in my domain, hedgepig?'

Trimp had never been called a hedgepig. Bravely she decided to retaliate, and swallowing hard she adopted a stern tone. 'Not that it's any of your business, bird, but I'm searching for my friend, a baby squirrel named Chugger!'

The goshawk twitched his head to one side. He had never been addressed as bird before. 'Prithee, have a care, spinedame. I am called Krar the Woodwatcher. None hath called me bird and lived!'

Trimp became bolder. She stared levelly at the goshawk. 'Aye, and I'm called Trimp the Rover by those with any manners. None have called me hedgepig and lived – er, that goes for spinedame also!'

It was Trimp's turn to take a backward step. She

thought Krar was about to eat her, but a moment later she realised that he was actually smiling at her, an unusual occurrence in a hawk.

'Thou art a bold beast, Trimprover. Thine enemies must be few methinks, or dead. Say again the name of this squirrelmite thou seekest.'

'Chugger, but he'll answer to Chugg. He's only a babe.'

The forest green was blotted out as Krar spread his colossal wings. He touched Trimp's head with a wingtip. 'Do you tarry here, Trimprover, whilst I make enquiries.'

Trimp was knocked flat by the backrush of air as Krar flapped his wings and rose among the tree trunks. Leaves drifted down through a golden shaft of sunlight as he shot like an arrow through the woodland canopy.

Gonff came trotting through the woodland, catching sight of his friend as he hurried in from the opposite direction.

'Ahoy, Martin, no sign of the liddle feller?'

'None, mate. Have y'seen Trimp?'

'Hi, you two, I'm over here!'

Both ran over to where Trimp was sitting with her back against the poplar, picking leaves from her headspikes. Gonff stood, paws akimbo, shaking his head at her.

'Well, missie, this's a nice how d'ye do, us two runnin' ourselves ragged along the streambanks an' through the woods, an' you sittin' here coolin' yore paws, very nice!'

Trimp stood up, brushing herself off. 'Actually I'm waiting for word of Chugger at any moment. Now I don't want either of you to be afraid.'

Martin looked about and spread his paws wide. 'Afraid of what, Trimp?'

She pointed upward. 'That!'

Entering the woodland through the hole he had made in the treetops, Krar Woodwatcher zoomed in like a thunderbolt. All three travellers were knocked flat by the wind from his wings as he landed.

Trimp patted one of Krar's talons. 'Now you'll have to stop doing that, Krar, it'll injure some poor beast one day. These are my good friends, Martin the Warrior and Gonff, Prince of Mousethieves. Meet Krar Woodwatcher, mates. These woodlands belong to him!'

Martin and Gonff gulped and bowed low at the same time. Krar closed both eyes and clacked his beak politely, as goshawks do when greeting friends. He turned to Trimp.

'Thy friend the squirrelmite is taken captive in the talons of laggardly carrion – crows, I fear. Alas, 'tis sad news.'

Trimp was about to speak when Gonff silenced her with a wink. The artful Mousethief addressed himself to the goshawk, cleverly using the bird's own antiquated mode of speech.

'Lackaday, sirrah, and thou callest thyself ruler of this fiefdom? Were I in thy place I'd say fie upon myself methinks, allowing carrion to hold innocent babes in durance. 'Tis not the worthy act of a just lord!'

Much to Martin and Trimp's surprise, the huge goshawk shifted from one leg to the other, his head hanging slightly. 'Thou speakest truly, O Mousethief. 'Tis my domain and 'twas fitting I stand chided for lack of vigilance.'

Gonff shook his head doubtfully. 'I fain would give thee a chance to redeem thyself, lord.'

Crouching low, the huge bird spread his wings wide upon the ground, his face a picture of abject misery, his very feathers seeming to droop. 'Then truly woe betide me, though I crave a boon from thee, Prince of Mouse-thieves. Give me leave to effect rescue of thy vassal, I beg ye. Grant me this favour and I will be in thy debt from this day henceforth!'

A wave of pity swept over Trimp as she watched Krar, prostrate at Gonff's footpaws. She could not keep from crying out, 'Oh, say you will, Gonff. Let him do it!'

The Mousethief folded his paws stubbornly. Turning his back on the goshawk, he winked at Martin and Trimp as he spoke. 'Silence, maid, cease thy prattling! For how doth the Prince of Mousethieves know this creature will cleave true unto his word?'

Martin drew his sword. Touching Krar's bowed head with it, he kissed the blade and announced dramatically, 'I, Martin of Redwall, do give my pledge and bond that Krar Woodwatcher, lord of this place, will honour thy trust, O Prince. For is he not a warrior born, like myself, and bound in word and deed to protect lesser creatures!'

Gonff paced up and down, as if digesting this statement. Then he placed his footpaw under Krar's beak. 'Say where is this place yon foul crows abide?'

A note of hope crept into the goshawk's voice. 'Some pines in a clearing, right close to here, O Prince. Thou and thy friends mayst follow me and watch whilst I free thy servant. But 'tis better it be done soon, for tarrying is unwise, methinks!' He watched avidly as Gonff nodded.

'Mayhap 'tis so. Go then, but hearken, thou hast this warrior to thank for his surety.'

A transformation came over the goshawk. He dipped his lethal beak and kissed Gonff's footpaw. 'My thanks to thee, O Prince!' Standing tall, Krar spread his immense wings, saluting Martin, who was dwarfed in his shadow. 'And my thanks to thee, sire. Karraharrakraaaaaaarrr!'

The goshawk's blood-chilling war cry rang out as he whooshed into the air, bowling the three friends over. Trimp sprang up, pulling leaves from her spines.

'I wish he wouldn't do that! Gonff, how did you know he'd act like that?'

The Mousethief flicked a paw at Martin. 'Oh, it was easy. I know how warriors think – I've lived with one most of my life, haven't I, matey?'

Martin tweaked his friend's tail. 'Cut the chatter or we'll lose sight of Krar!'

Running as fast as they could, the friends kept Krar in

sight as he winged slowly along, just beneath the tree-tops, taking care not to lose them. After a while they saw a broad green hillock thrusting itself above the woodland. At its top was a pine grove. Krar swooped down, landing alongside Gonff.

'Yonder lies the carrion stronghold, O Prince. I pray thee make no move. We have been seen!'

As he spoke a crowd of grey-black crows of the hooded variety came fluttering out of the pines like ragged dark pieces of cloth blown on the wind, coming to rest on the level sward below the hill. Their bold harsh chatter filled the air as they swaggered forward to meet the interlopers, wings folded, beaks thrust forth aggressively. In a less fraught situation the sight of their curious rolling gait might have been comical, but these were savage birds, who brooked no trespassers on their land. Krar whispered, 'Bide here, friends. Warrior, keep thy blade ready. Now, I will go hence and parley, for I know the carrion tongue.'

He strode out, erect and disdainful, and a big crow, far heavier than the rest, waddled forward to meet him. At a point between the crows and the travellers both birds halted. Eye to eye they stood, beaks almost touching. The crow leader hit the soil several times with his beak, casually, as if showing his contempt by digging for worms.

He made harsh cawing noises. 'Kraaaw rakkachakka krawk karraaaaak?'

The goshawk rapped sharply back at him. 'Arrakkarraka!'

The crow gestured carelessly with one wing. 'Nakraaaak!'

Evidently it was not the answer Krar desired. The goshawk made his move without a moment's hesitation.

Charging forward, he slammed the crow to the ground with a ferocious headbutt and began hammering him ruthlessly with beak and talons. Cawing and hopping

63

about excitedly, the crow gang called out encouragement to their leader, but he did not possess the warrior's heart or ferocity of the goshawk. It was over in a trice. A few long grey-black feathers flew in the air and the crow leader lay defeated.

With sharp pecks and talon scratches, Krar forced the crow to stand. The brave goshawk rapped out a command at his beaten foe. 'Chavaaragg!'

Humiliated, the crow turned to face his gang, spreading his wings limply and dropping them so they trailed upon the grass.

Trimp nudged Martin. 'I know Krar has won, but what's he doing?'

The Warrior had understood it all, he knew. 'Those feathers that you see are the crow's pinfeathers. Krar ripped them out. That crow will never be able to fly again. Krar forced him to show his wings to the others as a warning. Hush now, Trimp, I want to see what happens next!'

The goshawk took to the air. Sailing over the heads of the crows, he winged upwards, landing in the biggest nest, atop the highest tree. A female crow shot out of it with a terrified squawk. Krar dipped his beak into the nest and came up with an egg in it. He put the egg back. Spreading his wings he flapped them, screeching harshly at the crows. Then with a powerful thrust he ripped a chunk from the nest with his talons and cast it down to earth. Pandemonium broke out down below. The crows dashed into the pine grove, cawing and leaping about in distress. Martin spoke as he watched them, having interpreted the goshawk's move.

'He's threatening to rip all the nests to shreds, starting with the crow leader's, unless they bring out Chugger. Watch!'

'Trimp! Gonff! It me, Chugg, here I are!'

Dashing out of the pine grove, with the crows behind shooing him on, Chugger hurtled forward, tripping and rolling down the hill, giggling as he went. 'Heeheehee, yah yah ole fedderybums!'

Trimp swept him up into her paws, kissing the little fellow and lecturing him at the same time. 'Such language, master Chugg. Thank the seasons you're safe. Why did you go wandering off like that, eh? Oh, my little Chugg, you had us worried to death!'

Chugger threw his tiny paws wide, grinning broadly. 'See, it me, Chugg! I norra hurted, big birds frykkened o' me, I smacka smacka dem wiv big sticks, ho yes!'

Gonff hugged Chugger fondly, then turned stern. 'You liddle fibber, smackin' crows with big sticks indeed. But let me tell you, bucko, remember what Girfang did to young Riddig, eh? Well, any more fibs an' runnin' off when yore told to stay near camp an' you'll get the same off me!'

Chugger hid his face in Trimp's tunic and sulked. Martin threw a paw about Gonff's shoulders. 'Big old softie, I'll wager you wouldn't have the heart to lay a paw on Chugger, would you, O Prince?'

The Mousethief struck a regal pose, looking down his nose. 'Oh, I don't know, you'd be surprised what us royal types can do when we're in the mood. I usually have any mouse who leans upon me beheaded, so remove your paw, common fellow, afore you incur me wrath!'

Martin looked at Trimp in mock horror. 'Such an air of command these royal ones have about them!'

The hedgehog kicked Gonff lightly in the tail. 'Yes, O Prince, it's your turn to cook the supper when we get back to camp!'

Krar landed in their midst, managing not to knock anybeast over with his giant wings. He gestured with his beak. 'Best we begone from this place. Methinks there be but one of me and too many of yon carrion. Let us away now!'

8

As there was still plenty of daylight left, the travellers opted to sail further rather than lie about in camp. Krar Woodwatcher saw them off on the streambank.

'Fare thee well, O Prince of Mousethieves, fortune go with thee. Thou wilt not see me, but I will guard the air and watch o'er thee 'til thou art gone from my domain. Be you subject to thy Prince's commands and behave thyself, squire Chugg, or I will give thee back to yon carrion. Fortune attend thee, dame Trimp, my friend. Thou too, good Dinny, and thee, sir Martin. I'll not lightly forget that ye forswore thine honour for me. Go now, goodbeasts!'

Chugger began weeping as they sailed off downstream. 'Wahaah! Chugg not want Krar t'be gonned!'

Martin let the little fellow work one of the paddles. 'Krar isn't gone, Chugg, he's watching over us, even though we can't see him. Give him a wave, go on!' Chugger waved a chubby paw and felt somewhat better. As the Warrior held the paddle with the squirrel-babe, he explained as best he could. 'Sometimes friends do go from us – it will happen more and more as you grow up, Chugg. But if you really love your friends, they're never gone. Somewhere they're watching over you and they're always there inside your heart.'

66

*

Towards evening they saw fireglow in the distance. With complete silence and great caution, the friends approached it, hoping that if it were anybeast hostile, they might slip by unnoticed. But as a voice raised in song echoed on the dusky air, Gonff relaxed, chuckling.

'I'd know that barrel-bellied baritone anywhere, mates. Now there's a fine voice for ye, but don't tell him I said it. Haharr, listen to 'im, will you!'

It was a fine voice, more bass than baritone. Deep and rich, it thrummed out over the babbling streamnoises.

'Hoooooo rum tum toe, follah diddle doh,
Me boots are full of water,
An' the bread won't rise,
So I'm scoffin' apple pies,
An' swiggin' good dark porter.

Hooooooo bless my fur, an' you sit over there,
There's honeycake an' salad,
An' you've got no choice,
But t'listen to me voice,
As I sing you this ballad!'

A look of pure mischief spread across Gonff's face. Cupping both paws around his mouth he sang out in a perfect imitation of the singer's deep voice.

'Hoooooooo you sit there, an' I'll sit here,
An' I won't hear yore ballad,
But I'll scoff yore pie,
An' I'll look ye in the eye,
With me ears stuffed full o' salad!'

From round a bend in the bank a small neat logboat came shooting out, propelled by a fat shrew with an ash stave. Trimp knew that shrews were usually aggressive and short-tempered, but this one was different. He performed a joyful jig at the prospect of company. It came as no surprise that the shrew and Gonff knew each other. As the former leaped aboard the raft they pounded backs and shook paws.

'Log a Log Furmo, ye pot-bellied son of a water-walloper, as soon as I clapped ears on that warblin' I knew 'twas the best ballad singer this side o' Mossflower!'

'Haharr, Gonff Mousethief, ye light-pawed rogue, if I hadn't 'ave known that was you singin' back at me I'd 'ave thought 'twas meself. Pull over t'the camp an' bring yore pals with ye, supper's on the go. Ahoy, Martin, is it really yourself, Warrior? Good t'see you, matey!'

Dinny tapped the shrew Chieftain with a digging claw. 'Doan't ee know oi, zurr, furr oi'd know ee frum a buttyfly?'

Log a Log Furmo stood back, rubbing his eyes. 'Well sink me a log, is that the slim young mole I once knew as Dinny? Wot 'appened, mate, is there another beast inside that skin with ye?'

Dinny chuckled, patting his ample form. 'Nay, zurr Log, oi jus' growed more bootiful an' gurtly strong, since you'm bain't been round to rob moi vittles.'

Furmo turned to Trimp. 'And what is a gentle hogmaid like ye doing with such rogues?'

Trimp smiled. 'Keeping them in order.'

'I'd best watch my manners then, I'm thinking,' laughed Furmo.

The Guerrilla Union Of Shrews In Mossflower, Guosim for short, had always been headed by one traditionally named Log a Log. They ranged all the waterways in their logboats, a great tribe of them. Trimp was almost half a head taller than most of them. Small spike-furred long-snouted shrews, with brightly coloured headbands and rapiers tucked in their belts, watched as the newcomers made their way to the fire. Log a Log introduced them as friends, reassuring his band. Guosim shrews are excellent cooks, as the hedgehog maid soon discovered. Their apple and blackberry crumble was pure delight to taste. Two Guosim cooks stood over Trimp, watching anxiously as she sampled some, enquiring gruffly, 'Good crumble, that? Made it ourselves, y'know!'

'Aye, to our own recipe. D'ye like it, marm?'

Trimp's smile would have charmed the birds out of the trees. 'It's perfect, thank you. I've never tasted a crumble in my life that could compare with it. Beautiful!'

Unused to such compliments, the shrew cooks kicked their footpaws bashfully and began serving more food, calling to one another in bass growls to hide their embarrassment.

'Hoi, Rugger, pour 'er some pear cordial, will ye!'

'Aye, an' give 'er some shrewcheese an' watercress!'

'Look after pore liddle Chugger, will ye, Bindle? Pour some honey o'er the babe's hazelnut pudden!'

'Some streamside salad an' newbaked cornbread for ye, marm!'

Log a Log Furmo smiled at the antics of his younger shrews, trying to impress the travellers with their hospitality, particularly Trimp, for it is a fact that the Guosim had always been partial to a pretty face. Furmo passed Martin and Gonff a tankard of shrew porter apiece, saying, 'Haharr, young Trimp's gotten 'er paws well under the table there. They'll feed 'er 'til she bursts!'

Some of the little shrews had never seen a mole before, and they crowded around Dinny, haranguing him as he ate.

'Does all moles 'ave softy nice fur like you, mista Diggy?'

'Ho yuss, moi dearies, us'n's keeps it soft boi eatin' oop all us vittles loik goodbeasts.'

'You mus' be the goodest mole of all, mista Diggy, 'cos you be eatin' a h'orful big lot o' vittles!'

'Hurr hurr, thankee, young 'un, oi 'spect oi am!'

'You got very bigbig claws, mista Diggy, wot they for?'

A kindly shrewmum rounded the little ones up. 'Don't you be askin' mister Dinny foolish questions, now. Leave 'im in peace to eat 'is supper. Bedboats for you, 'tis late.'

Martin was relating the object of their journey to Furmo when the shrewmum stole up and whispered in the shrew Chieftain's ear. He excused himself, explaining, 'We'll talk later, friend. I've got to sing the liddle 'uns off to sleep. Won't be long.'

Moored to the bank was a logboat, padded thickly with warm cushions and blankets. The shrewbabes lay in it, rocked by the motion of the water, as their Log a Log sang them to sleep in his melodious deep voice.

'The stream flows by and time rolls by,
Now daytime flies so close those eyes,
It's been a long day little one, little one.
Small birds now slumber in the nest,
And fishes in their stream,
Know night has come to send us rest,
And give to all a wondrous dream,
All night hours go, so soft and low,
The lazy stream runs calm and slow,
It's been a long day little one, little one.
Our weary world is waiting soon,
Bright stars will pierce the sky,
As silent as the golden moon,
That sheds her light on you and I,
And when the darkness drifts away,
Some lark up high will sing and say,
Oh welcome to a newborn day, my little one.'

Gonff crept up, carrying Chugger. The squirrelbabe was fast asleep. Sliding him aboard the logboat with the dozy little shrews, Gonff patted his friend's shoulder.

'Wish we could take you all the way with us, Furmo

mate, ole Chugg went out like somebeast'd whacked him with a slingstone once you started singin'. How d'you do it?'

Log a Log Furmo shrugged, gesturing at the logboat. 'I've had plenty o' practice, mate. Eight of them are mine.'

It was about an hour after dawn when Trimp opened her eyes. The previous night had been a late one, with lots of good shrew food, singing, storytelling and even a bout of tail wrestling by two lithe young Guosim shrews to impress her. Some shrew cooks were up and about, rekindling the fire and preparing breakfast. The Guosim were very fond of sizeable breakfasts when they were at summer camp. Feigning sleep, the hedgehog maid peeped out from under her blanket, savouring the day. Downstream looked like a long winding green hall, with alder, bird cherry and weeping willow trees practically forming an arch over the sundappled stream, which was bordered by bright flowering clubrush, sedge and twayblade. Blue and pearly grey, the firesmoke hovered, making gentle swirls between sunshine and shadow in diagonal shafts. Snatches of murmured conversation between early risers were muted in the background, with the sweet odours of smouldering peat and glowing pinebark on the fire. Trimp wished that she could stay like this for ever, happy amongst true friends, in tranquil summer woodlands by a stream.

'Oatmeal'n'honey, fresh fruit an' hot mint tea, marm!'

It was the two shrewcooks from the previous evening, tempting her to partake of breakfast. Trimp needed no coaxing. She sat up gratefully, wondering how one night's sleep could leave her with such a fine appetite.

'Thank you, friends. My word, this looks delicious!'

Gonff and the Log a Log were in friendly dispute as they broke their fast.

'Hearken t'me, Mouseythief, we're sailin' with you, at least as far as the seashore, an' that's final, mate!'

71

'No no, Furmo, we wouldn't think o' pullin' ye away from yore summer camp. We'll be all right travellin' on alone.'

'Hah, will y'lissen t'the mouse, turnin' down an offer of safe voyagin' in convoy. He's mad, Martin, tell 'im!'

Wiping wild plum juice from his paws the Warrior agreed. 'Safety in numbers, Gonff, I'm all for it. Where's your manners, mate, d'you want to offend Log a Log Furmo by refusing his kind offer? Ignore him, Furmo, I accept!'

Dinny and Chugger seconded the Redwall Champion.

'An' h'i except too as well an' all, mista sh'ew!'

'Hurr, oi too, zurr, ee shrews be gudd company an' gurt cookers. Burr aye!'

Trimp licked her oatmeal spoon and held it up. 'That goes for me too, unless Gonff wants t'do all the cooking and paddling aboard that raft!'

The Prince of Mousethieves clapped the Guosim leader's back. 'Quit yore arguin', matey, 'tis no good wot y'say, yore goin' with us, like it or not, see. Yore goin'!'

A real shrewish voice rang out. Furmo's wife Honeysuckle bustled up, waving a ladle. She was bigger than him and had a temper that none could match on land or water. 'Goin'? Goin' where may I ask?'

Even though he was a chieftain, Furmo wilted under her fierce eye and sharp tone. 'Er, just down the stream apiece, my fragrant woodrose.'

Gonff interrupted, standing between both shrews. 'Ah Honeysuckle, you delightful morsel, we've asked your husband to accompany us with some of his shrews, to show us the way and guard us against attack. But of course he says he can't possibly leave yore side on such a foolish errand. Not that I blame Furmo. Anybeast leavin' a dark-eyed beauty like you to go off sailin', huh, he'd be out of his mind, mad as a frog an' daft as a bluebottle!'

Lips pursed grimly, Honeysuckle waggled the ladle under Furmo's nose and spoke threateningly. 'An' you, y'great lazy lump, you said you wouldn't go, eh?'

'But petal, 'ow can I leave you an' all the liddle 'uns?'

Furmo winced. His wife had hoisted him upright by one ear. 'In the boat, Log a Lazypaws, this instant. You Guosim there, wot are you standin' grinnin' about, eh? Now get those logboats ready t'sail, now, while I'm still in a good mood. Shift yore mossbound behinds!'

Four logboats were lashed to the raft's sides, each with six Guosim paddlers. Honeysuckle tossed supplies aboard with furious strength and energy. Gonff murmured under his breath as Dinny dodged a sack of vegetables, 'Matey, I'd hate t'see 'er in a bad mood if this is one of 'er good moods!'

Honeysuckle scowled at him. 'What was that you said?'

The clever Mousethief gestured at the provisions. 'I was just sayin', marm, after so much bad food 'tis nice to see some good food!'

She pointed a warning paw at the pair. 'Don't let me hear of you two wastin' any!'

Dinny tugged his snout respectfully. 'Hurr, 'ow cudd us'n's be a-wastin' vittles loaded aboard boi such ee furr paw as yourn, moi gurt booty?'

Honeysuckle dipped the mole a deep curtsy, actually smiling. 'Why thankee, sir mole, wot a gallant thing t'say!'

Halfway downstream between the camp and the next bend, Log a Log sighed with relief and shook Dinny warmly by the paw.

'You clinched it, Din, all that fair paw an' great beauty stuff. Where'd you learn it?'

The mole twitched his nose at Trimp. 'Burr, oi diddent lurn nuthin', zurr, h'oim jus' a reg'lar silver-tongued molerogue, bain't oi, miz Trimp?'

The hedgehog maid twitched her nose back at him. 'Aye, especially when it comes to lappin' up oatmeal'n'honey you are. Great fat fraud!'

Furmo did a perfect imitation of his wife's voice. 'One more remark like that, young 'og, an' I'll rap yore ears with my pudden spoon. That mole's a real gentlebeast!'

Meandering happily down the broad waterway through the sun and shade, the travellers and their shrew friends jested and chuckled with each other.

A watermeadow appeared on their left about midday. The Guosim had ceased paddling because the current was carrying them along with sufficient speed. All aboard both raft and logboats sat admiring the serene beauty as Log a Log pointed out its features.

'Looks peaceful, don't it? But mark my words, mates, midst all that brookweed, water lilies, crowfoot an' gipsy-wort, there're more skeeters than y'could shake a stick at. Mayfly, caddisfly, stonefly, alderfly, pond skaters, big lacewings an' o' course the ole Emperor dragonflies. Makes it a rare ole fishin' spot – fish all come there to hunt the flies.'

Gonff winked craftily at the shrew. 'Aye, an' Guosim go there to hunt the fish, I'll wager.'

A sturdy old shrew elder snorted at the Mousethief's remark. 'Yore jokin', of course. There's eels an' pike in there longer'n a logboat. 'Tis them'd be huntin' us if'n shrews was fool enough to try fishin' that watermeadow!'

Log a Log pointed downstream. 'Look, there's dragon-flies comin' up this way. They ain't tarryin', either. Wonder wot's upset 'em?'

A half-dozen of the huge insects came straight at the raft, suddenly veering off into the watermeadow, their iridescent wingbacks and black-green banded bodies making a brave sight. Log a Log addressed Martin. 'Somethin's upset the dragons. We'd best be on our guard, 'specially when we round that bend ahead – there's a creek to one side of it. Stay on the alert, Guosim!'

Trimp sat in the centre of the raft, holding on to Chugger. Half the shrews took to paddling the logboats lashed to the raftsides, the rest joined Martin, Log a Log, Dinny and Gonff, who stood for'ard on the raft, weapons close to paw. As they rounded the bend it became only too clear what danger they were in.

Like some fantastic snowstorm a male swan came billowing out of the creek entrance. The sight of it took Trimp's breath away. Spreading awesome wings, the colossal bird reared out of the water, its long neck bent, hissing loudly like a serpent. Log a Log roared at the paddlers, 'Back water! Back water, Guosim!'

Furiously the shrews backpaddled against the current, but the raft's stern hit the bank on the bend's incurve and lodged there. The elder shrew seized a long paddle and bravely swung it at the swan, sizing up the situation for his companions as he did so.

'He's a mute swan. Prob'ly the female's guardin' 'er young up that creek, an' this feller thinks we're goin' to 'urt 'em. Looks fairly mad t'me. Ain't goin' to let us pass or retreat. This is his stretch o' water, an' he'll protect his family an' this area with his life, mates!'

Though they were in great danger, Martin could not help admiring the giant bird. With its tough orange beak, which had a hard black lump at its base, and its neck thick as a rowan sapling, the mute male swan was a fiercely wondrous sight, snow white, with wings powerful enough to cripple and kill an adversary. The Warrior picked up a paddle to fend it off, knowing that he had not the heart to kill or injure such a magnificent creature with his sword. However, the swan had no such finer feelings, but came at them hissing and making a peculiarly strange squeak, far out of character given his bulk and ferocity. Gonff swung his paddle.

A gigantic wing descended on him, snapping the paddle like a twig and buffeting him from the raft into the water. Martin's paddle clacked hard against the bird's beak, sending a jarring pain through his paws, and the swan came at him. Dinny caught it a hefty blow in the neck, which merely seemed to bend gracefully under the impact. Two shrews were swept off into the water by another clout from the swan's wing. It reared high and gripped the raft timbers in its wide webbed claws, trying to hoist itself aboard. Trimp and Chugger slid backward, yelling, as the raft began tilting with the swan's weight pressing on its front end. Martin grabbed his sword and held it up quickly, so that the swan's beak hit it with a loud echoing sound. Pang!

Nobeast was expecting what happened next. Something hit the swan's head like a stone, sending a cloud of small white feathers into the air. There was an ear-splitting screech from above. It was Krar Woodwatcher! The courageous goshawk came in for another dive, even though it must have been dizzy from the first blow. The swan swung its beak and retaliated. There was a thudding noise as both birds struck one another simultaneously. Krar landed in a heap on the raft. Savagely shaking off Dinny, who was trying to help it recover, the goshawk struggled upright, panting, 'Use thy raftpoles and get thee off downstream. Hasten now, whilst I hold off yonder battler!'

Krar launched himself into the attack once more. Feathers flew amid the hissing and screeching, stream-water was thrashed into foam, leaves and branches showered wide. Punting the raft out from the bank, whilst shrews either side paddled madly, they skimmed out under the arch formed by the swan's neck and Krar's wings, into the midstream current and off down the waterway. Still paddling and poling with great vigour, they turned their heads to see what the outcome would be. Krar Woodwatcher was as brave and hard a fighter as the swan, but not so foolish. The moment he saw every-beast was out of danger he zoomed off into the wood-lands to nurse his bruises, leaving behind a bewildered and still angry mute swan. Trimp could not stop herself from trembling as she called out, 'He's coming after us, the swan's coming after us!'

Log a Log gritted his teeth. 'Don't look back, mates, it'll slow us down. Keep paddlin' fast as y'can. The swan'll only foller us to the edge of his territory, then he'll go back to guard his family.'

The shrew's prediction proved true, though it gave them a hair-raising moment. The swan came after them in no uncertain fashion. It was almost upon the raft, hardly two logboat lengths from it, when suddenly it gave a final hiss and turned about, traversing back upstream lest any other intruder had shown up to menace its brood. With a sigh of relief the friends collapsed to the deck, shaking all over from exertion and the shock of the swan's attack. The irrepressible Gonff grabbed the sailcloth, holding it wide and flapping his outstretched paws at Trimp. 'Wot's the matter, matey, never seen a swan before?'

The hedgehog maid hooked a paw under the teaser and pulled him flat on his tail. 'Oh, I've seen a swan all right, Gonff, though if I never see another one in my life 'twill be too soon, thank you!'

Through the thinning trees, Dinny scanned the sky. 'Hurr, whurr be ee 'awkburd gone?'

Martin indicated the changing terrain. 'We're coming out of the woodlands, Din, leaving Krar's territory too, I imagine. I wish I could have thanked him. What a great fight he put up on our behalf. I'll never forget that brave bird. Never!'

9

Once they left the trees behind there was very little shade. The water became deeper, the current more sluggish. Throughout a long hot day, the travellers did their share, taking turns to relieve the Guosim paddlers. Only little Chugger seemed unaffected by the blistering heat. With a damp shrew headband bound round his brow and an ash twig in his paw, he cavorted and leaped everywhere, doing battle against a score of imaginary swans.

No sooner had shadows begun to lengthen than Log a Log shipped his paddle, calling out the order they were all waiting upon. 'Pull into that curve on yore right, mates. We'll rest there an' camp until tomorrow!'

Gratefully Trimp watched their lumbering craft nose into the shallows of a cove. It had a good flat bank and protruding rock ledges to provide much-needed shade. Guosim cooks immersed canteens of drinks in water which was cool and shaded by the overhang. Some went out scouting for fresh food, others began preparing a meal from their supplies. Eyeing their leader hopefully, the rest sat on the raft in silence, awaiting his command.

Log a Log Furmo wandered up and down the bank, peering into the crystal-clear water. He scratched his chin, as if undecided, then wagged a cautionary paw at his crew. 'No further'n the end o' that raft, now. Stay out o' the current an' deep parts, an' keep close to the bank. I don't want to carry back news of any drowned Guosim to yore kin.' Before he had finished speaking, several of the younger shrews hurled themselves yelling into the stream.

'Yahahoooooo!'

Jumping ashore to avoid the splashes of the bathing party, Log a Log shook his head at Martin. 'Look at 'em, like a flippin' shower o' Dibbuns!'

A secret wink passed between Gonff and Martin as the Warrior shrugged free of his sword and belt. Grabbing Log a Log between them they leaped into the water. The shrew Chieftain surfaced breathless, blowing spray from both nostrils.

'Yah, y'rotten 'orrible creatures, what'd ye do that for?'

Gonff flung himself on Log a Log and ducked him. 'Gerrout, ye ole fogey, you were dyin' for a play in the water, weren't you?'

Log a Log swam deftly out of the Mousethief's reach. 'Of course I was, mate, but don't tell my shrews that. I'm supposed to be a serious leader who acts responsibly!' He sank beneath the surface again as Chugger landed on him.

'You norra leader, you a big fish, Chugger wanna ride on you back. C'mon, fishy, hup hup, gerra move on!'

Everybeast had tremendous fun in the stream, laughing and splashing, ducking and diving and behaving exactly as Log a Log had said, like a shower of Dibbuns. However, they deserted the water en masse when the foraging party returned, hailing them from the banktop: 'Lookit, mates, we found strawberries!'

Two haversacks filled with wild strawberries, small, sweet and juicy, were carried into camp. Refreshed after her swim, Trimp sat with Chugger and Dinny on the sunwarmed rocks, sharing a heap of the delicious fruit.

One of the foraging party reported to Log a Log. 'Saw

a pile of otter tracks on the heathland back there, mebbe fifteen or more, all big 'uns!'

The shrew Chieftain shrugged, selecting a big strawberry. 'Otters are goodbeasts, we've no reason to fear 'em. They're welcome to a pawful o' vittles if'n they visit us.'

As evening shades tinged the skies the otters came upriver and emerged dripping from the stream. A big wiry fellow, obviously their Skipper, held forth his paws in greeting.

'Peaceful evenin' to ye, friends. Is that a fruit salad with strawberries in it I see? Looks 'andsome, don't it?'

Log a Log smiled at the hungry otters, indicating that they were free to help themselves. 'Sit down an' welcome, friend. Haven't I seen you afore?'

Balancing back on his rudderlike tail, the otter answered, 'Prob'ly crossed paths once or twice, matey. I'm Tungro – my tribe have a holt on the river north o' here.'

The shrew nodded. 'Ah, Tungro. Heard yore name someplace. What are you'n'yore crew doin' hereabouts, mate?'

Tungro accepted food from Trimp and thanked her. He acted rather nonchalant, but Log a Log suspected he was either hiding something or not telling the full story when he replied airily, 'Oh, not much, y'know, jus' takin' a look t'see wot's on the other side o' the hill, so t'speak. Ain't you or none o' yore crew caught sight of an old-lookin' raggedy otter round here today, have ye?'

Log a Log threw a pebble into the stream, watching it sink. 'No, mate. Why d'you ask?'

Tungro did not reply. He nodded to his crew, finished eating and bobbed his head courteously. 'Obliged to ye for the vittles, friends. Go in peace an' good fortune travel with ye. Oh, if'n you should bump into the ole otter I mentioned, tell 'im that he can come back to the hold if'n he's mended his ways.' Tungro handed Furmo an otter tailring. 'Give 'im this an' say that yore all mates o' mine. Fare ye well, now!'

Without creating a single splash the otters slipped into the water and were gone. Martin and Gonff came to sit alongside Log a Log, and the Mousethief expressed his bewilderment.

'Phew, that was a speedy visit. What d'you suppose 'twas all about, Furmo?'

The shrew's answer was guarded. 'Ye'll forgive me if'n I don't tell all the story, 'cos I ain't certain of the full facts meself, but here's as much as I'm willin' to say, mates. I've heard of Tungro, aye, an' his brother Folgrim. Both great warriors, 'tis said, but Folgrim was knowed t'be fiercer, even though he was smaller than Tungro. Well, when their ole father died, they was joint Skippers of their holt. One winter they were attacked by a mixed band o' vermin, but otters ain't beasts to mess with. They gave those vermin scum a real good drubbin' an' drove 'em off. Now Tungro reckoned that was enough, but not Folgrim. Off he went alone in pursuit o' the vermin. Wasn't 'til two seasons later Folgrim returned 'ome. They say the vermin laid a trap an' captured 'im. Starved, beat an' tortured somethin' 'orrible he was, wounded, crippled an' with only one good eye. Sick in the brain too, 'cos Folgrim was never the same after wot those vermin did to 'im. I know from lissenin' to travellers, Folgrim be'aved so bad an' strange that Tungro's banished 'im more'n once from the holt, but Folgrim always returns, an' Tungro forgives his ways an' takes 'im back. Well, you couldn't banish yore own brother for ever, just 'cos he ain't right in the head, now could ye?'

Martin had to agree with the shrew. 'No, you're right, blood's thicker than water. What was that he gave you to give to his brother?'

Log a Log held up the beautiful otter tailring, carved from the backbone of some great fish. 'Nice, ain't it? Though I hope we don't meet Folgrim an' have t'give 'im it.'

Gonff took the tailring and inspected it. 'Why not, Furmo? He's not as bad as all that, is he?'

The shrew took the tailring back and stowed it in his pouch. 'I can't say, Gonff. I won't tell ye all I've heard 'cos I'm not sure I believe it, an' I can't tell ye what I haven't seen. I'm for a spot o' shuteye now. You two can sit up an' natter all night.'

Nothing further was mentioned of Tungro's brother Folgrim. The friends lay down to rest that night with their own thoughts about the story they had heard. Purely out of insatiable curiosity, Gonff wished that he could meet the strange otter. Finally the Mousethief slept, not knowing that he was to get his wish on the following day.

Next morning was damp and humid, with the sky clouded over a dirty grey and drizzle falling continuously. Pushing on downstream the craft sailed slowly along on the rain-flecked waters. Trimp and Chugger sat beneath the awning the shrews had set up from the single sail. The hogmaid watched the others, droplets spilling from their whiskers, soaked through, paws slipping on paddles, as they pushed doggedly on. As noon approached there was no change, and the drizzle persisted. Guosim paddlers looked pleadingly to their leader. Log a Log wiped moisture from his eyes, seeking a suitable spot along the same bank they had camped on the previous day. Eventually he called, 'Head 'er in, mates. Looks like an ole cave yonder!'

A tent was rigged over the cavefront, and the provisions were stacked under it to keep them dry. Everybeast crowded under the canvas and in the small cave. Chugger was wearing a rough hooded cloak which Trimp had fashioned from an empty apple sack. Evading the hedgehog maid, who looked after him like a mother duck, the little squirrel toddled off to explore the country. Trimp looked right and left. Where had the little imp gone? Poking her head from under the shelter she spotted him. Chugger had climbed the rock ledges and was up on top of the bank. He wrinkled his nose and waved at Trimp. 'No worry 'bout Chugg, jus' goin' to fight swans!' Waving his ash twig he vanished from sight. Trimp took off in pursuit, scrambling up the wet stones.

Martin had just lit a small fire when he heard Trimp calling urgently from above, 'Help! Come quick, mates!'

Grabbing his sword, Martin dashed out ahead of the shrews. Together he, Gonff and Furmo took the ledges in a series of bounds, with Dinny and the Guosim following swiftly behind. Trimp was crouched down, protecting Chugger. She pointed. 'There, Martin! Oh, help him, please!'

Two water rats were tormenting another creature. Martin peered through the curtain of misty drizzle. It was an otter, limping along, clad in a ragged cloak and bent almost double. Kicking him and striking him with whippy willow withes, the vermin spat at him, taunting, 'Move yerself, yew dodderin' ole ragbag, we're goin' to tie rocks to yer paws an' sink yer in the stream, nice'n'slow. Come on, yer hobblin' addlebrained idiot!'

Martin lifted his sword and took a pace forward. Log a Log placed a paw on his shoulder. 'Stop there, Warrior, don't interfere. That's Folgrim you see, fightin' the enemy!'

Gonff nodded towards the two rats, who were still unaware of their presence. 'He's fightin' them, d'ye say? Huh, it looks the other way round t'me, mate!'

Log a Log shook his head grimly, murmuring to his shrews, 'Get Trimp an' the liddle 'un back down t'the cave – this ain't fit fer 'em t'see. Keep silent, Martin, crouch down by me an' watch. You too, Gonff.'

One rat stuck out his footpaw and tripped the lame otter, who fell heavily. Both rats laid on savagely with their switches as he pleaded, 'Please, sirs, don't drown me, I'm nought but a pore wayfarin' beast who's lost his way, don't beat me. Owow!'

This continued for a moment. Until one of the rats got too close to the victim. Like a wolf, Folgrim was upon him with lightning speed. He seized the rat in a death hug, sinking his teeth deep into the vermin's throat. Shocked beyond belief, the other rat stood trembling a moment, then he dashed off wailing in terror. Folgrim lifted a bloodstained mouth from his prey's neck, calling, 'Run run run, ratty, I'll track ye down, Folgrim'll get yer.'

At a signal from Log a Log the travellers backed off unobserved and clambered down to their camp. Gonff sat by the fire, sipping a beaker of hot mushroom soup. He stared into the flames and shuddered. 'Ugh! I never seen a creature killed like that afore!'

Martin passed a beaker of soup to Log a Log. 'So that's Folgrim, brother of Tungro. Well, Furmo, d'you believe what they say now?'

Log a Log nodded. 'Every word, mate, every awful word!'

A sound of somebeast scrambling down the ledges alerted them. Next moment Folgrim limped in, still with a bloodsmeared mouth. Chugger's eyes grew big and round at the sight of the fearsome beast. The otter winked his single eye at them and sat by the fire. 'Ah, nice fire. Chills a beast t'the bone, drizzle does!'

Swiftly, Dinny filled a beaker from the soup pot. 'Yurr, zurr h'otter, drinkee summ noice 'ot zoop up!'

Smiling, Folgrim shook his head. Martin saw that his teeth were filed, or broken into jagged points. 'Not fer me, mole. I got food back up there.'

Trimp approached bearing a loaf and a hunk of cheese. 'Then take these with you for tomorrow, sir.' She took a step backward at the sight of the otter's face. It was painted thickly with plant dyes and mud, to cover the horrible wounds and scars etched into it. The single red-rimmed eye stared crazily at her.

'No thankee, missie, I'll 'ave more food by tomorrow when I track that other 'un down. You, shrew, can you let me 'ave tinder an' flint? Beast needs a good cookin' fire in this country an' I ain't got the makin's.'

Log a Log gave Folgrim a bag of soft dried moss and two chunks of flintstone to make fire with. 'Take 'em an' welcome, friend. Yore brother Tungro said that I should give you this tailring too. He says yore welcome back at the holt if'n you've mended yore ways. We're friends of your brother's.'

Folgrim reached out and grabbed Trimp's paw, pushed the tailring over it with a swift movement and released her. 'Pretty bracelet for a pretty maid, eh! If'n you see my brother, tell 'im that I said 'e's a good beast. The holt's better off widout me – it's far too late fer me t'mend my ways. Got t'go now, light a fire, do a spot o' cookin'. Travel on, catch the other rat, light another fire, do more cookin'!' Baring his pointed teeth at the horrified friends, Folgrim stood up and stumped out into the rain.

Trimp covered her mouth with both paws, her normal good pallor taking on a greenish tinge. Log a Log sat her down by the fire, placing a dry sack round her shoulders.

'D'you feel sick, missie? Y'don't look none too chirpy.'

Trimp took a deep breath before replying. 'Didn't you hear? That otter is going to cook a rat and eat it. Oh, I can't believe it!'

Gonff winked at the others as he patted Trimp's paw. 'You didn't believe him, did ye, Trimp? Haha, that's a good 'un, ain't it, Martin, ain't it, Furmo? An otter eatin' a water rat!'

They both laughed hollowly.

'Er, haha, shouldn't believe all y'hear, Trimp.'

'Aye, he was only joking, miss, haha . . .' Martin's half-hearted laugh trailed off miserably.

Further along the bank, in the shelter of another rock ledge, Folgrim was kindling a fire and holding a one-sided conversation with the slain water rat.

'Pity I never got yore mate, he was fatter'n you are. Still, don't fuss, I'll lay 'im by the paws afore sunset tomorrow night. Fire's nice, ain't it? Chills a beast to the bone, this drizzle does. Nice fire, I likes a good fire!'

10

They slept late next morning. The rain had ceased and sunlight was beaming from clear summer skies when Chugger roused himself and trundled out on to the bank. Steamy mist, from the rain, hung over the whole bankshore in a thick low layer, waiting for the sun to evaporate it. The tiny squirrel raced through it, giggling as he tried to catch the elusive tendrils in his paws. 'Yeeheehee! All be's covered in frog, lotsa frogs. Heehee!'

Gonff and Trimp emerged from the cave yawning. Upon hearing Chugger's cries, Gonff became alert. 'What frogs? Who's covered in frogs?'

Trimp shoved the Mousethief playfully. 'He means fog. Look out!'

The mist parted and Chugger bowled head over brush into them. Gonff swept him up, tickling the little fellow and swinging him about. 'I'll give ye frogs, y'villain!'

Soon the whole party was up and about. Furmo and his shrews lit a fire and began cooking breakfast. Dinny appeared out of the mist, toting a pail of water.

'Hurr, doan't be furr frum ee seashores naow. Lookit all ee frog yurrabouts, Marthen.'

Martin climbed halfway up one of the ledges and peered over the mist curtain. 'Right, Din. We don't

87

normally get heavy bankmist like this inland. Sea can't be too far off now. Hush! Everybeast be still. I can hear someone coming this way!'

It was the otters, Tungro and his crew. As soon as Martin recognised their voices he hailed them from the bank. 'Morning, friends. Breakfast's almost ready, y'welcome to share it with us!'

Tungro waded ashore, dripping from the stream. 'Thankee kindly, goodbeasts, we wouldn't say no to a bite o' brekkist. The crew ain't eaten yet t'day.'

Nudging Log a Log Furmo, Gonff raised his eyebrows. 'Better git more shrewbread on the hot stones. Here was I, thinkin' I was goin' t'get a nice big peaceful breakfast – now it'll be a small noisy one with this lot as guests!'

The rest of Tungro's crew came ashore in a huddle. They had Folgrim with them, a rope lead round his middle and both paws bound by a long hobble, which had allowed him to swim. He winked his one good eye at Trimp. 'Good day to ye, missie. 'Ope I finds yer well?'

The hedgehog maid shuddered, though she bobbed him a curtsy and managed a quick smile. 'I'm well, thankee, sir.'

Tungro drew Martin and Furmo to one side. He seemed slightly embarrassed and hesitant. 'Er, I 'opes you'll fergive me, er, bringin' my brother Folgrim to yore camp fer brekkist like this. He ain't a bad beast really, 'tis just that 'is mind's troubled.'

Martin nodded understandingly and patted Tungro's shoulder. 'Don't worry, friend, we know a bit about Folgrim and the bad times he's had. He dropped by here yesterday afternoon. There was no trouble, he behaved himself quite well.'

Tungro looked relieved. 'We caught up with Folgrim just after he'd tracked an' slain a rat. He'd lit a fire, that was 'ow we spotted 'im. Me'n'the crew had t'jump on pore Folgrim a bit, but we managed, tied 'im up an' buried the rat carcass afore he, er, well . . .'

Furmo poured a beaker of pennycloud cordial for the otter. "'Tis all right, y'don't have to explain, we know from the other rat Folgrim managed t'get his paws on, just over the banktop there. Come on now, get somethin' to eat.'

Furmo and his shrews had made a delicious breakfast. There was hot shrewbread, strawberries and a batch of vegetable pasties, with a choice of cordial or hot mint tea to drink. Tungro sat slightly apart with his brother, trying to make him eat a little, but Folgrim kept his mouth firmly shut, refusing the food in silence. Everybeast tried to get on with their meal, but they kept taking secretive glances as Tungro encouraged his brother. 'Come on now, Fol, these're prime vittles, made by the best o' Guosim cooks. Try some o' this pasty, me ole mate!' Folgrim merely shook his head stubbornly. Tungro noticed the watchers and shrugged with embarrassment. 'Sorry, he won't eat nothin', though there ain't a thing wrong wid yore food, friends, 'tis the best I ever tasted.'

Trimp was trying to hold on to Chugger, but he wriggled out of her grasp and went swiftly on all fours to Folgrim. Smiling up into the otter's scarred face, Chugger grabbed a pasty and lectured him like a mother squirrel. 'Eaty all up now, or y'don't grow bigga strong like me. H'i eatim up if'n you don't, silly ole riverdog!'

Suddenly Folgrim burst out laughing at the little squirrel's antics, and took a big bite out of the proffered pasty. 'You ain't eatin' all my brekkist up, liddle sir, ho no!'

Chugger nodded his head in agreement. 'Good h'otter, now Chugg getcher sh'ewbread an' minty tea!'

Folgrim gobbled another mouthful of pasty. 'Why thankee, mate, though I likes cordial better'n mint tea. Mebbe you could fetch me a couple o' them strawberries too, they look nice!'

Tungro shook his head in amazement at the sight of Chugger feeding breakfast to his brother, both of them chatting away amiably, as if they were old friends.

'Well wallop me rudder, will y'look at that? Folgrim never was the most civil o' beasts – back at the holt 'e spoke to nobody, much less smile an' chat like that. I reckon my brother's took a shine to yore liddle squirrel!'

Trimp was slightly apprehensive. She confided her fears to Dinny in a whisper that only he could hear. 'I'm not so sure I like Chugger being around Folgrim. He's an otter who's eaten his enemies and is troubled in his mind. Who can tell what he'd do if the mood took him?'

The mole put aside his food, watching Folgrim and Chugger. 'Oi doan't think ee gotten much t'wurry o'er, missie. Hurr, jus' you'm looka yon h'otter. Whoi, ee'm loik an ole molemum wi' 'er h'infant molebabe. Wuddent 'arm an 'air o' maister Chugg's liddle 'ead, burr no!'

Trimp watched as Chugger fed Folgrim some shrewbread. The little squirrel was talking to the otter as if he were a naughty Dibbun.

'Now if'n you don't eat alla sh'ewbread up, I won't not let you 'ave no st'awbees, mista Fol!'

The hedgehog maid nodded in agreement with her molefriend. 'I think you're right, Din. They're firm friends!'

When the meal was over, Martin and his group struck camp. Warm summer sun had lifted all the mist and the broad stream glistened invitingly. Tungro hailed them as they were packing supplies aboard.

'My 'earty thanks to ye, friends. We've got t'go now. Safe journey to you'n'yore mates, Martin, an' fair weather attend ye to the north coast!'

However, it was not that simple. Folgrim refused to go with his brother. Digging himself into the banksand he resisted all their attempts to move him. Tungro stroked his strange brother's head coaxingly.

'C'mon, Fol, let's go back 'ome together, matey. Yore ole bed's waitin' for ye, an' everybeast's wantin' to give you a great welcome. Wot d'you say, eh?'

Chugger leaped from the raft and threw himself upon Folgrim, hugging the scarred otter and wailing piteously. 'Waahaah! Don't take mista Fol 'way. Waahaahaa!'

As if this were not sad enough, Folgrim joined in, tears streaming from his one eye. 'Buhurr! Don't take me away from me liddle pal. I wants t'go with 'im. Buhuhurr!'

Tungro was greatly moved. Dashing a paw across his eyes, he appealed to Martin. 'Tell me, mate, wot do I do?'

The Warrior leaped ashore. Two swift slices of his sword set Folgrim free from the ropes at his waist and paws. 'There's only one thing to do, friend. Let your brother come with us. We'll deliver him safe to your holt on the return journey, I promise.'

Folgrim jumped up. With Chugger perched on his shoulders he boarded the raft, both of them grinning from ear to ear. Tungro shook Martin's paw fervently.

'I know my brother'll be safe with goodbeasts like you'n'yore friends, sir. Mayhap 'twill be good for 'im.'

They sailed off downstream, waving goodbyes to the otters standing on the banks.

'See you sometime about autumn!'

'Aye, we'll be waitin', with a potful of shrimp'n'hotroot soup to welcome ye!'

'Good, we'll be lookin' forward to it!'

'Watch out for Folgrim at night, he's a terrible snorer!'

'Hurr hurr, if'n ee can outsnore this lot, zurr, ee must be a good 'un!'

'You speak for yourself, Dinny mole, I don't snore!'

'Ho yuss ee do, miz Trimp. Don't 'er, zurr Gonff?'

'I wouldn't know, Din. When you're snorin' it drowns out everythin', even thunderstorms!'

The curious raft, with logboats tied to both sides, sailed off downstream into the soft summer morning. Tungro and his crew gave a final wave before sliding into the water and gliding sleekly upstream, home to their holt.

It was midday when Log a Log Furmo steered into a

curving recess. Martin looked up at the shrew as he scrambled atop the steep rocky bank.

'What've we stopped for, Furmo? Surely it's not time to eat already. We've hardly been afloat today.'

'Come up 'ere'n'look at this, Martin.'

The Warrior joined his friend on the banktop. Far ahead he could see thick extending pine woods, flanking both sides of the stream. Martin peered hard at the dark mass. 'Trouble, d'you think?'

The Guosim Chieftain voiced his thoughts. 'I noticed the stream's startin' to run swifter, so I thought it best t'pull in an' scout the land. No sense dashin' into danger, that's if there's any there.'

Martin mused for a moment, looking from the raft to the pines and back again, before making up his mind. 'Right, here's what I suggest. You take Gonff, I'll take Folgrim – I wager he can smell vermin a league off. We split up and go both sides of the bank to scout those pine woods out. Leave the rest with the raft. Throw a kedge anchor over the stern – that'll slow them up so they won't be speeding into the pine wood area.'

Furmo agreed with Martin's strategy. An old water-logged willow limb, forked at one end, was weighted by lashing big chunks of rock to it. When it was cast over the raft's stern it dragged heavily on the streambed, slowing the vessel's progress considerably.

Furmo and Gonff took the north bank, the raft dropped Martin and Folgrim off on the south bank. Chugger shook a tiny paw at the Warrior. 'You take good care of mista Fol, or I smacka you tail!'

Martin nodded seriously at the little fellow. 'Aye aye, cap'n Chugg, I'll watch out for him, never fear.'

Log a Log Furmo had been right. The broad stream was surely moving faster, running deeper too, Martin noticed as he trotted along the bank with Folgrim at his side. Without the kedge anchor on its stern, both raft and logboats would go hurtling downstream.

At mid-noon they reached the fringes of the pine woods. Gonff and Furmo waved across at Martin on the opposite side. He held both paws up, signalling them to wait. After a while Folgrim returned from scouting inside the fringe. He was carrying some ashes and a clump of grass, stained dark purple, along with a dab of ochre, still wet from the stream. Urgently he gestured for them to back off, away from the pines.

When he judged they were far enough from the conifers, the otter signalled them down to the shallows, where they could converse across the stream. Gonff and Furmo waded in as deep as they dared. Martin and Folgrim followed suit, the strong current pulling at them. The otter held up the stained grass and spoke. 'Painted Ones, in the woods. Beware!'

Gonff and Furmo waded back to dry land. Folgrim called after them, 'See you back at the raft!'

Trimp helped the Guosim shrews haul her friends aboard, and looked questioningly at Furmo as he ordered the craft into the south bank, behind a curve. 'What is it, what's happening?'

The shrew Chieftain explained. 'Painted Ones are in those pine woods ahead. Folgrim found traces o' the blaggards.'

Trimp was plainly puzzled. 'What d'you mean, Painted Ones?'

'Nobeast knows fer sure, missie, but most of us thinks they're some kind o' tree rats. My Guosim ain't been down this far in seasons – weren't any about then. I reckon they must've been driven out o' their own territory an' settled in the pines yonder. Painted Ones is vicious savages, never just a few, always come in big gangs. Those woods'd be ideal for 'em – they paints themselves all over, like sunlight stripes an' shadows. Painted Ones live up in the trees, an' woe betide any pore traveller tryin' to pass through their stampin' grounds.

Killin's second nature to 'em! They're very good at disguises – you could be walkin' in the pines, thinkin' nobeast is there, then bang! The villains 'ave got you, an' yore a dead 'un!'

Dinny shook his head sorrowfully. 'Et be a gurt pity, 'cos we'm be orfully near ee seashores. Oi cudd feel et in moi diggen claws.'

Trimp sighed sadly. 'But we can't go any further now.'

Gonff chucked her gently under the chin. 'Lackaday, lookit that long face, like a toad with toothache. Cheer up, pretty one, or you'll have it rainin'. Leave it to me, I've got a plan!'

Dinny wrinkled his nose. 'You'm got ee plan, zurr?'

Gonff adopted his devil-may-care expression. 'Why d'ye think they call me Prince of Mousethieves? Of course I've got a plan, you ole tunnel-grubber!'

Martin prodded his friend's well-fed middle. 'I hope 'tis a plan that'll work, matey?'

'Oh indeed, an' did you ever know any o' my plans that didn't work, O swinger of swords?'

'Aye, lots of them, O pincher of pies!'

'Well this won't be one of that sort, O noble whiskers!'

'It had better not be, O pot-bellied soup-swigger. Now tell on.'

'We won't wait 'til light – we'll set sail and shoot past them in the dark. They won't expect that.'

The raft stayed tied to the bank until midnight, then they cut loose the kedge anchor and hoisted the sail. Drifting out into a moonless dark midstream, Gonff nodded to Furmo, who was seated in the logboats with his Guosim. Digging paddles deep they shot the craft off downstream, with Martin, Dinny and Folgrim punting long poles at the stern. A light breeze caught the sail, billowing it out beautifully. Gonff and Trimp laid out slings and heaps of well-rounded stream pebbles where they could be easily reached. The Prince of Mousethieves chuckled. 'The speed she's goin', we'll be through an' past 'em afore they even guess we've arrived, eh, missie?'

Covering Chugger's sleeping form with foodsacks and loose canvas, Trimp snuggled down by him. 'I hope you're right, Gonff, for all our sakes, but mainly for this little mite's. I don't know what I'd do if any harm befell Chugger.'

Folgrim turned from his pole, file-sharpened teeth glinting in the darkness, his one good eye roving wildly. 'If'n yer wants t'see deadbeasts, pretty miss, take a look at any vermin puttin' a paw near my pal Chugg!'

Trimp shivered, certain that the scar-faced otter did not issue idle threats.

As the flotilla of raft and logboats neared the pine wood, myriad eyes, aglow with evil intent, watched it from the bankside trees on both sides. Small harsh excited whispers sounded through the conifers.

'Yikkyikkyikkyikk! Heerdee comm!'

'Many many lotsa shroobs'n'micers too. Yikkayikka!'

'Betcher deez viddlez too, loddza viddlez!'

'Fassta fassta inta dee trapp. Yeehikkayikka!'

'Fattee moledigga an' 'edgepiggee, avva fun wid dose!'

Then the raft was into the wooded area. Martin congratulated Gonff quietly on his daring scheme. 'Well done, mate. We're shooting through like a shaft from a bow. Not much can stop us now!'

No sooner had the words left his mouth than the raft hit a thick series of vine ropes, stretched at different heights above and below the water. Everybeast aboard was thrown flat with the impact, and both leading logboats and the front of the raft were jammed fast in the cunning trap.

11

Martin was first to spring upright. He lashed about with the long punting pole as Painted Ones dropped from the trees on to the raft. Several were sent screeching into the water. Furmo and his shrews began laying about them with their logboat paddles, hollow thonking noises sounding as they struck tree rats in mid-air. Screams and splashes mingled with roars and shouts rent the blackness of the stream between the dark spreading pines. It was a scene of total chaos. Folgrim groped his way to the canvas protecting Chugger and Trimp and stood over them, flailing viciously, the air thrumming as he wielded his long pole. Whack! Thwock! Thunk! Splat! Gonff and Dinny were hard at it with their poles. Panting heavily, Martin called to them, 'There's too many of 'em – we can't keep this up. Hold the vessel as best you can. I'll be back soon. If not, go without me. That's an order!' He broke his pole over the backs of three who were trying to climb aboard, then dived into the fast-flowing stream.

As soon as he felt himself hurled against the ropes by the current, Martin latched his footpaws into the heavy vines and unsheathed the great sword from his back. It was tremendously hard trying to swing his blade in the rushing water, but swing it the mouse Warrior did. He hacked and hewed with might and main until his grip was frozen to the sword by cold water and weariness. By a superb feat of will he forced himself to continue. Heavy wet strands struck his face as the razor-sharp blade whipped through them, and water filled his mouth as he roared like a wild beast, battling the powerful woven ropes of wet vine. Lowering the blade underwater, Martin sawed furiously at the ones that he had twined his footpaws into, ducking his head beneath the surface and hunching both shoulders to put more force into his efforts. Then the raft was running overhead, scraping his back as it was liberated from the trap. Martin went head over tail, automatically shifting the sword to one paw and reaching out frantically with the other as the vessel sped forward.

Dinny felt somebeast grab his footpaw as he stood astern, swinging his pole. He was about to deal whoever it was a resounding blow with the pole butt when Martin's head emerged from the streamwater.

'Dinn, the pole, quick!'

The mole shot his pole into the water and Martin grabbed it. Throwing his sword on to the raft, he struggled aboard with Dinny's help. The raft was still swarming with Painted Ones. Martin seized the fabulous blade, and whirling it aloft he gave full cry to the battle call of Badger Lords.

'Eulaliaaaaaa!'

Screeching with fright the tree vermin threw themselves from the raft, splashing frenziedly for shore.

Gonff threw back his head and roared with laughter. 'Hahahaha! Look at 'em go! The ole Eulalia's worth a dozen fighters, an' let me say, matey, that 'un of yores was a right blood-freezer. I near jumped out o' my fur!'

Martin was grinning as he slumped wearily down to the deck. 'Let's just say it was an additional idea to make your plan work. I was far too tired t'do anything except shout. Owow! What're you villains doing to me?'

97

Trimp and Chugger scrubbed roughly at the Warrior with clean dry foodsacks. The little squirrel growled, 'Be still an' stoppa shoutin', we dryin' you off. Don't wanna catcha deff o' cold, do ya?'

The hedgehog maid was hard put to keep a straight face. Her squirrelbabe was becoming quite a one for being severe with otherbeasts. She cleaned Martin's ears out roughly. 'That's the stuff, Chugg, you tell him. Warriors have to get dry too, same as any other creature!'

Luckily none of the friends were seriously injured, though there were the usual number of bumps, cuts, scratches and scrapes sustained, as in any rough-house encounter with vermin. Trimp and Log a Log Furmo set about ministering to the slight casualties, whilst Gonff and Dinny kept a weather eye out for any likely berth, now they had left the pine wood behind. A small mid-stream island loomed up out of the darkness, perfect as a resting place for the remainder of the night.

However, after their hazardous scrape with the Painted Ones, they were far too keyed up for sleeping. Guosim cooks built a small fire in the shelter of some bushes and cooked up a cauldron of vegetable soup. Gonff took some soft bread and chopped scallions, made Bubbling Bobbs and tossed them in the cauldron. Trimp sat round the fire with the rest, feeling a strong sense of camaraderie with them, laughing, chatting and fishing for Bubbling Bobbs with clean sharp twigs. Furmo regaled them with a comic song called 'The Festive Fight'.

'One dark an' stormy night,
As the sunset in the east,
To granma's house I went,
For to partake of a feast,
With frogs an' fat hedgehogs,
Some otters an' a sparrow,
An' a squirrel who attended too,

Armed with a bow an' arrow.
The seedcake had been served,
When a dormouse in a bonnet,
Took one bite, oh what a sight,
She broke her teeth upon it.
Then backward fell a mole,
Tail first into the custard,
Ole granpa grabbed his spoon,
An' lookin' quite disgusted,
He hit the mole a smack,
Then like a flash of lightnin',
An otter brained him with a flan,
That started off the fightin'.
We fenced with celery sticks,
With pies an' puddens pelted,
The squirrel with the bow,
By a pot of soup got belted,
A sparrow flung a scone,
It laid the otter senseless,
Then granma swung her pan,
An' left us all defenceless,
Two frogs sailed out the door,
A hedgehog up the chimney,
Whilst me an' ole granpa,
To the mantelpiece hung grimly.
So hark an' hear my tale,
Stay safe at home an' starve sir,
Steer clear of granma's house,
When there's goin' t'be a feast there!'

Chugger had fallen asleep leaning against Folgrim, a soggy Bubbling Bobb still clutched in his grubby paw. After the fight with the Painted Ones, Trimp trembled fitfully, thinking what might have happened had they fallen into the claws of the foe. However, the feeling passed as she looked around at the cheery faces of her friends. Ribbing one another good-naturedly and chuckling, they sat around the fire, finishing off the meal with gusto. Nobeast would guess that but a short while ago, they had been battling for their lives, and hers. Allowing her eyes to close slowly, she snuggled down on some dry moss. Who would not feel safe in the company of such brave creatures?

Murmuring streamwater soon had them all lulled, with the exception of Martin and Folgrim, who sat, outwardly relaxed, but inwardly alert. Fading to glowing embers, the fire burnt down. Somewhere a nightjar called, and moonshadows cast soft patterns through lazy breeze-stirred foliage. Peace lay over the little island in midstream, awaiting the calm hours of dawn.

Day broke fine and clear, with a warm summer wind blowing easterly. Log a Log Furmo hopped aboard the raft, wetting a paw and holding it up. 'Hoist that sail, mates, an' ship the paddles. We're on a good fast run t'the big sea!'

Picking up speed, the raft fairly zinged along the broad watercourse. With his bushy tail blowing forward over both ears, Chugger perched in the bows of a lead logboat, shouting aloud with exhilaration. 'Whooooeeeeee! Us goin' a sea!'

Dinny clung nervously to a stayrope, not too sure whether he was fond of the vessel's wild ride downstream. 'Hurr, zurr Log, bain't us'n's a-goin' ee bit farst yurr?'

Log a Log laughed and performed a nimble jig round the edges of the logboats flanking the raft. 'Fast, me liddle fat mate, fast? See the way those banks down yonder take a deep dip? When she 'its there you'll know wot fast means!'

The mole shut his eyes tight, grabbing the stayrope tighter as Furmo gave it a mischievous twang. Folgrim and Trimp rescued Chugger from his precarious position and tied a line to his chubby middle, whereupon he promptly hopped back to his former position. Furmo began booming out a song in his wonderful bass voice.

'You stay aft mate, I'll stay fore,
Mind the rocks an' watch the shore,
Like good shipmates you an' me,
Roll down t'meet the sea!
Fast as fast as you can wish,
Through the waters like a fish,
Our ole craft do wend its way,
On this bright summer's day!
Wid spray in yore face,
An' a crackin' pace,
An' a runnin' stream afore,
If y'never lack a wind at y'back,
Then who could ask for more!
Ooooooh rum a doodle aye doh
Go where I go
Rum a doodle aye doh follow me!'

The raft bucked sharply, entering a canyon of buff-hued rock. Everybeast yelled and held on to something. Chugger was thrown into the water from his perilous perch. Trimp screamed in alarm, but Folgrim had a good grip on the line, and with a powerful heave he swung the little fellow back on board.

'Up y'come, rascal. 'Ere, Gonff, look wot I caught, a Chuggfish! Funny liddle critter, never seen one wid a tail that long!'

Shaking water from his ruffled fur, the baby squirrel drew himself imperiously to his full height. 'I norra Chuggfish, h'i a likkle squiggle!'

White water boiled about the surface, whilst high banks narrowed and dipped sharply downwards. Furmo gave orders to stow the sail, and his Guosim shrews took up their positions at the logboats' oars, keeping the vessel in midstream with strong skilful strokes. Soon they were all thoroughly drenched by spray and unable to hear each other talk because of the roaring waters. Log a Log and Martin with long poles sculled at the after end. The Warrior mouse noticed that the shrew Chieftain was no longer singing and smiling. Grim-faced and silent, he struggled to keep the raft on course.

Now the raft really began to buck, side to side and up and down, sometimes rearing high out of the stream and returning to hit the water with a resounding splash. Twice it was whirled completely round on the treacherous current, Martin and Furmo poling furiously to turn it. Trimp knew they were in trouble when Gonff pushed her and Chugger flat, shouting at them to hold tight. Gripping the tough vines that held their craft together, Trimp locked both footpaws around her little friend. Lifting her face, the hedgehog maid took a quick glance ahead. What she saw took her breath away.

A rainbow bridged either bank, shining through a misty curtain of cascading watermist. The raft rushed through it. Then there was nothing!

Martin heard himself yell with surprise as his pole snapped on a rock at the waterfall's edge. The entire vessel, raft and logboats, sailed out into space. Log a Log's voice cut across the sudden silence.

'Hang on, maaaaaaaaaaates!'

Then the thunderous roar of falling water took over. They were falling, down, down, with a view of beach and sea to the front and an awesome sheet of rushing water at their back. Gripping fiercely to anything within reach, the breath torn from their mouths, they plunged downwards, tilting as the raft went head first, for what seemed like an eternity. Down, down, down . . . Whooooooom!

The broad surface of a pool at the bottom exploded with the impact. By its own momentum the vessel was plunged deep into the pool, breaking into pieces as it went.

Water rushed into Trimp's mouth. Her eyes opened.

Everything was cold, silent and vague. Half conscious, she stared about. Somewhere high above the water was billowing in thick white clouds, and she tried to fight down panic as she felt Chugger pawing feebly at her. They were both trapped under a log from the raft, which had become wedged in the rocks at the pool's bottom. Then the little squirrel's paws went limp. Panic surged through Trimp with the sudden realisation that both her and Chugger's lives were going to end, trapped underwater and alone. Bubbles burst from her mouth as water flooded relentlessly in. Forgetting her plight for a moment, the hedgehog maid felt a tremendous wave of pity tug at her heart for Chugger. The little squirrel was still a baby. What a sad way for him to end a tragically short life. She reached down and held his paw, thinking that at least he would have her with him. Then the arrival of Folgrim jolted her failing senses.

Setting himself between the rocks he bent his body, levering outward with all four paws, veins standing out on his neck as he added the strength of his rudderlike tail and the back of his broad skull. Folgrim pushed until the scars on his face stood out like blue ropes. There was a grinding crunch, followed by a muffled clonking noise. The log floated upwards, free, the rocks trapping it having been forced apart by the otter's wild strength. Folgrim seized Chugger by his tail and Trimp by one paw. Setting himself firm in the sand, he thrust mightily upward, tail and footpaws working in unison. In a stream of bubbles all three shot to the surface. Willing paws pulled them ashore.

Martin took a quick check of his crew. 'Dinny, where's Dinny?'

The words had hardly left his mouth before Folgrim plunged in again, streaking underwater like an arrow. White sand and shell fragments, together with weeds and grains of rock, clouded the bottom a pearly grey colour. Folgrim swam to an overturned logboat and wormed his way underneath. The otter's head broke water in a small air pocket trapped in the upturned vessel, and Dinny's head was facing him. The mole tugged his snout in polite relief. 'Gudd day to ee, zurr. Oi 'oped sumbeast'd cumm afore ee air runned out in yurr. Oi doan't moind tellin' ee, oi'm gurtly affrighted o' liven unnerwater. Us moles be loik that, 'appy unnerground, but sad unnerwater, ho urr!'

The otter showed his filed teeth in a smile. 'Then shut yore eyes, 'old yore breath an' 'ang on t'my paw, mister Din. Soon 'ave y'back on land, matey!'

Chugger shot fountains of water everywhere as he recovered. Trimp, who was no worse for her ordeal, sat watching Furmo anxiously. 'Oh, say he's going t'be all right, sir?'

Chuckling, the Guosim leader pressed gently on the little squirrel's stomach and another jet of water arose. 'This 'un'll be fine, missie, don't git yoreself in a fret. I seen shrewbabes swaller twice that amount – it never seemed to 'arm the liddle fellers a bit!'

Chugger opened one eye, his paw rising to point accusingly at Furmo. 'You keep punchin' Chugga's tummy an' I swirt water in you eye, sh'ew!'

Furmo held Chugger upside down and shook him thoroughly, letting the baby squirrel go as he snapped at his footpaws. 'See, I told yer, miss, he's stronger'n a growed eel!'

Dinny rolled himself into the warm sand until he looked like a white moleghost. He went and sat by Martin, who shook his head and burst out laughing.

'Have a rest, go to north shores, make it a holiday, take all summer! Some rest, eh, Din? Some holiday!'

Gonff dug a big raft splinter from his tail and sighed with relief. 'Well, look at me, mates, I'm enjoyin' meself no end. Only one thing missin' though . . .'

Martin knew what was coming, so he interrupted

Gonff. 'Food! That's what it is, isn't it, you felonious famine-faced soup-stealer!'

Gonff picked his teeth nonchalantly with the splinter. 'How'd you guess, noble britches? Ahoy there, Furmo, wot's the position on vittles, matey?'

One of the Guosim cooks answered for his leader. 'Flour's ruined, fruit's all right though, plenty o' fresh water in that pool. Biscuits we baked this mornin' are lost in the stream. I reckon we could stand a few fresh supplies of wotever the land has to offer 'ereabouts.'

Martin took charge, issuing orders. 'Right, anybeast who feels up to it can forage for food. We'll split up around these hills and dunes on the shoreline. Dinny, you stay here with miss Trimp and Chugger and take a rest. See what you can salvage from the wreckage.'

12

Trimp was still feeling a bit sick and dizzy from her ordeal in the pool, but with Chugger about it was difficult to rest.

'Chugger, come away from that water, it's very deep!'

'Ho, Chugg know it deep, I beena bottum of it!'

'Yes, well that's where you'll find yourself again if you don't come away. Come on, this instant!'

'Yah, lea' me alone, me an' mista Din doin' a job, see!'

The mole picked him up with one huge digging claw. 'Oi can doo ee job on moi own thankee, maister. Naow, you'm do loik miz Trimp tell ee an' no cheek frumm ee!'

A fox appeared as if from nowhere. Behind him were four roguish-looking vermin, an assortment of rats and ferrets.

The fox looked the wickedest of all five. He was obviously their leader, and wore big hooped brass earrings and tattered silks. Faded tattoos showed on the paw holding a sharp single-headed axe. He gestured at Chugger.

'Haharr, young 'un, you lissen t'yore elders an' don't be cheekin' 'em. Avàst now, cullies, wot 'ave we 'ere?'

One of the vermin sniggered. 'Dinner, that's wot we got!'

Shaking his head in censure, the fox growled, 'Stow that kind o' gab, Fribb, these 'ere are gentlebeasts – a mite grubby, but respectable. Ain't that right, missie?'

Trimp had decided instantly that she did not like the vermin, or their leader, but her voice showed no fear. 'Who are you and what do you want?'

Strutting insolently about, the fox rummaged through the salvaged supplies with his axeblade. He chose an apple, polishing it on his ragged sleeve. 'I could ask you the same question, me pretty.'

Trimp picked up a solid spar of raftwood. 'I'm not your pretty, and 'tis usually considered good manners to ask before helping yourself to the food of others!'

Scornful sniggers echoed from the four vermin. Pausing with the apple halfway to his mouth, the fox grinned. 'This 'un's got me quakin' in me boots, mates. Gut me, she's a right mouthy liddle baggage, ain't she?'

Trimp brandished her wooden spar, trembling slightly, but still game for trouble. 'Aye, but you'll find I can back up my words when dealing with bullies. Now who are you and what do you want here?'

Making as if to go, the fox sidled past Trimp. Suddenly he turned, knocking the spar from the hogmaid's paw with a deft flick of his axeblade. Dinny went for him with a deep growl, but one of the vermin tripped him with a cutlass blade. He tried to rise, only to find another one menacing his throat with a pike. Biting into the apple, the fox pulled a face and spat the piece out. He held the axe under Trimp's chin, his voice hard and commanding.

'I'm Sholabar, lord of these coasts. See that boat out there? Well, 'tis mine. I patrols these waters an'—'

Trimp interrupted him sharply. 'I don't see any boat out there!'

Sholabar growled at one of the vermin. 'Where did ye berth the boat, Grimleg?'

'Be'ind the point, like y'told me to, cap'n.'

The fox shrugged. 'Well, no matter. Point is, missie,

yore on my land. All around ye, far as y'can see, belongs t'me. Even this freshwater pool. So yore a trespasser, see!'

Trimp pushed the axe away from her chin and laughed in the bully's face contemptuously. 'Haha! Don't talk stupid, nobeast owns the shores and sea!'

Shaking with rage, Sholabar raised his axe at her. 'Snotnosed liddle spikeback, I'll skin yer alive!'

Chugger bounded forward and sank his teeth in the fox's leg.

'Yahowww! Leggo! Gerrim offa me! Yaaarrgh!'

The little fellow clung like a limpet, sinking his teeth deeper and growling fiercely. One of the vermin grabbed him by the tail. Trimp seized Sholabar's paw, trying to stop him swinging the axe at Chugger. The fox roared, 'Aaaargh! Stretch 'im out, Grimleg! Yaaaah! I'll chop the liddle brat in two!' He shook his arm, trying to loosen Trimp's hold, while Chugger's little teeth dug deeper and deeper. 'Fribb, get this brat offa me! Eeeyarrr! He's bitin' me leg t'the bone! Owowow!'

Before the fox could issue another yell, Folgrim came hurtling out of nowhere and struck him like a thunderbolt. There was an ominous crack. The fox's head went backward at a crazy angle under the force of the otter's blow, and he fell slain upon the sand. Taking one swift look at Folgrim, the four vermin fled for their lives. Martin and Gonff were rounding the corner of a nearby dune, carrying wild onions and dandelion shoots, and two of the fleeing vermin ran straight into them. Gonff butted one in the stomach, laying him out, gasping for air. Martin tripped the other one and grabbed him hard by the scruff. The other two vermin ran the opposite way, only to find themselves surrounded by Guosim rapier points.

Hauling the four vermin roughly along, the foragers arrived back at the poolside. Martin had to place himself between the captives and the scar-faced otter, who was trying to get at them with the dead fox's axe. Martin spoke calmingly to him. 'No more slaying, friend, they've had enough. You four, sit down there and explain yourselves. What's been going on here? The truth, now!'

Grimleg the ferret managed a good act, whining pitifully. 'We're nought but porebeasts, sir, we roams the sands, lookin' fer vittles t'keep skin an' bones together, sir. Woe is us, sir, we fell foul o' this robber band. We begged 'em for food but they attacked us. That liddle 'un tried to eat our cap'n, er, Sholabar, an' yon 'ogmaid was goin' t'brain us wid a club. Sir, 'tis the truth I tell ye. See that savage riverdog? That 'un slew our mate Sholabar fer no reason at all, sir. An' that mad mole 'ad a sword 'e was goin' t'kill me wid!' Grimleg picked up the cutlass he had dropped when he fled. 'Aye, this is the very blade, I swears it on me mother's eyes, sir. They'd 'ave murdered us if you 'adn't arrived!'

Trimp noted Martin's wink before he turned to her stern-eyed and demanded, 'Is this true, did you attack these poor creatures? Speak!'

Trimp caught on immediately. Cringing and rubbing her paws nervously, she grovelled on the sand, performing a passable imitation of a vermin lying its way out of trouble.

'Oh, 'tis true, yer honour, 'tis true, we 'ad a wicked upbringin' y'see. But spare our lives an' we'll give up bad livin', on me granma's whiskers I swear we will. Kind sir, just let us sail off in our boat, that's moored be'ind the south point, an' you'll never see 'ide nor 'air of us agin, on me oath!'

At the mention of a boat, Furmo exchanged glances with Martin. 'So they've got a boat. What d'you think, matey?'

Surveying the wreckage of what had once been their vessel, Martin nodded, as if considering the matter. 'Aye, it'd save us long days of walking, eh, Gonff?'

Gonff drew his dagger and stood over the four vermin. 'Fear not, friends, justice has come to yore aid. These ruffians, the hogmaid an' her crew that attacked you so wickedly, here's how we'll deal with 'em. My friends an' I will confiscate their boat an' take them with us as deck slaves for punishment. That way they'll bother honest creatures like yoreselves no more. What d'ye say to that?'

Grimleg and his vermin companions were nonplussed. In one fell swoop they had been foiled of their prey, lost their boat and also their captain to boot. The ferret was about to object when Furmo drew his rapier and stood facing him, cold-eyed. His voice, when he spoke, was like ice.

'I'd say 'twas a good idea. These honest beasts should make no objection, as long as the tale they told us is true. 'Cos I can't abide a liar, y'see! Liars is worse than thieves or murderers, I always say. Show me a liar an' I'll silence his untruthful tongue for ever. Gurr! I can't stand liars!'

Gonff placed his paw on Furmo's rapier hilt. 'Put up yore blade, matey, these are honest creatures!' Grimleg and his vermin nodded furiously, trying hard to look poor but honest. Gonff pointed an accusing paw at Trimp and her friends. 'Now this lot, they're a different kettle o' fish. They've got the look o' savage murderin' villains t'me!'

Folgrim narrowed his one eye and squinted wickedly. 'Aye, I'm a bad lot, allus 'ave been. Ain't 'appy 'less I'm slayin' pore honest beasts wid me axe.'

Chugger bared his teeth and emitted a small growl. 'Ho, we's villings sure nuff, choppa tail off an' cutcha froats us will. Gurrr!'

Dinny squinched up his snout and made evil gestures with his digging claws at all and sundry. 'Burr aye, an' stuffen ee tails up'n ee noses. Gurrurr!'

Trimp kicked sand at the seated vermin. 'Hah! Gimme a sharp blade an' a cookin' pot, an' I'll show ye what I do to pore honest beasts. Yarrrrr!'

Gonff gave a shudder of mock horror. 'Enough o' that foul talk, ye blaggards! Off t'the boat with you an' keep a bridle on those wicked tongues!'

Martin drew his sword and marched the miscreants off. Gonff and the Guosim shrews had to bite their lips to keep from bursting out laughing.

Log a Log Furmo kept his face solemn. He patted the backs of the four miserable vermin heftily, then shook each one by the paw, with a grip that caused them to wince. 'Lucky for you we came along, my friends, very lucky!'

One of the Guosim cooks whispered to Gonff in a voice that all could hear. 'I 'opes they thanks the Chief – he can't stand ungrateful beasts. Why, I've seen Furmo take 'is blade an' . . .' Before the sentence was finished the vermin were gabbling aloud in panic.

'Aye, lucky indeed fer us, sire, thank ye!'

'Don't know wot we'd 'ave done without ye, Chief!'

'True, true, we'll never forget 'ow you saved us!'

'Thankee, thankee kindly, sir!'

Gonff gathered up the vermin weapons, tut-tutting like an old mousewife. 'Nasty sharp things. Don't fret, friends, we'll take care o' these lest you injure yoreselves on 'em!'

Furmo presented them with the piece of wood that Trimp had intended using. 'Sorry about yore friend the fox. You can dig a nice restin' place for him with this. Goodbye to ye.'

As they marched off down the beach, one of the vermin, a big skinny rat, kicked the sand ruefully. 'Huh, why did we ever come 'ere in the first place, that's wot I'd like ter know?'

Grimleg whacked him over the head with the piece of wood. 'Ah shuddup, screwnose!'

Log a Log Furmo was delighted with the new vessel. He splashed about in the shallows, admiring it as the others clambered aboard. It was a long flat-bottomed skiff, with a single square midsail. Bluffed at the stern and pointed at the bows, fashioned from seasoned beech, elm and rowan wood, it had oarlocks and paddles, four to each side, plus a fine carved tiller and rudder. There was a stern shelter of canvas, stretched over a frame of willow, for cover in rough weather.

When Furmo climbed aboard he went beneath the shelter, then emerged crowing with joy. 'Lookit, Guosim, a liddle stone hearth an' a clay oven, an' three good bench seats. I reckon this craft'd hold a score an' a half of crew. I tell ye, mates, whoever built this vessel knew wot they were doin', true craftsbeasts they must've been. A real beauty, eh, Gonffo?'

The Mousethief shook his head in amazement. 'I wager 'twill go like the wind too. Where'd those ole badbeasts ever lay paws on a marvellous craft like this?'

Chugger swaggered about, now immersed in his new role as a pirate captain. 'Us robbed it offa ole frogdad an' boiled 'is tail for vikkles. Heeheehee!'

Trimp reprimanded him sharply. 'That's quite enough of that kind of talk, thank you, Chugger.'

The miscreant shot up the mastpole scowling darkly. 'I norra Chugger no more, h'i a villyun, a orful bad 'un!'

Dinny went to sit beneath the stern awning. 'Well oi bain't a bad 'un no more, zurr, ho no, et 'urts moi face, a-scowlin' an' a-snarlin' all ee toim. Oi'm nought but a good ole mole, oi surpose.'

Tacking close to the shore they threaded northward. Furmo and his Guosim shrews were in absolute ecstasies about their new craft. Being great boatbuilders they could readily appreciate the skill and ingenuity which had gone into its construction.

'I thought you were only travelling with us as far as the shore, my friend,' Martin reminded the shrew gently. 'Weren't you supposed to return to your camp and tribe, once we were safely downstream?'

Furmo was sniffing the deck, licking the mast, listening to the prow timbers and rapping his paws experimentally on the carved elm oarlocks. He smiled absently at Martin. 'Oh, y'mean goin' back upstream t'the domestic life? Well I tell ye, matey, I'd get a right ole tellin' off from me wife if'n I went back to tell 'er we lost the logboats an' raft together. Huh! I might be a Log a Log, but my missus Honeysuckle, she's the real ruler of our tribe. She'd skelp the ears off me if'n I went back boatless!'

Martin nodded his agreement. 'So what are you going t'do?'

A crafty smile flitted across the shrew's rugged face. 'I'm goin' t'stay with ye, 'til yore adventure's done. Then you can sail back 'ome with me an' explain to me darlin' wife how you couldn't 'ave done without me'n'my Guosim crew. In fact you'll be so pleased with me that you'll present me with this boat, t'make up fer the ones we lost. In return I'll throw a smashin' feast for you'n'yore crew, an' we'll top it all off by namin' the vessel *Honeysuckle* in me dear wife's honour. Done?'

Grinning broadly, Martin clasped Furmo's paw. 'Done, you golden-tongued rascal!'

13

The days that followed were sunny and uneventful, and good progress was made by the little ship *Honeysuckle*. She was ideally built for skimming the coastal waves, responding quickly to any vagrant wind, sliptide or rockshoal by just a touch on her tiller. Chugger was a constant source of amusement. The little squirrel had promoted himself to captain, still keeping up his new identity as a villainous sea rover. Folgrim and Trimp often had to stifle smiles and chuckles at his antics. Swaggering about the deck, armed with a stick for a sword, he growled out orders to all and sundry.

'Gerra vikkles cooked, or I fro y'to a sharkers!'

'Keepa tiller straight, mista Furmo, or cap'n Chugg make ya scrubba deck!'

'All singa funny song, or I choppa tails off!'

Gonff saluted him smartly. 'Cap'n Chugg sir, I've checked the provisions, an' we're runnin' low on everythin'. We need more vittles.'

Chugger stroked his chin reflectively, as he had seen Martin do, then he waved his tiny paws irately. 'Well saila ship to d'shore an' get lotsa more vikkles. Hmph! Don't 'nnoy me, mouse, I busy bein' cap'n!'

Gonff looked to Furmo. 'Well, we do need more provisions.'

The shrew Chieftain tacked the vessel artfully across two cresting rollers, watching the shoreline intently. 'We'll sail 'til evenin' then put in t'shore. A night on dry land'll do us good. Tomorrow will be time enough to send out a foragin' party. Er, if'n the cap'n approves.'

Chugger was binding a coloured shrew headband around his brow to make himself look more dashing. He nodded. 'Good good, dat's wot we do. All 'ush now an' be quiet. Cap'n Chugg gonna take 'is nap!'

By evening the weather had grown noticeably brisker. Folgrim pointed shoreward, to where the beach was sandy and rockstrewn, dotted with dunes and backed by grassland with stunted trees and bushes. 'Best chance a landfall there, afore the light fades.'

Leaning on the tiller, Furmo sent the *Honeysuckle* skimming towards the beach. Wading ashore, the crew took up the ship's bowline, waiting on Furmo's word. Watching the incoming waves carefully, he yelled as a high one caught the stern. 'Take 'er in, me hearties. Heave!'

Without any difficulty they ran the vessel up high and dry above the tideline, where it lay safe.

Dinny immediately trundled up the beach, pleased to be on dry land, calling back to them, 'Thurr be an owd boat up yurr. Oi thort et wurr a rock!'

Upside down and half buried in the sand, the boat lay, long forgotten on the deserted shore. Folgrim viewed it wistfully. 'Wonder who it belonged to?'

Trimp ventured closer, peering into the dark cavern formed by the upturned craft. 'I don't know, but it'd make a snug shelter for the night. We could get a fire going and make a decent meal with the last of our rations. Come on, it'll be fun!'

Before anybeast could stop her, the hedgehog maid stooped and scurried under the wrecked hull.

'Yeeek!' She came scampering out hastily, with a huge redbacked crab chasing her, its claws open and extended aggressively. She hopped clear, but the crab stood outside on the sand, menacing them, protecting its shelter. It was joined by another crab of equal size and ferocity. Trimp was shaking like a leaf, and Chugger hid behind her.

'Yaaah! It a bigga spider! No, two bigga spiders now!'

Martin stayed Folgrim's paw as it strayed to the axe he had taken from the vermin. 'Easy now. Killing's not necessary, friend. They're not spiders, Chugg, they're crabs, pretty big 'uns too. But not to worry, our Prince of Mousethieves knows how to deal with crabs, don't you, O chubby one?'

Gonff bowed low, muttering to his friend, 'Less of the chubby one, matey.' He turned to Trimp. 'Fear not, pretty one, crabs an' I are ole chums. Furmo, build a fire over yonder an' bring me two long pieces o' wood, will you? Stand clear the rest of ye!'

Whilst Furmo and his Guosim shrews built a fire of driftwood, both crabs held their ground, never going forward or back, but scrabbling sideways with their fearsome pincers wide open, giving out danger signals to the intruders. Gonff took the two long wooden spars offered by a shrew and bound them at both ends with rags soaked in lamp oil, keeping one eye on the crabs.

'These should do fine. Now watch this an' remember, mates, a crab's the daftest creature livin'. Once he latches on to somethin' he won't let go, unless 'tis food he can push into his silly mouth, an' these poles ain't food!' He charged the nearest crab, with the pole held out horizontally, shouting, 'C'mon, ole shellback, bite on this!'

Clack! The creature's powerful claws seized the pole.

'Now one for your ole pal there. Bite on this, stalkeyes!' Gonff thrust the second pole at the other crab in like manner. Obediently the fearsome pincers grabbed it. Boldly the Mousethief stood a hair's breadth from both crabs and turned his back on them to face the audience. 'Y'see, they ain't got enough brains between 'em to let go of those poles, an' while they're hangin' on to 'em they can't hurt us with their nippers. Now, they'll stand there like that 'til the crack o' doom if I let 'em. But here's the best way to get rid o' crabs. Watch!'

Taking a blazing piece of wood from the fire, Gonff raced nimbly round both crabs, touching the flames to both ends of each pole. Agitatedly the big crustaceans continued their sideways patrol, stalk eyes waving wildly in the firelights they were carrying, stumbling and tripping in dumb panic. The Mousethief advanced upon them, swinging his crackling torch.

'You rock-backed oafs, go on, get out o' here afore yore nippers get burned. Go on, into the water with yer!'

He chased them a short distance down the beach, until the crabs' tiny brains realised the answer to their burning problem. They scuttled off sideways into the sea. Gonff skipped back up the beach, chuckling. 'Ain't got the sense they was born with, those two!'

Everybeast waited whilst the fearless Gonff went beneath the boat hull with his lighted torch. 'Come on in, buckoes, the place is empty!'

Guosim cooks like nothing better than to improvise with their cooking. That night they did the crew proud. Barley broth with wild onions and dried watershrimp, hot mint and dandelion tea, and the *pièce de résistance*: a big pan, lined with thick slices of honey-soaked shrewbread, into which they placed all their dried apples and pears and hazelnuts, mixed with the last of their fresh berries – blackcurrants, strawberries and raspberries. The pan was covered with a flat slab of stone and placed on the fire. After a while, the aromas drifted temptingly around in the shelter formed by the upturned boat. Whilst Folgrim was not looking, Chugger emptied his barley broth into the otter's bowl and sat happily licking his seashell spoon.

'Cummon, mista Fol, eaty up all barley broff, or you don't get no pudden. See, Chugg eat all his up, yum yum!'

The scarred otter tugged his friend's bushy tail fondly. 'Ain't it strange 'ow a bowl can fill itself up agin? Yore a forty-faced liddle skinnamalinker, cap'n Chugg!'

The pudding was perfectly cooked, a triumph. Everybeast had their bowls heaped, and they tucked in willingly.

'Mmmm, this is marvellous!'

'Best I ever tasted, pipin' 'ot an' delicious!'

'Burr aye, gurtly noice an' turrible tasty et be's!'

'Any chance o' second 'elpings there, cooky?'

'If'n you wants to end up in the sea wid yore crabmates, Gonff, jus' keep callin' me cooky!'

'Oops, sorry, O well-furred an' beautiful Guosim Boss!'

'Oh, all right, pass yore bowl 'ere!'

Outside the night grew cold, with a stiff wind driving sand spirals across the shore. Fortunately the shelter was in the lee of the wind, and they sat around the cheery fire amid the good food and banter. During a lull in the conversation, Trimp cocked an ear to the opening. 'Listen. Can you hear anything, Martin?'

Martin listened. 'Aye, like a sort of moaning.'

Furmo refilled Dinny's bowl. 'Prob'ly the wind.'

But Martin's paw was on his sword. He leaned forward, alert. 'That's not the wind. Listen carefully!'

In the silence that followed they all heard the audible moaning from outside, eerie, ghostly.

'Oooo oo ummmm, ooo oooo aaaahhhh . . .'

It seemed to fade and rise with the lonely wind out on the moonless stretches of coastline. Furmo shuddered. 'Don't sound like nothin' livin' t'me!'

This remark started off a lot of fearful speculation.

'Mayhap 'tis the spirits of deadbeasts?'

'Aye, mate, could've been the long-dead crew o' this boat!'

'They say strange things 'appen on ole lonely shores!'

'I've 'eard tell o' that, too. Bet they comes back on dark nights, to visit the spot where they perished!'

'Ooh urr, us'n's should've stayed aboard ee boat on ee sea!'

'Hark, I can 'ear 'em singin' words!'

Sure enough, the words came clear and distinct. Beneath the boat fur stood on end, paws trembled and creatures drew closer to the fire. They could not avoid hearing the wailing dirge, which rose and blended with the sighing winds.

'Ooooo ooo ummmm! Ooooo ooo aaahhhh!
From the deep cold seas afar,
Spirits of the dead arise,
Rattling bones and sightless eyes,
From the deep mysterious sea,
Wand'ring lonely beach and shore,
We must walk eternally,
Wand'ring, seeking evermore,
When the pale moon sends its light,
Or in dark and starless night,
Roaming near and travelling far,
Ooooo ooo ummmm! Ooooo ooo aaaaaaahhhhhhhhh!'

Trimp's face was blanched with fear. Chugger was trembling like a leaf, and she hugged him close to her. The breath caught in her throat as a spectrally hollow knock sounded on the upturned boat hull – Whock! Whock! Whock! – followed by unearthly-sounding voices.

'Leave the coast, desert our shore,
Or stay here for evermore,
Go by land or go by sea,
Heed these warning words and fleeeeeeeeeeeeee!'

Martin looked at the terror-stricken faces around him. Drawing his sword, he turned to the only one, beside himself, who did not appear to be affected by the eerie chants. 'Well, what d'you make of that little lot, Gonff?'

The Mousethief drew his dagger. 'Don't see how a ghost could be solid enough to knock its paws on a boat hull, mate. You stay here in case it's some kind o' trap – take care of these ditherin' daisies. I'll go an' take a look out there!'

Gonff slid out into the night. A moment later he reappeared, a great deal faster than he had left. Martin gripped his friend's paw as the dagger slid from it. This was not like Gonff, who sat ashen-faced and trembling. The Warrior gazed into his haunted eyes. 'What is it, mate? What did you see out there?'

Gonff swigged down a beaker of dandelion and mint tea. He regained his composure slightly, though it was some time before he managed to speak. 'I tell ye, matey, I never want to see aught like that again. Tall they were, very tall, with 'orrible faces an' long white bodies that seemed to flutter'n'float!'

One of the Guosim shrews recoiled in horror, his paw shaking as he pointed out beneath their shelter entrance. 'Eeaaargh! I see one! There 'tis!'

A vague misty shape was gliding about outside. Martin sheathed his sword and seized a long paddle. 'I've had enough of this nonsense. Let's see what these ghosts have got to say for themselves!' As the apparition drifted by again, Martin struck out with the paddle, giving it a good hard sweep.

The ghost gave a yell of surprise and collapsed into a heap. Martin grabbed the struggling mass and dragged it inside the shelter. Ripping off the flowing white cloth, he exposed a hedgehog on stilts.

The creature's face was daubed thickly with some kind of white clay, and long seabird feathers were stuck into the clay. Blackened beneath the eyes and painted bright red about the mouth with plant dyes, it gave the hedge-hog a fearsome appearance. It glared at Martin defiantly. 'Arrah now, an' aren't you the bold ould Sea Rogue! Goo on now, cullie, kill me an' get it over wid. That fine blade you carry looks fit t'do the job. You durty murtherin' omadorm!'

Martin grabbed the hedgehog firmly by its clay-encrusted ear. 'Listen, my friend, keep a civil tongue in your head or I'll box your ears for you. We're not Sea Rogues and we don't go about slaying others willy nilly!'

A huge grin cracked the white-clayed face. 'Muther of all the seasons, now ain't that a mercy! By the spikes o' me fat uncle, does that fine pudden taste as good as it smells? Could y'not serve me up a large morsel of the luverly stuff, an' could meself not sit next t'that pretty darlin' hogmaid whilst I show her the powers o' me turrible appetite, sir?'

Martin was smiling as he extended a paw. 'I'm Martin the Warrior of Redwall, and these are my friends, who no doubt will introduce themselves.'

The hedgehog shook the proffered paw vigorously. 'An' 'tis pleased I am to meet ye, Martin sir. I'm Murfo, son o' Chief Dunespike, Allcoast Champion Spinetussler.'

Gonff immediately took to Murfo. Sensing in him a kindred spirit, he exchanged a wink with the newcomer. 'Don't y'think you'd better ask yore dad an' the others in out o' the weather, Murfo? They'll catch their death o' cold, stumpin' about in long white nighties on a night like this. Go on, give 'em a shout.'

Murfo stuck his head outside and roared, 'Hoi, da, these beasts are friends, an' they've got pudden on the hob. Bring the boyos over, will ya!'

In the blink of an eye, the shelter and the beach sur-rounding it was packed with hedgehogs, all untying stilts from their footpaws and casting aside their long white ghost robes. Murfo's father, Dunespike, was possibly the biggest hedgehog Martin had ever set eyes on.

Introductions were made all round, with Dunespike offering his apologies for frightening them.

'Ah, 'tis sorry I am for puttin' the fears into honest craturs like yerselves, but we've seen that sleek boat of yours afore, so we'd be forgiven for thinkin' that you were the durty scut of a fox an' his flotsam that usually sail in it. Ah yis indeed, Martin me ould son. Well now, isn't this all grand?'

As one all the hedgehogs nodded and chorused, 'Ah, 'tis grand, grand indeed, sir!'

Furmo scraped his ladle around the big pan, commenting, 'Sorry there ain't enough pudden t'go round all yore tribe.'

Chief Dunespike accepted the last bowl and passed it to his son, shaking his head ruefully. 'More's the pity, but those who get none'll never know what they missed an' be no worse for the missin' of it! Here, me son, get that down yer gob an' don't go tellin' your ould da how grand it tastes. Bad cess t'this rotten tooth o' mine, it won't abide the sweet stuff an' torments the very life o' me if I go near anythin' sweetish, so it does.'

All the hedgehogs' spikes rattled as they shook their heads and chorused in unison, 'Ah yis, the ould tooth torments the big feller turrible!'

Trimp could not resist asking a question. 'But why do you parade around the shore at night dressed as ghosts?'

Whilst Dunespike sat nursing his tooth, Murfo explained, 'Sure, to scare off the sea vermin. They're all superstitious wretches. Scarin' them is far simpler than gettin' the half of our tribe slain in battle. It works just grand, missie. Ain't that right, boyos?'

Again all the tribe nodded their heads and spoke together. 'Ah yis, 'tworks just grand, grand grand!'

Still nursing the side of his jaw, which looked painfully swollen, Dunespike glanced admiringly at Martin's sword. 'By the spike of the great hog himself, 'tis a grand an' powerful blade you have there, Martin sir!'

Martin unsheathed his sword, holding it forth for all to see. 'Aye, that it is. The hilt was my father's and the blade was forged by a Badger Lord from a piece of a star that fell from the skies. This sword is a magic weapon!'

Dunespike shook his huge head in amazement. 'Magic, you don't tell me! How so?'

He did not see the wink that passed between Martin and Gonff. Martin turned the sword, so that the red pommel stone at its hilt top twinkled in the firelight. 'This stone can soothe pains and heal wounds!'

The big hedgehog Chief stared reverently at the stone. 'And toothaches?'

Martin smiled. 'Aye, toothaches too!' Digging a hole in the sand with his swordpoint, he pushed the sword in upside down. He held it in the deep wet sand until he judged the stone was cold enough. 'Sit down here, sir. Gonff, will you get the other side of the Chief and hold his head?'

Dunespike sat down gingerly. Gonff braced the hedge-warrior's head still by leaning against the uninjured side. The hog looked uncertainly at Martin, who was withdrawing his sword from the sand. 'You wouldn't be goin' to hurt me now, would you, Martin?'

The Warrior smiled reassuringly. 'Me, hurt you? I'm not even going to touch you, Chief. 'Tis the pommel stone does all the magic. Sit still and relax.' Very gently, Martin began moving the cold stone in slow circles around the patient's swollen jaw, murmuring as he did so, 'Easy now, easy. How does that feel, nice and cool?'

Dunespike closed his eyes, leaning heavily against Gonff. 'Ah, 'tis grand, grand, like a butterfly's breath on a morn in spring. Don't stop, Martin, keep doin' that, round an' round me ould rotten achin' tooth.'

Martin whispered soothingly in Dunespike's ear. 'Round and round with the magic stone, that's the stuff. Is your tooth in the middle of this area I'm circling?'

Dunespike sighed contentedly. 'Yis, so 'tis, so 'tis.'

Gripping the crosshilt with both paws, Martin whacked the pommel stone, hard and sudden, right at the middle of the swelling, where the tooth was located. Thump!

'Yaaaargooooogh! I'm destroyed, he's killed me! Aaargh!'

The entire tribe of Dunehogs leaped forward. Martin swung his blade aloft, halting them with his fearsome war cry. 'Eulaliaaaaa!'

Dunespike stopped roaring. He opened his eyes, felt the side of his jaw, then spat out a blackened molar. 'Haharrharr! Look at that now! I'm free of pain – me ould tooth's out! Oh, seasons preserve y'grand name, Martin sir!'

Trimp put a pawful of sea salt in warm water and stirred until it dissolved. She gave it to Dunespike, saying, 'Take this and swish it around where the tooth came out, sir. 'Twill clean the hole and help it to heal.'

The big hedgehog patted Martin's back so heartily that he almost knocked him flat. 'Sure, an' I wish ye'd done that when we first met, then I would've been able to tackle that grand pudden of yours. Martin of Redwall, yer a mighty cratur, sir, heroical, y'are.'

The Dunehog chorus echoed their Chief's sentiments.

'Ah yis yis, heroical indeed!'

'Isn't he the grand mouse!'

'Oh, that he is, grand, grand!'

Murfo appealed to his father. 'Da, would y'have Martin an' his friends sittin' the night out under some battered ould boatwreck? Sure an' 'twould only be good manners to invite them back t'the roundhouse.'

14

Trimp walked ahead of the main party with Murfo and a party of admirers, all of whom, it seemed, wanted to hold her paw lest she slip. They were deep among the dunes when Murfo stopped and tapped the side of his nose. 'Well, missie, what d'you think of our roundhouse?'

Trimp looked round. All she could see was sand dunes. 'Where? I can't see any roundhouse?'

The hedgehogs danced with glee, highly amused.

'Can ye not see it at all, pretty one?'

'Ah sure, maybe she's got her eyes shut!'

'An' the roundhouse starin' her right in the face!'

'She's pretty all right, pretty short-sighted. Hahaha!'

At that Trimp lost her patience. 'Very funny, I'm sure. Now would one of you stilt-legged, clay-faced buffoons show me this roundhouse?'

Murfo stepped forward to the side of the biggest dune and slid aside a screen of brushwood and dead grass, revealing an opening. Bowing low to Trimp he bade her enter. 'How d'you like it, me beauty? This whole big dune is our roundhouse, an' none can find it except the Dunehogs.'

It was an ingenious structure, built from stones, timber, clay and wattle, completely disguised as one massive sand dune. Inside it was lit by lanterns and a fire glowing beneath a stone oven, with secret air vents to the outside. Everybeast sat upon woven rush mats, and a silence fell as Dunespike entered and threw up his paws. 'Do we know who we are?'

Every hedgehog held up their paws and answered, 'Sons o' the sand an' daughters o' the dunes!'

The Chieftain looked round until he had selected a very young beast, who was still learning the tribe's rules. A question and answer session started between master and novice. Older Dunehogs watched, nodding sagely.

'Do we fight our enemies?'

'Dunehogs would rather use fright than fight!'

'How tall is a Dunehog?'

'As tall as his stilts!'

'Where do Dunehogs live?'

'In a roundhouse where nobeast knows!'

'Why don't they know?'

''Cos we cover our tracks!'

'An' when is it your turn to cover tracks?'

'Dawn 'til night, first quarter o' the moon!'

'Right. You did grand, young 'un, just grand!'

'I thankee, Chief Dunespike!'

Food was served amid a babble of chatter. Dunespike plumped his huge bulk down between Martin and Trimp, knocking Murfo out of the way. 'Ah, that's better now. My turn t'sit next t'the pretty maid.' He tweaked Trimp's headspikes before turning to Martin. 'These young 'uns must learn the rules, y'know. Sit ye an' welcome to our ould home. Eat hearty now.'

The crew of the *Honeysuckle* soon got into the habit of eating like Dunehogs. There was a board, piled high with wafer-thin ryeflour pancakes, and between each four creatures two earthenware pots were placed, steam arising from both. One of the pots contained a thick stew, consisting of overboiled potato, finely chopped cabbage, wild onions and various types of shellfish. This was spooned on to a pancake and rolled up carefully. One end was twisted a couple of times to stop the contents spilling out.

Gonff was an expert within seconds. He nudged a nearby Dunehog. 'Good idea, this, mate. Saves a lot o' platewashin'.'

'Oh, that it does, sir. 'Tis a grand ould idea!'

Gonff, the perfect mimic, answered him in Dunehog idiom. 'Ah sure 'tis. Grand, grand!'

Everybeast within hearing chuckled appreciatively.

When the first pot was finished, there was still about half the amount of pancakes left. These they used in like manner with the contents of the second pot: a sweet hot mass of pulped berries and honey, with some strange tangy spice mixed in.

Dunespike chomped away blissfully. 'Ah, thank ye, Muther Nature, for the good ould sweet stuff. 'Twas meself was thinkin' I might never taste it again until yourself magicked me rotten tooth away, Martin!'

For entertainment the Dunehogs laid on an exhibition of Spinetussling. A circle was cleared and two contestants tied on pairs of half-size learning stilts. They stood balancing at the ring's inner edge. Then a few oldsters, acting as referees and judges, shouted, 'Hold y'circle, no paw touchin' now. Get set. Tussle!' The pair stumped adroitly out, charging one another. They were two fully grown males and had lots of supporters.

'Ah, g'wan there, Doggle, make him eat sand!'

'Get into the great lump, Paykel, throw him spike o'er stilts an' let's see the soles of his footpaws!'

'Watch the divvil now, Doggle, look out fer those sweeps with his stilts!'

'Go on, Tussle will ye, Tussle!'

Both hedgehogs circled awhile then met in the middle with a resounding bump of heads. They locked head-spikes and began trying to throw each other over. Not being allowed to touch one another with their paws made it very hard. Sweating and grunting they pushed back and forth, every now and again trying a side hop to unbalance the unwary one.

'Now, Doggle, now, give him the ould sidehead twist!'

'Use the one two forward butt, Paykel, an' you'll Tussle him!'

In the end Doggle triumphed. He took the advice, using a combination of the sidehead twist and a left stilt-sweep. With a roar of surprise, Paykel spun once in the air, stilts flying high, to land flat on his back. Cheers rang out from Doggle's supporters as he leaned down and rapped on his opponent's stilts thrice, which is considered a very sporting gesture in Spinetussling circles.

Now the Dunehogs were calling for the Chief to enter the ring, but he shook his head, smiling. Murfo yelled across at him. 'G'wan, da, show 'em how a real champion Tussles, or is yer belly gettin' too grand?'

This aroused jeers and laughter. Still smiling, Dunespike plodded down to the ring's edge. 'Are you fit to be thrown, Doggle?'

Doggle performed an agile dance on his stilts. 'Aye, Chief, I am that. Though I'm thinkin' 'twill take somehog younger an' faster than yerself to throw me, ye fat ould omadorm.'

Dunespike raised one eyebrow. There was menace behind his smile as he tied on one stilt. 'Ah sure mebbe I am gettin' on in seasons, but let's see if we can't make ye kiss the sand wid yer backspikes!'

A gasp arose from the audience as Dunespike stood erect.

'Will ye look at that, he's goin' to Tussle wid only one stilt. Doggle will make crab bait of the ould fool!'

One of the judges pointed at Dunespike. 'D'ye not know yer wearin' only one stilt, Chief?'

'I do!'

'An' y'wish to Tussle like that tonight?'

'I do!'

The judge shook his head in resignation. 'Right. Hold y'circle now, no paw touchin', get set. Tussle.'

The agility and skill of one so old and heavy shook Martin. Dunespike bounded across the ring on his one stilt, meeting Doggle who was yet not halfway across. Down went the Chief's huge head, spikes bristling, and he caught his opponent a mighty butt, locking spikes and twisting powerfully. Doggle went sailing through the air sideways, to land amid the spectators. Roaring with laughter, Dunespike hopped over to knock his opponent's stilts thrice amid wild applause. Then he looked at Martin. 'Would ye like to tie the ould stilts on an' Tussle wid me, Martin of Redwall?'

Shaking his head, Martin held up both paws, laughing. 'I'd sooner tangle teeth with a shark than Tussle with you, sir. You're a warrior born!'

Gonff chimed in. 'Martin's a warrior too, y'know, an' sure he's a grand one with the ould sword. Let him show ye!'

Martin shook his head wearily at the Mousethief. 'Gonff, if you want any exhibitions of sword dancing you can do them yourself. I don't like showing off every time we meet new friends.'

Gonff shrugged glumly. Trimp felt sorry for him and immediately tackled Martin.

'It's not a case of you showing off, Martin, it's wanting to show you off to our friends. He's so proud of you, as we all are. Couldn't you manage just one little example of your bladeskill?'

Martin threw his paws about them both. 'When you put it like that I've no option, missie. Forgive my bad manners to you, Gonff. Right, let's see what we can do with these stilts!'

At Martin's request the Dunehogs thrust two stilts upright in the sand and balanced another one across their tops. The three stilts looked like a doorframe standing freely in the middle of the ring. The Warrior bade everybeast stand clear. A silence fell as they eagerly watched Martin take up position, holding the sword over one shoulder in a classic fighting stance. After weighing the stilts up, he hopped a half-pace back and went into action with a roar. 'Redwaaaaaaaallllllll!'

Like a shimmering blur of light the fabulous blade hit the topmost, horizontal stilt, sending it flying in the air. Almost within the same breath the sword zipped left and right, chopping both the upright stilts clean through their middles. Before the top stilt had hit the ground, Martin's sword severed it in mid-air. Even before the thunder-struck audience could shout or applaud, Martin had sheathed his battleblade and was sitting calmly next to Dunespike.

Amid the tumultuous applause, stamping footpaws and rattling spikes, the hedgehog Chieftain found his voice. 'Well stagger me spikes an' pickle me paws! Martin of Redwall, ye'd be a useful mouse t'have around any-place! I thought me own two eyes were tellin' fibs t'me. Sure an' I still don't believe I seen y'do what y'did, sir!'

It was enough to end the battleplay. A great old hogwife took out a curious stringed instrument and began twanging it with her headspikes, another began shaking a tambourine, and a third took up his little paw-drum and beat a lively tattoo.

Murfo seized Trimp's paw. 'Haharr, can y'dance an' sing, miss?'

Trimp skipped down to the ring ahead of him. 'Just try me. I recognise that tune, 'tis "Hogstamp Pawclap"!'

Setting the sand flying, both young creatures went at the dance with a will, putting in all the fancy steps they knew.

'Hogstamp pawclap all around the floor,
Shake those spikes that's what they're for.
Day is ended work is done,
Hogstamp pawclap everyone!

Curtsy the pretty maid bow down sir,
You've never danced with one so fair.
Take y'partner one two three,
Swing to the left love follow me!

Rap rap rap! Let's hear those paws,
I'll stamp mine if you stamp yours,
Round an' round now jump up high,
Lookit that young hogmaid fly.

Hogstamp pawclap, move to the right,
I could dance with you all night,
Skip into the middle o' the ring,
Raise y'voice let's hear you sing!

Can't you see, merry are we,
Here's the land and there's the sea.
Promenade let's hear you say,
Honour your partner, jig away!

With a hog an' a stamp an' a clap clap clap,
Raise the dust up slap slap slap,
Beat that drum an' pluck those strings,
Ain't we all such lucky things!
Easy with the spikes now . . . Hedgehogs!'

As Trimp and Murfo halted, the music struck up
again and nearly everybeast began dancing. Dunespike
and Martin sat tapping time with tankards of Seafoam,
a fine beer that the Dunehogs brewed themselves.
Martin smiled as he watched Chugger kicking up his
heels with a tiny hogmaid, and leaned towards
Dunespike. 'Guess who's just changed from a squirrel to
a hedgehog. Haha, yesterday he was a Sea Rogue
captain!'

Dunespike took a deep swig and wiped a paw across
his mouth. 'An' good luck t'the liddle sprig, sez I. See,

Martin, yore pal the otter thinks he's a bit of an ould hedgehog too!'

Martin was amazed at the transformation that had come over Folgrim. The scarred otter was roaring with laughter as he whirled a hogmaid round and round. Dunespike nudged Martin. 'Sure an' I wish that otter was one o' me hogs. The boyo looks as if he'd stand no ould buck from anybeast!'

The Warrior winked at his friend. 'That's the truth, mate, nobeast messes with Folgrim twice!'

Dunespike was still watching Folgrim as he answered, 'Beasts without fear are far'n'few. I knew soon as I clapped eyes on you'n'Folgrim that you were two of that rare ould stock. Only other two I ever heard of was a mouse like yerself an' a black squirrel. 'Twas said that they were a grand ould pair of battlers who didn't know the meanin' o' the word fear, no sir!'

Martin came alert. 'What were their names? Where did they come from, Chief, do you know?'

Dunespike had eaten and drunk copiously, and he was tired. 'D'ye know, I'm not certain. The mouse had a short kind o' name, the squirrel now, was her name Rangfarl or somethin'? I can't think properly some days, me ould head must be turrible muddled from all that Spine-tusslin'. Wait now! I heard it said that the mouse came from north of here, up the coast a ways, though 'tis meself'd be lyin' if I told ye any more. Sometimes I wonder if there are more butterflies flyin' round in me head than there are out on the dune flowers.'

Martin patted the old Chieftain's paw. 'Never mind, matey. Though I'd be obliged if you could tell me how far the north shore is?'

Dunespike lay back on the rush mats and yawned cavernously. 'Oh, four days about. You'll easily know, 'cos the weather gets much colder an' you'll see a great ould rocky point stickin' out into the sea. Martin, I can't keep me eyes open, so I'll bid ye goodnight an' peaceful dreams.'

132

When the festivities had ceased and the lanterns had been doused, Martin sat awake in the firelight's glow. All around the Dunehogs' shelter creatures sprawled, snoring, murmuring, some even chuckling or singing broken snatches of song in their sleep. For some reason unknown to himself, a great weight lay on him, and tears sprang unbidden to his eyes. Then the Warrior realised what the cause of his distress was. He had been laughing, singing, drinking, eating and dancing, with hardly a thought for them.

'Them' being the father and mother he could hardly remember, who had lived only four days away from the place where he now sat. A vision of a ship, sailing off into a snowswept day, sprang into his mind, a memory of overwhelming sadness and pain. He gripped his sword tightly, knowing it was the only link between himself and the small young mouse who stood on the shore, watching the ship vanish into swirling snow and heaving waves. Weariness overtook Martin of Redwall. He lay down and let his eyes close. The small mouse, the ship and that long ago day grew dimmer and dimmer, then vanished into the realms of merciful dreamless sleep.

15

Over the following days and nights Martin hardly rested or ate. He was unusually silent, and spoke only when he had to. Draped in a blanket and sailcloth, he sat at the prow of the *Honeysuckle*, regardless of the hostile weather, which grew colder by the day. Dunespike and his tribe had given them a marvellous send-off, plying the crew with stores of food and delicacies. Trimp and the others had been sorry to sail off, the hedgehogs were so hospitable and funny. Martin's sombre mood affected the crew of the *Honeysuckle* deeply, and they were not the jolly bunch of companions who had travelled downstream together.

Log a Log Furmo cooked a special damson crumble, with Trimp assisting two of his Guosim shrews to make tempting arrowroot and redcurrant sauce for it. They sat beneath the stern shelter whilst Gonff dished it up to the crew, filling each bowl brimful and remarking, 'Dig in, mateys, this'll put the roses in yore cheeks an' a smile on yore faces. Best skilly'n'duff I ever saw!'

Furmo raised his ladle warningly. 'Ahoy, Gonffo, I'll raise a good lump 'twixt yore ears if'n I hear ye callin' my best damson crumble an' miz Trimp's sauce skilly'n'duff. Hmph! Skilly'n'duff indeed! What does he think we are, missie, a pack o' sea vermin?'

Trimp held out a bowl to Gonff. 'Fill it up, friend. I'd better take some to Martin. He only had a beaker of mint tea for breakfast, and 'tis late noon now and he hasn't had a thing since.'

Gonff heaped a good portion into the bowl. 'Best let me take it, pretty 'un. I know him better'n anybeast, 'cept my Columbine. Wish she was here now – liddle Gonflet too. They'd cheer him up.'

Dinny's homely face creased in a smile. 'Hurr, oi'm thinken ee h'infant an' yore pretty woif wudd cheer you'm up gurter'n anybeast, zurr Gonffen.'

Gonff sat down. Putting the bowl to one side he wiped at his eyes with a piece of rag. 'That's the truth, Din. I miss Columbine an' the liddle feller a lot. I ain't the cheerful rovin' type I used t'be.'

Chugger leaped on to the Mousethief's lap and hugged him. 'Shush now, mista Gonff, I be yore likkle one, eh?'

The Mousethief could not help smiling through his tears. 'Bless yore 'eart, Chugg, course you will, though I 'ope you ain't a Dune'og no more – they're too prickly to hug. Beggin' yore pardon, miz Trimp. No reflection on you.'

Martin came striding astern. He threw off the blanket and sailcloth, nodding to Furmo. 'Tell your shrews to trim the sail and take up oars. I can see the rockpoint standing out in the distance!'

Furmo went up the mast like a squirrel. He peered ahead at the dark jutting line far off, then came back down. 'Aye, that'll be the start o' the northlands right enough. Folgrim, will ye take the tiller an' keep 'er dead ahead? Gonff, 'elp tie off the lines. We'll make landfall tonight if'n she holds a tight sail. Stir yore stumps, Guosim, show our friends wot a shrew rower looks like!'

The *Honeysuckle* sprang forward, only having to tack the slightest bit, running before a wind out of the south-east. Martin took the for'ard port oar, with Gonff plying the opposite one. The Warrior set a vigorous pace, though

Trimp cautioned him. 'Easy now, Martin, not so fast, think of the others.'

Gonff blew off spray that was tickling his nose. 'That's the stuff, Trimp, you tell 'im, otherwise we'll all be flat on the deck afore we're halfway there. Don't forget, it's not safe to row like a madbeast on a full stomach of skilly'n'duff. Yowch!'

The Guosim rowers chortled gruffly as Furmo stood over Gonff armed with his stout wooden ladle. 'I told ye wot I'd do, you insultin' rascal. Now, say after me. Damson crumble with good hot sauce!'

Gonff repeated it dutifully, and Furmo made him say it again. The phrase made such a good rowing chant that the Guosim shrews took it up, bending and straightening their backs in time to the cadence.

'Damson crumble an' good hot sauce! Damson crumble an' good hot sauce!'

Chugger was acting captain again. He strode officiously up to Gonff and nodded approvingly. 'Mista Gonff, you like a damser crum an' good 'ot sauces?'

The Mousethief licked his lips appreciatively. 'I certainly do, me liddle mate!'

Patting his tiny stomach Chugger growled fiercely, 'Well you can't avva no more, I eated it all up, an' I not yore likkle mate now. I cap'n Chugg, see!'

Not stopping for anything they rowed doggedly on, trying to keep up the pace, which Martin had unconsciously increased again. Midnight had gone by an hour when they rounded the point. Everybeast lay back, panting with exhaustion, as Furmo gave orders to ship oars. Everybeast except Martin. As the *Honeysuckle*'s hull scraped to a halt in the shallows, he was upright, staring at the deserted shore, which was bathed in pale moonlight. Like lonely sentinels, the cliffs stood high in the background, topped by sparse vegetation. Darkened caves, partially covered by weather-warped driftwood and rubble, which had once disguised them from hostile eyes, lay forlorn and abandoned. A floodtide of memories poured in on Martin's senses. Every rock, even the wind-driven sand drifts, looked familiar to him. Turning to his tired companions, the Warrior spoke in a hoarse whisper.

'I was born here, I know this place!'

Slipping overboard he waded through the shallows.

Drawing his rapier, Log a Log Furmo signalled to his Guosim. Folgrim picked up his axe, determined to go ashore with them. Gonff backed to the rail and stood in their path, holding up both paws.

'No, mates. Let our friend go alone. 'Twould not be right to intrude on him this night!'

The crew of the *Honeysuckle* laid aside their weapons and sat down to await Martin's return.

Striding slowly up the beach, Martin turned to his right, the cave which had once been his home drawing him to it like a magnet. At first he thought his eyes were deceiving him. Halting, he stared hard at the feeble glow emanating from the cave. It *was* a light. Somebeast had lit a fire there recently, which had died to glowing embers. Drawing his sword, the Warrior of Redwall crouched, moving forward silent as moonshadow. Entering the cave he flattened himself against the rock wall, waiting until his eyes were accustomed to the dim light.

Covered by a long travelling cloak, an old mouse sat dozing by what was left of the fire. Martin crept close, extended his blade and tapped the mouse's paw lightly with its point. He did this once again, then the creature stirred, turning its face to him. The old mouse spoke in an awestruck voice. 'Luke, is that you?'

Wordlessly Martin placed some broken twigs on the fire. Laying aside his sword he sat down opposite the ancient creature, staring at it through the rising flames. A slow smile of pure joy stole across the old one's lined face.

'Oh, Luke, Luke, it is you! But how . . . ?'

The Warrior spoke softly, so as not to frighten the old

fellow. 'I'm Martin of Redwall, son of Luke the Warrior. Pray, what is your name, sir?'

Rising slowly, the old mouse shuffled round the fire. Sitting next to Martin he reached out and touched the Warrior's face. Martin watched in silence as tears rolled down the mouse's cheeks and his head began to shake.

'Ahhhh, so many seasons, so long ago. I've returned here through snow, rain and sun, many many times, and sat waiting alone, always alone.'

Tears overcame further speech. Martin drew the old mouse to him, placing a paw about his scrawny back and wiping away the tears with the cloak hem. He rocked him gently. 'There, there, no need to weep further, friend. I am Luke's son and I have come. You are not alone.'

The old mouse's eyes searched Martin's face. 'Aye, you are Martin, so like your father, so like him. D'you not remember me? I'm Vurg, I was Luke's best friend.'

Martin could not remember him, but he nodded. 'Of course. I didn't recognise you in the dark. Vurg, my father's strong right paw. I recall you now. How are you, Vurg?'

Holding forth his withered paws, Vurg chuckled. 'How am I? I'm old, Martin, old, old, old! Heeheehee, I've got more seasons on me than a hedgehog has spikes!'

Martin hugged the scrawny form to him fondly. 'Nonsense, I think you look just the same as you always did. I'll wager your appetite's still as good. Are you hungry, Vurg?'

'Heehee, anybeast tough enough t'be livin' on the northlands coast is always in need o' good vittles!'

Martin sheathed the sword across his shoulder. 'Right, come on back to the boat with me. I've got a crew of Guosim shrews there who'll feed you 'til you burst!'

Vurg rose creakily, retrieving a beaded linen bag from the sand. This he stowed beneath his cloak. 'Well, young Martin, what're we standin' round here waitin' for? Lead me t'the grub!'

Together they crossed the shore, Vurg leaning heavily on Martin's paw for support, chattering away.

'Guosim shrew cooks, eh? Bet they know 'ow to serve up proper-made vittles. Not like ole Cardo, now there was a mouse who'd burn a salad. Cook? Cardo couldn't boil water to save his life. You remember Cardo, don't you?'

Martin lied as he kept the oldster on a steady course. 'Oh, Cardo! How could anybeast forget that buffoon!'

Gonff was on watch, sitting in the prow. He saw the two mice approaching the *Honeysuckle* and roused the crew from their slumbers.

'Ahoy, mates, Martin's comin' back. Looks like he's brought company, too. Stand by – he might need help.'

Furmo and Folgrim assisted in getting Vurg aboard. The old mouse winked at the scarred otter. 'Heehee, bet you could take care o' yerself in a scrap?'

Folgrim's pointed teeth bared in a savage grin. 'I've taken care of a few in me time, sir!'

Vurg mused absently as they seated him comfortably under the stern awning. 'Aye, so did Luke an' Ranguvar, they took care o' more'n a few. Heeheehee!'

Furmo patted the old one's paw fondly. 'How's yore sweet tooth, grandad?'

'I tell ye, young whipsnout, a sweet tooth's about the only one I got left in me mouth. Heehee!'

The shrew stoked up his stove with seacoal and drift-wood. 'Then how does a baked river roll with hot maple syrup sound t'ye? I makes it with sweetflour an' all manner o' candied fruit, folds it careful-like into a big roll, bakes it to a turn an' pours 'ot maple syrup over it. Got a beaker or two of Dunehog Seafoam ale t'go with it. Sound good?'

Vurg wiped a paw across his lips. 'I'll tell ye when me mouth quits waterin', young 'un!'

Morning came, with overcast skies and a bitter wind.

Martin sat beneath the stern shelter with his friends, sipping barley and carrot broth. Vurg lay behind them, close to the oven, wrapped snugly in his cloak, sleeping off the feast he had consumed.

Gonff sat Chugger on his lap, allowing him to steal his beaker of broth. 'You finish that all up, matey, an' don't be dashin' about kickin' up a rumpus. Old Vurg needs lots o' sleep. Well, Martin, did y' find out what you needed to know from the ole feller, about yore dad an' so on?'

Martin shook his head as he watched Vurg sleeping. 'Didn't want to rush him. Vurg will tell me when he's ready. Though I did hint that I needed information.'

Dinny looked over the top of his beaker. 'Wot did ee'm owd feller say 'bout that, zurr?'

Martin shrugged. 'Not much, though he did say I'd find out all I needed to know when we took him back home to someplace called Tall Rocks.'

Chugger was beginning to wriggle out of Gonff's grasp. Trimp took charge of him, stroking the tiny squirrel's head soothingly. She looked enquiringly at Martin. 'Tall Rocks? Where's that?'

The Warrior stared out at the grey wintry seas. 'Somewhere up north of here. Vurg said he'd show us the way.'

Furmo picked up the linen bag from where it had fallen out of Vurg's cloak, and passed it to Martin. 'What d'you suppose is in this?'

Martin sighed deeply, and placed the bag carefully back in the folds of Vurg's cloak without disturbing him. 'He'll tell us when he's ready, I suppose. Though I'm not certain I want to know now. I have a feeling inside that 'tis going to be a long and tragic tale.'

Vurg woke before noon feeling much refreshed, and to prove it he ate a huge breakfast. Under his directions they pushed off and continued north. Martin watched, silent and pensive once more, as his birthplace faded into the distance.

16

It was a late noon, two days out from Martin's former home, when Tall Rocks hove into view. Rain was falling heavily and the wind had died completely. The sea surface, though pitted constantly by rainfall, was relatively calm, with a notable absence of the huge foam-crested rollers usual in the area. Vurg stood in the bows, Martin at his side, and relayed directions. Furmo and Dinny held the tiller between them, listening out for instructions.

'Keep her head out to sea a bit. Stick to that course!'

Furmo obeyed, but voiced his doubts. 'Wouldn't we be better tackin' in closer to the land side?'

Martin swiftly gave him his answer. 'No, no! Stay seaward. Vurg says the underwater reefs are close to the surface inshore. Out here the sea runs very deep, so the reefs are far below us. Keep her head out!'

'Right enough. Just as well the tide's runnin' smooth t'day.'

Martin agreed. 'Aye, Vurg says that if any waves start up you must steer right out to sea, away from Tall Rocks, and forget the whole thing until ebb tides arrive. Otherwise the *Honeysuckle*'d be smashed against the rocks!'

Dinny glanced fearfully to the horizon. 'O seas, keep ee

gurt waves clear of us'n's. Thurr be nuthin' wurser'n a drownded molebeast, no zurr!'

Trimp and the remainder of the crew stood aghast at the size of Tall Rocks. Monumental pillars of stone, they reared out of the sea like monsters from the dawn of time, huge and forbidding. For leagues of the coastline the seas were dotted with them, colossal and weirdly shaped, some cylindrical, others triangular or square-sided, their bases festooned with seaweed, kelp and dark moss above the columns of dark basalt stone. The *Honeysuckle*'s sail was taken in, and the most expert Guosim oarbeasts sat at the rowlocks, knowing their lives depended on the accuracy and sureness of their strokes. The order came when they were almost abreast of a cluster of columns, fronted by one half as big again in girth and height as the rest.

'Take 'er in steady. Keep the big 'un on yore portside!'

Trimp held tight to Folgrim's paw. 'Good grief! Look at the size of those rocks, Folgrim!'

Chugger, who had climbed on to the otter's shoulders, clung there like a leech, whimpering. 'I frykened, mista Fol, Chugg no like this!'

Folgrim tickled the little squirrel's footpaw. 'Aye, I'm frightened too, matey. So is the whole crew, an' even Martin, so we're in good company, I reckons!'

All else was forgotten as the monstrous pinnacles loomed close. Fear echoed in Furmo's high-pitched yell. 'Bring 'er round! Round the big rock! Push 'er off'n'take 'er round, mates! Now!'

Rising in a smooth high swell, the sea swept the skiff, like a cork, straight for the big rock. Paddlers on one side banked her, rowing furiously, whilst Martin and Gonff joined the others, fending the rock off by pushing against it with oars and long poles. With an audible sucking and gurgling the swell receded. Down they shot into a deep trough, with the *Honeysuckle* swerving bravely in a swift arc round the basalt monolith. No sooner were they on the lee side of the rock than the peril of their position increased. Now they were in a narrow channel betwixt the main column and the others grouped behind it. Obeying Vurg's orders, the Guosim Chieftain sang out, 'I'm steerin' for that pack o' rocks! Make ready to tie up, for'ard, aft an' amidships! But don't tie 'er fast, mates, leave slack so she can ride the swells!'

The moment they were in reach of the grouped pinnacles, Martin whirled a weighted line, as did Folgrim in the midships and Gonff at the prow. Again the swell lifted them and Furmo shouted, 'Heave those lines out, mates!'

The strong slender ropes snaked out and up. Three iron grapnels clanked simultaneously into the stone crevices. The *Honeysuckle* was secured safely, and bobbed up and down alongside the rocks, with the slack lines allowing her to ride easily on the swells.

Log a Log Furmo could not stop his paws shaking. He wobbled along the deck and leaned against Martin, pale, breathless and shaken. 'By the fur'n'blood o' the great Guosim, at least ten times there I thought we was a goner, matey!'

Martin grasped his friend's paws, steadying them. 'You did it superbly, Furmo. Nobeast could keep her on course like you did – 'twas nothing short of a miracle!'

Stamping his footpaw against the deck, Furmo smiled proudly. 'Aye, an' no other craft in all the rivers'n'seas could've done it like our *Honeysuckle*. Wot a ship! I'll tell some stories about 'er t'my tribe when we gets back!'

Vurg took a deep breath. Cupping paws around his mouth, he called out in a quavery voice, 'Ahoy the *Arfship*! Ahoy there, can you 'ear me?'

There was no answer. Furmo felt recovered enough to roar out in a thunderous baritone, 'Ahoy *Arfship*, 'tis Vurg an' some company. Ahooooy!'

Martin pulled the shrew to one side just in time to avoid a hefty rope ladder with timber rungs which came down out of the rocks and clattered to the deck.

Gonff stared in puzzlement at Vurg. 'Who are we shoutin' to, an' wot's an arfship, mate?'

On the ledge above them a hare appeared. He looked as ancient as Vurg – older, in fact. Shaking a tremulous paw at Vurg he called down, 'Where in the name of my auntie's apron have you been, wot? I've been sittin' up here like a blinkin' sickly seagull, worryin' about you, sah! Now y'come sailin' up here, pretty as y'please, in charge of this jolly old rats' regatta. Wot!'

Vurg mounted the rope ladder with Trimp's assistance, followed swiftly by her friends. The old mouse argued with the hare as he climbed up to the ledge.

'Oh, give yore flappin' jaws a rest, Beau, these creatures are friends, they brought me back from the north shore. Which is more'n I can say for you. I'd grow whiskers t'me footpaws waitin' on you t'come an' fetch me, y'great flop-eared bag-bellied droopy-pawed rockrabbit!'

The old hare's ears stood up indignantly as he helped Vurg on to the ledge. 'Hah, rockrabbit is it, you blather-bottomed old dodderer, wot wot. I've had a barnacle casserole bubblin' here for two confounded days waitin' for you. Bad form, sah! I was goin' t'make a plum pudden too, but I flippin' well ain't now. So you can go an' jolly well whistle f'your blinkin' dessert for all I care. An' I hope the casserole keeps you awake all night. Ungrateful bounder!'

Martin popped his head over the ledge. 'When you two creatures have stopped arguing, would you mind moving aside? We've got a ship's crew to get up this ladder.'

The hare fitted a rock crystal monocle into one eye and glared down at Martin. 'Oh, have you now? Well my compliments t'you, sah, an' your crew, wot! I s'pose you've come to eat us out of house an' home without a by your leave or jolly old toodle pip!'

Vurg interrupted the hare's tirade. 'Ahoy, Beau, mind yore manners. Take a close look at yon mouse an' tell me who ye think he is?'

Beau crouched down, holding his back and grimacing. He brought his face level with Martin's. The eyeglass popped out with surprise as he stared at the Warrior mouse.

'Luke! Well burn my auntie's taters, wot! You're a bounder, a rotter an' a curmudgeon, sah! How is it that you've stayed so jolly young whilst we've grown old? Not the done sort o' thing, I'd say. Bally cad!'

Martin sprang up on to the ledge. Smiling, he grasped Beau's paw and pumped it up and down.

'I'm Martin of Redwall, son of Luke the Warrior. Whom have I the pleasure of addressing, sir?'

The hare shook his hoary silver head, returning the smile. 'Knew y'father well, sah. Excellent chap! I'm Beauhair Fethringham Cosfortingsol. No I ain't, I'm Beausol Fethringhair Cosfortingclair. No I ain't, wait a tick. I'm Beauham Fethringclair Confounditall. Tchah! I'm so old I've forgotten me own name. What a disgrace, wot!'

Vurg sniggered. 'Heehee, try Beauclair Fethringsol Cosfortingham. That's yore silly long name.'

The hare scratched his scraggy whiskers. 'Ah! Of course it is. Thank you, old chap.' Then, scratching his whiskers again, he turned on Vurg. 'On the other paw, who asked you, sah, you battered old mouserelic? When I need somebeast to tell me m'name I'll jolly well ask m'self. Pish tush! The very idea, tellin' a chap his own moniker!'

Vurg approached him until they stood nose to nose. 'Battered ole mouserelic? Well of course I am, an' who wouldn't be, lookin' after you all these seasons. Should've left you on Twin Islands, that's wot I should've done!'

Martin clapped a paw to his brow, looking beseechingly to Gonff. The Mousethief pushed Beau and Vurg apart. 'Quiet now, you two, an' lissen t'me. Aboard our ship we got a way of settlin' arguments. We let any

145

quarrelsome beasts settle things by challengin' our argument counsellor. Folgrim, come over 'ere!'

Testing his axe edge by licking it, Folgrim strode over. Baring pointed teeth he turned his scarred face from Vurg to Beau. The otter's voice sounded like a blade hacking ice.

'Well now, anybeast got an argument t'settle wid me, choose yore weapons. Axes or teeth, it don't make no odds t'me!'

Vurg immediately hid behind Beau, whose throat bobbed like an apple on a string as he gulped. 'Arguin'? Who's arguin', old chap? Merely a bit o' humorous banter 'twixt my erstwhile companion and m'goodself, wot? I say, Vurg, hadn't we better get these seagoin' types aboard the good vessel *Arfship*? They look jolly hungry an' tired t'me. We could fricassee a shark or two for friend Folgrim, or maybe he'd prefer just to gnaw on the messdeck table. Er, ahaha, follow me, chaps. No offence, mister Folgrim sir, merely a jocular jest, wot wot!'

Vurg and Beau led them through a perfectly round tunnel in the rock. They emerged on the other side amid the massed pinnacles and stood gazing up in open-mouthed awe at the sight that greeted them. Beau managed to make an elegant leg and bowed slightly. 'Welcome to the vessel *Arfship*!'

Jammed between the column they stood upon and the one immediately next to it was half a ship. High overhead it stood, lodged between both pinnacles, more than two-thirds of the way up. From midships to for'ard end it was wedged firmly, a huge rusting iron spike at its forepeak driven into the rock by some tremendous force. The thing had once been red, but now through seasons of harsh weather, seaspray, sun and rain, it was faded to a rose-pink hue.

Dinny's voice cut the silence. 'Well fill moi tunnel! Arf a ship oop in ee air!'

*

Ascending another rope ladder, they climbed up to the old habitation. Trimp stared about in astonishment at the immensity of it all. It was like being in some great chamber. Timbered bulkheads with holes for oarports let in the light, as did the opened hatch covers high above them. Furmo's voice echoed spectrally in the vast space as the crew of the *Honeysuckle* walked through it wide-eyed.

'An' this is supposed t'be only arf a ship! I tell ye, mates, could you imagine it afore it was broken, with the other arf attached? It must've been like a floatin' village! I wager there wasn't anythin' that size ever sailed the seas!'

Vurg nodded his old head. 'Oh but there was, an' this is what's left of it. See through those open hatch covers? There's another deck above this an' another one above that again. Yore lookin' through three decks up t'the main one, which if y'count it makes four altogether. We keeps the 'atches open to give light, battens 'em down in bad weather. Up these stairs is the for'ard cabins. Come on, I'll show ye!'

Martin shook his head as he passed rows of benches, with chains dangling from them and long broken oars hanging through the ports. They looked well worn from constant use. 'Beau, was this a slave ship?'

'Indeed it was, old lad, the foulest, most evil vessel that ever plied the ocean. Now 'tis our home, our beloved *Arfship*. Actually, 'twould have been *Half Ship* if I'd had me way, but the others called it *Arfship*, so *Arfship* it is, wot. Come an' eat now, questions later, that's the drill!'

Following him up the ornately carved staircase, they entered a roomy cabin with its skylights thrown open. It was a complete living area. Tables, chairs, bunks and cupboards were all about, clean and neat. Two mice, old and grey, were working at a table next to a big glowing stove with its smokepipe thrusting through the edge of the skylight. Vurg introduced them.

'This is all of us left from those who sailed off long ago from the north shores. Myself, Dulam and Denno.'

The mouse called Denno went straight to Martin and took the Warrior's face gently in both his flour-dusted paws. 'No need to tell ole Denno who you are – I know. Luke's son Martin. Couldn't be no otherbeast. Yore the spittin' image o' the great Luke, though you got yore mother Sayna's eyes.'

Martin shook visibly, blinking hard. 'You knew my mother?'

Denno nodded. 'Course I did, an' a prettier, more gentle creature there never was. I knew 'em all, Martin, everybeast. But we've got all night to talk of that. Sit and rest now, the food will be ready soon.'

Barnacle casserole was a delicious concoction of sea vegetables and shellfish. Guosim cooks hurried back to the *Honeysuckle* and brought up more supplies. Beau relented, and aided by Folgrim and Trimp he began mixing a big plum pudding. Gonff helped the Guosim cooks to bake scones and bread. Martin and Chugger cut up an excellent cheese, studded with beech mast and hazelnuts. Dinny put together a salad with any spare vegetables he rooted out. Mint tea was put on to boil and dandelion and burdock cordial poured from a keg into serving jugs.

After the tables were pushed together and set, they sat down. Gonff proposed a toast.

'To the end of a journey, to my best friend Martin the Warrior an' to the wonderful vittles an' good hospitality showed to us by the crew of the *Arfship*!'

Everybeast raised their beakers and drank cheerfully. As they ate, Furmo could not resist asking the question which was puzzling him greatly.

'Tell me, Vurg, 'ow did the for'ard half of a great ship land up 'ere? It just don't seem possible.'

Vurg munched shrewbread and cheese as he explained. 'Yore right, mate, I wouldn't 'ave believed it meself if'n I hadn't been aboard at the time, but 'ere's how it came about. Durin' the biggest storm anybeast'd ever seen, the *Goreleech* – for that was once wot this ship was called – struck that big rock pillar out in front. I tell ye, waves twice as high as this vessel were runnin' on a sea driven by wind an' rain. 'Twas more like a hurricane than a gale. Well, she whacked that big rock side on, with a force you couldn't imagine. Smashed the *Goreleech* clean in two, like an 'ot knife goin' through butter. On board the for'ard part were oarslaves an' Sea Rogues doin' battle. We were flung to the decks like wet leaves in a wind. There was screamin', shoutin' an' weepin' – everybeast was sure they'd met their deaths. The stern half fell backward into the sea, and sank in the blink of an eye. Now, the same great wave that sank it carried us, an' the other half, swirlin' round to the back of the big rock. Down, down we went as the wave ebbed away in a torrent of suckin' an' whirlin', an' we thought we was surely done for. Then another giant wave rounded the rock an' lifted us, easy as a paw lifts a grain o' sand. Up we rose, up, up, high in the air. From where I lay on the deck, I saw the two pinnacles as the wavecrest flung us forward. Suddenly a shudderin' shock ran through me from tail to eartips. Then everythin' went still.

'I opened me eyes and stood up. We were wedged fast, right up 'ere, the broken midships restin' flat on a ledge of one column, the prow on another, with the big iron spike that stuck out front, driven like a nail, deep into the rock!'

Gonff forgot the beaker which was halfway to his lips, and sat shaking his head. 'An' what happened next, Vurg?'

The old mouse chuckled as he speared a scone with his knife. 'Me'n'Beau rallied our fighters fast an' finished off those scummy Sea Rogues afore they 'ad a chance t'get us. We've lived 'ere ever since. Nothin'll shift the ole *Arfship*, she's weathered time'n'tides, storm an' seasons, aye, an' never budged a splinter. After a while we made a rope cradle an' rigged a line over t'the cliffs on shore. Many creatures left an' went off t'find their ole homes. A score of us stayed 'ere. But that was long ago. Now there's only Dulam, Denno, me'n'Beau left out o' them all. Most o' our mates died. They're wrapped in sailcloth, weighted down with stones, sleepin' on the seabed far below us. Fates be kind t'their memories!'

Martin decided that the time had come. 'Tell me, Vurg, what became of my father, Luke the Warrior?'

Beau rose stiffly and went to a cupboard. He returned to the table with a large, dusty volume. ''Tis all within these pages, Martin, everything, as best as the four of us can recall. We spent many a winter an' autumn night recordin' the entire tale. 'Twas a joint work. D'y'know, I thought it might be found by somebeast, long after we were gone. But fate an' fortunes've smiled on us, laddie buck. There's food'n'drink on the table an' a long night ahead of us, wot! Here, Denno, you young whipper-snapper, you can understand your own writing best. Read the journal to our friends, there's a good chap!'

Denno polished a tiny pair of glasses. Perching them on his nose, he looked over at Martin. 'I was the scribe, y'see. Right, let's start at the beginning. I 'ope you like the title. 'Tis called "In the Wake of the Red Ship", this being an account of Luke the Warrior, written by his friends.'

Outside, the eternal seas washed against Tall Rocks, and breezes sighed a wistful dirge about the basalt columns where seabirds wheeled and called. In the cabin, high among the pinnacles, Martin of Redwall listened as the saga of his father, Luke the Warrior, unfolded.

BOOK TWO

Luke

17

There were other mice in the tribe, older and more experienced, younger mice also, bigger and stronger. But everybeast regarded Luke as their natural leader. As mice go, he was nothing special to look upon, of average height and stocky build. However, on closer observation it became obvious that Luke was a warrior born. Behind his calm dark eyes there lurked a flame; his stance bespoke fearlessness, some indefinable quality in his whole attitude marked him as one in whom others could put their unquestioning trust. A mouse tribe could look to him for guidance, and he could always be counted on for fairness and wisdom in his decisions. Such a creature was Luke the Warrior.

Over many seasons the tribe had wandered under his leadership. Long ago they had left the warm areas of abundance, those places where verminous villains preyed upon any who sought the peaceful life. Constant warfare against outnumbering odds had forced Luke's tribe into the nomadic way, always seeking and searching for some place where they would not have to sleep paw on sword, with one eye open. From the fertile middle lands they roamed north, where the weather was cold and the land bleak and sparse. On the day they reached

153

the northland coast, Luke thrust his sword into the earth. This would be his tribe's new home. It was a lonely place, quiet and undisturbed.

The tribe approved Luke's decision. Hardworking beasts could wrest a living from the ground here, providing they were left in peace to do so. There were caves in the base of the cliffs which backed the shore, a high rocky cape thrusting out into the sea at the southern point. It felt safe, with cliffs at the back and the seas in front of them. There was good soil on the clifftops, which could be planted and farmed in spring, summer and autumn.

For the first few days they kept a low profile, living off what supplies they had stored, making the caves habitable. During this time, Luke and his friends patrolled the area, watching out for enemies, robber bands and vermin raiders. Luke knew that his tribe was only a small one, wearied by constant travel, and would not be able to resist any major attack from a large force. But happily there was neither sight nor trace of foebeast.

Then, on the fourth day, Luke strode ahead of the rest as they made their way back to the caves. His step was light, and a shudder of joy ran through him. He felt that this forsaken northland coast was already bringing him happiness. Only two days before, his wife Sayna had given birth to their first little one, a son. They would call the new baby mouse by the name of Martin. Luke's grandsire had been named Martin, and when he was young Luke had often listened to tales that were told of the formidable Warrior mouse. It was his sword that Luke carried in the sheath on his back, given to him by his own father. Luke was the third of his family to carry the old battleblade, and one day, when the time was right, little Martin would be the next.

The tribe were busy preparing a feast for Luke and Sayna's son, the first little one to be born on the northland coast. There was to be a great bonfire, too. As Luke came within sight of the caves, he could see the ever growing mound of driftwood and dead timber being piled above the tideline. Two young mice were struggling to drag a big chunk of driftwood along the shore. Luke approached them, a smile hovering on his face at their efforts.

'Well well, Timballisto and Fripple, when d'you plan on gettin' that log to the bonfire pile, next season?'

Both mice were little better than three seasons old. They sat down wearily on the log, big round eyes imploring Luke.

' 'S too blinkin' big for us, Luke. Will y'lend a paw?'

The Warrior mouse drew his ancient battlesword from its sheath on his back and swung it high overhead, bringing the sharp blade down to bite deep into the wood.

'Righto, you two rascals, grab ahold of the swordhilt with me. We'll see if it moves any easier with us three strong beasts pulling it. Come on!'

Heaving energetically, Luke tugged the lump of wood through the sand. He watched fondly as the two little mice pulled valiantly, each latched on to the crosshilt.

When they brought the log to the pile of timber, Luke allowed Fripple and Timballisto to help him loose the swordblade, though he could have easily done it alone. He passed a paw across his brow, winking at them. 'Whew! Thankee, mates, 'twas a job well done!'

The little mousemaid Fripple took hold of Luke's paw. 'Please Luke will y'take me to your cave to see your new baby Martin please Luke?'

Luke could not help chuckling at the beseeching look on Fripple's face. He tweaked her paw gently. 'Of course I will, pretty one. What about you, Timbal?'

Timballisto scowled fiercely. 'I'll stay 'ere an' guard our wood 'til y'get back!'

Martin's cradle was a hollowed-out log, lined with soft moss and a woven blanket. The only family Luke had left in the world sat by it, his wife Sayna and her mother Windred. Crowing with delight, Fripple leaned over the cradle and took the baby's paw in hers. 'Oh my my, isn't he a lovely likkle feller!'

Sayna held the mousemaid's smock, lest she fall into the cradle. 'Aye, he's a good baby, no trouble at all. I think he will grow bigger and stronger than his daddy.'

Martin's eyes watched solemnly as his father loomed over him. He raised a tiny paw, reaching for the hilt protruding over his father's shoulder. This delighted Luke.

'Hoho, look at this bucko, tryin' to draw my sword!'

Windred hovered around the cradle anxiously. 'Be careful, he might cut himself on that blade!'

Luke reassured the fussing old mousewife. 'Oh no he won't. Martin's a warrior born, I feel it. Let my son hold the sword. It'll be his one day.'

Sayna watched her serious-faced babe trying to wrap his little paws round the blackbound haft with its redstone pommel. She shivered slightly. 'May the fates forbid that he'll ever have to use it in war.'

Luke released Martin's hold and stood up straight. 'Don't worry, Sayna. That'll never happen whilst I'm around. Besides, I don't think we'll be bothered here, being this far north. We searched the shores an' cliffs both ways. There's nothin' much to the south, an' if you go further north there's only some great tall rocks stickin' up out o' the sea about three days from here. Not a pawprint of vermin anywhere. Now, what about our son's feast?'

Windred turned to the cave entrance. Out on the shore the mice of the tribe were setting out what food they had foraged by the unlit bonfire. Each had brought what they could afford to spare, but it was not much. Windred spoke. 'Hah! Feast, you say? 'Tis a wonder we keep fur around bone on this forsaken coast. You've brought us to a cold an' hungry place, Luke!'

Sayna checked Windred reprovingly. 'That's not fair, mother. 'Tis not Luke's fault. Where the food was plentiful, so were our enemies. At least we have safety up here, and when spring comes we'll be able to farm and plant the clifftop lands. Luke says there's good soil up there. What about those berries old Twoola saw yesterday?'

Luke glanced from one to the other. 'What berries? Where did Twoola see them?'

Sayna explained. 'He took a walk last evening, north along the shore, and said he saw lots of berries growing in a rift near the clifftop. But there were great seabirds up there too, nesting. I thought it might be dangerous, which is why I didn't mention it yesterday. Seabirds can be very fierce creatures.'

Luke patted his swordhilt. 'Aye, an' so am I when our tribe needs food. Leave it to me. I'll take some good well-armed fighters with me, and Twoola can show us the spot. We won't harm the seabirds if they don't attack us, and I don't think they will, for what need have they of berries? Seabirds live on what they can scavenge from the sea and the tideline. We'll gather the fruit and uproot a few young bushes to plant on the clifftops back here. Now there's no cause for worry or fuss. I'll leave some warriors back here to guard our camp, and I'll be back as soon as I can, with whatever we find up there. Carry on with the feast – the youngsters are expecting it. I'll try to return before 'tis finished.'

Sayna placed Luke's warm cloak about his shoulders. 'You'll need this. It gets cold out there at night. Bring me back a little blackberry bramble, and I'll plant it so that Martin will be able to help me pick the berries in a few seasons.'

Windred adjusted the cloak around Luke's sword. 'Aye, and be careful out there. This is still strange country to us, Luke.'

With a score and a half of good mice that he could depend upon, Luke set out north along the shore. However, they could only travel as fast as old Twoola, and the ancient mouse hobbled along at a slow creaky gait. It was close to midnight when the foraging party reached the high crag where the berries grew. Twoola sat down wearily upon the sand, pointing upward. 'That's the place, Luke, but I ain't goin' up there. Some o' those seabirds are big as eagles!'

Luke took off his cloak and wrapped it round the old fellow. 'You did well getting us this far, Twoola. Stay here and rest – we'll go up. Vurg, Denno, bring those ropes.'

By those who knew the coasts and high seas, one name was whispered with terror and loathing.

Vilu Daskar!

The pirate stoat was known by other names. Butcher, thief, torturer, murderer. But none more frightening than his own.

Vilu Daskar!

Captain of the biggest vessel ever to plough the main. A trireme, with three banks of oars, pulled by wretched slaves. Crimson red, from the pennants fluttering at its forepeaks, down through the four mighty sails to its gigantic keel. Always leaving behind it a thin red wake, from the dyes which oozed out of its timbers. Jutting out from the prow stood an immense iron spike, rusted red by long seasons of salt water. Such was the red ship, named the *Goreleech* by its master.

Vilu Daskar!

Evil was his trade, the red ship his floating fortress. Aboard it he could disappear into the trackless wastes of seas and oceans, materialising again to prey on the unwary. Coastal settlements, inland hamlets, even the island havens of other Sea Raiders and Corsairs. None were safe from the *Goreleech* and its bloodthirsty crew, a mob of wild cruel vermin. Mercenaries, assassins, cutthroats, the flotsam and jetsam of earth and waters. These Sea Rogues were ruled by two things alone: a lust for plunder and slaughter, and a blood-chilling fear of their lord.

Vilu Daskar!
He revelled in the dread his name instilled into all.

In the 'tweendecks of the *Goreleech* relentless drums
pounded incessantly. Chained to the oars, masses of
gaunt slaves bent their backs and pulled, straightening
with a joint groan as they heaved on the long wooden
sweeps. To the accompaniment of slave drivers cracking
their whips and the ever present drumbeat, the red ship
sailed into the waters off northcoast.

Vilu Daskar leaned against the stern gallery rail, his
alert dark eyes watching constantly, like a snake about to
strike. Unlike other seagoing vermin he was highly
intelligent, well-spoken and modestly garbed. He wore a
long red cloak, beneath which was a plain black tunic,
belted by a broad red calico sash through which was
thrust a long bone-handled scimitar. The only concession
to finery was his headgear, a white silken scarf bound
about his brow, atop of which he wore a rounded silver
helmet with a spike at its centre. Tall and sinewy, he cut a
quietly elegant figure, unlike the crew under his command, all arrayed in a jumble of tattered finery and
sporting heavy tattoos and masses of gaudy earrings,
necklets and bracelets.

Evening light was fading fast over the cold seas when,
from high on the mainmast, a searat called Grigg sang out
from the crow's nest: 'Laaaand awaaaay off larboard,
cap'n. I sees a light onshore, sire, to the north o' that rocky
point!'

Vilu flicked his eyes in the direction given, without
moving his body. Akkla, the ferret steersbeast, held the
ship's wheel steady, awaiting his captain's command.
Even if it meant running the *Goreleech* on to rocks, he
knew better than to change course without Vilu's order.

The stoat spoke without raising his voice. 'Sweep south
and take her in behind that big rock point.'

Two other vermin stood waiting as Vilu peered hard at

159

the faint glow, far off on the shoreline. He issued orders to them without turning, knowing they would obey instantly.

'Reef and furl all sails, and increase the oarstroke to double double speed. We need to get out of sight quickly.'

Abruptly he strode off for'ard, where his bosun, the searat Parug, had a better view of the shore.

'So, my keen-eyed bosun, what do you see?'

Parug scratched at his beribboned whiskers, plainly bewildered. ''Tis 'ard to tell, cap'n. Ho, that's a fire right enough, an' a good big 'un, t'be seen from this distance, sire.'

A thin smile hovered on Vilu's lips. 'But?'

The bemused bosun shook his head. 'But anybeast'd be mad t'light a fire that big on northland shore. Wot are they up to, cap'n?'

Vilu lost sight of the glow as the *Goreleech* turned south, the headland blocking his view. 'Well, no creature in their right mind would set up a signal beacon on that shore, so they are either out of their minds, or ignorant of the danger. Maybe that's it, Parug, they might merely be simple beasts having some kind of celebration, eh?'

Parug's dull face broke out in a grin. 'Oh, like a kinda feast, y'mean, sire?'

The stoat's paw strayed to his bone-handled scimitar. 'Quite. Not very courteous of them. The least they could have done was to invite us!'

Parug's grin widened. 'So we anchors the other side o' yon point, comes over the rocks, an' invites ourselves, eh, cap'n?'

Vilu stroked the white bone scimitar hilt. 'Exactly. We might not attend the feast, but the least I can do is present my calling card.'

Parug stared blankly at his captain. 'Callin' card? Wot's a callin' card, sire?'

With lightning speed the scimitar blade's tip was

touching the bosun's throat. 'This is my calling card!'

Parug's throat bobbed nervously under the sharp bladetip. 'Oh, er, I see, sire, er, haha!'

Vilu Daskar tired of the one-sided conversation. He put up his sword and strode off.

Darkness had fallen. Luke's tribe laughed and sang around the bonfire, unaware of the big red ship anchoring the other side of the south point.

18

Luke threw the first rope up into the darkness. A moment later he heard the wooden bar tied to its end clack upon some rocks. He tugged it, making sure the bar held in the rocks it had wedged itself among. Paw over paw Luke went up, whispering to Vurg, 'Follow on with the other rope, mate, but be quiet. We don't want to disturb any of those seabirds.'

Vurg climbed up after him, and they balanced together, lodging their footpaws in the sides of the fissure. Luke took the second rope and began twirling it, paying the coils out as he swung it wider before throwing it strongly upward.

This time there was no sound of wood striking stone, but the rope went taut. A gruff friendly voice called down in quaint speech, 'Oi got et, zurr, oi'll make ee rope farst whoilst ee clamber up yurr!'

Vurg grabbed Luke's paw in the darkness. 'Sounds like a mole t'me. What d'you think, Luke?'

'Aye, 'tis a mole sure enough, though what he's doin' up a cliff I don't know. He sounds friendly enough, anyway. Come on!'

Both mice climbed until they reached a flat ledge, where there were several other moles and some hedgehogs to meet them. The mole who had hailed them took tinder and flint and lit a lantern, rumbling on in his curious mole dialect.

'Burr, us'n's doan't be gettin' mouseybeasts a-clamberin' up to call on uz, zurr, but welcumm to ee anyways. Oi be Drunn Tunneller, these 'uns be moi fambly, yon 'ogs be ee Tiptip brood, an' that 'un be Welff.'

A friendly-looking hedgehog wife in a broad rough apron twitched her spikes and curtsied. 'Pleased t'meet ye, I'm sure, but what be you goodbeasts a-doin' up 'ere in the dark night?'

Luke introduced his party as they climbed up to the ledge. Then he explained the reason for their visit.

'We came to take some o' those berries an' maybe some young plants whilst the seabirds were sleepin', marm. I'm sorry, though, I didn't realise they were your property.'

Welff brushed the apology aside cheerfully. 'Oh, you take all the berries an' shoots y'need, my dearie. Rain's washed good soil into this crevice for many a season. We got raspberry, blackberry, all manner o' berries growin' 'ereabouts. Ole Drunn's father tunnelled through to 'ere from the clifftops long ago. We've got a cave back there. Now don't ye be afeared o' the seabirds. We leaves 'em be an' they don't bother us a mite. Matter o' fact, they makes good watchbeasts in daytime, warns us if'n Sea Rogues be a-comin', so we can go an' hide in our cave.'

Luke stared questioningly at Welff Tiptip. 'Sea Rogues?'

'Oh, lackaday, sir, ain't you knowin' about those badbeasts? Why, they comes to this northcoast often as not.'

Luke began to feel the first stirrings of unease. 'But there's nothing t'be had on northland coast. Why do they choose to put in here?'

Drunn Tunneller waved a huge digging paw. 'Thurr be nobeast yurr to wurry abowt, zurr, so they'm cummin' to take on fresh water, patch ee sails, repair ee ships an' so forth. Burr, they'm all scum'n'villyuns!'

Welff nodded agreement with her molefriend. 'So they are. We hides in our caves an' stays well clear until those badbeasts are gone. Else we'd get slayed, or taken for slaves by 'em. Oh, Luke sir, what be the matter wi' ye? Do y'not feel well?'

Though the night was cold, Luke felt suddenly hot and sick. 'Further south, down the shoreline, my tribe have lit a big bonfire on the shore. We didn't think there'd be any danger this far north!'

Drunn's big digging claws took hold of Luke's shoulders. 'You'm must 'urry, zurr. Do ee take yore mouseybeasts an' get ee back with all 'aste, dowse ee flames, an' put out yon fire. Et be loik ee beacon to Sea Rogues. Oi beg ee, 'urry!'

Welff called after the party of mice scrambling down the cliff, 'Good luck go with ye, sir Luke. We'll follow ye on in the morn, with baskets o' berries an' wotever plants you may need. Aye, an' Drunn's moles will show ye how to hide yore dwellin's from the sight of Sea Rogues!'

Welff's words were lost upon Luke and his friends. They were already down and charging along the shoreline headlong, with old Twoola hobbling in their wake.

Dawn came wild and angry. Cold howling easterly gales swept the shoreline sand, piling it in buttresses against rocks and whipping grains widespread across the ebbing tide. Drunn Tunneller and Welff Tiptip led their little band along the beach, bearing between them the promised baskets of berries and young plants. Wearing cowled cloaks and mufflers over their noses and mouths they pressed on gallantly towards Luke's encampment, heads bowed against the weather's onslaught. To cover her anxiety Welff chattered feverishly to her molefriend.

'Now if 'twere late spring an' the weather milder a

body would expect Sea Rogues visitin' our shores. Anybeast afloat in stormy seas like we get this time o' season is nought but a fool. I know 'twasn't wise for Luke an' his mice to light great fires in full view onshore, but I reckon mayhap no harm will've befell them, eh, Drunn?'

The mole was about to agree with her when a fierce gust of sandgritted wind caused him to turn his face seaward. He groaned aloud and dropped his basket. 'Guhuuuurr noooo! Look yon, 'tis ee gurt redship!'

Through the fleeting spume of sand and seawater, Welff glimpsed the mighty bulk of the *Goreleech*, her crimson stern riding high on the main, red sails bellying tight as she sped westward out on to the deep. The good hogwife stood watching the fearful sight, tears mingling with the grit sticking to her face, and she moaned like a stricken beast. 'Waaaow, lackaday, the redship! Fortunes an' fates 'a' pity on those pore mice!'

Drunn grabbed her paw, signalling to his friends to follow. 'Coom on, missus, ee beasts be needin' our 'elp!'

Vurg was covered in swirling wood ashes from the scattered fire embers. He sat on the shore, lost in a dumb trance. Between them, Drunn and Welff shouldered his paws, steering him to the meagre knot of survivors who huddled forlornly in the mouth of Luke's cave. Old Twoola was the only mouse who seemed able to explain what had taken place. 'Friends, you come at a terrible time for us. Many graves will need to be dug in these bloodstained sands.'

Welff spoke softly to the old one. Now that she had recovered from her first shock, she was all business. 'Aye, 'tis so, but first we must attend to the living. Drunn, will you light a fire in this cave and set water to boil? Our family will prepare food for you. Dig out any ole linen you possess – we'll need bandages!'

As the moles and hedgehogs took care of the shoremice, their dreadful tale came out piecemeal.

'There was hundreds of 'em. We didn't stand a chance!'

'It was a massacre. Only those out lookin' for firewood escaped. We could do nothing to stop those evil killers!'

'Windred was lucky. She ran out on the shore with the babe, stumbled an' fell. Her cloak was over them both, an' the wind covered it with sand an' hid them. 'Tis a wonder little Martin wasn't smothered.'

Windred sat by the fire, bathing sand from the babe's face with warm water and the hem of her dress. 'Aye, an' he never made a single sound the whole time. Pore liddle mite, they slew his mother. Scum, they are! I'll remember that 'un's name to my dyin' day. Vilu Daskar! She tried to fight him off with a stick, but he had a big curved blade. He was shoutin' his own name, Vilu Daskar, an' enjoyin' what he was doin'. That stoat was laughin' as he cut my daughter down. Laughin' like a madbeast!'

Drunn looked up from a wound he was attending to. 'Ee maister o' redship shows mercy to nobeast, marm. Yurr, but whurr be zurr Luke gone to?'

The young mouse Timballisto, who had survived by climbing the cliff face, nodded towards the sea. 'Luke's out there, but nobeast can come near him, sir.'

Waist deep in the sea stood Luke, buffeted by the cold waves, with ice forming on his tear-stained features as he gazed westerly, after the red ship which was now nought but a blurred dot far out by the horizon.

Twoola shook his head sadly. 'He will not even look upon his own son, or his wife's mother. Alas, he has no ship to sail after the murderers. But he would have ended up slain if he did. Either way, I think Luke will die and be swept away when the tide turns. His life has been destroyed and he cannot exact a warrior's vengeance upon the Sea Rogues. Luke has no will to live.'

Welff hitched up her apron decisively. She turned from the sight of the forlorn creature standing in the sea to those who stood watching. 'I ain't havin' this, by the paws'n'prickles I ain't! You there, Cardo, go and fetch a stout rope. Vurg, give that stave you carry to Drunn. That liddle mousebabe's not growin' up without a father. Twoola, get every able-bodied beast out here. Move!'

Galvanised into action by Welff's no-nonsense manner, they dispersed quickly to their allotted tasks.

Drunn Tunneller tied the rope end around his middle and gripped Vurg's stave tight. 'Hurr, oi never was one furr pagglin' in ee sea, marm.'

The hogwife eyed him sternly. She was not about to be disobeyed in any circumstances. 'Go to it, Drunn, afore Luke freezes t'death!'

The mole trundled dutifully into the sea. 'Hurr, 'tis a good job oi trusters ee, missus!'

Luke was totally unaware of the mole wading up behind him, his eyes fixed on the horizon where the *Goreleech* had disappeared from sight. Drunn heaved an unhappy sigh. 'Whurrrr! Oi 'ates t'do this, zurr Luke, but 'tis furr thoi own gudd an' furr ee h'infant too, burr aye!' With one blow of the stout beech stave he knocked Luke unconscious. Looping the rope about Luke so that they were bound together, Drunn called back to the watchers onshore. 'You'm 'eave away farst. Oi'm most colded t'death out yurr!' Willing paws pulled the rope swiftly in to dry land.

The days that followed were hard upon the survivors. They buried their dead and would have gone on mourning all season, but for the help of the moles and the hedgehogs. Welff chided them ruthlessly and Drunn bullied them cheerfully, until they began to pick up the pieces and get on with the business of living. Luke recovered, but he spoke to none, sitting silently at the back of his cave, gazing into the fire. Every once in a while he would wander out into the night, and then sleepers would be awakened by his roaring down at the water's edge, shouting one name.

'Vilu Daskar! Vilu Daskar! Vilu Daskaaaaaaar!'

The morning following one such night, Luke's cave had become the meeting place for everybeast. They were gathered around the fire, breakfasting on hot oatcakes and blackberry preserve. Welff brewed a big pot of mint and comfrey tea, which they sipped as they ate. Luke had returned from the sea's edge, and he lay on a rocky ledge, wrapped in his cloak, sleeping. Cardo had a flat driftwood board, and his knife was heating in the flames as he announced to the gathering, 'I'm going to burn the names of our lost ones on to this wood with my knifepoint. Don't let me forget anybeast. I'll fix it in the sand on top of the big grave, agreed?'

Young Timballisto sniffed and rubbed a paw at his eyes. 'Will you put Fripple's name on it, sir?'

Cardo took his blade from the fire. He smiled sadly. 'Of course I will, Timbal. How could I forget my own daughter? I'll put a little flower after it, she'd like that.'

To break the atmosphere, Welff turned their attention to the baby Martin. 'Dearie me, will you lookit that mite, he's out of his cradle again. Where's he a-crawlin' to now?'

Windred knew. 'He's after his father's sword again. Watch.'

The solemn chubby mousebabe crawled over until he could get his paw on Luke's swordhilt. He sat quietly enough, trying to lift the weapon, which was twice his height.

Drunn squinted his eyes admiringly at the babe's efforts. 'Ee vurmints beware when that 'un grows!'

Windred looked across to Martin's sleeping father. 'Aye, an' bad fortune to any Sea Rogues when Luke awakens properly. He will, you mark my words. I know him!'

19

In the seasons that followed, Luke and his surviving tribe did well, and learned many things. No longer were they hungry, farming the clifftop land, foraging further afield in good weather, and gathering molluscs, shrimp and shellfish from rockpools and tide shallows. Drunn and his moles taught them how to create screens of rock, driftwood and overhanging vegetation for their caves, disguising them from the gaze of unwanted visitors and providing windbreaks against harsh weather. Windred looked after little Martin, who had become a sturdy toddler, living the simple life, still as solemn and well behaved as ever. Luke, however, was a different creature from the easy-going, good-humoured leader he had been before his wife's death. His tribe learned to give him a wide berth and ask no questions of him. He kept a cave apart from the others, in which he was making and storing weapons. He came and went at odd times, returning with materials he had gathered in his wandering. Martin was the only one he would confide in, though he constantly questioned Drunn and Welff on the habits of Sea Rogues. How often did they visit the north coasts? Did they ride at anchor or beach their vessels? What sort of discipline did they employ, what was the average size of a crew, what type of weapons and tactics did they favour? If a ship was sighted out on the main, all creatures ran for cover, but Luke would lie on the cliff-tops with Martin, watching it. The little fellow listened carefully to what his father had to say.

'I hope that vessel doesn't put in here, son. I'm not ready for them yet. Better that it stays out to sea and sails off. But when I'm ready, the day will arrive when I'll be looking for a ship to land here, and then we'll see what the seascum are made of. Look, she's veering off southward. We won't be bothered by that one, thank fortune. Come on, you can help me to build up our weapon supply.'

Luke showed his son how to make arrows, whilst he himself attended to the bows. 'See these, they're ash branches, good heavy wood. I've chosen the ones that are medium thick and straight, and dried the ends out by standing them in warm sand around the fire. Now, we make a slit in the opposite end and fit a piece of feather in it, like so, then bind above and below the feather with twine. Next, I place the dried end of the wood in the fire, let it burn, but not too much, then rub it to a point on this rock, burn a little more, rub a little more. Here, Martin, try the end of this with your paw. Be careful.'

Martin dabbed his paw gently on the needlelike point his father had rubbed on to the fire darkened ash. He smiled. 'Oo, it shark!'

Luke smiled at his little son, who was still learning to pronounce words. 'Aye, 'tis shark all right, very shark. Sea vermin don't wear armour, so an arrow doesn't need a metal or flint tip. A good hefty ash shaft with a firepoint will stop 'em!'

Vurg entered the cave, and indicated Martin with a nod. 'His grandma Windred is lookin' for him. Dinner's ready in the big cave. Are you coming, Luke?'

Luke glanced up from the bowstring he was twining and greasing. 'I'll be along. There's still work to do here.'

Vurg looked around at the rows of stakes waiting to be

sharpened, flint axeheads, unstrung yew bows, and gnarled driftwood limbs waiting to be fashioned into clubs. 'A fair ole bit o' work I'd say, Luke. Why don't me'n'Cardo an' some of the others help you?'

Luke knotted off the end of his finished bowstring. 'My son's a good little helper, but I could do with some like you to lend a paw. Why didn't you offer sooner, Vurg?'

His friend smiled wryly. 'Because none of us fancied gettin' our heads bitten off.'

Luke offered his paw. 'Sorry, mate. I accept your help gratefully. 'Tis not your heads I'm lookin' to bite off, just the Sea Rogues'.'

Vurg took Luke's paw and shook it warmly. 'Good. Let's go an' get some dinner, then every able-bodied beast in camp will pitch in with pleasure!'

From then on Luke became a real Warrior Chieftain, directing his creatures in the making of weaponry, drilling and training his fighters and marking off the shoreline around the caves in various strategies and plans for when the time was ripe.

It came unexpectedly, one evening the following summer. Having finished their day's chores the tribe sat about after dinner in the big cavemouth, their backs warmed by the fire within, enjoying the pleasant evening. Windred was singing an old song which had been passed down through her family.

'Old Ninian mouse and his goodwife,
Needed a house to build,
They had a family grown so large,
Their tent was overfilled.

To setting sun the old wife toiled,
From daybreak in the east,
But Ninian was a lazy mouse,
Who loved to sleep and feast.

The wife heaved stone and carried wood,
For door and wall and beam,
Whilst Ninian idly in daylight,
Snored on in peaceful dream.

She raised the gables, built a roof,
Her back was bent and sore,
As Ninian ate up all the food,
And loudly called for more.

So when the house at last was built,
His wife nailed up a sign,
Which stated "THIS AINT NINIANS!"
She said, "That shows 'tis mine!"

Then when the countless seasons passed,
And all within had died,
The rain and storm of ages long,
Had swept the sign outside.

It washed the first three letters out,
But left the rest intact,
That sign now reads, "S AINT NINIANS!"
A church? A joke? A fact!

So traveller if you read the sign,
Then take my word 'tis true,
A dreamer can become a saint,
So can a glutton too!'

Welff applauded with the rest, chuckling and shaking
her head at Windred's song.

'Tell me, Windred m'dear, is it true, is there such a
place as Saint Ninian's, or is it really a joke?'

Luke answered for her. ''Tis a fact, marm. I was born at
Saint Ninian's, as was Sayna my poor dear wife. We were
driven out, when I was a babe, by an evil warlord, a

wildcat named Lord Greeneye Verdauga who had a horde of vermin at his command, so they told me, but I was far too young to remember. This is our home now, and nobeast will ever drive us from here whilst I am about.'

Drunn Tunneller dashed towards them, waving. He was panting hard, having clambered down from the clifftops.

'Burr, git ee insoid, guddbeasts all, ee Sea Rogue ship be a cummen yurr!'

Immediately the tribe began pulling out driftwood and vegetation to disguise the cave's entrance as they had been shown. Luke nodded to Vurg and Dulam to accompany him down to the tideline.

Shading their eyes against the westering sun the three mice stood in the ebbing tide shallows watching the ship. Vurg scratched his head and looked to Luke. 'Doesn't look quite right t'me, mate. What d'you make of it?'

Luke scrutinised the vessel keenly. It was still a good distance from land. 'Hmm, could be just an honest merchant trader, but in these waters I doubt it, Vurg. It doesn't seem to be making good headway – if it's trying for land it won't make it here until near daybreak tomorrow at the rate 'tis goin', eh, Dulam?'

Dulam watched the strange craft take a north tack, as if trying to catch the wind. He pointed. 'See, she's got a broken mast, I think. That's why the going's so hard for that ship!'

Luke checked Dulam's sighting. 'You're right, mate. Maybe this is just what we've been waiting for. Back to the cave and rouse our fighters!'

Reynard Chopsnout, captain of the vessel *Greenhawk*, was in high bad humour. His ship was taking on water, and to make matters worse add a broken mainmast and ten days on short rations. Moreover, the crew were becoming mutinous and he was hard pressed to maintain command. The Corsair fox pawed irritably at the hard polished blob of pitch which served him as a snout. It was stuck on where his nose had been until he came off worse in a swordfight with a skilful ferret.

Chopsnout roared at the hapless weasel who was wrestling with the tiller. 'Hold 'er fast to the wind, Bootbrain. What's the matter with ye? To the wind I said, wagglepaw, the wind!'

Some of the vermin crew were aloft, trying to rig a jury mast. One of them called down mockingly, 'Don't shout too 'ard, Choppy, yer nose'll fall off!'

Chopsnout grabbed a belaying pin and hurled it up at the rigging. It fell back, almost hitting him. Amid the hoots and jeers of the crew, he yelled, 'Who said that? Come on, own up, ye lily-livered poltroon!'

Another insult rang out from below, where other crew members were baling out the water the *Greenhawk* was shipping. 'Bootbrain'd 'andle the tiller better if yer fed us proper, yew ole vittle robber!'

Chopsnout could not see who made the remark. He danced and stamped in anger on the deckplanking. 'Liar. Filthy foul-tongued liar. I get the same amount o' vittles that everybeast aboard gets!'

There was an ominous clack. Chopsnout quit stamping and dropped on all fours, scuttling about the deck. This caused great hilarity among the crew, and bold ones began yelling.

'Oops, ole Choppy's lost 'is hooter agin, mates. Hahaharr!'

'Let's 'ope it don't bounce down 'ere an' kill somebeast.'

'Give 'im a chance, mateys, 'e's on the scent of it. Heehee!'

'Arr now, don't say that, bucko, 'e'll go an' get all sniffy on us. Hohohoho!'

The irate fox soon found his pitchblob nose and stuck it on hastily. He paced the deck waggling his cutlass ominously. 'Go on, laugh, ye slabsided slobberin' swabs, but don't come whinin' t'me for aid or advice. I'm finished, d'ye hear, finished!'

He strode off huffily to his cabin. Bootbrain dithered at the tiller, not sure of which way to swing it. 'Harr, cummon, cap'n, we was only funnin'. Wot course d'yer want me to set?'

Chopsnout poked his head round the cabin door and cast a withering glance at the weasel. 'Course? I couldn't give a frog's flipper wot course you set. Sail where y'fancy, let the ship leak 'til she sinks, leave the mainmast broken. 'Tain't my bizness. I'll leave the command o' the *Greenhawk* to youse clever-tongued beasts, an' see 'ow *you* like it!'

There was an uneasy silence from the crew. Darkness was falling fast and nobeast was about to take on the responsibility of running the vessel. Chopsnout smiled triumphantly. 'So, what've ye got to say t'that, me fine buckoes?'

Bootbrain, who was never given to teasing or insulting his captain, could not help making an observation. 'Cap'n, yore nose is on the wrong ways round. Ye've stuck it on backwards.'

The final straw came when a strangled titter rang out from below. Reynard Chopsnout slammed his cabin door shut and sat sulking in his cabin.

Sometime after midnight there was a rap on the cabin door. Chopsnout snarled at the beast without, 'Go 'way an' leave me alone!'

The rapping persisted, accompanied by a voice. 'But cap'n, lissen, 'tis yore ole mate Floggtail. I've spotted somethin' on the shore. Come an' look!'

Adopting a stern face, Chopsnout emerged from his cabin. The crew were gathered on deck, peering at a fire burning on the beach some distance away. The Corsair fox could not help smirking as he addressed Floggtail, the searat first mate.

'Well well, a fire, eh? Looks no different from any other I've seen. What d'ye plan on doin' about it, mate?'

Floggtail stared hard at the firelight, scratching his fat stomach distractedly. 'Er, er, Scritchy an' Wippback reckons we oughter tack a bit an' sail beyond that point stickin' up south'ards, cap'n.'

Chopsnout smiled encouragingly at the two searats. 'Hmm, clever thinkin', you two. Wot next?'

Both searats hastily explained their plan.

'We drops anchor t'other side o' the point, cap'n.'

'Aye, then, er, we climbs over that point an' drops in on 'em.'

'That's right, then we slaughters 'em all an' robs any vittles we find!'

Chopsnout shook his head in despair at their stupidity. 'How d'ye know that those creatures on shore ain't already sighted us an' armed theirselves up, eh? An' tell me this, wot's t'stop this ship sinkin' if'n you takes the time to tack around be'ind yonder point? Well cummon, I'm waitin' fer an answer off'n some bright spark?'

There followed a deal of paw shuffling and blank looks, then Floggtail appealed sheepishly to Chopsnout. 'Er, cap'n, 'ow would yew go about it, sir?'

Chopsnout snorted airily. 'Ho, yore in trouble now, so youse need yore ole cap'n agin, eh? Well I ain't makin' a move 'til I gets a full apology off'n this crew for the insults I've bore!'

Staring at the deck as if the answer lay there, the vermin crew mumbled disjointedly.

'Sorry, cap'n, er, about yore no . . .'

'About wot we said to yer.'

'Aye, we didn't mean it, cap'n.'

''Twas on'y a joke, cap'n, we won't say nothin' no more.'

'Yore the best cap'n ever t'sail the seas, sir!'

Chopsnout attempted a sniff, holding on to his nose, which was starting to wobble slightly. 'Well all right, so be it. But next time you start any o' that I'm done with ye for good. Now, 'ere's the way I sees it. That fire onshore is only a liddle 'un, an' all I can see is two beasts sittin' by it, mouses mebbe. If'n there was a full tribe o' them there'd be a great big fire, so I figgers there's on'y the pair of 'em, prob'ly some ole hermit an' his wife. They're either daft or blind, 'cos they ain't seen us, or they wouldn't've lighted a fire an' give themselves away. Hark t'me now, this is my plan. Leave off fixin' the mast an' balin' out water, all four paws on deck 'cos the tide's starting to ebb. Grab any spare planks, timbers or oars an' start paddlin' 'er for the shore double quick. We'll run the *Greenhawk* up on the sand an' beach 'er high'n'dry. Then we'll capture those two mice an' torture 'em 'til we finds out where they've hid all their vittles. After they've cooked us a good feast the rest's simple. We fixes the leaks an' the mainmast, chops the ole mouse'n'his wife up fer fishbait, then sails off south fer a bit o' sun an' plunder!'

Bootbrain nodded his head in admiration of Chopsnout. 'Stripe me, 'ow d'you remember it all, cap'n? Yore a clever 'un, no two ways about it!'

The Corsair fox drew his ragged frock coat about him haughtily, staring down his imitation nose at the astounded vermin crew. 'Aye, that's why I'm a cap'n, so mind yore manners an' git about yore business, you dumbclucks!'

Vurg raised his eyes from the fire on the beach that he and Luke were sitting by. 'She's headed straight for us. They've put out paddles. You were right, Luke, that ship'll land here around dawn.'

Luke reassured himself by touching the sword concealed beneath his cloak. 'Good. Is everything ready, Dulam?'

The mouse who had crawled up in the sand behind Luke made his brief report. 'Aye, ready. Old 'uns an' the

177

babes are well away, hidden beyond the cliffs, an' our fighters are waitin' in the caves.'

Luke watched the *Greenhawk* moving closer to land, speaking to Dulam without turning his head. 'Tell them to make every shaft count – 'twill be kill or be killed. We'll only get one chance to capture that vessel.'

Dulam wriggled off back to the caves. Luke sensed Vurg's trembling, and he placed a steadying paw on his friend. 'Take it easy, Vurg. This is the best chance we're ever goin' to get of startin' to avenge our loved ones. Trust me.'

His companion stole a glance at the hard-eyed warrior sitting beside him. There was not a shred of pity or unsureness showing on Luke's face, just cold wrath and determination. Vurg suddenly stopped trembling.

'I'm all right, Luke. I trust you. All of yore tribe do!'

The *Greenhawk* was aided by a light breeze caught by her square-rigged after sail, speeding up the vessel's progress, drawing her closer to the pair of forlorn figures huddled about the guttering fire onshore. Reynard Chopsnout drew his cutlass and climbed up to the prow. He crouched there, putting a final edge to his blade on an iron cleat. Already he could mentally hear the whimpers of the two shorebeasts, pleading for their lives. This was going to be as easy as falling off a log!

20

Somewhere on the clifftops a small bird raised its beak to herald the dawn, as day's first pale streaks washed the sky outward from the east. The crew of the *Greenhawk* sweated and cursed as they pushed their craft onshore with makeshift paddles. She rose on a swell and forged forward, scraping her hull into the sand and listing to port, keeling slightly as the ebbing water dropped her on the beach. Roaring and shouting, Chopsnout urged his vermin over the side. 'Grab 'em, mates, I want those two alive!'

Luke shrugged off his cloak. Raising his sword he watched the savage-looking Sea Rogues pounding up the beach. Vurg took up his position, spear at the ready, steeling himself against the wild war cries of the charging foe.

'Haharr, let's see the colour o' yer innards, mice!'

'Lop off'n their footpaws so they can't run away!'

'Gimme a cloak made out o' mouse's skin!'

'Eeeeeyaaaaargh!'

Chopsnout could scarce believe his eyes. Leaping down from the prow to bring up the rear, he saw the first wave of ten or so crewbeasts vanish into the ground.

*

Halfway up the beach, Luke's fighters had dug a trench, lining it with sharpened stakes and covering it with rush mats strewn thinly over with sand. Vermin screamed in shocked agony as they plunged into it. Luke gave the signal, letting his swordpoint dip as he bellowed aloud to his companions, 'Now! Strike now!'

Both Luke and Vurg dropped into a crouch. Arrows hissed angrily overhead, thudding into the vermin who were hovering on the edge of the spiked trench. Two more flights of shafts followed speedily, then Luke leaped upright, wielding his sword as the archers dropped their bows and seized fire-hardened lances.

'Chaaaaarge!'

They dashed forward, with Luke and Vurg out in front, leaping the trench and hurling themselves upon the enemy.

Chopsnout had lost his pitchblob nose as soon as he hit the sand. He stood yelling hoarsely at his vermin crew. 'Retreat, back to the ship, retreat!'

However, they were suddenly outflanked. The rest of Luke's small force thundered out from a cave situated on the far edge of the point, armed with long cudgels and slings. Rocks whistled through the morning air, cutting down several of the routed vermin, then they were hit from both sides by Luke's lances and the swinging clubs of grim-faced, ruthless mice. Reynard Chopsnout leaped ineffectively at the high beached bulwarks of the *Greenhawk*. He slid awkwardly back to the moist sand, half raising his scimitar as Luke's battlesword found him. It was over in less time than it had taken for the vermin to beach their boat.

Luke was now every inch the Warrior Chieftain of his tribe. Sheathing his blade, he nodded curtly at the stunned faces of the fighters surrounding him. 'Well done, we've gained ourselves a ship!'

Cardo let his lance drop, obviously shocked. 'Luke, they're dead. We've slain them all.'

Luke picked up the lance, pressing it into his friend's paw. 'Aye, that was the idea, mate. Or would you sooner that we were caught nappin' an' murdered like our families were?'

There were loud cries of agreement with Luke. Friends crowded round to shake his paw or pat his back.

Luke glanced up at the clifftops. 'Steady, mates, plenty o' time for that later. Some of you fill in that trench. Dulam, you an' the others roll those vermin carcasses into the sea, the ebbin' tide'll carry 'em out. I don't want the young 'uns to see any of this. Vurg, come with me. We'll have to rig up some means o' haulin' the ship above the tideline, so she don't get carried back out on the floodtide.'

Luke and Vurg hurried to the cliffs, intercepting Drunn, who was climbing down to see the result of the battle.

'Burr, you'm winned, zurr Luke. Oi allus knowed ee wurr a gurt Wurrier, ho urr!'

Luke took the friendly mole's outstretched paw and shook it heartily. 'Drunn my old mate, how are ye at movin' ships up beaches?'

The mole sized up the situation immediately. 'Et be the least oi c'n do furr ee, zurr!'

Before the incoming tide had arrived Drunn, with the aid of his moles, some mice and the hedgehogs, had dug a shallow channel from the *Greenhawk*'s prow to a spot above the tideline. This he lined with slabs of cliff shale, well wetted down with seawater. On the vessel's forepeak was a windlass, a simple mechanism for hauling up the ship's anchor, with a horizontally revolving barrel. Welff Tiptip and her hogs helped to carry the anchor up onshore, where they wedged it firmly between two big rocks jutting up out of the sand. Now the ship was attached to the land by its anchor rope. Drunn chose the stoutest creatures to turn the windlass, which they did by ramming home stout poles into the housing. Once the slack of the rope was taken up they began turning the windlass in earnest.

The young ones and oldsters had come down from the clifftops. Extra paws were needed, so they all joined in. Windred and old Twoola ran back and forth, splashing more water on the shale slabs as the ship slid forward, up on to shore, creaking and groaning. Martin and young Timballisto pushed with all their might against the windlass spokes, along with the rest.

It was a happy day. A sprightly breeze moved the clouds away, sunlight beat down on the workers. Joyfully they toiled, turning the windlass bit by bit, moving their ship up the shore on its own anchor rope. Some even improvised a shanty to keep up the rhythm of the task, and soon everybeast was singing it.

'Oh don't it make a sight so grand,
A ship that travels on the land,
Keep that windlass turnin', bend yore backs an' push!

We'll soon have her above the tide,
Then we'll clean an' scrape each side,
Keep that windlass turnin', bend yore backs an' push!

We've got to find a good tree fast,
Then we'll build a new mainmast,
Keep that windlass turnin', bend yore backs an' push!

With pitch an' rope we'll make her right,
All shippyshape an' watertight,
Keep that windlass turnin', bend yore backs an' push!

You vermin scum, oh mercy me,
Beware when Luke puts out to sea,
Keep that windlass turnin', bend yore backs an' push!'

Gradually the ship slid over its runway of wetted shale slabs bit by bit, finally coming to rest above the tideline, with the bow end firmly wedged between the two standing rocks that had secured the anchor. Luke was smiling broadly as he patted the barnacle-encrusted hull. 'Well, there she is, a right old slop bucket if ever I saw one, mates, but by winter I guarantee she'll be good'n'ready.' He called to Martin, who was down by the tideline with Timballisto, stowing things behind a rock. 'Ho there, son, what are you doing?'

Martin beckoned his father to join them and explained, 'We collected all the weapons for you, see.'

He unrolled an old length of sail canvas, revealing a jumbled assortment of swords, daggers and various blades that had been once owned by the crew of the *Greenhawk*.

Luke ruffled his young son's ears approvingly. 'Well done, Martin. You too, Timbal. These are far better than our makeshift weapons!'

Timballisto selected a short sword for himself. Martin picked up a longish curved blade and began thrusting it into his belt. But Luke took the sword from his son and tossed it back with the other weapons.

'No, you're far too young to carry a blade yet, son. Timbal, you may keep your blade. 'Tis about time you had one – you'll be fully grown in another couple o' seasons.' Seeing the disappointment on Martin's face, Luke threw a kindly paw about his son's shoulders. 'Martin, you don't need the blade of any seascum. My sword is yours by right. It was passed on to me by my father and one day I will give it to you.'

The young mouse's piercing grey eyes searched his father's face. 'When?'

In his mind Luke saw himself asking the same question of his own father. He gave Martin the same answer he had received long ago.

'When I think you are ready.'

Throughout the remainder of summer and all of autumn, the tribe of Luke worked long evenings, after their day's chores of farming food and foraging the shores was done. Gradually the once rickety Sea Rogue ship took shape. The hull was careened, ridding it of weed, barnacles and other saltwater debris. Unsound and rotten planking was torn out and replaced with good stout oak, which they travelled far to find and haul back. Cauldrons of pitch and pine resin bubbled continuously, lengths of rope were woven and hammered in between the ship's timbers. Then the pitch and resin were poured into the joints, sealing them and making the vessel watertight. Any spare food was cooked and preserved in casks for ship's stores, along with new barrels for fresh water to be carried in. Luke oversaw everything, paying careful attention to the slightest detail.

'Do it proper and 'twill serve you well!' Everybeast in the tribe became familiar with their Chieftain's constant motto.

Winter's first icy breath was coating the northern coast with rimefrost when the new mainmast was raised. Vurg and Drunn had chosen a good tall white willow, which would bend with the wind where other wood might crack and break. Newly patched and hemmed, the wide single mainsail was hoisted, fluttered a moment, then bellied proudly out in the cold north breeze. A cheer went up from the creatures who had worked so hard to repair the vessel. Luke stood back upon the shore with Martin and Windred, surveying the new craft. It had three curving sails from the bowsprit to the mainmast, with the big triangular sail and a tall oblong one either side of the new willow. At the stern was a smaller mast with one other triangular sail. It obviously met all Luke's requirements. He smiled at Martin. 'She'll have to have a new name, son.'

Martin, like all youngsters, always had a question. 'Why do they always call ships she?'

Luke had to think about that one for a moment. 'Truth t'tell, son, I'm not sure, but I think they call ships she because, well, she's like a mother to her crew.'

Another enquiry followed immediately from the serious-faced young mouse. 'I haven't got a mother. Will she be my mother?'

Luke's eyes were sad as he replied, 'No, son, I'm afraid not.'

Windred stared reprovingly at Luke. 'D'you mean you're not taking Martin along with you? He's your son, Luke!'

The Chieftain nodded. 'Aye, he is, and that's why I'm not goin' to risk his young life out there on the seas. Beside that, Windred, you're his grandmother, so he'll have to look after you – the only family I have left in this world is you two. Now let's hear no more of it. Would you like to name the ship, son?'

Martin would not let anybeast see tears in his eyes, so he rushed off along the shore, calling back to Luke, 'Call her *Sayna* after my mother!'

Windred watched her grandson dash down to the sea, where he stood throwing pebbles into the waves. 'I'm sorry, Luke, I should have kept my silly mouth shut.'

Luke rested a paw gently on her shoulder. 'Don't be sorry, Windred, I'd have had to tell him sooner or later. Martin's made of tough stuff. He'll grow to be a fine warrior, though the only way he'll learn is to be told the plain truth. 'Twould be no good telling him lies.'

That night a feast to mark the completion of the vessel *Sayna* was held in Luke's cave. Autumn's harvest had been good and the cooks had excelled themselves. Martin cheered up as he and Timballisto joined a young hog-maid called Twindle and Drunn's nephew Burdle. The four sat together, giggling and joking beneath a lantern at the rear of the cave, ruddy firelight twinkling in their eyes. They had never seen such a sumptuous spread. 'Yurr, lookit ee gurt plum pudden!'

'Oh, an' see those likkle tarts, they've got cream on top that looks like a twirl. Bet my mum Welff made those!'

'Mmm! Have you tasted the soup yet? 'Tis full o' rockshrimps an' veggibles!'

'I want a slice o' that big cake, the one with honey an' redcurrants all over the top!'

They sipped Drunn's fizzy apple cider and munched hot wheat scones that contained chunks of candied pear. The elders drank special barley beer and cut off slices of celery and onion cheese to go with it. Old Twoola raised his beaker and broke out into song.

'Oh the weather's cold outside outside,
But we're all snug in here,
With thee an' me, good company,
An' lots o' barley beer!

Oh the snow comes down outside outside,
An' winter winds do moan,
But sit us by a roarin' fire,
An' you'll not hear one groan!

Oh the night is dark outside outside,
But the soup is good an' hot,
Good food, fine friends an' happy hearts,
I'd say we've got the lot!'

Amid the laughter and applause that followed, old Twoola poured himself another beaker, crying out, 'That's the stuff. 'Tis a feast an' we be here to enjoy ourselves. Who's got a song?'

Drunn began using a gourd as a drum, beating out a rhythm on it with two wooden spoons. 'Goo urr, missus Welff, show 'um 'ow ee can sing!'

186

Goodwife Welff was immediately up, apron swirling as she danced a jig, clapping her paws and singing.

'Two plums grew on a pear tree,
A wise old owl did say,
Oh dearie me I'm certain,
They shouldn't grow that way.

For beechnuts come from beech trees,
Whilst Mother Nature rules,
As long as acorns come from oaks,
No wisdom comes from fools!

Then came a little hedgehog,
Who said with simple smile,
Good day to you wise creature,
Now list' to me awhile.

Why does a tree stay silent,
And yet it has a bark,
An' why do shadows fall at night,
But never leave a mark?

Though you may think me silly,
I know 'tis only fair,
Most any fool can tell you,
That two plums make a pair!'

The mice had never heard this quaint ditty before, and they chuckled at the logic of the little hedgehog.

Dulam poured Welff a beaker of cider, offering her his seat, so that she could catch her breath. 'Good song, marm, that was very clever.'

The hogwife winked at him. 'If'n you think that's clever then ponder on this. How many pears in a dozen pair, six or twelve?' She watched the bemused mouse trying to work it out.

'Er, six, I think, aye 'tis six.'

Goody Welff chuckled. 'Then I wouldn't send you to the orchard for my pears.'

Dulam scratched his head and did some more figuring. 'No, twelve, the answer's twelve!'

'Twelve pair o' pears, are you sure?'

'Er, er, aye! I'm sure, marm!'

Goody Welff drained her beaker, eyes twinkling. 'But that's twenty-four, twelve pairs o' pears.'

Dulam scratched his head furiously. 'You've got me all mixed up, marm!'

Drunn patted the puzzled mouse's back heartily. 'Ee try wurkin' et out in apples, zurr!'

Late into the night they carried on feasting, singing and setting riddles. The fire was burning low when Windred moved the cave barricade a little and peered outside. She shuddered and hurried back to the fire. 'Brr, snow's beginnin' to fall out there!'

Luke took his cloak and spread it over Martin and Burdle, who had drowsed off together in the corner. Windred waited until Luke returned to the fire, then asked, 'Couldn't it bide until the spring?'

Luke stared into the red embers. 'No. I have stayed too long already. Snow or not, I'm bound to sail in the morning.'

Windred sat silent awhile, listening to the snow-laden winds sweeping the shore outside. Suddenly she leaned forward and gripped Luke's paw fiercely. 'Go then, and seek out Vilu Daskar. Slay him and destroy his blood-coloured ship. Steal the life from him who robbed us of our Sayna. I'll take care of Martin and when he's grown enough, he'll care for me. But swear to me that one day you'll return here to the creatures who love you, Luke the Warrior!'

Holding his swordblade over the fire, Luke watched the embers reflecting red against it. 'I swear that when

I'm done the seascum will murder no more innocent creatures. On my oath I will return here when my work is done!'

21

It was a bitter winter noon when the ship *Sayna*, crewed
by Luke and a score of his fighting mice, slid down its
shale runway on the ice the season had provided. With
one fluke buried in the sand, the anchor held the ship
against an ebbing tide. Even though her sails were furled,
the *Sayna* strained against the anchor rope, as if eager to
be gone. All the farewells had been made, and the crew
had sent their friends and families back into the caves, not
wishing them to stand out tearful and freezing to wave
the ship off. Luke was last to leave. Martin sat stone-faced
outside the cave. Luke could not reason with him.

'Son, son, you would not last two moons out there on
the high seas. I cannot risk your life pitting you in battle
against the seascum I am sworn to do war with. Listen to
me, I know what is best for you!'

But Martin would not listen. 'I want to sail on the ship
and be a warrior like you!'

Luke spread his paws wide and sighed with frustration. 'What am I going to do with you, Martin? You
have my warrior spirit and your mother's determination.
Listen, son, take my sword.'

It was a fighting sword and well used. Luke pressed it
into his son's paws. The young mouse gazed wide-eyed

at the battle-scarred blade and gripped the handle tight as if he would never let go.

Luke smiled, recalling the time when his father had passed the sword on to him. Tapping a paw against the crosshilt, he said, 'I can see it is in you to be a fighter, Martin. The first thing warriors must learn is discipline.'

Martin felt as though the sword were speaking for him. 'Tell me what to do and I will obey.'

Relief surged through Luke as he commanded the would-be warrior. 'You will stay and help defend our cave against all comers, protect those weaker than yourself and honour our code. Always use the sword to stand for good and right, never do a thing you would be ashamed of, and never let your heart rule your mind.' He tapped the blade once more as its pitted edge glinted in the winter morning. 'And never let another creature take this sword from you, not as long as you live. When the time comes, pass it on to another, maybe your own son. You will know instinctively if he is a warrior. If not, hide the sword where only a true warrior who is brave of heart would dare to go and find it. Swear this to me, Martin.'

'I swear it on my life!'

The young mouse's grey eyes reflected the wintry sea as he spoke. Luke saw that the tide would soon be turning.

'It might be some seasons before I return, but I'll be back, son. Meanwhile, Timballisto is a promising and sensible creature, with more seasons under his belt than you, and I have left him in charge of our tribe. Obey him.'

A determined smile, reminiscent of his mother, hovered on Martin's lips. 'Of course I'll obey him, but one day I shall be in charge.'

A great feeling of pride enveloped Luke. 'I'm sure you will. Farewell, my son.'

Rigging ropes hummed around broad-bellying sails as the *Sayna* skimmed the deeps like a great white swan, headed west out on to the main. Luke turned for a moment from the tiller and looked back astern. He saw the small figure standing on the pebbled strand alone, waving the sword in a warrior's salute. The vessel dipped, bow into a rolling trough, and when she rose on the next wavecrest the shoreline was lost in an afternoon of snow and icy winter spume. Luke turned back to his crew, certain he had chosen fighters whom he could trust to be at his side through thick and thin. Vurg, Cardo, Dulam, Coll and the rest, they stood waiting his orders, clinging to the taffrails to stay upright on the heaving deck. Cardo was not looking too well. Luke shook his head. 'Get below decks, all of you. Batten down everything and stay there, 'tis goin' to get rough. I'll take tiller an' first watch. We have t'learn to be sailors now, seabeasts, so like all beginners we can expect to be sick – me too. There's nothin' to be ashamed of. We'll get used to stormy seas in a few days.'

Cardo had definitely taken on an unhealthy pallor.

'Permission to jump over the side an' drown myself, cap'n!'

Just looking at his friend made Luke feel queasy.

'I'll drown you myself if you start that cap'n business. My name's Luke an' that's what you'll call me. Permission denied, now get below, all of you!'

The entire crew shouted back at him, 'Aye aye, cap'n!'

Luke was glad they had not lost their sense of humour.

It was three days before they were out of the stormy latitudes. The evening of the fourth day saw calm seas with no trace of snow. Luke realised they must have drifted south-west instead of holding the north-west course. A meeting was held in the captain's cabin, and Luke told the others what had happened. ''Twas my fault, really. I'm still only learning about bein' at sea. You may've noticed the weather's changed for the better – well, that's because we've drifted south.'

But Vurg would not hear of his friend taking the blame. 'Oh, frogfeathers, mate, it's the fault of everybeast here, we've all taken our turn at the tiller. Bein' seasick or sleepy didn't help things. Little wonder we drifted off course. Ain't that right, pals?'

The crew agreed, though Coll had a question.

'Er, just what *was* our original course? Seems to me we've just been sailin' willy nilly, eh, Vurg?'

'Well, I s'pose there's little else y'can do when you're searchin' the seas for that red ship.'

Luke gestured at the empty shelves round the cabin. 'What were we supposed t'do? There's not a chart or a map aboard the vessel. Most of these pirates sail by instinct. I've been thinkin', maybe 'tis best what we're doin', lettin' the winds an' currents carry us.'

Cardo had regained his colour, as had the rest of them. 'Why do you say that, cap'n, er, sorry, Luke?'

'Well, look at it this way. Seascum hate the cold stormy seas as much as we do, so it stands to sense they'd sail to warmer waters. I've a feelin' the further south we sail the more chance we have o' meetin' up with Vilu Daskar.'

Dulam spoke up as he headed for the door. 'Great idea. I'm with ye, Luke. But after three days sick I'm feelin' much better, 'cept that I'm famished. Let's break out some vittles an' get a decent feed inside us!'

Dulam's suggestion was welcomed wholeheartedly. The crew were much happier now they were in calmer climes with a plan of action worked out.

A full moon beamed down on the *Sayna* as she drifted south on calm seas. Luke let Denno, a fat jolly mouse, take the tiller.

'Let her sail easy, Denno, just keep your eyes open and check the tiller from swingin' wide in another direction. I can tell by the smoke comin' from our galley there's some serious cookin' goin' on. Better take a peek, eh?'

Denno shook his head, chuckling. 'You'll prob'ly get

chased away. There's more cooks in that galley than y'could shake a stick at, an' that Cardo's the worst of all. Thinks 'e's cap'n o' the stewpot!'

Lantern light and steam came from the open galley window. Out on the darkened deck, Luke shook with suppressed laughter as he watched the antics of his crew. They bustled and bumped into one another, each trying to advise or outdo the other with tips on cooking expertise.

'Not too much o' that dried barley, Vurg, go easy.'

'Oh, rubbish, my ole mum always put plenty o' barley in everythin' she cooked!'

'Aye, I thought yore mum's fruitcake tasted a bit funny.'

'Well it didn't stop you scoffin' it, y'great lard bucket!'

'Lard bucket yoreself, mate. Hoi, Dulam, where are you goin' with the salt? Ship's stew needs lots of salt!'

'How d'you know? 'Tis the first time you've been on a ship. Put any more salt in that stew an' we'll drink the water barrels dry afore mornin'.'

'Aye aye there, chop those carrots smaller, mate!'

'Gerrout, I like big cobs o' carrot!'

'So that means we've all got to 'ave great lumps o' carrot?'

'Huh, won't 'urt you. Hey, 'tis my turn to stir. Gimme that ladle.'

'I'll give ye it on yore nose, see 'ow y'like that!'

A large cauldron of stew was carried into the big cabin, where Luke had set out beakers of ale and an oatcake by each place. Doing his utmost to keep a straight face, he tried sniffing appreciatively. 'Mmm, that smells good. What is it, Cardo?'

A heated debate broke out over the cauldron's contents.

'I call it Cardo's Carrot Seastew!'

'Ho, do you now, well I calls it Vurg's Veggible Delight!'

'I did all the work, so 'tis goin' t'be called Coll's Combination Concoction!'

'No it ain't, it's Dulam's Delicious Shipstew!'

Luke banged the mess table with the serving ladle. 'Enough! I won't have mutiny aboard my ship over a pot o' grub. I'll name the stew. Put it down here!'

They watched as Luke ladled a portion into his bowl. Blowing on a spoonful he sampled it gingerly, with his crew looking on anxiously. Bravely Luke chewed at the stew, his face expressionless. He put down the spoon and took a deep draught of ale.

They all spoke the word at once. 'Well?'

Luke picked something from between his teeth and looked at it quizzically before returning his verdict.

'I think it should be called crunchy barley, half cooked carrot lump, far too salty 'otwater stew. So if you'll excuse me I'll just stick to oatcake an' ale for tonight's meal, mates. Eat up, an' see how you lot like it!'

Luke wandered out on deck with his frugal meal. 'I'll take the tiller for a while, mate. You go an' get somethin' to eat.'

Denno immediately stopped gazing at the peaceful moonflaked waves and relinquished his watch. 'Certainly smelled great when they carried it to the cabin, Luke. Thankee, mate. I'll enjoy some o' that stew.'

Luke smiled wryly. 'Oh aye, I'm sure you will!'

Soft pastel-hued skies heralded the dawn. A mouse named Cordle dozed at the tiller, a canteen of water held loosely in his paw. Coll came to relieve him, sipping from a beaker.

'Huh, fine one you are, sleepin' on watch. Good job Luke never caught ye or he'd 'ave whacked yore tail off!'

Cordle blinked sleepily and took a quick swig of water. 'Leastways while I'm sleepin' I'm not drinkin'. I tell ye, Coll, I never drank so much water in all me life!'

'Aye, no more o' that blinkin' stew fer me, mate. You

could've stood a spoon up in the salt that went into it! If we capture any Sea Rogues, I reckon we should feed it to 'em, that'd teach 'em a lesson.' But Cordle was not listening – he was staring eagerly out to sea. 'What's up, Cordle?'

'Look, land! I'm sure of it, that's land of some sort dead ahead. Laaaaand hoooooooo!'

Instantly the ship came alive. The mousecrew tumbled from their bunks and staggered out on deck, rubbing sleep from their eyes as they followed the outstretched paw of Cordle.

'It's land! Land!'

'Dead ahead, Luke. Cordle's spotted land!'

Luke climbed to the bowsprit and viewed the dark blot on the horizon. 'Aye, 'tis land sure enough, an island by the look of it. Take in the bow an' mainsails, Coll, an' steer north. We'll sail in nice'n'easy round the other side of that island. No sense in chargin' at it full sail. Right, mates, I want you all armed an' alert. Cordle, Denno, Dulam, stay with the ship an' guard it close, the rest of you'll come ashore with me. Make no noise, tread careful an' follow my lead. There's no tellin' what we might meet!'

The *Sayna* dropped anchor in a sheltered inlet on the island's west side at early noontide. It was sunny, silent and windless. Luke inspected the high rocks surrounding the cove. Seabirds nested in the crags beneath a jumble of trees and vegetation growing on the clifftops. Climbing over the ship's side, the shore party waded through clear sunwarmed shallows to a narrow strip of sandy beach.

Vurg gripped his spear tight, whispering to Luke, 'I don't like it, mate. 'Tis far too quiet – place gives me the creeps. I feel like somebeast's watchin' us!'

Luke drew a scimitar he had chosen from the former crew's weaponry. He pointed it at a strange sight, a flight of steps carved into the cliffs. 'I wonder who took the trouble t'do that? Looks as if they've been there a long time. Let's take a look.'

In single file they climbed the smooth, well-carved steps, which, though narrow, were easily negotiable. They ascended in several zigzag shapes to the clifftop. From above, the *Sayna* looked very small in the cove below. Cardo uprooted something from the ground which he wiped on his tunic before beginning to eat it.

'Mmm, young onion. Wonder how that got here?'

A loud, frightening cry rang out from the trees.

'Oohoohoohaaaaaarrrrreeeeeegharr!'

The hair on Cardo's nape stood straight up, and he dropped the onion. 'What'n the name o' frogs was that?'

Luke and Vurg began creeping forward, gesturing to the rest not to follow them. 'Stay here. We'll go an' take a look.' Crouching low, they made their way into the thickets.

A small bird whistled somewhere, but other than that the only sound the two mice heard was their own footpaws rustling through the ferns. After a while Luke straightened up. 'Well, whatever it was there's neither sight nor sound of it now, matey.'

Vurg uncrouched and something bumped lightly against the back of his head. He turned cautiously. 'Hoho, pears, a whole treeful of 'em!'

It was a pear tree, laden with fine ripe fruit.

Vurg picked one, squeezed it gently, nodded approvingly, then took a huge bite. 'Mmm shlumphh! Sweet'n'juicy, mate, wunnerful!'

Luke reached for a pear, grinning at his friend's juice-wetted face. 'Ole greedyguts, are you eatin' that pear or takin' a bath in it?'

Fffffssssst . . . Splack!

A thick piece of wood with a metal point at either end whipped out of nowhere and thudded deep into the tree trunk between them both. It was followed by a loud booming voice echoing out of the stillness of the trees.

'Seascum! Touch not my food. Go from this place or Werragoola will tear you limb from limb and devour you!'

Luke threw his pear to the ground. 'Do as I say, Vurg. Drop your pear an' let's get back t'the crew. Don't argue!'

Vurg was not about to disagree. He dropped the half-eaten pear as if it were a poisonous reptile and followed Luke back the way they had come. When he figured they were both out of sight, Luke dropped down behind a fallen tree.

Vurg was still wide-eyed and trembling. 'Did ye hear that voice, matey? It must've come from a beast ten times bigger'n a badger!'

'You lay low here 'til I get back. Give me your spear.' Before Vurg had a chance to argue, Luke plucked the spear from his paws and was gone.

Bellying down, Luke crawled back to the pear tree. Then he lay still, checking the area keenly, eyes darting back and forth as he searched the trees for any sign of movement. Satisfied he was not being watched, Luke picked up his fallen pear and stuck it on the point of Vurg's spear. Acting speedily he flung the spear, butt end first, into a thick bush, where the pear on the spearpoint remained clearly visible, sticking out of the leaves. Next Luke gave the pear tree a good shake, calling out aloud, 'Hah! These must be the pears the cap'n tole us about!' Then he wriggled off into the shrubbery with his teeth clamped tight around the scimitar, and lay still, watching.

Suddenly another metal-tipped wooden club struck the pear from the speartip and a mad, booming voice howled angrily, 'You did not heed my warning! Now Werragoola says you must die! Yakkahakkaheeeyhooooo!'

A wild, ragged figure hurtled across the tiny clearing and flung itself into the bush, undoubtedly hoping to come to grips with whoever was holding the spear. Luke was after it in a flash. The beast was immediately at a disadvantage, trapped with its bottom sticking out of the bush. The sturdy mouse dealt the target a tidy whack with the flat of his blade and shouted sternly, 'Come out o' there, ye savage!'

The reply came back after an agonised gasp. 'Haharr! Stabbed me from the rear, eh, seascum? You pirates are all the same. Just wait'll I get out of here!'

Luke gave the bottom another whack with his blade-flat. 'Mayhap this'll help ye, Wellaguller, or whatever y'call yoreself. Here, have another taste o' my blade!' He laid on another stinging blow and the beast almost somersaulted out of the bush in a cloud of leaves and broken twigs.

'Owowowouch! Typical vermin pirate type, wot! Can't slay a chap without jolly well torturin' him t'death first. Oooh! My posterior's aflippin'flame, y'great lout!'

It was a hare, garbed ridiculously in rags, seashells and strands of vegetation, its face stained purple with berry juice. Luke watched it cautiously as he put up his sword.

'I'm no seascum. My name's Luke an' I'm a chieftain from far across the seas.'

The hare stood up, rubbing his tail area ruefully. 'Oh I see, and that gives you the blinkin' right to land up here an' whale the tar out of chaps' bottoms with your sword. Huh, prob'ly why you had to leave the place you came from – everybeast got fed up with you wallopin' all an' sundry round the nether regions with swords an' what-not, so they banished you from the blinkin' land. Say then, scurvy cad, beaten up any other poor creatures t'day, wot wot? Speak up, sah.'

Luke was astonished at the nerve of the hare. 'Hold on a tick, flop-ears! First you go terrifyin' my crew with your howlin' an' wailin', then you try to kill me by flingin' those funny-lookin' spears of yours, an' then you got the brass neck to complain when you get caught at it. Just who d'ye think you are?'

Puffing out his narrow chest, the hare clapped a paw to his stomach and bowed curtly. 'Who do I think I am, sah?

I am smoke on the wind, a creature of many resources! To the vermin inhabiting this island I am Werragoola the purple-faced terror. In a far more elegant life than this I was known as Beauclair Fethringsol Cosfortingham. Fondly referred to as just Beau by m'family, friends an' dear old nanny, wot!'

Vurg stole cautiously up, brandishing a stick. 'Ah, there y'are, Luke. But who's this creature?'

Luke made the introductions. 'This is the one who was doin' all the shoutin' an' throwin' weapons at us. Vurg, meet Beau.'

The hare regarded Vurg's outstretched paw suspiciously. 'Vurg, eh? Sounds a right murderous vermin name if ever I heard one. Chap looks shifty, too. D'y'know, I'm not totally convinced that you two aren't Sea Rogues.'

Luke sighed impatiently. 'Well we're not standin' round all day just to convince ye. Come on, Vurg, let's round up the crew an' get back aboard the ship. We're wastin' time here.'

They had only gone a few paces when Beau leaped in front of them with a broad grin pasted on his purpled features.

'You're mice, silly old me, wot? Mice aren't seascum, they're good chaps like m'self. Have y'really got a ship, Admiral Luke? Are y'sailin' away from this confounded isle? Take me with you, sirs, I beg of you. I'll even provision your vessel with the food I grow here. You won't be sorry. Old salty Beau they call me on shipboard, can turn m'paw to anythin' nautical. Hoist me mains'l, loose those anchors, take a turn round the riggin' an' boggle me bilges, wot wot! I can spout that sort o' rot all season . . .'

Luke could not help smiling at the lanky excited creature. 'Keep that up, Beau, an' we'll make ye swim behind the ship to give us a bit o' peace. You say you've got provisions?'

'Provisions, grub, rations, scoff, vittles, tucker, you name it, Luke m'mouse, an' I've got it!'

Luke was forced to place a paw across Beau's mouth. 'Enough, mate. You can sail with us, but on two conditions. Cut the cackle an' show us to the provisions!'

22

The crew of the *Sayna* spent the rest of the afternoon gathering produce which Beau had grown. They carried pears, apples, wild grapes, mushrooms, carrots and all manner of fresh food back to the ship. Luke was wondering whether he would regret his decision, because the hare never once stopped chattering.

'Heave ho, me hearties, that's the ticket, wot wot! I say there, what a jolly little ship, absolutely tiptop! Far nicer than the great red monstrosity that delivered me here, by the left, I should say so!'

They were filling pails from a lively trickle of fresh water running down the cliff face to the shore. Forming a chain, the crew passed it aboard, where it was emptied into the casks to top up the *Sayna*'s water supply. Beau was chattering on as he shoved another pail beneath the running water.

'Oh yes, this's the stuff t'put fur on y'tail, wot! Good fresh water, sweet an' clean, drink it m'self, y'know, mornin' noon an' night. Feel those muscles, see how my eyes sparkle, have y'ever seen teeth as white as mine, wot!'

Luke pulled him to one side. 'Beau, did you say a great red ship brought you here?'

'Indeed it did, sah, filthy great thing, name o' the *Goreleech*.'

Luke's paw tightened like a vice over Beau's. 'Tell me everything you know about the red ship!'

Beau rubbed his paw and looked quizzically at Luke. 'Of course, old chap, no need to crush a fellow's paw. It all started some seasons ago when yours truly got the jolly old urge to go seafarin'. Shipped out on a small merchant craft, tradin' round the coast, y'know. Good crew, couple o' shrews, some hedgehogs an' a mouse or two. We were doin' quite well, until one night our ship was lyin' at anchor an' we were all in our hammocks snorin'. Well, the *Goreleech* sailed up an' took us by surprise, rammed our little boat with its great iron spike, sunk us like a stone, wot. Sea Rogues everywhere, slew most of the crew, took the remainder captive. I'll never forget the captain of the red ship, a stoat, Vilu Daskar, cruel murderin' villain! I spent two seasons chained to an oar in the red ship's middle decks, starved, whipped, kicked an' beaten. Still got the scars if y'd like to see 'em. I was the only beast out of my old crew left alive after a while, then I fell sick, too weak'n'thin to be of further use at the oar. Vilu Daskar had me thrown overboard. Prob'ly thought I was about t'die, so the fish an' the tides could finish me. Hah! But I came off stern stock. My old nanny could have told him that I was a Cosfortingham, an' we don't die too easily, y'know. I was washed up here an' this has been my home ever since. Island's full o' vermin, though, searats an' such, deserters, runaways an' some who've been marooned – evil lot. The rogues would've skinned an' scoffed me, but I've spent my seasons here livin' in secret, growin' my own tucker an' fightin' 'em from the shadows'n'tree cover. That's when I became Werragoola Purpleface, regular one-hare army, wot!'

Luke smiled in admiration at the brave hare. 'You did well, Beau. Tell me, have you ever sighted Vilu Daskar's vessel again?'

'Rather. Passed here three moons ago, put in for water an' sailed off bound south. I hid on the clifftops an' watched the red ship come an' go. D'you know, your ship's the first decent craft with honest crew I've ever seen put in here. Jolly lucky for me I'd say, wot wot!'

Screeching war cries cut the conversation short, and Beau hurled himself at Luke, knocking him to one side. A rough sharp spear buried itself in the sand where Luke had stood a moment before. Down the steps in the cliff face a huge mob of ragged vermin were dashing towards the *Sayna*'s crew.

The Warrior mouse acted swiftly. Grabbing the spear, he ran forward, shaking it to feel the balance. From halfway between the tideline and the stairs he made a mighty throw. A searat, slightly ahead of the rest, took the spear through his middle and toppled over screaming. Those behind could not stop their mad charge and stumbled over the slain rat. Luke's roar snapped the crew out of their shock.

'Back to the ship at the double!'

The vermin who had tripped on their fallen comrade did not have far to fall. They sprawled in the sand momentarily, then scrambled up and gave chase after the mice.

Weapons drawn, Luke, Vurg and Beau stood in the shallows, hurrying the crew past them. 'Get aboard quick, mates, loose all sails an' up anchor!'

Cordle, Denno and Dulam helped the first few over the side and set to, turning the windlass to haul up the anchor.

Wild with their desire to capture a ship, vermin thundered recklessly into the water. Luke swung back and forth with his sword, slaying and wounding wherever he struck. Vurg hit out with his spear and Beau went at them, a club in each paw. 'Yaaah! Back, back, ye scum!'

Other vermin were coming in from both sides now, to

cut the trio off from their vessel. Aboard the *Sayna*, Coll and some others went to work. Hanging over the stern, they whizzed arrows and slingstones at the mob in the shallows. It was Cardo who saved the day, though. Grabbing an axe, he chopped the rear anchor free of its rope, then, heaving until he had pulled a fair length from the windlass, the resourceful mouse cast the thick line into the sea. 'Grab ahold, mates, we'll haul ye aboard!'

Luke held off the closest foes whilst Beau seized the rope and knotted it into a wide loop, which he threw over Vurg and Luke with one wide cast, then ducked inside to join them. Bound together within the noose of anchor rope, they struck out at the surrounding attackers, with Vurg bellowing back to the ship, 'Heave away, mates, fast as y'like!'

Billowing sails caught the wind, whipping the *Sayna* out to sea. Every available crewmouse bent his back at the windlass spokes, making it fly round. Luke smashed a spearhead with a swipe of his swordblade, but before he could strike at its owner his footpaws left the seabed and he was swept away backwards with Vurg and Beau pressed either side of him. Even spraying seawater sloshing at his mouth could not silence the hare.

'Fare thee well, vermin, glub glub! G'bye, chaps, gluggle!'

With the *Sayna*'s outward momentum and the windlass winding them in, they soon outdistanced the maddened vermin. Vurg felt his back bump hard against the ship's side as Beau hooted, 'Steady on, chaps, glub! We ain't the blinkin' enemy. Gluggle ug! D'ye mind lettin' us live a trifle longer! Pshaw! This seawater tastes jolly foul, wot!'

Willing paws pulled them aboard, and Luke wriggled free of the rope. They stood astern, watching the island recede as the enraged mob fought among themselves in the shallows. Luke put aside his blade and took off his sopping tunic.

'How did we do, Cardo? Everybeast safe?'

'Aye, they're all alive, mate, one or two wounds. I took a slingstone right across the paw meself!'

Vurg inspected the cut on his friend's paw. 'Nasty! Is that the paw you use t'cook with?'

Cardo smiled cheerfully. 'No.'

Vurg gave a disappointed sigh. 'Wot a pity!'

The crew laughed heartily at the indignant Cardo.

Beau looked from one to another, unable to fathom the joke. 'What's so funny? Is the blighter an awful cook?'

This caused further laughter and more indignation from Cardo. 'Take no notice of 'em, Beau. They're all lousy cooks. You'll be sorry you signed aboard this ship, mate, 'specially when y'taste the grub. It's dreadful. Even the fishes throw the scraps back aboard!'

Immediately the hare cast off his raggy garb and began wrapping a length of canvas around his waist like an apron. 'Lucky you found me then, chaps. Aboard my old ship I was voted the choicest chef to be chosen from all chief chefs!'

Coll nudged the hare. 'Bet you couldn't say that again?'

Beau dismissed him with an airy twiddle of both ears. 'Couldn't I though, hah? I was the cheese chofen chief of all choosers, no, wait a tick, I was choked by a chosen chief chook, no, that ain't right . . .'

Luke interrupted him. 'If y'can cook, then stow the blather an' get t'the galley. Cardo, you can be Beau's assistant. Denno, attend the wounded, you were always good at healin'. Coll, you take the tiller. Keep that westerin' sun at your right shoulder – we're followin' the red ship south. The rest of you trim the sails an' see she moves along steady!'

Beau turned out to be an excellent cook. That night he served the crew of the *Sayna* a meal to gladden their hearts. Being a hare, he cooked victuals in generous portions, so there was more than enough for all.

'Right ho, I know this'll be wasted on you famine-faced chaps, but here's tonight's menu, wot. Starters, cheese an' onion turnovers, with my own flaky pastry, followed by shrimp an' mushroom bake in a parsley an' turnip sauce. For afters there's a pear an' plum pudden. To drink, mint an' dandelion tea or some rather good cider I found in your ship's stores. Hold hard a moment there, don't touch a bally crumb till I've said grace, you savages!'

Luke lowered his eyes, admonishing the crew. 'He's right. No need to get sloppy an' bad-mannered 'cos we're not at home. Carry on, Beau.'

The hare intoned the grace at tremendous speed.

'Fate'n'fortunes smile on us,
An' of this crew take care,
But let no greedy robber try,
To guzzle up my share!'

Before anybeast could raise an eye or pick up a spoon the hare was tucking in as if there were no tomorrow.

Vurg passed the turnovers to Luke. 'Our cook can certainly shift the vittles, mate!'

Luke sniffed the hot turnovers appreciatively. 'Beau can do wot he likes, long as he keeps servin' up meals as good as this 'un!'

'Aye. Better put some aside for Cordle – he's on tiller watch.'

The *Sayna* ploughed steadily south on fair seas under a waning moon. Weary after the day's exertions her crew lay down to rest, though food seemed to have the opposite effect on the garrulous cook. Beau quoted endless rhymes, danced and sang ceaselessly, now that he was not alone but in the company of friends. Luke sent him on deck to guard the tiller, and he did a double watch, serenading the sea and the night skies. Dulam wadded his cloak about both ears, complaining bitterly. 'A good cook he may be, but a tuneful singer he ain't. Sounds like somebeast attackin' a plank wid a rusty saw out there. Hoi, give yore gob a rest, will ye, Beau!'

But insults and pleas had no effect on the off-key warbler.

'Oooooh flunky dee an' a rum tumtum,
The good ship *Flinkydogg*,
Set sail with a crew o' fishes,
An' fat ole cap'n frog.

Oooooh doodle dey make way make way,
The frog said to the fishes,
"All fins on deck an' use yore tails,
To wash these dirty dishes!"

Oooooh skiddle deedoo, a fig for you,
The fishcrew boldly cried,
"Just chuck 'em in the ocean,
They'll be washed up by the tide!"

'Tis mutiny oh woe is me,
The frog did croak so sad,
"If I'd a crew o' boiler crabs,
They'd not be'ave so bad!"

'Twas after dark, a passin' shark,
Heard what was goin' on,
So for his tea, impartially,
He ate up everyone.

Oooooh goodness me hoho heehee,
The shark smiled, "Lackaday,
I can't abide a feckless frog,
Nor fish who won't obey!"'

Beau neatly dodged an apple core flung at him from

the cabin. His ears stood up indignantly. 'Rotten bounders, fancy chuckin' missiles at a chap who's doin' his level best to sing y'to sleep, ungrateful cads!'

He was answered by an irate bellow. 'Y'great lanky lollop-eared breezebarrel. Shuttup!'

Beau lay back on the deck, tending the tiller with a long footpaw.

'A wink's as good as a nod t'me, old lad, if y'don't appreciate good music then I'll withdraw the privilege of my melodious meanderings. But I'll finish this little ditty first. Stay calm, there's only another forty-six verses to go.'

23

In the following weeks the *Sayna* covered many sea leagues. They were well out of the cold latitudes and the weather became almost tropical, with constant sunshine beating down out of clear blue skies. But Luke was getting edgy and frustrated. There had been no sign of the red ship, which could be anywhere in the trackless wastes of ocean they were searching. Between them, he and Denno began drawing up a chart, from the northern shores to the isle where Beau had lived and onward. Luke was disappointed that there were no other landfalls to act as route markers.

'We're sailin' blind, mate. At least if we sighted land there might be some news of the red ship, but all we've seen for ages now is nothing but sea on every horizon.'

Denno put aside his quill pen, nodding agreement. 'Aye, we could do with takin' on some fresh water, too, an' the supplies are runnin' low. That hare must think his one job in life is dishin' up mountains o' vittles to the crew. Lookit the stomach I've put on!'

Luke, however, was not about to criticise his cook. 'You leave ole Beau out o' this, Denno. That hare can do no wrong as far as I'm concerned, mate. I never tasted such wonderful food in all my seasons.'

But Denno's words proved prophetic. It was on the afternoon of the following day that Vurg scraped bottom of one water cask with the dipper.

'If'n we don't sight land soon then I reckon we're in trouble, matey. Water's all but finished!'

Beau emerged from his galley swinging a ladle. 'No water? Well, we'll have t'make do with cider an' whatnot. Cardo, what's the jolly old position on drinks other than water? You're my assistant seacook.'

There was a rattling and scuttling from the galley, then Cardo popped a mournful face round the door. 'Down t'the dregs, Beau, down t'the very dregs!'

The irrepressible Beau began climbing the rope ladder of the centre mast. 'Well, no use standin' round with a face like a squashed apple, comrade o' mine. Just have t'scan the bloomin' horizon for land, wot wot!'

Cardo cast a withering glance up at Beau. 'Oh, just like that?'

The hare was now clinging to the mainmast top, one paw shading his eyes as he gazed eagerly all around. 'Well of course just like that, y'silly fat mouse. Hello there, chaps, is that a smudge way out to the south-west? Land ho! Or at least I'll bet it's somethin' jolly close to land. Hah, well done that hare! Mentioned in dispatches, maybe jot down a line o' praise or two in the ship's log at the very least!'

Luke shoved Denno playfully. 'Y'see, matey, told you I wouldn't have a word said against ole Beau! Cordle, set a course sou'west. If that's land we might make it before tomorrow mornin'.'

Tacking against the prevailing breezes, the *Sayna* lay off the island three hours before dawn. A huge cone, of what Luke took to be an extinct volcano, reared dark and forbidding against the night sky. Though it was difficult to see much in the darkness, Beau noted that there were forests of trees growing on the slopes and a shoreline of kinds. Luke spoke his thoughts to the hare as he sized up the situation.

'We'd best stay offshore until 'tis light – there might be reefs 'twixt here an' the beach. Don't see any signs o' life ashore, but we'd best not chance anythin' until daylight. You go an' get a bit o' shuteye with the crew, Beau, I'll call ye when 'tis light.'

'Wouldn't think of it, old lad. You and I shall stand watch together, 'til the ravenwinged shades of night are flown and earth is reborn in fiery sunlight to day!'

Luke leaned on the taffrail, eyes searching the shoreline. 'Well said, Beau, very poetic, mate.'

The talkative hare perked up. 'Thank ye kindly, Luke. I'm rather glad you appreciate poetry. Here's a modest effort I composed m'self, to while away the hours back on my island. "A mole and a duck went strolling one day—"'

Luke's strong paws clamped round Beau's jaws, holding his mouth tight shut. 'Either be quiet or go t'sleep. If you don't I'll put ye to sleep with a belayin' pin!'

As dawn broke Luke roused the crew, and they sailed cautiously in towards the shore. Now the island could be viewed clearly. The beach was dark bluey-black volcanic sand. A thin plume of white smoke drifted lazily from the top of the rock cone which dominated the place, denoting that the volcano was not altogether extinct. Purple and scarlet flowers bloomed thick in the foothills, and many of the trees had huge spear-shaped leaves. It was an exotic scene, though the total silence made it rather sinister. As Vurg watched the *Sayna*'s prow nose into the sandy shallows, he conveyed his misgivings to Luke.

'I'm gettin' that same feelin' I had last time we came to an island – I don't like it, matey. Too quiet for a place that looks so fertile. There's got to be some sort o' creatures livin' here!'

Luke pointed to the shore. 'You're right, Vurg. See there? Slightly above the tideline? What d'you make o' that?'

Beau elbowed his way to the prow. 'A great pile o' fruit! The creatures must be jolly friendly leavin' a gift like that for us.'

Luke frowned. 'Too friendly, perhaps. Let's not be too hasty. There's something about this little offering that doesn't ring true.'

But Beau was already leaping the side. 'C'mon, you chaps! I'll be food taster. My stomach's as steady as a jolly old rock, wot wot.'

Before Luke could stop them, most of the crew had followed the hare, bounding overboard into the shallows and splashing ashore towards the heap of luscious fruit piled on the beach. Vurg chuckled as the hare picked a grape, tossed it and caught it deftly in his mouth. He waited a few seconds and then waved a large bunch of wild grapes at the ship. 'Still standin', me hearties. Delicious! C'mon, everyone, tuck in!'

Luke and Vurg watched as they all pounced hungrily on the mysterious gift. 'Ahoy, Beau,' called Vurg. 'Bring some back for us.'

'Right y'are, Vurg. I say, chuck the empty casks overboard an' we'll see if we can find a stream to fill 'em from.'

Being the only two left on board, Vurg and Luke rolled all the casks out and tipped them over the side. Vurg tied the tiller in position so the ship would not drift.

'I was wrong, Luke. This island seems quite friendly now. P'raps Beau was right, an' whoever left the fruit out doesn't mean us any harm. Mayhap they'll show themselves before the day's out.'

A stream of freshwater actually flowed across the shore, not far from the heap of fruit. Dulam and Cardo filled the casks and got them back to the ship. Luke rigged a rope through the mainsail's top block, and between them he and Vurg hoisted the casks of water aboard. Dulam and Cardo waded back to join their friends ashore.

Luke called after them. 'Make the most of it. Tell the crew I want them back on deck by sunset. We sail at first tide tomorrow.'

Luke was busy stowing the casks in the galley when Vurg shouted urgently from out on deck. 'Onshore, mate. Come an' see!' He left what he was doing and hurried out.

Some of the crew were lying down amid the fruit, some were sitting aimlessly nearby, whilst one or two of the remainder were staggering oddly about. All appeared to have slack grins on their faces. Luke yelled, 'Ahoy, Coll, Dulam, Beau, what's the matter, mates?'

Dulam collapsed on the sand, Coll fell on top of him, only Beau remained standing. The hare gave a faint giggle, tried to wave, then his legs gave out and he sat down awkwardly, staring at the ship, smiling foolishly.

Luke smote the taffrail. 'That fruit, I should've known it. C'mon, Vurg!'

But Vurg was pointing to where the foothills met the shore. 'Wait, those bushes are movin'!'

Halfway over the side, Luke checked himself. He could scarce believe his eyes. The entire hillside had come to life, literally hundreds of bushes were moving across the shore in a massive screen of foliage. On instinct he leaped back aboard and dragged Vurg down flat.

A veritable hail of missiles struck the boat: arrows, javelins, spears and stones. Drums began pounding aloud and an eerie wailing rose from the bushes, followed by another salvo of missiles. Luke grabbed a long boathook.

'Get your spear, Vurg. Pole her off into deeper water.'

Scurrying forward, they pushed the vessel into the ebb tide, grunting with exertion as they pressed hard against their poles. An arrow thwacked into Vurg's shoulder, and Luke ignored a deep javelin graze across his cheek.

'Push, Vurg, let's give it all we've got, mate!'

The *Sayna*'s keel scraped free of the sand. Luke dashed

recklessly astern and slashed the rope which held the tiller rigid. Wheeling sideways, the *Sayna* caught the tide. Luke flattened himself as another rain of death peppered the ship, then she was bow out, sailing free. Arrows, sticking up from the deck timbers as if from a pincushion, snapped against Luke's footpaws as he dashed back to Vurg's side.

Wincing, the brave mouse tugged the shaft from his shoulder. 'Lucky that arrow's flight was near spent an' my tunic's a good thick 'un. I'm not bad hurt, Luke, what about you?'

Luke pawed blood from the cut on his cheek. 'Only a scratch, mate, I'll live. Whoever they are 'tis plain they can't shoot straight. Great seasons, look!'

Vurg stared in amazement at the diminishing shoreline. Silent and deserted the beach lay, as if nobeast had ever been there. All that remained was a pile of squashed fruit. Vurg turned in bewilderment to his friend. 'Where've they gone? Denno, Cordle, Beau, the whole crew are gone. What do we do now?'

Grim-faced, Luke gazed at the shoreline, his warrior blood pounding furiously as he strove to control himself. 'Let's make sail, it'll look as if we're runnin' away. We'll wait 'til dark, Vurg, then we'll go back an' get 'em!'

Drums pounded everywhere. At first, Cardo thought they were inside his skull, causing the massive headache which woke him. However, he saw that they were all too real when he opened his eyes. It was a scene that turned his blood to ice water, though strangely, everything was wrong side up. Like the rest of his crewmates, he had been bound tight and slung lengthways on a stout pole, so that his head hung down. The poles had been hoisted up on ropes, close to the ceiling of a big cave, with a fire burning at its centre. Rock ledges had been carved around the cave walls in tiers, and these were crowded with hundreds of small fierce ratlike rodents, unlike any

Cardo had ever seen. They were covered with intricate patterns of red, orange and white dyes, with clattering seashells affixed to ears, paws and tails.

At the rear of the cave were two massive drums, atop of which forty or fifty of the rodents performed a stamping dance. The sound boomed and banged relentlessly, increased fourfold as it echoed around the cave's interior. Crouching by the fire was a figure far larger than the rest, obviously a female weasel, draped from ears to tail with long necklaces and bracelets made from painted crab claws. Her face was daubed thick with white clay, black charcoal lines accentuating the features.

Beau was hanging alongside Cardo. He opened his eyes, looked around, then squinched his ears flat peevishly and called downward to the rodents, 'Put a flippin' bung in it, you chaps, wot! Those drums are makin' my old noggin throb dreadfully. I say there, you! Yes you marm, tell these blighters t'desist. Hmph! Rank bad manners t'go thumpin' drums like that when a body's feelin' out o' sorts. Now pack it jolly well in!'

As if by magic complete silence fell. The remainder of the crew had awakened, and Beau winked at them knowingly. 'Voice of command an' discipline, that's the thing t'give the blinkin' troops, wot wot!'

The weasel sprang upright. Grabbing a long wand ornamented with dried sea urchins, she shook it, pointing first at the captives, then to somewhere at the back of the cave between the two drums, and finally making a long sweeping gesture at the crammed masses of rodents.

'Rabbatooma! Slarissssssss! Ya Aggoreema!'

This seemed to drive the rodents into a frenzy. They laughed savagely, howling back at their leader, 'Ya Marrahagga! Slarissssssss! Ko, Slarissssssss!'

Coll strained his head over towards Beau. 'Huh, 'ope you ain't said the wrong thing, mate.'

The hare was quite indignant. 'Wrong thing, laddie? Me? I should say not. Tact an' diplomacy are the pawmark of us Cosfortinghams. Hang on a tick, I'll have a word with that vermin lady, see what the position is as regards loosin' us from our bonds, wot. Now then, my good villainess, d'you think y'could spare a few of those runty types to unbind me'n'my stalwart comrades? Sort of save us hangin' around, pardon the pun.'

Ignoring the hare's request, the weasel crouched and began making mysterious weaving patterns upon the cave floor with her wand. The small ratlike creatures pointed at the captives and chanted aloud, 'Ko Slarissssss Rabbatooma! Slarissssss eeeeeeyoh!'

Denno shook a droplet of perspiration from his nose-tip. 'Phew! I'm roasted!'

Dulam closed his eyes, as if trying to block out his thoughts. 'Quiet, mate. That could be a bad choice o' words. They might be flesh eaters.'

Now the rodents who had been dancing on the drumheads deserted their posts, swiftly scrambling on to the ledges alongside the rest. Casting something into the fire, the weasel caused the flames to burn green. Then she went to the drums and began tapping her wand alternately against the side of each one, calling out in a sibilant voice, 'Slarissssss Slarissssss Slarissssssssssss!'

Ever the optimist, Beau suggested brightly, 'D'y'know, I'm not familiar with their lingo, but I'll wager Slariss is some sort o' greeting, like how d'ye do, or good evenin', chaps. P'raps I'd better return the compliment, show some manners, wot. I say, marm, Slariss t'you too. Slarissssssssssss. Howzat?'

From a hidden opening behind the two drums Slariss emerged.

Beau's mouth went suddenly dry with fear – even he was not ready for this. The snake's head was bright green and huge. It slid slowly out in a seemingly never-ending ripple of sleek coils. As if searching, its flickering tongue quested in and out restlessly, eyes glittering in the fire-light, twin diamonds of primitive evil. Lazily the green and black chevroned coils formed into several loops, one atop the other, with the flat reptilian head resting at their peak. Standing at the other side of the fire, the weasel poked the tip of her long wand in the flames until it was glowing. Not one creature in the cave made a sound or moved a muscle. The snake was hunting, seeking a victim. The crew hung motionless, stiff with terror. Beau was not aware of the glowing wand's end approaching behind his head. Suddenly the weasel touched it against the tip of his long right ear.

'Yowchowoop!' He shook his head.

'Slarisssssss!'

Not a paw's length away the snake swayed its head, mouth open, fangs bared dangerously, hissing its challenge. The hare found himself staring into the reptile's eyes. Frozen with nameless dread, he hung there helpless.

24

The night was humid, still warm from the day's sun. The *Sayna* came back to the island on the floodtide, showing no sail. Luke and Vurg dropped anchor offshore.

Vurg was muttering to himself as they went over the side. 'Can't tell if'n any beast's watchin' us. I 'ope none spotted us comin' in. Suppose they did, though? Mebbe one of us should've stayed behind as guard on board.'

Luke chuckled dryly. 'I thought o' that meself, mate, but it'll take the two of us to rescue our crew. Besides, if we get caught too then what use is a ship to us? Stow your chunnerin', Vurg, y'gettin' to sound more like an ole mousewife every day.'

They stole up the deserted beach, using any rocks they found as cover. Closer to the foothills Vurg held up a paw. 'Sssh, lissen, can you hear anythin'?'

Luke stood quite still and listened closely. 'Thought it was the waves at first, but it sounds like some sort o' chant – drums, too. Aye, that's the sound o' drums!'

Vurg pointed to the foothills, slightly to the right of them. 'Comin' from there, matey, I'm sure 'tis!'

Sword and spear at the ready they pressed on into the foliage stretching uphill before them. The sounds of drums and chanting grew louder, closer. Luke whispered, 'Stay there, mate. I'll go an' take a peek.'

The cave entrance was a short winding tunnel. Luke sized up the lie of the land, then beckoned to Vurg. They crouched behind a bush at one side of the entrance whilst Luke explained his plan.

'See that round boulder, just uphill there? D'you reckon we could shift it between us, Vurg?'

'Aye, at least we'll give it a try, mate!'

'Good, but first we need to dig a bit of a hole here.'

'Where, right here in the entrance to the tunnel?'

'That's right. Ground's pretty soft, we'll use our weapons.'

Between them they scraped out a shallow depression in the tunnel's mouth. Luke searched about until he found a sizeable chunk of rock, which he placed to one side of the hole, tamping it down firmly.

'Right, now let's move that boulder.'

It was a large round stone, but it moved slowly when Luke set his back against it and Vurg used his spearbutt as a lever. Luke fought for control as they rolled it down towards the entrance.

'Whoa, go easy now, mate, easy does it, just a touch more. There, that should do it!'

The boulder was checked from rolling into the hole at the cave entrance by the rock Luke had placed there, which now served as a wedge to hold the boulder back.

Luke drew his sword, then paused. 'Those drums've stopped. Come on, somethin' must be goin' on in there. Be careful not t'make any noise, matey.'

The friends crept through the tunnel and, keeping to the shadowed walls, entered the main cave, hardly able to believe their eyes at what they saw. Sinister green firelight flickered over the massed faces of the rodents packed on the ledges, all staring fascinated at one thing. The great snake! The reptile's thick neck was quivering as it prepared to strike at Beau, rearing back and hissing coldly.

Luke sprang into immediate action. Grabbing Vurg's spear, he hopskipped forward a pace and hurled the hefty weapon with all the force he could muster.

Speechless with horror, Beau saw the reptile's mouth open wide, revealing sharp deadly fangs as it struck forward at his unprotected face. Then, like a lightning bolt, the spear went smashing into the gaping mouth, driving half its length out through the back of the neck column. Thrashing wildly in its death throes, the snake fell back to the floor, its powerful body flailing like an immense bullwhip, battering rodents from the lower ledges and scattering the fire into a cascade of flying sparks and embers.

The weasel scarce had time to turn before Luke was upon her, ramming the vermin leader flat against the rock wall, his swordblade at her throat. 'One move an' yore dead meat, scum!' the Warrior roared into her painted face.

Though the weasel could not understand Luke's language, the message was clear. The only part of her which moved was her throat, as she gulped against the swordblade.

"Tis Luke, mates. We're saved!'

A ragged cheer rang out from the crew. Below them the dead snake was still causing great damage. Rodents were flung high, smashed against the cave walls, crushed and beaten senseless by the writhing coils of the monster. It seemed like an eternity before the reptile's body went limp and still. However, a great number of the rodents had escaped serious injury, huddling together on the highest cave ledges. Several of them now grabbed weapons and advanced on Luke and Vurg, screeching savagely.

'Marrahagga lagor Rabbatooma! Lagor!'

Vurg swiftly freed his spear from the snake's carcass and joined Luke, pressing his spearpoint at the weasel's heart. Luke kept the sword at her throat as he growled,

'Tell 'em to back off an' cut my crew loose!' He nodded to the bound figures hanging on their poles from the cave ceiling. 'My crew. Cut 'em down afore I cut you down. Now!'

The weasel raised a paw slowly and pointed at the crew. 'Rabbatooma, lagor, Ko!'

One rodent, obviously some kind of minor chieftain, bowed curtly to the weasel. 'Ya Marrahagga!' Turning sullenly to the rest he indicated the prisoners. 'Lagor Rabbatooma.'

Beau had recovered from his shock and rediscovered speech.

'I should jolly well say so, you foul little fiends. You heard him, let us Rabbatoomas go, this very instant!'

The rodents obeyed. Swinging out on ropes, they perched on the poles and sawed through the crews' bonds with their daggers. With shouts of relief and pain Beau and the *Sayna*'s crewmice fell to the dusty cave floor, where they lay groaning.

Cardo whimpered as he tried to rise. 'Paws've gone numb with bein' tied tight for so long!'

Luke's reply was brusque. 'We can't linger here, mates. Crawl out on your bellies, move yourselves, that's an order!'

Luke and Vurg were still menacing the weasel as the crew hauled themselves out in a sorry complaining bunch.

'Ow ow, I got pins'n'needles in all me paws!'

'My pore head's achin' fit to split, mate!'

'Look, that rodent slashed m'tail when he cut the ropes!'

'Huh, you should complain, my backfur's all scorched from hangin' over that blazin' fire!'

Luke kicked the last one's tail lightly. 'Mebbe next time you'll wait my orders afore dashin' ashore to stuff drugged fruit down yore faces!'

When the crew were gone Luke spun the weasel round

and held the blade across her throat from behind.

'Keep an eye on those savages, Vurg, stick 'em if'n they get too close. Right, weasel, we're backin' out of here nice'n'easy. Don't move or yore a dead 'un!'

As they retreated the rodents followed them, crying, 'Lagor Marrahagga!'

Luke was beginning to understand what they said. 'Don't fret, buckoes, we'll let go of yore Marrahagga as soon as we're out o' this stinkin' place. Now back off!'

They negotiated the short winding tunnel. Waiting outside, the crew were massaging life back into numbed paws. Luke guided the weasel round the shallow pit they had dug, and the rodents had just reached its edge when he nodded to Vurg. 'Knock that wedge aside, sharpish!'

Vurg hit the piece of rock a sharp tap with his spear-butt, moving it aside. The boulder rolled forward half a turn and landed in the shallow hole with a bump. It blocked the tunnel entrance off completely and muffled the squeaks of rage sounding from behind it.

Vurg leaned on his spear, grinning. 'A good tight fit, I'd say, mate!'

Luke ordered his crew to get back aboard the *Sayna*, whilst he and Vurg took the weasel and forced her to sit next to the pile of squashed fruit. With his swordpoint Luke drew a picture of the *Goreleech* in the sand, then he transferred the point back to the weasel's throat.

'Marrahagga see red ship sail by here? Red ship, big one?'

The weasel watched Luke's face as he repeated the question several times over. Carefully she drew three circles in the sand, with squiggly lines radiating from them and an arrow pointing south. Whilst Vurg squinted at the drawing, the weasel tapped Luke's sketch of the ship thrice.

Luke understood. 'Three suns, that's three days,' he explained to his bemused friend. 'She says the red ship sailed by here three days back, bound south.'

Vurg dusted his paws off in a businesslike manner. 'That means we ain't far behind her, mate. Better get under way. What do we do about this 'un, Luke?'

The weasel looked unhappily at the Warrior. Touching the swordblade with a paw, she tried to shake her head. A mischievous smile crept over Luke's face, and he thrust a big squashed plum at the weasel's mouth. 'Eat!' She shut her lips tight in revulsion. Luke swung his blade aloft as if to slay her with one blow. 'Marrahagga eat! Eat!'

The weasel gobbled the fruit with great alacrity.

Vurg giggled like a mousebabe, and selected a bruised pear. 'Cummon, Marryhaggit, try some more o' yore own medicine!'

The weasel was forced to down two more plums and a peach. She sat unhappily, juice dribbling down her chin.

Vurg turned to Luke, full of mock sympathy. 'Dearie me, she don't look too 'appy, mate. D'ye think she's still hungry?'

Luke passed the weasel a half-eaten apple that one of his crew had sampled earlier on. 'Oh, I wouldn't worry about ole Marrahagga, mate, she'll cheer up soon. Come on, let's get goin'.'

When they looked back, the weasel had picked up a piece of fruit and was about to hurl it at them. She swayed, dropped the fruit and sat down with a bump, a silly grin plastered on her painted face.

Vurg waved to her. 'G'bye, ole Marryhaggit, 'tis nice to see we're leavin' you happy. I can't abide sad farewells!'

Luke waved too. 'Aye, an' take care of that headache you'll have tomorrow!'

As the *Sayna* left the island in her wake the crew sat sipping hot tea of a herbal remedy brewed by Denno. Cardo, voted spokesmouse by his crewmates, addressed the Warrior.

'Luke, we're sorry we raced ashore an' ate that fruit,

'twas silly of us. But we'd like to offer a hearty vote of thanks to you for savin' our lives. Yore a true warrior!'

Luke held up his paws to silence the cheers. 'Aye, I saved you because I was able to, mates. Pity I wasn't there when the red ship hit the northlands shore. Every night an' day I think of my son Martin back there, growin' up without a mother to care for him, nor a father, with me off here chasin' the red ship. But we'll catch her, I swear we will. An' I'll make the name Vilu Daskar just a dirty memory in the minds of honest beasts!'

The crew went off to their sleeping places as the ship sailed south in the soft warm night, each with their own memories of family lost or left behind. Luke stood in the prow, keeping watch, lost in thoughts of Martin's small figure on the strand, waving his father's old battlesword. He stared forlornly at the gentle bow wave dispersing into the calm dark sea.

'Someday I'll come back and find you waiting for me, son.'

25

On an island many leagues to the south, black smoke billowed above the crackling flames of what had once been a peaceful community of squirrels. Vermin, armed to the fangs, roamed in bands through the forestlands, slaying anybeast who dared to oppose them. Screams rent the air, whips cracked as pitiless rogues rounded up those left alive. Bound neck and paw into a straggling line, the bewildered captives were dragged out of the sheltering trees, into the dunes above the tideline. Akkla, the ferret mate, sniggered evilly, watching the prisoners' horror as they glimpsed their home to be. The red ship *Goreleech*, riding at anchor in the sea offshore.

'Move yerselves, me beauties, we'll soon find yer a snug liddle berth aboard the pretty red boat!'

Vilu Daskar sat on the beach, chin on the bone handle of his scimitar, pensively watching whilst Parug, his bosun, forced the terrified squirrels to kneel and bow their heads before the master of the red ship. Vilu stayed silent until the pitiful heap of provisions and plunder was piled in front of him. Lazily the stoat's eyes flicked over the crewbeasts standing around the pile.

'Is this the best you could do?'

One, a burly weasel called Rippjaw, shrugged. 'Dat's all we be findin', cap'n!'

Vilu stood slowly, his eyes fixed on a necklace of yellow beads, which Rippjaw sported about his neck.

'So, where did you get that trinket, my illiterate friend?'

Rippjaw glanced down at the necklace with his good eye. 'Oh, diss. I take 'im offa deadbeast, cap'n.'

Vilu's scimitar made a noise like an angry wasp as he slew the weasel with one powerful stroke of the sharp blade. With a look of bored disdain, he flicked the necklace from Rippjaw's severed neck on to the pile.

'Must I keep reminding you addlebrained fools that all loot belongs to me? You do not steal from Vilu Daskar.' He turned to the prisoners, as if noticing them for the first time. 'Hmm, you're a pretty wretched lot. No mind, though, you'll soon learn to pull an oar – either that or die. Well, lost your tongues? Nobeast got anything to say?'

An ancient squirrel, silver-grey with uncounted seasons, raised his bound paws and pointed at Vilu. 'The one that follows upon the wave, will steer you one day to your grave!'

The stoat could not explain the shudder that ran through him, but it was gone in an instant. He dismissed it, observing to Akkla, who stood awaiting orders, 'I make it a rule never to take notice of threats by those I've conquered. If any of them were true I'd have been dead long ago. Take that dithering old relic and the rest of his tribe aboard the *Goreleech*, and chain them on deck.'

The captives were being moved off when wild commotion broke out at the woodland fringe. More than a score of crewbeasts fought wildly to control a single squirrel. Vilu leaped nimbly on to a grass-topped dune, viewing the scene with evident enjoyment. Noosed ropes held the maddened squirrel by her paws, neck, tail and waist. The vermin dug their footpaws into the sand, hauling on the lines to keep them taut and prevent her attacking them. She was a huge sinewy creature, with unusually black shining fur which glistened in the sunlight. Though wounded and scarred in several places, she heaved and bucked against the ropes, sending vermin sprawling, baring strong white teeth at them.

Stopping safely out of reach on his perch, Vilu smiled. 'Whoa! What have we here, a real fighter?'

The searat Grigg, his paws cut and burning from rope friction, reported in a strained voice, 'This'n's killed four crew single-pawed, cap'n. 'Tis like tryin' to 'old a pack o' sharks at bay!'

Vilu leaped down from the dune. 'Hold her tight, now!' Advancing on the bound squirrel, he soon had his scimitar tip under her chin, forcing her head back.

'Be still now. I am Vilu Daskar and I could kill you with a flick of my blade. Be still!'

Snorting for breath against the noose around her neck, the squirrel fixed her blazing eyes on the stoat, hatred and loathing ringing fearlessly in her harsh voice.

'I know who you are, scumface. Let's see you put down that blade an' loose me. I'm Ranguvar Foeseeker an' I could rip *you* t'bits without need of a weapon to do the job!'

Vilu pressed his bladepoint harder, causing a drop of blood to stand out against the jet black fur.

'Ranguvar Foeseeker, eh? Hearken then, you're in no position to throw out challenges, and I've no intention of fighting you. I don't do battle with my slaves.'

Ranguvar tried to push her chin further on to the blade. 'Coward! Then slay me an' be quick about it!'

Vilu withdrew his scimitar, shaking his head. 'Never thought I'd live to see the day, a berserk female squirrel! No no, my friend, I'm not going to slay you. What a waste that would be. With mad strength like that you could do the work of a score of oarslaves alone. A few seasons of Bullflay's whip and short rations will humble you. Down on the bottom deck, front row. The seaspray day and night should cool you down a bit. Take her away!'

'You won't break me, dirtbrain,' Ranguvar yelled as she was being dragged off. 'Don't close your eyes to sleep whilst Ranguvar Foeseeker is aboard your cursed ship!'

Vilu Daskar picked up a pawful of dry sand and watched the breeze carry it away, remarking to Grigg, 'Huh, insults and threats, they're like sand in the wind to me, Grigg: here one moment, gone and forgotten the next.'

Minus the use of oars, using only her sails, the red ship coursed south. Bullflay the chief slave driver and his assistants unchained all the galley slaves and herded them up on the trireme's high maindeck. The *Goreleech*'s new squirrel captives were shocked by the sight of the oar-wielders. Starved to emaciation, hollow-eyed and ragged, barely alive in some cases, the wretched slaves blinked against the bright afternoon. Bullflay cracked his long sharkskin whip low, pulling several of the slaves flat as it curled around their footpaws.

'On yer knees, ye worthless fishbait, don't yer see the cap'n's present?'

Ranguvar had been chained and covered with a weighted cargo net, through which she watched the scene.

A huge baulk of timber had been attached to a rope reeved through a block halfway up the mainmast. Vilu stuck his scimitar into the mainmast at shoulder height.

'I've brought you thirty-six new oarbeasts, Bullflay. How many do you need?'

The big fat weasel saluted with his fearsome whip. 'I'll take every one you got, cap'n Vilu!'

The pirate stoat signalled for some refreshment and a seat. Hurriedly four crew members brought his chair, a flagon of his favourite damson wine and a grilled fish. Seated comfortably he picked delicately at the fish and sipped wine from a crystal goblet, watched by the hungry slaves. Wiping his lips on a silken kerchief he nodded briefly to his chief slave driver.

Bullflay grabbed the rope which had been reeved through the block and hauled on it until the baulk of timber was hoisted level with the scimitar sticking from the mast. 'Haul the wood this high, or else!' He let the baulk drop to the deck. The weary oarslaves stood in line for their turn to haul up the baulk. Then he picked up his whip and cracked it over the new arrivals. 'Come on, you lot, get below. We'll get yer chained up to an oar nice an' tidy like. Hahaharr!'

Getting the black squirrel Ranguvar below was an awesome task. Keeping her bundled in the cargo net a score of vermin dragged her through the decks until she was at the front seat of the vessel's bottom level. Eight of the Sea Rogues suffered wounds and injuries, but they finally got the berserker chained alone to a long thick oar handle. Ranguvar sat relatively quiet. She waited until the other oarslaves were brought down and shackled into place at the sweeps. She questioned one, a tired old otter, who looked as if he had seen many seasons slaving.

'What was all that about up on deck, the timber an' the rope? Why did you have to haul it up, all of you?'

The otter blinked back a tear from his craggy face. 'Didn't yer know, mate? Vilu Daskar an' Bullflay got to 'ave their bit o' fun. Thirty-six new oarslaves means they got to get rid of thirty-six old 'uns, so they finds the sickest'n'weakest by makin' us hoist the log.'

'What happens to those who can't haul the log?' Ranguvar could not stop herself asking.

The otter's husky voice shook as he explained. 'That's when the real sport starts, mate. They sails the red ship out 'til land's too far away for a fit beast to swim back to it, then they runs out a plank. Vilu gives the pore creatures their freedom, tells 'em they're free to swim back t'shore an' forces 'em t'walk the plank.'

Ranguvar's fur stood up on the nape of her neck. 'Do any ever make it, friend?'

'What d'you think? You saw the state of some o' those slaves. If'n the big fishes don't get 'em the sea does.'

Ranguvar turned and murmured softly, 'Well at least you survived it. What's yore name?'

Bowing his head until it touched the oar the otter replied, 'Norgle's my name. My father's name was Drenner, he used to sit where yore sittin' now, that's his oars yore chained to. My ole dad was one of those who couldn't haul the log.'

Slaaaash! Crack!

'Shaddup, yer scurvy bilge swabs!'

Slavemaster Bullflay swaggered up to his rail, directly in front of Ranguvar. He wielded the whip at Norgle, but the black squirrel sat up straight and took the blow. A big skinny rat positioned himself alongside Bullflay. Picking up a drumstick, he stood ready at the big drum which was used to keep the oarslaves pulling in time with each other.

Bullflay winked at him, nodding towards Ranguvar. 'See that, Fleabitt? Cap'n Vilu said this squirrel's a real tough 'un. We'll 'ave ter pay 'er some special attention, won't we?'

Fleabitt's narrow frame shook with unconcealed glee. 'Special attention, right, chief. We'll learn 'er!'

Ranguvar's piercing stare raked the rat scornfully. 'What could I learn from you, cocklebrain?'

Craaack!

Bullflay's whip struck her. Ranguvar transferred her dead stare to him without even blinking.

'Is that the best you can do, barrelbelly?'

Choking with rage the burly weasel flogged away at his new oarslave, using all his strength. When he finished his stomach was heaving in and out, and both his paws were shaking violently with the exertion.

'You . . . you dare talk ter Slavemaster Bullflay like that! I'll flay yer to dollrags!'

Ranguvar, who had ducked her head to protect her face, raised her eyes. There was death dancing in them as she growled at Bullflay, 'You big useless lump o' mud, one day I'll kill yer with my bare paws, even if'n I have to bite through these chains to get at yer. Remember that, weasel!'

Bullflay could not bring himself to answer, or raise his whip again. Ranguvar's eyes had frightened him. He strode off down the walkway, laying left and right with his whip at the other oarslaves.

'Silence there, quiet! An' be ready ter row when my drum starts to beat, if you want t'keep fur on yore backs!'

Two hours after daybreak next morning a searat called down from his watch in the crow's nest, 'Away to the north, a sail, cap'n, a sail!'

Vilu Daskar leaned out over the stern of the *Goreleech*, shading his eyes, peering hard at the faraway smudge.

'Sail? Are you sure? What kind of craft is she?'

'Too far off t'tell, cap'n sir, but 'tis a sail fer sure!'

Akkla kept the tiller steady, awaiting Vilu's order.

Striding the afterdeck, the pirate stoat stroked the yellowed bone handle of his scimitar pensively. 'Hmm, a sail, eh? How far off are the Twin Islands, Akkla?'

'We could make 'em by tomorrow midday wid all sail an' full speed on the oars, cap'n.'

His eyes still fixed on the far-off object, Vilu replied, 'Too fast, we'd lose her. No ship can keep up with mine under full sail and oars. Take her to half sail and tell Bullflay to set the rowers a steady beat. We'll let her keep us in sight, and that way we'll land at Twin Islands tomorrow night. Set your tiller south and a point west.'

The red ship sailed off on her new course, with the whips cracking on all three decks below. Oars rose and fell, pulling the *Goreleech* through the waves. The fresh captives groaned miserably as they bent their backs under the lash.

26

Vurg snuggled deeper in his hammock. Morning sunlight streamed through the cabin window, and he tried to ignore it, closing both eyes tight, but he could not close his ears to the raucous duet which the cook and his assistant were yelling from the galley. Other crewmice were already awake, hurling objects at the galley door, haranguing the singers within.

'You'll turn the grub sour wid that noise!'

'Aye, belt up, you two, stop that awful racket!'

'I thought somebeast was tryin' to squash a dozen frogs!'

But Beau and his assistant Cardo were in full cry and not about to give up for mere threats and insults.

'Ho wot d'you give to a saucy crew,
Stew! Stew! Stew!
Wot's better than a bowl o' stew?
Why a bowl o' stew or two!
We fries the varnish off the mast,
Then adds some ole rope ends,
An' the cap'n's boots all boiled up slow,
Good flavour to it lends.
So scoff it up 'tis good for you,

Stew! Stew! Stew!
Made with a drop o' lantern oil,
An' a barnacle or two,
Some fine sail threads an' fishes' heads,
Then roast the cook's ole socks,
An' add to that some o' the fat,
They use to grease the locks!
Ho stew, stew luvverly stew,
No skilly'n'duff or brown burrgoo,
Just swallow the lumps that you can't chew,
An' fill a plate for yore worst mate,
Then sit an' watch him temptin' fate,
With face so green an' nose all blue,
Stew! Stew! Steeeeeeeeeeeeewwwww!'

Luke was guiding the tiller, smiling as he listened to the crew voicing their doubts about breakfast.

'D'you think they really mean it, Cordle?'

'I don't know, mate. Mebbe they're just jokin'.'

'But they wouldn't use lantern oil an' lock grease, would they, Vurg?'

Vurg winked at Luke as he answered Denno, who was prone to bouts of seasickness at the slightest thing. 'Who knows, mate? Ole Beau's a great 'un for playin' pranks an' I remember that salty stew Cardo made when we first set sail. Wot d'you think, Luke?'

The Warrior was hard put to keep a straight face. 'No, Vurg, I don't think Beau an' Cardo'd do that to our vittles, though I couldn't find my seaboots this mornin'.'

The cook and his assistant staggered out of the galley, bearing between them a steaming cauldron. Denno's usually ruddy face took on an unhealthy pallor. 'Urgh! I ain't eatin' none o' that stuff!'

Grinning wickedly, Beau dipped a beaker into the cauldron. 'Wot? After all the blinkin' trouble we went to preparin' this delicious stew? Now see here, Denno m'laddo, I'm goin' to see you eat this, even if I have t'feed it t'you m'self. It'll put the jolly old roses back in your cheeks. Now open your mouth wide, old chap!'

'Yaaaah! I'm too young t'die!'

The crew of the *Sayna* shook with laughter as Beau chased Denno round the deck with the beaker of stew.

'Oh, c'mon, you great big silly, stan' still an' open wide!'

'Gerraway from me, you lop-eared poisoner! Help, somebeast stop 'im! Do somethin', you rotten lot!'

Beau pursued Denno from stem to stern, stew slopping from the beaker as he coaxed and cajoled. 'Never grow up strong an' handsome like me if you don't eat all your blinkin' brekky up, wot wot?'

Denno scrambled up the mainmast for the crow's nest, with Beau scaling the rope ladder close behind him. When he reached the topmost point, Denno suddenly yelled, 'Sail, I see a sail!'

Beau grabbed his footpaw, chortling. 'No excuses now, laddie buck. I'll pour it down your ear if you don't hold still!'

Luke's sharp command caused the hare to release the crewmouse.

'Beau, let him be! Are you sure it's a sail, Denno?'

'Aye, Luke, I saw it a moment ago, but it's gone now!'

Beau let the beaker drop and clambered swiftly up alongside Denno, his keen eyes following the mouse's paw.

'Over there it was, south, mebbe a touch west!'

The hare concentrated his gaze upon the horizon for a while, then he climbed down to the deck and made his report to Luke.

'There was somethin' out there, but bad weather's risin' from the sou'west – sea's gone quite choppy an' the clouds are lowerin'. Mayhap 'twas a ship – couldn't really tell.'

Luke came to a decision speedily. 'Vurg, steer her over that way – south goin' west. Coll, Dulam, Cordle, pile on all sails. Beau, get the food to my cabin, an' the rest of you, make sure everythin' is battened down tight. Looks like we're in for a storm.'

When the orders had been carried out the crew gathered in Luke's cabin to share the meal. Contrary to Denno's belief the stew was delicious. Beau was quite huffy that anybeast should think it otherwise.

'Phuff! Never cooked rubbish or wasted good food in all m'life, wot. Vegetable stew, sah, with lots of carrot, dandelion root, leeks, dried mushrooms, onions, taters an' my own special barley'n'oat dumplin's. Puts fur on the chest, a glint in the eye an' a splendid spring t'the paw. Stuff t'give the crew, eh, Luke?'

The Warrior cleaned his bowl with a chunk of bread. 'It certainly is, mate. D'you think we should allow Denno a second helpin'?'

Denno licked his spoon sheepishly. 'Not my fault. The way they were singin' that song, well, I thought . . .'

Beau kindly ladled him another portion. 'Thought, laddie? Y'know what the shortsighted vole thought. Listen an' I'll tell you.

'A shortsighted vole climbed out of his hole,
His glasses he'd lost I fear,
Some blossom petals in the breeze,
Fell on his head, oh dear!

"I thought 'twas summer but winter's come,
'Tis snow!" that vole did shout.
"I think I'd better go and warn
The creatures hereabout!"

He bellowed round the woodland wide,
"I think 'tis going to freeze!"
He shooed some sparrows from a nest,
"Back to your hive you bees!"

236

And squinting dimly at the ground,
He lectured tufts of grass,
"All hedgehogs now should be indoors,
'Til wintertide does pass!"

"Go join your family round the fire,
Don't sit there all alone,
'Tis no fit weather for a mole,"
He scolded at a stone.

"And as for you," he told a bush,
"You badgers aren't too smart,
I thought you'd be the first to know,
When winter's due to start!"

So gather round and listen all,
My moral's clear and true,
I think 'tis best to stop and think,
When thoughts occur to you!'

As Beau finished his poem the ship gave a lurch. Luke
saved the stew cauldron as it slid by and laid it safe on the
deck, wedging it 'twixt the table and his chair.

'Don't panic, crew, it's the bad weather. Sit tight an'
wait it out in comfort – there's little else we can do. I'm
goin' out on deck. Vurg, you come with me. We'll take
tiller watch two at a time until the storm passes. When
you go out there, use ropes an' tie yoreselves to that tiller.
I don't want any crew washed overboard.'

The little ship began to sway crazily as mounting
waves buffeted her, up and down, side to side. Luke
gritted his teeth as he and Vurg strove to hold the tiller on
course. Spray lashed both mice until, despite their heavy
cloaks, they were saturated. A high-pitched whine, like
that of a stricken beast, rose above the storm's din. It was
the wind, playing on the tightened rigging ropes as if
they were the strings of some instrument. Pawing

saltwater from his eyes, Vurg glanced anxiously up at them.

'If we don't slack off some sail this gale might rip us t'pieces, Luke. Can't we take her t'half canvas?'

The Warrior stared straight ahead into the onslaught. ''Tain't possible, Vurg. I couldn't risk the crew's life by sendin' 'em up into the riggin' to shorten sail. Also I'm near certain 'twas the red ship that Denno an' Beau sighted. I don't figger on losin' her. We're bound to follow!'

Beau and Cardo struggled back to the galley across the seesawing deck, bearing the empty stew cauldron between them. Coinciding with the boom of thunder overhead, the galley door slammed open wide. A flash of white lightning illuminated the scene as they were both swept inside by a wave crashing over the ship. Smoke wreathed them as the galley stove was extinguished into a hissing mess by the water. The seacook staggered inside, yelling to his assistant, 'Lock all y'can in the cupboards – keep the blinkin' vittles dry. I'm goin' to fetch a rope and secure those water casks before they start rollin' about!'

No sooner was Beau out on deck again than a crackling bolt of chain lightning struck the *Sayna*'s foremast. Like a dry twig the stout timber split, sending the long lower jib swinging like a scythe. Vurg saw the danger and shouted, 'Beau, look out, mate!'

As Beau turned the jib caught him a mighty clout in the midriff, hurling him ears over tail into the sea.

Luke was already on the move. Releasing the tiller he quickly tied the stern line about his waist and plunged in after Beau, with Vurg bawling above the mêlée, 'All paws on deck! Hare overboard! All paws on deck!'

Down, down went the Warrior, into a world of boiling confusion, with the roar of storm and sea ringing in his ears. Luke felt his progress checked as the line pulled tight, and immediately began striking upward, his eyes searching the racing bubbling surface for signs of the hare. Air started escaping his nostrils and mouth as he fought his way bravely to the wavetops. Gasping for breath, he surfaced in a deep green valley, then the maddened seas crashed down upon him. Next moment he was swung up high on the crest of a huge roller. Luke took the opportunity to scan swiftly about for Beau. Below him he could see the stern of the ship, but no other sign of life upon the watery wilderness. Then he was dropped into another deep trough, only to be swept aloft again. About his middle, the line tightened painfully as he was pulled along in the ship's wake, spitting seawater, paws flailing, searching constantly for Beau, despite his own predicament.

Vurg called out to the crew, 'Haul Luke in, mates, afore the line snaps an' he drowns. Beau's gone, can't do nothin' about that. Haul in there!'

Willing paws heaved on the line. Luke felt himself pulled through the buffeting waves, and relaxed, half stunned and too helpless to resist. Vurg was waiting with a dry cloak and a beaker of elderberry wine, and Cardo helped to carry Luke to his cabin.

The Warrior coughed and spluttered as the wine revived him. He sat up, shaking his head.

'It was too wild t'see anythin' out there. No sign of Beau?'

Cardo was weeping uncontrollably. 'None at all. That ole hare was my best matey, an' the finest cook afloat. The sea's a cruel beast, cruel!'

Luke passed the remainder of the wine to him. 'Drink this, now, Cardo. 'Tis a terrible thing, poor Beau. But we must concentrate on keeping this ship afloat or we'll all finish up on the seabed if'n this storm keeps up.'

He was interrupted by joyous shouts from out on deck as the ship gave a mighty shudder and stopped rolling.

'The wind's turned. We're saved, mates!'

Wrapping the cloak about him, Luke hurried from the cabin.

Evening was streaking the skies westward, and to the east the thunder boomed dully, with a sporadic bolt of lightning far off. Vurg scratched his head in amazement. The wind was still blowing, but strong and warm, flattening the sea with its power. The *Sayna* was shuddering lightly, her damaged rigging thrumming as she responded to Dulam's touch on the tiller and sped southwest.

Relief among the crew was evident. Coll laughed. 'Hahaha! Quickest thing y'ever did see, Luke. One moment we're near sinkin' in a storm, then swift as a flash the wind turns east an' suddenly veers west. We're saved!'

Dusk was creeping in. Luke's cloak fluttered straight out behind him as he stood, with the crew, looking back over the stern at the distant area where Beau had been lost. Cardo had composed a short verse.

'Our friend was taken by the sea,
He rests now, who knows where,
A good an' gen'rous beast he was,
A brave an' cheerful hare.

We've got no flow'rs or blossoms,
To cast out on the deep,
No stone will ever mark the spot,
Where he sank down to sleep.

Beau Fethringsol Cosfortingham,
Sweet as long summer days,
Your memory lies in our hearts,
You'll be our mate, always!'

The crew stood in silence, heads bowed, tears falling on to the deck. Everybeast had loved the hare dearly.

Luke took a deep breath and wiped his eyes. 'Cordle,

take first watch aloft, keep yore eyes peeled for the red ship. Coll, your turn at the tiller. Right now, while me'n'Cardo put the galley straight an' piece together a meal, the rest of you get rope an' pitch, bind that mast as best you can, then take in all sails. She's runnin' fast enough in this sea. In future storms I don't want to see anybeast out on deck without havin' a lifeline attached to 'em. 'Twas a terrible thing that happened to Beau, but I know he'd want it to serve as a lesson to us all.'

The sun's fiery orb sank below the westering horizon, and the *Sayna* sped smoothly into the night. A splash announced that the shattered jib had been jettisoned overboard. Luke stood at the galley fire, which he had rekindled, longing to hear just one merry chuckle from Beau, but knowing it was not possible. They would have to sail onward without their friend the hare.

27

Vilu Daskar was used to freak weather in tropical waters.
When the storm struck he ordered his oarslaves put to
work. With no sails to aid them they were forced to row
double time as the drums pounded out and whips
cracked. Daskar himself took the wheel, tacking the
Goreleech skilfully on a direct westerly course. As the
tempest began slackening he swung the vessel due east,
came round the far side of the Twin Islands and anchored
a safe distance offshore, behind the easternmost of the
two massive hills.

Savouring the night air, Vilu sat out on deck, sating his
appetite on a plate of baked fish and a flagon of nettle
beer. Akkla the ferret hovered nearby, watching the stoat
pick his teeth with a fishbone. Vilu dabbed at his mouth
with a silken kerchief and stood up. Akkla gazed
anxiously at the remains of the meal, hoping Vilu had
finished.

'Had anything to eat yet, Akkla?'

Edging eagerly near the barrelhead table, the ferret
bowed cringingly. 'No chance ter eat durin' that storm,
cap'n.'

Vilu held out a paw, as if inviting Akkla to finish the
meal, then clouted the ferret's face sharply, knocking him

to the deck. 'Go and get your own food, famine-face!'

From below decks there was a bellowing roar which mounted to a screech, quickly followed by the thudding of paws up the companionway. Bullflay the weasel slavemaster, assisted by some of his cronies, stumbled out on to the deck. He was pressing a wadded rag to staunch the blood from one side of his head.

Vilu could see he was in great pain. 'Hmm, nasty injury. How did you come by that, Bullflay?'

The weasel's toadies took up the tale with relish.

' 'Twas the black squirrel, sire!'

'Aye, the berserk female. Tore master Bullflay's ear off, sire, with 'er teeth!'

'She'd 'ave 'ad 'is other ear if'n we 'adn't rescued 'im, sire. Madder'n a shark that 'un is!'

'No use floggin' 'er, sire, two whips master Bullflay's broke on 'er. Two!'

Vilu sat back, a smile hovering across his eyes. 'So, and what would you have me do with this berserk warrior, Bullflay my friend?'

The weasel's flabby jowls quivered with rage. 'I wants yer t'let me kill 'er, sire, tie rocks to 'er neck'n'paws an' slide 'er into the water nice'n'slow, let the other oarslaves watch 'er drown bit by bit!'

Vilu nodded understandingly. 'You'd like that, eh, Bullflay?'

A drop of blood spattered the deck as the slavemaster nodded. 'Aye, sire, I'd like it fine after wot she did t'me!'

Vilu dallied with the bone handle of his scimitar. 'I've no doubt you would, but I'm captain aboard this ship, not you. I decide who lives or dies and that squirrel is not ready for death yet. Cut her food and water for a few days, that should do the trick.'

Bullflay was about to protest when he saw a dangerous glint in Vilu's eyes. He saluted sullenly. 'As y'say, sire.'

Vilu smiled sweetly, perilously. 'Precisely, my lard-bellied friend. As I say!' He beckoned to Akkla, who was still crouching on the deck, holding his face where he had been struck.

'Stop slobbering about down there. Get up! Take four crew and go ashore. Climb that hill, and mount a lookout for the ship that was following us. Report to me when you sight it. I'll lay an acorn to an apple that they'll do like any other vessel does when they come to Twin Islands. Parug, do you know what they'll do?'

The searat bosun shook his head. 'No, sire.'

Vilu closed one eye and squinted towards the channel separating both islands. 'They'll sail straight up the middle of there, always do. We'll be waiting for them when they emerge from the channel mouth and meet them head on with our spike, eh, Parug?'

A quiver of evil joy shook the bosun. 'Stick 'em like a gnat on a pin, sire!'

Vilu filled a beaker with nettle beer, passing it to Parug. 'Like a gnat on a pin. What a quaint turn of phrase!'

Far below on the bottom deck of the trireme, Norgle the otter sat on the second row, staring in admiration at the back of Ranguvar, sitting alone on the front bench. Lashmarks scored and quartered the black squirrel's back, where Bullflay had done his best to flog her into submission. He had failed – every slave chained to an oar throughout the length and breadth of the *Goreleech* knew it. It brought fresh life and the spark of defiance into the hearts of even the oldest and most timid. Norgle heard the heavy pawstep of Bullflay descending and murmured softly to Ranguvar. ''Tis Bullflay, matey. Get yoreself ready for the worst. Like as not he'll slay ye for bitin' off his ear.'

The black squirrel's eyes glowed with fierce battle light. 'Hah! Not before I've bitten his other one off!'

'Silence down 'ere. One more peep an' I'll flay yore backs t'the bone, y'bilge scrapin's!'

A hush fell as Bullflay's whip cracked aloud. Still

holding the rag to his ear, he strode up and stood by the drum. Raising the whip high he glared at Ranguvar. 'An' you'll be the first t'git flayed, squirrel!'

The eyes of Ranguvar bored into her hated enemy. 'An' you'll be the first to die, lardbucket!'

Bullflay quailed under the berserk stare of Ranguvar. He let the whip fall and strode off, muttering, 'We'll see 'ow bold yer are after a couple o' days without vittles or water. That'll cure you!'

However, when food was served up to the oarslaves, even though it was only a crust, one bowl of thin gruel and a cup of water, everybeast saved a small portion. When the oardecks were quiet, the food was passed from paw to paw until it reached the captive berserker.

Mid-morning of the following day saw Dulam, whose watch it was at the topmast, bellowing, 'Laaaaaaand hooooooooo!'

Luke joined him at the lookout point. The high, humped hills of Twin Islands stood out fresh and green in the warm sunlight. He patted Dulam's back.

'Well done, mate. You'll get an extra portion at lunch for bein' the first to spot land!'

Dulam sighed mournfully. Luke was a warrior, not a cook. 'An' will I have to eat it too?'

Luke tweaked his friend's ear playfully. 'There's gratitude for ye, after me slavin' over a hot galley stove since dawn makin' skilly'n'duff for ye.'

Dulam sighed wistfully. 'My ole mum used t'make the best skilly'n'duff on the northland coast.'

Luke chuckled as he climbed out of the rigging. 'Well, I ain't yore ole mum. Mayhap we should've brought her along, Dulam.'

'Aye, mayhap we will next time. She's as good with a ladle as you are with a sword. Dear ole mum, yore liddle Martin used to come round to our cave for her apple pies. Sweet apples, golden crust, steamin' hot, dusted with spices an' warm arrowroot sauce poured over 'em. I can taste 'em right now.'

Luke helped Dulam down to the deck. 'Well, let's hope she's still feeding my son, make him grow up big'n'strong. Now will you stop natterin' on about those pies, 'tis turnin' me off my own cookin'!'

'Huh, that wouldn't be hard to do!' Vurg remarked in passing.

Luke heard him. 'What was that you said, Vurg?'

'I said the sky's far up'n'blue, mate!'

Luke glanced upward, remarking quietly to Vurg, 'There's far worse cooks aboard than me.'

Vurg cupped a paw to his ear. 'What?'

The Warrior winked slyly at his friend. 'I said, the sky's as blue as the sea.'

Afternoon shadows were starting to lengthen as the *Sayna* lay offshore of the Twin Islands. Luke called up to the topmost watch, 'Any sign of the red ship?'

Cardo shielded his eyes. 'None at all, Luke!'

Vurg leaned against the tiller. 'So what now, mate?'

Luke studied the Twin Islands carefully before replying.

'No good chasin' out into unknown waters with the *Sayna* in a bad state. No tellin' what might become of us. I think we should sail her into that channel which separates the two islands, 'tis calm an' sheltered in there. We could make the *Sayna* shipshape again, fix the mast properly, make a new jib an' sew up those torn sails. Sort of put everythin' to rights afore we set sail again, eh, Vurg?'

'Aye, sounds sensible, but what about the red ship, Luke?'

'Well we ain't in a fit condition to chase her right now. We'll have to make up two days when we're sailin' again. Strange though, Vurg, I've got a funny feelin' that red ship isn't too far off somewhere. Hmm, mayhap 'tis just a fancy an' it'll pass. Right, head 'er in there, mates. We'll make fast to the east channel bank about halfway along.'

Later that evening Akkla tapped nervously at Vilu Daskar's splendidly carved cabin door.

Vilu put aside the charts he and Parug were studying. 'Come!' the pirate stoat's voice called imperiously.

Akkla entered respectfully and made his report.

'Sire, 'tis like you said: towards evenin' a ship sailed into the channel an' put in 'alfway up on the east side.'

Vilu could not resist a triumphant smirk at Parug. 'Just as I predicted.' He turned back to Akkla. 'What manner of vessel is it?'

'Like an ole Corsair barque, cap'n, but ain't no Corsairs aboard of 'er, they're all mice, tough-lookin' beasts. She took some storm damage, sire – I think they've put in there for repairs.'

Parug drew his cutlass and licked the blade. 'It's dark outside, cap'n. We could come stormin' up the channel like an 'awk on to a wren, jus' when they're least expectin' us!'

Vilu shook his head despairingly at the searat bosun. 'No no, my impulsive friend, why wreck a ship that's in need of repair? Leave the mice awhile, let them work and sweat fixing up their craft, get it all good and seaworthy again. Then we'll swoop on them and sink it, let them see all their efforts destroyed. Much more subtle, don't you think?'

Parug thought for a moment, then his features creased into an evil gap-toothed cackle. 'Haharrhahaharr! Yore a bad 'un all right, cap'n!'

Vilu adopted a modest expression. 'Oh, I do my best to be the worst. Akkla, what was the name of this ship?'

'I don't know letters, sire, but Fleabitt does, an' 'e said 'twas called the *Sayna*, I think. Aye, that's the name, *Sayna*!'

To both Sea Rogues' surprise, their captain poured

247

wine for himself and them. Akkla and Parug sipped appreciatively at their goblets. Vilu Daskar's wine was the best.

Vilu himself merely wet his lips as he mused, 'Hmm, *Sayna*. What do you think, my friends, 'twould have been saner for *Sayna* to give Twin Islands a miss?'

Akkla and the bosun stared at him in dumb silence. Vilu put aside his wine and sighed.

'That's called a play on words, you bumpkins. Saner, *Sayna*, 'twas a pun, don't you see?'

The pair stood in slack-jawed silence, trying to understand what their captain had said. He turned his back, dismissing the slow-witted crewbeasts. 'Dimwitted idiots, get out of my sight before I lose patience with your thick-skulled ignorance. Begone!'

Akkla and Parug set their goblets down gingerly, not daring to finish the wine, and hurried from the cabin. Vilu's former good humour had deserted him. He detested being surrounded by stupid witless vermin.

Slouching in his chair he began to focus his mind upon the *Sayna* and her crew. Why would a vessel of such small size be pursuing a ship as huge as the *Goreleech*? What possible harm could a score or so of mice inflict upon Vilu Daskar, terror of the seas? They must be totally insane, or recklessly brave. Well, one way or another, he would soon find out. Hah! And so would they, the fools!

Vilu left his cabin and strolled out on deck, almost colliding with a searat called Drobna. His claws dug viciously into the rat's cheek, drawing the frightened rodent close. Vilu smiled disarmingly at him. 'Tell me, what chance does a minnow stand if it chases a shark?'

Drobna's cheek was pulled awkwardly on one side, and spittle trickled from his lips as he blabbered out a reply. 'Nuh . . . nuh . . . none, sire, minnow agin a shark's got no 'ope!'

Vilu released him, patting Drobna's cheek tenderly.

'Well said, my friend, well said. Even a moron like you can solve a simple problem now and then.'

He strode on up the gently swaying deck, leaving Drobna rubbing a stinging cheek, completely baffled.

28

Luke was already up, having taken last watch of the night. The *Sayna* lay moored on the east bank of the canal-like channel running between Twin Islands. Luke leaned on the starboard rail, watching the day break still and humid, with leaden overcast skies. Cardo came out of the main cabin, bearing an old shield that he used as a tray. On it was a beaker of hot mint and dandelion tea, accompanied by a warm scone spread with stiff comb honey.

He winked at Luke. 'Mornin', mate. Here, get that down you. I was up awhile before dawn, so I tried me paw at bakin' scones.'

Luke seated himself on a coil of rope, sipping gratefully at the hot tea and nibbling gingerly at the scone. He surveyed the islands' two massive hills, which looked silent and oppressive with the heavy grey sky cloaking their summits in mist.

'Hmm, wouldn't surprise me if'n we had a spot o' rain today, Cardo. Well, this scone tastes good, matey. Where'd you learn to bake stuff like this?'

Cardo stared down the channel to the open sea beyond. ''Twas a recipe Beau taught me. I miss that ole hare. He was a good friend t'me.'

Luke put a paw round Cardo's shoulder. 'Aye, so do I.

Strange, but we never know the true value of friends'n'family 'til they ain't with us any more. Come on, matey, buck up. I can hear our crew wakin'. Mopin' about won't help us. Best t'keep ourselves busy, eh?'

The crew of the *Sayna* had nothing but praise for Cardo's good cooking, and it cheered him greatly. After breakfast Luke reviewed their position and gave orders.

'Cardo, see if y'can cook up a lunch t'show us that breakfast wasn't just a flash in the pan. Cordle, pick a couple o' good patchers to help you repair the sails. Coll, Denno and Dulam, I want you to strip down the mainmast an' bind it round tight with strong greased line. That willow never broke, it only cracked. 'Twill be good as new once it's bound an' tightened proper. Vurg, get yore weapons an' come with me. We're goin' up that big hill yonder. Let's see if we can find a decent piece o' wood to fashion a new jib from. Right, off t'work now, crew, an' keep yore wits about you an' both eyes open. 'Tis strange territory.'

The hill turned out to be a complete disappointment. There were no proper trees with trunks and stout limbs growing there. Luke snorted in disgust as he swiped with his sword at one of the tall feathery bushes which grew in profusion on the slopes. Vurg picked up the branch his friend had lopped off and inspected it.

'Huh, too thin an' brittle. Wouldn't even make decent firewood. Won't find a decent jib spar growin' 'ereabouts.'

Luke peered uphill into the warm humid mist. 'Looks pretty much the same all over, Vurg. Why don't we go back down an' try searchin' the channel edges for a good piece of driftwood? Might've been some timber washed up there. Vurg? What's the matter, mate?'

Vurg was rubbing his paws together furiously and flapping them as if he were trying to fly. 'Yukk! Some kind o' filthy insects. Must've come off those bushes. Look, they're all over me paws!'

Luke pushed his companion forward, urging him downhill. 'Well don't stand there flappin' y'paws, mate, let's get to the channel. Good salt water'll wash 'em off!'

Further uphill than the two mice had ventured, Vilu Daskar's spy patrol lay among the bushes. They watched Luke and Vurg hurry off down to the water. Ringpatch, the ferret in charge of the group, said, 'If they'd reached the 'illtop they'd 'ave seen the *Goreleech* anchored below on the other side. Good job they never.'

'Yah, they woulda never got past us,' a small searat called Willag scoffed airily. 'There wuz only two of 'em. We'd 'ave chopped 'em up fer sure!'

Ringpatch eyed him contemptuously. 'Huh, what d'you know about it, spindleshanks? Those two mice looked like warriors to me. I wonder why they turned back an' ran off?'

'Said it was some kind o' insects, least that's wot I thought I 'eard one of 'em say,' replied one of the patrol vermin.

'Huh, insects,' Willag sneered. 'They can't 'ave been much as warriors if'n they ran from insects!'

Suddenly, one of the patrol leaped upright, hitting himself left and right with both paws and dancing wildly. 'Yaaaagh! Insec's! I'm covered in 'em! Yeegh!'

Tiny moist brown slugs from the surrounding bushes were all over the patrol, writhing and crawling, sticking to any patch of fur they came in contact with. The vermin thrashed about in the bushes, beating at themselves.

'Yuuurk! Gerrem offa me, I can't stand insec's!'

'Uuugh! Filthy slimy liddle worms!'

'Yowch! They sting too. Owowow!'

'Sputt! One got in me mouth. Oooogh!'

Ringpatch dashed off uphill. 'Patrol, retreat. Let's get out o' here afore they eats us alive!'

Stumbling and crashing through the bushes, they

retreated over the summit, driven by the sticky slugs to seek a saltwater bath.

Vurg had just finished scouring his paws in the channel shallows when he cocked an ear upward. 'Listen, did you hear something? Like a kind of high-pitched squealin' noise? Came from up near the hilltop there.'

Luke stood still, cupping both paws about his ears. 'Aye, I heard it, mate, though I couldn't imagine anythin' but insects wantin' to live on this forsaken place. Prob'ly some seabirds, feedin' off those horrible grubs.'

Vurg dried his paws in the coarse grass. 'Well let's 'ope they eat 'em all. I detest squigglies!'

It was noon by the time they got back to the ship. Denno was atop the mast, binding the last bit tight with greased line, and he saw them approaching.

'Ahoy, crew, looks like Luke'n'Vurg found us a jib spar!' Willing paws helped the pair carry a long stout limb of some unidentifiable wood aboard the vessel.

Coll inspected it, nodding his approval. 'Tough oily-lookin' wood. Let's strip the bark off an' measure it agin the broken jib for size.'

It proved an ideal replacement for the old spar. By midnoon they had it fixed. Rigging and fresh-patched sails were hauled, and Luke paced the deck, checking all was shipshape.

'Good as new the ole tub looks, mates. I'm famished. What happened to that lunch Cardo was supposed t'be cookin'?'

Cardo popped his head round the galley door. 'Go an' seat yoreselves in the cabin. 'Tis about ready.'

The *Sayna*'s cook had triumphed again. Cardo had used most of the dried fruit to make a hefty steamed pudding, covered with a sauce made of pureed plums and arrowroot, and there were beakers of old amber cider to drink with it. Luke voted the meal so delicious that he proposed Cardo be made Ship's Cook for life. Ladle clutched to his chest, Cardo bowed proudly as the crew applauded.

'Hoho, good ole Cardo. More power to yore paw, mate!'

'Any second 'elpings there, cooky me darlin'?'

'Aye, an' keep them scones comin' for brekkist every day!'

'Wot's for supper tonight, matey, anythin' tasty?'

Knowing he had a new-found power to wield, Cardo laid the law down to them, shaking his ladle officiously. 'So I'm Ship's Cook now, eh? Then cook it is! But I ain't washin' dishes an' scourin' pots'n'pans, so there!'

To appease his touchy cook, Luke sided with Cardo. 'Agreed! From now on everybeast washes their own dishes. We'll take turns with the pots'n'pans. I'll do first duty!'

A splatter of heavy drops pattering on the bulkheads announced the arrival of rain. Vurg opened the cabin door and slid his plate and beaker out on to the deck. 'I vote that the rain washes our dishes tonight, buckoes!'

Soon, raindrops could be heard pinging merrily off the crew's dishes scattered across the deck. Through the open door Luke watched a distant lightning flash, and he heard the far-off rumble of thunder.

'Looks like we're in for heavy weather, mates. Best batten down an' lay up in this channel 'til it's over.'

Rain continued into the late evening, but the crew were snug and dry in the cabin, glad of the respite from sailing. Cardo sat apart from the rest, his face gloomy.

Vurg tweaked the cook's ear. 'C'mon, wot's up now, y'great miseryguts?'

Cardo shrugged. 'Don't know, Vurg, just got a bad feelin' an' I can't explain it. Somethin' seems wrong.'

Denno nudged Vurg, pulling a wry face at the unhappy cook. 'Oh dearie me, just like the ole farm mouse, nothin's right.'

Coll winked at him. 'Which farm mouse was that, matey?'

Denno began tapping a beat on the tabletop.

'There was an ole farm mouse, lived in an ole
    farmhouse,
Who always thought of a reason,
To rant an' complain, again an' again,
Whatever the weather or season.

If rain came down, he'd scowl an' frown,
Shake a paw at the sky an' say,
"Rains like these are good for the peas,
But they ain't much use for me hay!"

Then if wind came along, he'd change his song,
Cryin' out "Oh woe lackaday,
'Tis all I need, a wind indeed,
To blow all me apples away!"

He'd gnash his teeth about shaded wheat,
At the sign of a cloud in the skies,
An' the very sight o' cloudless sunlight,
Would bring tears to both his eyes.

He'd simmer'n'boil, as he pawed the soil,
An' got himself worried an' fussed,
"Lookit that sunlight, 'tis far too bright,
'Twill turn all me soil to dust!"

Oh botheration trouble an' toil,
Life don't get peaceful or calmer,
If I'd gone to sea, a sailor I'd be,
Instead of an ole mouse farmer.'

The crew were all laughing heartily when Cardo said,
'What's so funny? We were all farmers once.'

The laughter died on their lips. Luke patted Cardo. 'Aye, yore right there, mate. Farmers we were, fightin' the weather an' seasons to put food on the table. We didn't have much, but we were happy with our wives an' families until Vilu Daskar an' his red ship showed up. Now we're seamice, rovers, fightin' evil an' ill fortune. Though I tell you this: one day, when 'tis all over, we'll return home an' pick up the threads of our old lives again.'

Outside the elements increased their fury. Thunder reverberated overhead, rain lashed the heaving seas and flaming webs of chain lightning threatened to rip the darkened skies with their ferocity. The crew of the *Sayna*, without guard or watch on the galeswept decks, allowed sleep to close their weary eyes.

Most of the night the storm prevailed. Three hours before dawn a strong warm wind blew up from the south. Driving the tempest before it like a rumbling cattle herd, it hurtled on northward. Peace and calm was restored to the seas in its wake. Humidity returned, bringing with it a dense foggy bank, which hung over the Twin Islands and their channel like a pall.

The *Goreleech* put out to sea, then Vilu Daskar ordered her turned about, a league out, to face the channel. An hour before dawn he gave the command.

'Bullflay, tell your drummer to beat out full speed. Don't spare the whips. I want this ship to run up that channel as if hellhounds were chasing it. Stand ready, my scurvy Sea Rogues, there's slaves to be taken!'

29

Vurg woke with a raging thirst. He got up quietly, so as not to disturb his sleeping crewmates, and picked his way through the darkened cabin to the door. It was foggy on deck, silent and damp. Vurg padded to the galley, dipped a ladle into the water barrel and drank deeply. A second measure of water he tipped over his head to waken himself properly. He was about to start lighting the galley fire from last night's glowing embers, so that Cardo would have a good fire to cook breakfast, when he heard the sounds.

It was like a steady drumbeat and a deep swishing noise which grew louder by the moment. The noises seemed to be coming from somewhere further up the channel. Vurg made his way to the forepeak. Leaning out, he strained his eyes against the blanket of milky white mist. The sounds increased in volume, and the *Sayna* began to bob gently up and down on some kind of swell. That was when the world turned red!

Towering over him like an immense leviathan, the *Goreleech* came thundering down upon the ship *Sayna*. Vurg was flung high into the air, and landed hard on a rock in the shallows, swallowed by the merciful blackness of unconsciousness. A horrendous rending of ship's timbers rent the air as the *Goreleech* ploughed into the *Sayna*, ripping the entire starboard side out from stem to stern. Masts fell before the wicked iron spike on the red ship's prow, snapping off like dried twigs. Vilu Daskar roared with evil joy at the sound of screaming crewbeasts in shock.

Half stunned, Luke splashed about in the water. He grabbed a floating object for support. It was Cardo. The dead cook's eyes stared unseeingly into his until Cardo sank slowly beneath the channel. Luke came to life then. Bellowing like a creature possessed, he seized a rope trailing from the red ship's side and began hauling himself, paw over paw, up the *Goreleech*'s massive hull. Soaked, bruised and weaponless, the Warrior climbed with the speed of fury, grappling his way over carved galleries, swarming over the heavy seawet mats of rope fenders.

Vilu Daskar was just turning to shout further orders to his vermin crew when Luke came storming over the gallery rail. He was upon the pirate stoat like a wolf, grabbing him round the neck. Both beasts crashed to the deck, Luke's eyes filled with bloodlight as he throttled his mortal enemy. Vilu Daskar could do nothing against the Warrior's furious strength. He saw crewbeasts dashing to his aid and managed a panicked gurgle. Akkla swung a belaying pin, once, twice, thrice, to the back of Luke's unprotected skull. Another two crashing blows laid the Warrior mouse low, and Vilu slipped from his faltering grasp. Vermin crewbeasts rushed the stoat captain to his cabin, where he lay on a table, making a croaking sound as they forced warmed wine between his lips. He reeled off the table, nursing his neck with a silken cloth.

'Dirr . . .we . . . sinkam?'

Bullflay stared at Akkla. 'Wot did 'e say?'

The ferret turned to Vilu. 'Don't try to talk, sire, yore throat's damaged. Aye, we sunk 'er all right. Crew's just draggin' aboard any mice that are still livin'.'

Still clutching the silken cloth about his neck, Daskar

staggered out on deck. Bullflay waddled ahead of him, drawing a cutlass and straddling the limp form of Luke. 'This's the one who strangled yer, lord. Let's see if'n I kin take off 'is 'ead wid one swipe!'

Vilu kicked the slavemaster, sending him sprawling. 'Gggghaaa, I wan' 'im alive. Hhhhraaaggghh!'

The pirate stoat tottered unsteadily back to his cabin. When the door slammed, Fleabitt whispered to Grigg, 'Talks awful funny, don't 'e?'

'So would you if'n you'd been near throttled ter death,' Grigg whispered back. 'Better not let 'im 'ear y'say that 'e talks funny, or you won't 'ave a tongue t'talk wid at all, matey!'

Dulam was chained to deckrings like the others of the *Sayna*'s crew who had survived the ramming. He dabbed gently at the back of Luke's head with his wet tunic, but it was some considerable time before the Warrior began to stir and show signs of coming round. On his other side, Denno pressed Luke gently back to the deck. 'Lie still, mate. You should be dead by rights, the poundin' yore head took back there. I saw it as I was hauled aboard.'

Luke lay still, eyes closed, head throbbing unmercifully. 'What about our crew?'

He felt Denno's tears drip on to his paw as he said, 'There's only us three left, Luke: you, me'n'Dulam.'

Luke felt numb. He could hear his own voice echoing in his ears. 'I saw Cardo, but Coll and Cordle and the others . . . Vurg! Where's Vurg?'

A seaboot thumped cruelly into his side. Bosun Parug stood over them, grinning.

'Fishbait the lot of 'em. Bit of a mistake, us 'ittin' yore ship so 'ard. Shoulda just sneaked up an' burned it, then we would've caught ye one by one as y'dived inna water.' He kicked Luke once more, obviously enjoying himself. 'Huh, three mis-rubble prisoners. 'Twas 'ardly worth it. Three mice! Hah! May's well call it two, 'cos cap'n Vilu's got special plans fer you, bucko. I never knew a beast laid paws on Vilu Daskar an' lived t'see the sun go down. I'd 'ate t'be you, mouse. Death'll come as a mercy to ye when the cap'n's finished wid yer!'

But Luke was hardly listening. He was consumed with grief and guilt over his slain crew. Mentally he told himself that this was the second time he had lost dear ones by leaving them unguarded. It did not matter what happened to him now, though there was one thing he longed for ere death claimed him. One chance, just one opportunity to slay Vilu Daskar!

Twin Islands lay bright and still in the afternoon sunlight. The fog had gone; so had Vilu Daskar and the *Goreleech*. Slowly Vurg became aware of a tickling sensation on his face. A tiny hermit crab, burdened by a periwinkle shell, was dragging itself across his cheek. He brushed it aside and sat up, wincing. From jaw to ear his cheek was purple and swollen. Finding a pawful of cool wet kelp he bathed it gingerly as memory flooded back. The *Sayna*, her crew, Luke, the red ship looming out of the fog!

Vurg leaped up. Sloshing through the shallows, he climbed up on his ship's wrecked hull, looking desperately this way and that. Far off out to sea, sailing north by east, he saw the *Goreleech* ploughing the main. Scrambling down into the wreckage, Vurg ignored the splitting ache in his face and head and shouted aloud, 'Luke! Cordle! Denno! Ahoy, mates, anybeast aboard? Coll! Dulam! Where are you?'

Ripping away broken spars and dragging damp canvas out of his way, Vurg forced an entrance to the shattered main cabin. Coll was there, pierced through by a splintered bulkhead spar, his body swaying gently in waist-deep seawater. Yelling in horror Vurg fled the cabin, flinging himself from the wrecked vessel on to the shore. Cardo was the second one he found, lodged underwater beneath the prow.

Vurg sat on the warm sand, his head in both paws, sobbing uncontrollably. He was alone, all the friends he had sailed with from the northlands shore gone, slain or taken captive aboard the hated red ship.

Sometime towards evening he fell asleep, stretched out above the tideline, numb with grief and aching all over. How long he lay there Vurg had no way of knowing, other than that it was dark when he opened his eyes. But that was not what had wakened him. Somebeast was close by. Vurg did not move. He lay, fully alert now, with his eyes half open, scanning the area around him. He heard noises, a damp scraping sound, coming from behind the *Sayna*'s smashed stern.

Vurg rose until he was on all fours, carefully, silently, making his way to the water's edge. Gritting his teeth with satisfaction he found a broken spearhead, with half the shaft still attached. Wading quietly into the water, he made his way along the *Sayna*'s hull to the stern. He saw a dark shape on the beach, scraping away at the sand with a chunk of flat wood. Gripping the broken spear tightly, Vurg sneaked up from behind and flung himself upon the creature, yelling as he locked a paw about its neck, 'Yaah! You filthy murderin' sum, I'll kill ye stone dead!'

However, killing the creature was not so easy. It lashed out with long hind legs, batted Vurg hard with the chunk of wood, doubled up and sent him sailing over its head. Like a flash his adversary was upon him, forcing his face down into the sand.

A familiar voice rang in Vurg's ears. 'I say, steady on there, old lad, wot wot!'

Vurg managed to push his head up and shout, 'Beau, it's me, Vurg!'

The hare rolled off him, pulling him upright and dusting sand away from his face.

'Well bless m'paws, so it is. Why didn't y'say so, instead of pouncin' on a chap like that? Didn't hurt you, did I?'

Vurg could not help himself. He hugged Beau and kissed both his cheeks soundly, weeping unashamedly.

'Oh, Beau, Beau, I thought you were drowned long ago!'

The hare managed to extricate himself from the tearful crewmouse and held him off with both paws. 'Well, if I wasn't drowned then I soon would be with you jolly well cryin' an' weepin' all over me, wot!'

Vurg stood staring stupidly at Beau. 'Then you weren't drowned when you fell overboard?'

Beau could not resist striking a noble pose. 'Drowned, me laddie? Pish tush an' fiddledy wotsit! Us Fethringsol Cosfortinghams don't sink that easily, just 'cos some confounded storm chucked me in the briny, an' not for the first time let me remark. Well, says I to m'self, let blinkin' Ma Nature use other fools as fish food, not me, sir! So I struck out for the old terra firma, an' stap me vitals if I didn't land up at Twin Islands. Had t'live on the far isle, of course – pesky little insects on this one would eat a body alive if you let 'em, wot.'

Immensely cheered by the fact that he was no longer alone, Vurg smiled and clasped his friend's paw firmly. 'But you're alive, that's the main thing!'

The irrepressible hare winked fondly at Vurg. 'Pretty much alive, apart from havin' me paw squashed by some hulkin' great mouse. Righto, companion o' mine, come on. We'll cross the channel on to my island an' have a bite to eat whilst we swap yarns. Howzat suit you, ole mousechap?'

Vurg released Beau's paw and turned away. 'There's something I've got to do first. My shipmates . . .'

Beau sniffed. One of his long ears flopped down to wipe an eye before he answered, 'Say no more, friend. I buried them m'self while you were sleepin'. Just finished the job when you sneaked up an' tried playin' piggyback with me, wot! Don't fret, old fellow, I've put the *Sayna*'s crew t'rest in the shadow of their own ship.'

Together they waded into the channel. However, Vurg still had a question to ask. 'Was the whole crew slain, Beau?'

'Sadly most of 'em were, Vurg, though I never found Luke or wotsisname an' the other chap, er, Dulam an' Denno, that's 'em. Which means they were certainly taken for slaves aboard that foul vessel *Goreleech*. So, all in all there's four of the old gang left, five countin' yours truly. Hang tight to my paw now, gets rather deep here. We'll have to jolly well swim for it, wot wot. Chin up an' strike out!'

When they reached the far island it was quite a climb to Beau's den. He had made it over the far side of the hill, facing out to the open sea. Because of this, Beau had not known about either the *Goreleech* or the *Sayna* until it was too late. But, as Vurg realised, there was little he could have done anyway against the red ship's crew.

The den was a small cave halfway down the big hill. Beau had made it comfortable and foraged around the island to provide food. Kindling a fire he put dandelion tea on to brew and produced a meal with his own gatherings and a few things they had managed to salvage from the *Sayna*'s galley.

Warming himself by the fire, Vurg allowed Beau to inspect his wounds.

'Hmm, that's a rather attractive shade of purple on your face there, old thing. Have t'make a compound, take out the pain an' swellin'. Cheer up, Vurg, you'll be as good as new in a day or two, my old nautical matey!'

Vurg heaved a sigh and gazed out to sea. 'What do we do then, Beau?'

The hare sliced himself a wedge of fruitcake from the *Sayna*'s stores, adding it to his plate of island salad. 'What do we do then? Why, we sit here an' chunner whilst we grow old together, like two proper desert isle hermits, m'friend. Huh, an' if y'think that you're a nincompoop! Do? I'll tell you what we're goin' t'do, laddie buck. Make a boat from the wreckage of our ship *Sayna* an' sail after the red ship. Rescue our friends an' if we get half a bally chance we're goin' to put paid to that evil blaggard who calls himself a captain. Disgrace to the blinkin' rank. Right?'

Vurg locked paws with his friend. 'Right, Beau. And the sooner we get started the better, mate!'

30

The crew of Vilu Daskar had a special name for the *Goreleech's* bottom deck: the Death Pit. After two days chained to an oar down there, Luke knew the place was aptly named. In hot weather it was airless and foul; when seas were rough it was awash with stinking bilgewater. Wretched slaves, chained in pairs at each oar, port and starboard, lived and died there under the lash of Bullflay, the fat sadistic slavemaster, and Fleabitt the drummer, his cruel assistant. Both these creatures delighted in tormenting the helpless oarslaves, withholding drinking water, taunting the sick and generally enjoying the misery they heaped without mercy on their helpless victims.

Luke found himself up at the for'ard end, pulling an oar alone, singled out for special treatment under Bullflay's watchful eye. Before chaining his paws to the oar, Parug shackled the new slave's footpaws to a long running chain, stapled at intervals to the deck. The searat bosun pointed out the reason for this.

'Just in case the oar snaps an' you thinks yore loose to escape, well you ain't. This 'ere chain joins youse all to the ship. If it sinks, you go t'the bottom with 'er!'

If Luke turned his head slightly right, he could see

Dulam and Denno, manacled to an oar on the other side of the aisle, about three rows back.

Bullflay's whip cracked, its tip catching Luke's ear. 'Git yore eyes front, mouse, or I'll flick 'em out with this whip. Yore down 'ere t'row, not look at the scenery!' He strode off down the centre aisle, laying about him. 'Bend yer backs, lazy scum, put some energy into it, cummon!'

Fortunately a strong breeze sprang up later in the day. Fleabitt stopped drumming and gave the order to ship oars. A pannikin of brackish water and a hard rye crust was issued to each slave. Bullflay and Fleabitt went up on deck, to eat in the fresh air. Luke tugged at his pawchains, calling across to his neighbour, 'Do they often leave us alone like this?'

Norgle the otter, seated behind on the right, answered, 'Huh, where are we goin' to run to, matey, or are we fit enough t'bite through these chains?'

Another voice growled, 'I'll find a way to break 'em someday!'

Luke could not help himself staring across at the creature who had spoken. Directly opposite, chained singly to an oar, just as Luke was, sat a ferocious black squirrel. Everything about her, from the scars to the savage glowing eyes, bespoke the fact that here was a warrior. He felt an immediate kinship with the dangerous beast. She spoke again.

'Look around. All these poor creatures are defeated, because they are slaves, in chains. But Vilu Daskar could not chain the heart, mind, or blood of Ranguvar Foeseeker. Aye, I'll bite through these chains one day, then I'll slay Vilu Daskar, Bullflay, Fleabitt an' as many of 'em as I can, until they bring me down an' slay me!'

Luke stretched his paw until the chains cut into him. 'I am Luke the Warrior and I swear on the memory of my dead wife Sayna that we will break these shackles together, Ranguvar Foeseeker. I will stand beside you when the time comes, and we will take many with us before we fall!'

Ranguvar stretched her paw across to Luke. Where the chains cut the flesh, blood mingled from both creatures' wounds.

'We will do it together, Luke. I have waited long for another warrior to come to the red ship. You are here now!'

Gazing into the fearless dark eyes of Ranguvar, Luke had no doubt that they could accomplish anything together. Murmurings came from all around the bottom deck. Denno spoke for everybeast as he called out, 'We'll be with you, to the death!'

Luke smiled grimly. 'Good! But we need a plan.'

By next morning Vilu Daskar had regained his voice, though he still kept the dark bruises on his neck covered with a white silken scarf. Accompanied by Parug and Akkla he descended to the lower deck and paid Luke a visit. The stoat captain held the scarf end to his nose as the vile reek of the Death Pit assailed his nostrils. Luke kept his eyes down as Daskar addressed him.

'So, mouse, why does a creature in a small ship follow my *Goreleech*? Surely you must have known you had no chance against the red ship. Why did you do it?'

Luke made no reply. The blade of Vilu's bone-handled scimitar slid along Luke's neck and lifted his chin until he was looking into the stoat's eyes. Still he did not speak. Daskar raised his eyebrows and nodded. 'Speak or I'll slit your gizzard. Why were you following me?' Though the sharp blade was pressing on his neck, Luke closed his eyes and held the silence. 'I warn you, mouse, talk, or you're a deadbeast!' To add weight to the threat, Vilu swung the blade high over Luke's head, bracing himself for the strike.

'No, wait! Don't kill our cap'n. I'll tell ye, sire!'

All eyes turned on Denno, who was waving his paws agitatedly. 'Please spare the cap'n, please, sire. I'll tell you all!'

Vilu strode over to Denno, chuckling. 'Loyalty to one's captain, a wonderful thing. I wish that my crew of sea scrapings showed that faith in me. But then they wouldn't be Sea Rogues, would they? So, loyal mouse, save your captain's life. Tell me why your silly little tub was pursuing the mighty *Goreleech*?'

Denno's face was a picture of simple honesty as he explained, 'Do you recall the northland shore, sire? We followed you from there to avenge our families.'

Vilu's paw tapped the bone scimitar handle pensively. 'Northland shore, hmmm. Ah yes, I remember now. Bunch of mice, fools, burning a fire like a signal beacon on the beach. Aye, they were all either too young, too old, or too weak to make oarslaves of. We slew them for fun and ate their food. Oh dear, were they your families? Well, never mind, they provided a bit of amusement for my crew. By the way, where were you and all the able-bodied ones whilst this was going on, eh? Probably hiding somewhere to save your own skins, I shouldn't wonder.'

Seated next to Denno, Dulam's fetters clanked as he struggled to rise, tears streaming down his cheeks. 'That's a lie! If we'd've been there we would have fought you murderers down to the last beast!'

Vilu smiled condescendingly. 'But instead you chose to go off and gather daisies.'

Dulam's whole body was shaking with rage. 'No we never!' he blurted out. 'We were up the coast by the tall rocks, keepin' lookout while Luke and the others buried our tre—'

'Shut yore mouth, idiot!' Luke shouted.

Vilu turned to Parug and Akkla, smiling triumphantly. 'Unchain these two and their captain. Bring them to my cabin.'

As they unshackled Luke, he glanced across to Ranguvar and winked. The plan was beginning to work.

The three mice were hustled roughly into Vilu Daskar's

cabin, where they were lined up in front of an ornate table. Lounging behind it in a magnificent carved chair, Vilu watched as his servants laid out wine, baked fish, preserved fruits and bread, fresh from the ovens. He picked at the feast, whilst Luke and his friends stood dull-eyed and hungry, trying to ignore the wonderful food. Akkla, Parug and Bullflay stood by awaiting orders.

Vilu dabbed the silken scarf across his lips, weighing the three slaves up carefully. He addressed Denno.

'You, tell me what it is you were hiding up the coast in the tall rocks. But take care. One false word, one little lie, and I will hang both your friend and your captain from the mainmast, where their bodies will stay until they rot and seabirds pick at their bones. But speak truly and I will give you all your freedom, once I have what you hid in the tall rocks. That is your choice. Now speak.'

Denno glanced apologetically in Luke's direction, then said, 'It was the treasure of our tribe, sire. We had travelled many seasons, guarding it from foebeasts. Havin' chosen the northland shore as our new home, we searched out a safe place to hide it. Among the tall rocks, further north.'

Luke was glaring angrily at Denno. Vilu smiled at the Warrior mouse in mock surprise.

'Now now, don't pull faces at your friend. He's just saved your life and bought your freedom. Let's hear you speak your piece now. Tell us about this treasure, or I'll hang both of these mice in your place and you can watch them dangle!'

An expression of defeat replaced Luke's glare, and he sighed. 'Only if you promise to spare our lives and set us free once you have the treasure.'

Vilu spread his paws disarmingly. 'Akkla, Parug, Bullflay, tell this mouse about my word.'

The three vermin nodded vigorously.

'Oh aye, the cap'n never lies!'

'You can rely on that, mouse!'

'I'll take me oath on it!'

Vilu took a sip of wine and dabbed his lips. 'See?'

Luke told him what he wanted to hear. ''Tis a great treasure, plates, chalices, daggers an' swords, all wrought of gold'n'silver, studded with many jewels.'

The pirate stoat nodded approvingly. 'Just as I thought. Now tell me the exact location. Where did you hide it?'

Luke stared levelly at Vilu Daskar.

'Only three creatures went among the tall rocks to hide that treasure, myself, Vurg and Cardo. I am the only one you left alive out of the three, so only I know the true location. But I am not a fool, Vilu Daskar. I do not trust the word of a murderer, so I will not tell you, no matter what you do to me or my friends. However, I have a proposition for you. Set sail for the northland shore, and when we reach there I will pilot your red ship up the coast and steer you to the spot. That way you will have to keep us alive, at least until you have the treasure. Agreed?'

Bullflay grabbed Luke and raised a belaying pin, but Vilu held up a paw and stopped him.

'Release him, Bullflay. I like this mouse. It will be a change to do business with a creature who has a brain. Good enough. I agree to your proposition, mouse.'

Luke could not resist a parting dig at his enemy. 'You have no choice but to agree. Dead mice cannot find the treasure for you.'

Vilu popped a piece of preserved fruit into his mouth. 'How wise of you. Of course I must keep you alive. Meanwhile, days and nights spent in the Death Pit will make you realise how wonderful freedom will be when you eventually gain it. Bullflay, you can be as hard on them as you please, as long as you keep them alive. Go now!'

That night, as Bullflay lay snoring on a heap of old fenders and Fleabitt dozed with his head resting on the drum, Luke winked at his two friends. 'Well done, mateys. You played yore parts well!'

Ranguvar Foeseeker whispered across to Luke, 'I think I can feel this staple startin' to move!' The black squirrel had wrapped a piece of rag around her pawchains, and had been silently heaving and levering for many hours. Only after much strain and effort was the heavy iron staple, which held the running chain that connected all the footpaw shackles to it, beginning to move in the damp solid deck timbers. For the first time since he had been aboard the *Goreleech*, Luke smiled.

'Keep at it, Ranguvar. Once you've got the staple out pass it over to me, mate!'

The *Goreleech* dipped her high bows into the trackless waste of the main, bound north into the night, the red sails bellied to the wind. On she went, like a giant blood-coloured bird of ill omen, sated on a cargo of misery.

Vurg was sweating in the sun, prying timbers loose from the wreckage of the *Sayna*. Beau was sawing away at some sail canvas with a rusty dagger. Beside them on the sand a mishmashed pile of timber and cordage was bound together in the rough shape of a raft.

'I say, old thing,' the hare called up to his companion, 'we'll need somethin' a bit straighter than that rib plank t'make a blinkin' mast, wot?'

Vurg wiped his brow in exasperation. 'Well it's the straightest piece I can find. I'm a farmer, not a boat builder. If'n you can find a better bit o' wood, matey, then yore welcome t'try!'

As he hacked away at the canvas, Beau nicked his ear when the dagger point tore free and shot upward.

'Well keep your fur on there, mousey, I thought the flippin' agreement was that I built the perishin' raft an' you supplied the bally materials. Hold y'temper in the ranks, wot wot, I nearly chopped my ear off there whilst you were yammerin' on at me like an old frogwife!'

Vurg left off prying loose timbers. Sucking at a splinter in his paw, he climbed down to join Beau.

'Owch! There's so many splinters in me I'd float if'n I fell into the sea, mate. How's our raft comin' along?'

The hare stood paws akimbo, surveying his work. 'Oh, splendid, absojollylutely spiffin'! All she needs is a jib boom, spanker, top royal gallants an' mizzen shrouds!'

Vurg peered at him questioningly. 'D'you know wot yore talkin' about?'

Beau leaned against the raft. It collapsed. 'No, d'you?'

'Yeeeehawhawhaw! Y'ain't figgerin' on goin' ter sea on that thing, are yer, mates? Yukyukyukyuk, worra mess!'

Beau and Vurg were astonished to see a large fat sea lion basking in the channel, watching them. Patting a bulging stomach with both flippers, he snorted a cloud of droplets from his bristling whiskers and chortled heartily.

'Yukyukyukyuk! Looks more like a mad seagull's nest than a raft. Only place you'd go on that termites' brekkist is straight t'the bottom. Yukyukyuk!'

Vurg stood open-mouthed, but Beau recovered his composure smartly, twitching his ears disdainfully at the creature.

'Mad seagull's nest? Termites' breakfast? Have a care there, chubbychops, wot wot! My old auntie used t'say, don't criticise what y'can't do y'self. Pity you never met her!'

Floating flat on his back, the sea lion blew a jet of water on to his stomach and watched it evaporate in the sun. 'Aye, more's the pity, flop-ears. I 'ad an ole auntie once, got 'erself et by a shark, cheered my ole uncle up no end. She was a grouchy beast at best o' times.'

Beau drew himself up to his full lanky height. 'Call me flop-ears once more an' I'll wade out there an' chastise you severely, m'good feller. Name's Beauclair Fethringsol Cosfortingham, Beau f'short. Now, what appellation d'you answer to? Speak up, wot?'

Paddling into the shallows, the sea lion beached himself like a glistening grey rock on the sand. He grinned as he extended a flipper the size of a small table.

'Ain't got a h'allepation. They calls me Bolwag, pleased t'meet ye, Beau, an' yore liddle mouseymate there.'

Vurg shook the proffered flipper. 'My name's Vurg!'

Bolwag heaved his bulk further up, and galumphed around the raft, inspecting it.

'Seen a lot better, an' one or two worse. Not much of a craft t'go chasin' after the red ship, though, is she?'

Vurg looked up curiously at the gigantic sea lion. 'How did you know we were goin' after the red ship?'

Bolwag sorted through the mess of timbers with flipper and muzzle, sending planks flying. 'Watched it come'n'go fer many a season, Vurg. Saw what happened to your mates. That ole cap'n, Vilu Daskar, he's worse'n any shark, evil beast!'

Beau began picking up the planking. 'I say there, Bolwag, d'you mind not chuckin' our raft around like that? Took us long enough t'put it together, wot. Of course we'll be sailin' blind, haven't a bally clue where old Vilu wotsischops has sailed off to.'

Bolwag nodded his great head wisely. 'I know which way the red ship's bound. Always goes the same course when it leaves 'ere. North'n'west two points, to Wood Isle. Takes on water'n'provisions there.'

Vurg peered upchannel to the open sea. 'Wood Isle? Have you been there, Bolwag? Will you show us the way to this place?'

Bolwag frowned, then his whiskers split into a huge grin. 'Suppose I'll 'ave to, matey. Couldn't let a pair o' liddle sardines like you two go twiddlin' round alone out there. Beau's ole auntie might never clap eyes on 'im agin, and we can't 'ave that now, can we? But first let's git yore raft built proper'n'seaworthy. You lay out a good crisscross of timbers on a big piece o' canvas, I'll go an' fetch some bladderwrack – grows big in these warm waters. Git t'work, an' I'll be back afore you knows it, mates!'

Neither Beau nor Vurg had the least idea what bladderwrack was. They stretched the biggest canvas sail on the sand and began laying a grid shape of ship's timbers on it. Bolwag returned, though at first it was hard to tell whether it was he, because a huge clump of sea-weed surrounded the sea lion's body as he swam, towing it with him. With a powerful heave he flung it ashore.

'Bladderwrack, buckoes. Nothin' like it fer keepin' afloat!'

It was slimy, slippery seaweed, but studded with big inflated air bubbles.

Bolwag winked at them. 'Cover those timbers with it, an' lay on more timber atop o' the bladderwrack. I'll go an' get some more.'

The process was repeated three more times, after which they cloaked the lot with the sailcloth ends. Under Bolwag's directions, Vurg and Beau laced the canvas casing tight with rope until the sea lion was satisfied with the job. It looked an ungainly bundle.

Vurg bounced up and down on it. 'Haha, 'tis springy enough. Will we need a sail, Bolwag?'

'Nah, I'll be either pushin' or pullin' all the way. Well, it don't look like much, me 'earties, but 'tis tight'n'strong an' 'twill get you to Wood Isle without sinkin'.'

Afternoon was well advanced when they loaded the last provisions aboard and launched the odd-looking raft into the channel. Bolwag grabbed a trailing line in his mouth and went off like a fish. At first Beau and Vurg clung to one another on the skimming, bobbing raft as it bounced and cavorted across the wavetops. However, after a while they became used to the momentum and sat sharing some bread and cheese. Heading north and west they sped onward, creating a small bow wave of spray, though it was hard to tell exactly where the raft's bows were located, as it swivelled from side to side. Bolwag kept the sunset in the corner of his left eye as he pulled them effortlessly along.

Beau waxed lyrical at approaching evening. 'Does somethin' to a chap, the old sunset, rather jolly, wot. Sky goes the colour of meadowcream when y'stir it into a plate of damson pudden, sea's as dark as blackcurrant cordial, an' the sun looks like a rosy apple covered with honey. I say, Vurg old lad, rather poetic, wot wot?'

Vurg hid a smile. 'Did you compose that with your stomach?'

Beau grinned. 'Yes, it did sound rather gutsy, didn't it! Oh I say, nothin' to ruin a perfect evenin' like a great pack o' sharks. Just look at that lot!'

Vurg saw the ominous fins cutting through the water until they surrounded the raft. Suddenly the whole craft swayed threateningly as Bolwag flopped aboard. Beau threw himself on top of the sea lion, grabbing at his slippery hide with all paws and roaring heroically.

'I've got you, old fellow. They'll have t'deal with me before I'll let 'em get to you. Ahoy an' belay, you slab-sided swabs. Scuttle me bilges an' other nautical terms, show me a shark an' I'll show you a coward! Take one bite out of our raft, just one munch, I dare you! I'll leap into the briny an' give you a sound drubbin'! Hah, y'dealin' with a Cosfortingham now, wot wot!'

Bolwag shrugged his huge bulk, sending Beau toppling into the sea. The hare yelled out in panic.

'Didn't mean it, only jokin' you chaps, there, there, nice sharky, good sharky. Yowoops!'

One of the big fishes flicked his tail, catching Beau and sending him sailing back on to the raft.

Bolwag chuckled. 'Yukyukyukyuk! Don't yer know a bottlenose when y'sees one?'

Beau clung to Bolwag's flipper, shivering. 'Keep mum, old chap. Don't go callin' 'em names like bottlenose – you'll get 'em mad an' they'll scoff the raft. Nice sharks, good sharks. I say, aren't sharks handsome chaps?'

Bolwag's stomach shook as he laughed. 'Yukyukyukyuk! Those aren't sharks, ye great booby, they're pals o' mine, bottlenosed dolphins. They offered t'push awhile an' let me 'ave a rest!'

Vurg smiled at his irrepressible friend. Beau regained his composure quickly in any situation.

'Pish tush, sah, I knew that all along, what d'ye take me for, wot? Sharks indeed. What gave y'that idea?' He leaned over the raft's edge and patted the strange beak-shaped snout of the nearest dolphin, which stuck its permanently smiling face out of the sea as Beau nodded to it. 'Ahoy there, you jolly bottlenosed rogue, what d'you mean by impersonatin' a flippin' shark? Wipe that smile off your face an' answer me, laddie!'

The big fish gave an earsplittin' squeak and shot a jet of water into Beau's astonished face. He sat back wiping water from his eyes, remarking to Vurg, 'Pity that chap never had an auntie to teach him a few manners, wot. Spittin' seawater into a feller's fizzog, huh, very nice, I don't think!'

Bolwag flapped Beau's ears gently with his huge flipper. 'Don't you go talkin' about my pals like that, matey. Kweekum an' his school 'ave been friends o' mine since I was a pup!'

Whilst Bolwag held an unintelligible conversation, which consisted of exchanging varying degrees of squeaks with Kweekum, Beau whispered to Vurg, 'Tchah! School indeed. Only school that chap ever attended was the school of spittin'. I'd give him detention or a few whacks of the cane if I was his schoolmaster, wot! Blighter can't even speak without squeakin' like a confounded seagull. I'll bet all the baby bottlenoses are a right shower of yahoos. Still, y'can't expect any better if you're brought up with a name like bottlenose, I suppose, wot wot?'

Over a score of dolphins were around the raft, propelling it along at an alarming rate. Every so often, an extra frisky one would jump out of the sea and leap clear over the raft. Vurg sat awake, excited and astounded by it all. Beau tried to sleep, stuffing a piece of bladderwrack in both ears, muttering to himself, 'Fat chance of shuteye a chap's got round here. Great lump of a Bolwag, snorin' away like a thousand frogs on concert night, an' those pesky bottlenoses squeakin' like a pile o' rusty gates, not the sort o' thing a Cosfortingham's used to at all. Indeed not. Good job auntie's not here!'

However, despite the intrusions, Beauclair Fethringsol Cosfortingham was soon adding to the din, snoring uproariously and chunnering on in his dreams through the night watches as the strange craft hurtled towards its destination over the sprawling main.

'Hmm, mm, wot? Pass the salad there, auntie, an' tell the cap'n to stop the boat rockin', will you? Mmm, mm. No thanks, old chap, couldn't touch another bowl of that bladderwrack pudden, foul stuff. Give it to old bottlenose for school lunch, will you, sharks like that sort o' thing. Mmm mm, wot!'

31

Bullflay cracked his whip over the heads of the wretched rowers chained to the decks of the Death Pit.

'Back water an' ship oars, you idle bunch o' landspawn! Sit still there, not a word or a move, or I'll 'ave the hide off yore backs 'til yer bones shows through!'

Luke heard the anchor splash as he drew his oar inboard. Placing a cheek flat on the oarshaft he tried looking through the rowing port, but it was a very limited view. Shallow clear water, a white sand beach and just a glimpse of heavily wooded rocks. Norgle the otter, who had his head bent in similar fashion, murmured to Luke, 'I always hate makin' landfall. Makes me sick t'me stummick, thinkin' of green growin' things, firm ground under me paws, an' livin' free like I once was.'

The otter flinched numbly as the lash descended across his back. Fleabitt the rat stood wielding his own personal whip, sneering at the chained Norgle.

'Then don't think, oarscum. Mister Bullflay told yer not to move or speak, now I'm tellin' yer not to think, see!' He turned as chains rattled nearby. Ranguvar was sitting up straight, her mad eyes boring into the rat.

'Try that on me, ratface. I'm thinkin' – aye, *thinkin'* I'd like to get just one paw round your louse-ridden throat.

Go on, swing that lash, see if y'can stop me thinkin'!'

Fleabitt wilted under the black squirrel's gaze, and fled the bottom deck, following Bullflay without a word.

Vilu Daskar came out of his cabin, the silken scarf still bound round his neck, which was permanently marked from Luke's attack upon him. He cleared his throat painfully and beckoned to the two ferrets, Akkla and Ringpatch. They hurried to his side for orders.

'Break out the neckchains. We need watercask carriers and food gatherers. Choose a party, but only from the top deck. Take enough crew with you, so that you have two to each one slave. We'll lay over here two nights for provisioning. If any slave escapes you'll answer to me with your lives.'

Vilu stood waiting whilst two searats set up a chair and table on the stern deck. When a canopy had been rigged over the chair and food put on the table, he sat down. 'Willag, Grigg, Bullflay, bring the mouse Luke to me.'

Luke was freed from his oar shackles and fitted with a neckchain attached to paw manacles. Bullflay raised his whip. 'Up on deck, mouse, move yerself!'

Luke smiled contemptuously at the slavemaster. 'Bring that whip down on me an' I'll strangle ye with it!'

Bullflay's paw faltered, and he let the whip fall to his side. Sometimes he was not sure who he feared the most, the black squirrel, or the Warrior mouse. Luke strode past him, head held high, giving a broad wink to Dulam and Denno as he passed them on his way to the stairs.

Vilu Daskar popped a wild grape into his mouth, chewing it slowly as he looked Luke up and down. 'Willag, bring a chair for our guest.'

The Warrior dismissed the offer with two words. 'I'll stand.'

Indicating the roast seabird, fruit and wine, Vilu said, 'Suit yourself, Luke. Here, you must be hungry. Have some food and drink. It's good – I'm only served the best.'

Though Luke's mouth was watering at the sight of the victuals on the table, he shook his head. 'I don't eat food from the table of a murderer.'

Vilu shrugged. 'Have it your own way. I brought you up here because I want to hear more about this treasure you have hidden. Where did you come by it?'

The reply Vilu received was flat and harsh. 'I've told you all, I'll take you to it, there's nothing more to say.'

Vilu's bone-handled scimitar was out, its tip under Luke's chin.

'There are many ways to die: quickly, with a single stroke, or slowly, painfully, bit by bit. Now talk!'

Luke's chained paws rose, and he pushed the blade aside. 'If I die swift or slow, you will never find the hiding place. Remember, murderer, I am the only beast alive who knows where it is. Kill me or my friends and you will never possess a single piece of my tribe's treasure.'

Vilu stuck the bladepoint down into the deck timbers, and the scimitar stood quivering. He nodded and smiled. 'You're a strange and reckless creature, Luke, different from the rest. A brave beast like you would go far in my crew, maybe even standing at my side, second in command.'

Luke smiled back at him. 'Aye, Daskar, then you could make me a real warrior, teach me how to plunder defenceless ones, murder innocent creatures and run away to hide aboard this red ship. You and your Sea Rogues would never stand up to real warriors in combat. Cowards, assassins and the scum of oceans, that's all the captain of the *Goreleech* and his crew are!'

A burly weasel named Clubface was working nearby and heard Luke's words. Thinking to gain the admiration of Daskar, he drew his dagger and leaped upon the manacled slave, roaring, 'Nobeast talks to our cap'n like that an' lives. I'll gut ye!' The weasel was big and strong, but he did not possess Luke's speed. The Warrior mouse's pawchains rapped him hard between his eyes, and Luke grabbed the paw holding the dagger, twisting it inward. Clubface felt himself tripped, and fell backward. Luke slammed his weight down on top of the weasel, falling with him and driving the dagger deep into his attacker's heart. Like a flash, Luke was upright, the dripping blade in his paw, facing the pirate stoat. Daskar laughed aloud, thumping the tabletop with his scimitar handle, applauding.

'Neatly done, Luke, you are a real warrior. Come on now, you've got the dagger, try to kill me!'

Sea Rogues had come running to surround Luke. He relaxed and stood with the blade hanging loosely from one paw. Vilu Daskar stood and bowed slightly. Motioning his crew to stand off, he pointed the scimitar at Luke. 'My compliments. You are not only brave, but wise also.'

Luke nodded towards the vermin all round him. 'The numbers are a bit one-sided, Daskar. I'll slay you one day, but I'll pick the time and place!'

Smiling and shaking his head, the pirate stoat replied, 'Well said. I like an enemy who uses his brains. Take him below and chain him back to the oars.'

Zzzzipthunk!

Before anybeast could move, Luke had thrown the dagger, embedding it deep in the mast alongside Daskar's head.

'Sometimes a knife can reach further than a sword. Remember that, stoat!'

Luke went down under the press of crewbeasts. Vilu Daskar stood over him, shaking with rage. He raised the sword, holding it trembling over the fearless slave, then, thinking better of his actions, he snarled, 'Get him below, out of my sight!'

Sea Rogues hoisted Luke upright and dragged him off, back to the Death Pit of the lower deck.

Bolwag's flipper, damp and heavy, touched Vurg's face, wakening him. The sea lion was back in the water; it was midnight of the second day since leaving Twin Islands. The dolphins were gone.

'Vurg, wake up, liddle friend. Give Beau a shake. Look yonder. Wood Isle an' the red ship!'

Moonbeams danced on the phosphorescent sea. No more than an hour's sailing time away, the *Goreleech* could be seen, riding at anchor, close to the shore of the island, which looked for all the world like a chunk of forest sticking out of the main.

Beau rubbed his eyes drowsily. 'I say, does look jolly pretty in the moonlight, wot!'

Bolwag drifted off from the raft. 'Aye, pretty dangerous too, mate. Well, shipmates, this's where we parts comp'ny. I wouldn't be of much use to ye on land or aboard a vessel. But I got ye here.'

Vurg waved at the friendly giant. 'So you did, Bolwag, an' our thanks to ye for that. You've done more'n enough for us. Good fortune to you an' those bottlenoses – give 'em our thanks if'n you see 'em again!'

Beau added his farewells to those of his friend. 'Toodle-oo and farewell, you old rascal, wot. I'd watch out for sharks if I were you. Remember how they scoffed your ole auntie, bit careless that, keep your eyes peeled, sir. Oh, an' give my regards t'those bottlenose chaps, not bad types really, except for all that pesky spittin' an' squeakin'. G'bye now!'

Bolwag sank beneath the surface and was gone.

Now they were alone, with only their wits to rely on. Lying flat on the raft, they paddled with their paws, discussing the situation, whilst they were still out of earshot of the *Goreleech*.

'Well, Beau, we've got this far. What's the next move?'

'Patently obvious, m'dear feller. Got to free our friends from durance vile, wot!'

'Huh, I know that, but we won't get very far jumpin' aboard the *Goreleech* an' challengin' 'er crew now, will we?'

'Of course not, we'd need at least three of us t'do that. We need a scheme, a plan, an idea, or a combination of all three. C'mon now, Vurg, get the old mousey thinkin' cap on. I'm more a leader than a planner, don't y'know.'

As they drew closer to the monstrous red ship, Vurg weighed it up carefully, an idea forming in his mind.

'Beau, d'you see those rope'n'canvas fenders hangin' over the sides to protect the *Goreleech* from rocks?'

'Indeed I do, whackin' great things they are too, some of 'em, bigger than our little raft. Why d'you ask?'

'Because I been thinkin', we could be a fender too!'

'The deuce y'say, an' what good'll that do, pray?'

'Well, I notice that the stern fenders hang a bit low. S'pose we was to cut one loose an' let it float off. Then we ties our own up in its place an' hides there.'

Suddenly Beau was thinking along the same lines as Vurg. 'Rather! Spiffin' wheeze, wot. From there we could contact the oarslave chaps at night, when nobeast's about!'

'Aye, get word to them we're here, see if we can't pinch a few weapons t'help Luke an' the others!'

'By the left, I'm glad I thought o' that little plan. Don't slack, Vurg, paddle harder please. Hmph! It's one thing strainin' m'brain t'think up these plans, but it's a bit much to expect me t'do all the paddlin', old chap!'

'Oh, button up, Beau, y'make more noise than a squeakin' bottlenose!'

'I beg y'pardon, sah! Confounded nerve o' the mouse, wot?'

'Stop natterin' an' keep paddlin'!'

'Pish tush, I could say the same for you, whiskerface!'

'No you couldn't, floppylugs!'

'Yes I could, bottlenose!'

'Bottlenose y'self, gabbyguts!'

Glaring at one another and arguing heatedly they ran smack into the *Goreleech*'s stern. Thud!

High up near the afterdeck a window swung open.

Poking his head out, a searat, blinking from the cabin lanterns, called, 'Ahoy, who's out there? C'mon, show yerself!'

The two friends grasped the bottom of a fender, pulling the raft close in beneath the stern. Huddled together they held their breath, listening as somebeast joined the searat.

'Aye aye, wot's goin' on 'ere, mate?'

'Thought I 'eard a noise out there. Sounded like two beasts arguin', then summat struck the ship.'

A third voice joined the conversation angrily. 'Somethin' will strike you if'n yer don't shut that winder. Can't a beast gerra bit o' rest without bein' blown outer the bunk by draughts from the seas at night!'

The window slammed amid sounds of muffled argument. Both friends gave a quiet sigh of relief. Vurg whispered, 'Better wait until later, when they're all asleep, then we'll see what can be done. What's the funny face for, Beau?'

'Funny face nothin', old lad, I'm blinkin' well famished!'

'Wot, y'mean the vittles are all gone?'

'Exactly, an' the water too. We'll starve t'death!'

'Don't talk rubbish. You could live off'n yore fat for ages.'

'Yukk, urroogh, blaaaah!'

'Don't make so much noise. What're you up to now, Beau?'

'Yurkk, this bally bladderwrack tastes absolutely foul!'

'I ain't surprised, matey. Bet even the sharks turn their noses up at that stuff. Beau, where are ye goin'? Come back!' But Beau was shinning up the stern gallery with the alacrity that only a hungry hare could muster.

'Won't be a tick, old thing. Hold the fort 'til I get back.'

A moment later the gluttonous creature had vanished into the darkness. Vurg perched on the raft, nibbling anxiously at his paw, wondering where his friend had gone to.

*

A ferret and a searat were working in the galley. The ferret laid out loaves of hot bread to cool at the open serving hatch, whilst the rat was occupied chopping up fruit, which he mixed in a bowl with honey.

'Good fresh fruit they got from the island t'day, cullie. Cap'n doesn't go much fer it, but it'll look nice on 'is table fer brekkist.'

Sampling a slice of apple, the ferret licked honey from his paws and winked at the rat. 'We'll 'ave it fer lunch, after we clears the cap'n's table.'

Wiping his paws on a rag, the rat took down a dead pigeon from a hook. 'Lend a paw ter pluck this willyer, mate?'

They both bent to the task until the bird was plucked. Shuffling to the cupboard for a roasting spit, the rat stopped, looked at the empty space on the table, just inside the window ledge, and turned angrily on his mate.

'Think yore funny, don't yer? Cummon, put it back!'

'Put wot back? Wot's up, matey?'

'Hah, don't you matey me, y'fat robber. Where's me fruit salad got to? Now give it back 'ere.'

'I never touched no fruit sal— Hoi! Where's me bread gone? It was laid out there t'cool a moment ago.'

'Lissen, slopchops, never mind usin' yore bread as an excuse, I saw yer pinchin' slices of apple outta that fruit salad. I'll chop yer thievin' paws off wid me cleaver!'

'Ho, thief is it? Well you kin explain t'the crew where the bread's gone when there's none fer brekkist, so there!'

'Don't you accuse me o' stealin' yore lousy bread. Take that!' Swinging the dead pigeon, the rat caught the ferret a smack.

'Ooff! That wuz a foul blow. 'Ere, you 'ave some o' this!' The ferret dealt the rat a stinging blow to his rear with a wooden rolling pin, and they fell to fighting in earnest.

Beau watched from his hiding place on the deck, munching on a hot loaf. The sound of approaching paws caused him to slide into the shadows of the galley bulkhead. As he did, a loaf of bread fell to the deck. Fleabitt stopped in passing, noticed the loaf and grabbed it. Gnawing away happily he went to see what all the noise was about in the galley. Poking his head round the door, he said, 'Nice bread this is, mates. 'Ope you got plenny more fer brekkist tomorrer. Likes good bread I does!'

Instantly he was dragged into the galley and set upon by the two cooks, who pounded him mercilessly.

'So yore the one, yer scringin' liddle thief!'

'Owow! Yowch! Murder! 'Elp, they're killin' me!'

The ferret swung his rolling pin with relish. 'Kill yer, y'durty grubswiper, I'll murder ye. Take that!'

Brandishing a copper ladle the rat leaped on the hapless Fleabitt, pounding him severely. 'Aye, an' after he's killed an' murdered yer, I'm goin' to slay yer, yew filthy vittle plunderer!'

A sound overhead caused Vurg to look up. Beau's muted whisper came out of the darkness. 'Stand by the raft there. Here, catch these!'

Two long hot loaves dropped down on Vurg, then Beau was alongside him, placing a bowl between them both. 'Nothin' like fresh fruit salad'n'honey to keep a chap's chin up, wot. Don't hog all the bread, there's a good chap, chuck a loaf over here. Oh, I found a flask an' filled it from the water cask, better than nothin' I suppose, wot wot.'

Vurg was glad of the food, though he lectured Beau severely. 'Your stomach could've got us both caught and killed. That was a foolish risk you took, Beau, don't ever do it again!'

The garrulous hare twiddled both his ears carelessly. 'Oh, fiddle de dee, mouseymate, what d'you expect a bod t'do, sit here and jolly well starve? Fat chance!'

Vurg could not help smiling at the devil-may-care Beau. 'Oh, all right, but be careful. Great seasons, lookit the size of these loaves. There's enough here t'feed most of the crew. Did you have to take so much bread?'

Beau tore off a chunk and dipped it in the honey. 'Waste not want not, old bean. Bet Luke an' company'll be glad of fresh bread. Don't imagine they get it too often, wot wot. When we've had a nap we'll go an' seek 'em out!'

It was still some hours to dawn. Luke sat shackled to his bench, head bent as he slumbered over his oar. Bullflay lay snoring on his makeshift bed. All was quiet amid the smouldering lanterns of the lower deck, save for the odd whimper of some wretched oarslave, dreaming of home and happier times. Ranguvar was dozing too. She flicked at something tickling her ear. It was a dried stem of bladderwrack. It tickled again, and this time she caught it in her paw, opening her eyes as somebeast whispered, 'What ho, old thing, y'don't happen to have a chap down there named Luke, do you? Warrior type like y'self?'

Ranguvar immediately became alert. She looked to the oar port and saw a bewhiskered hare smiling in at her, holding a paw to his lips as a caution to silence. Ranguvar nodded. Pointing across to Luke, she murmured quietly, 'Over there, first oar port on t'other side. Who are you?'

'Formal introductions later, friend. Here, chew on this.' Completely mystified, but grateful, Ranguvar accepted the big chunk of fresh bread packed with fruit salad. 'Don't eat so fast, marm, twenty chews to each mouthful now. Bye bye!' With a wave the hare vanished.

Ranguvar shook Luke awake by waggling the end of his oar. 'Ssshhh! You've got a visitor, Luke. Look to your oar port.'

Beau peeped in at Luke, his face a mask of mock accusation. 'Why aren't you dead, sah?'

Luke shook his head in disbelief. 'Why aren't you?'

'Far too hungry to let things like dyin' interfere with my plans, old feller. Vurg's alive too, y'know. Listen, I can't stop t'chat. Here's some food, share it about. Be back tomorrow night, keep y'chin up. I'll see what I can do about bringin' somethin' to deal with those chains. Meanwhile, sit tight an' smile, the rescue party's arrived at last, wot!'

When Beau was gone, Luke and Ranguvar took the hare's advice. They sat tight and smiled, sleep forgotten, now that the first bright rays of hope had started to glimmer.

32

The voyage to the northern coast was well under way. Fortunately, the weather remained fair with favourable winds. Parug, the rat bosun, however, was not a happy Sea Rogue. Vilu Daskar had sent a command, through Akkla, that he was to report to the captain's cabin. Parug was all of a tremble as he rapped hesitantly on the door. Vilu Daskar was sly and unpredictable – who could tell what he wanted to see his bosun about? Whip in paw, the slavemaster Bullflay opened the door to admit Parug. It did not bode well by the look on Bullflay's ugly face.

'Get in 'ere. Cap'n wants to see you.'

Vilu was seated at a table, his wicked bone-handled scimitar before him. Parug came to attention in front of the pirate stoat, shaking visibly. Vilu Daskar sat in silence, his face betraying nothing as he stared levelly at the dithering bosun, who managed to gulp out a word. 'Sire?'

Vilu touched the silken scarf at his neck, extending the silence until it became almost unbearable, before he spoke. 'There is a thief aboard my ship.'

'A th-thief, sire?'

'Yes, Parug, a thief. I have a dagger to match this sword, bone-handled, with a curved silver blade. Last night it was on this table, where it usually is, this morning it is gone.'

'G-gone, sire?'

Vilu got up and walked round the table. Halting behind Parug, he dug his claws hard into the bosun's shoulder. Parug whimpered in pain and terror as the stoat hissed viciously in his ear. 'Stop repeating everything I say, or I'll slice the foolish tongue from your slobbering mouth. Have you been walking round this ship with your eyes shut? Other things are being stolen. Food, water, equipment, ship's gear. Now I want to know the names of those who are robbing me. Do you understand, Parug? Speak!'

The bosun knew his life was at stake. Words babbled from him like water pouring from a barrel. 'Sire, cap'n, I've noticed it meself, all kinds o' things are disappearin', 'specially vittles an' drink, sire. But on me oath, cap'n, I'm keepin' a sharp weather eye out fer the villains, I swear I am, sire, day'n'night!'

Vilu released him and went to sit back in his chair. 'But you haven't a clue who the thieves are, right?'

Parug nodded miserably, unable to stop his head from bobbing up and down. Vilu glanced across at Bullflay. 'I don't suppose you've any ideas about the culprits?'

Shuffling awkwardly, the gargantuan weasel shrugged. 'Can't think o' none, cap'n, unless 'tis like the crew sez, the Sea Bogle! Some of 'em even sez that—'

Bullflay got no further. Vilu Daskar moved like lightning. Clearing the table at a bound, grabbing his scimitar as he did, the stoat laid Bullflay low with a resounding blow to his face from the flat of the glittering blade.

'Enough! Do you suppose I am as big a fool as the idiots who serve me? Don't dare speak to me of Bogles or phantoms! What need would ghosts have of food? You addle-witted moron, the thieves are living breathing beasts, with the same need for food and drink anybeast has! Out! Get out of my sight, both of you. Search the *Goreleech* from stem to stern!'

Lined up on deck, the crew of the red ship were made to stand fast all morning as a search was made of their living quarters. Vilu Daskar sat beneath an awning, watching as each one was called out to accompany Akkla, Parug and Bullflay below decks.

'Foulscale, yore next, step forward, lively now!' The weasel Foulscale went with the searchers into the crew's accommodation. They searched his hammock and the area around it, and he was then made to gather up his belongings and taken up on deck. Bullflay ordered him to unroll his bundle and display the contents. Then the slavemaster called out, 'Righto, crew, take a look at this gear. Is it all the property of Foulscale?'

A brass-earringed searat stepped forward, pointing. 'No it ain't, that belt's mine. I'd know it anywheres, sharkskin, wid a green stone in a round brass buckle!'

'I found it lyin' by me bunk!' Foulscale protested.

Vilu Daskar strode over to Foulscale's belongings. With his swordpoint he flicked the belt to its owner, then addressed Foulscale.

'You stole the belt. Get over there with the others!'

Ashen-faced, the weasel walked over to join an ever growing band of Sea Rogues who had been caught with the property of fellow shipmates among their gear.

It was high noon by the time the search ended. Those who were innocent stood in line, looking greatly relieved. More than a score of vermin, who had been caught in possession of stolen property, huddled miserably around the mainmast, awaiting the consequences.

Vilu Daskar delivered his judgement for all to hear. 'I know you are not the thieves I seek. Somebeasts are plundering wholesale from this ship. Make no mistake, I will find them and punish them slowly to the death. There will be an end to thieving aboard my *Goreleech*. But you who have been caught, you are still guilty of stealing from your shipmates and must be punished. Thank your lucky stars I am in a lenient mood, and keep your paws to yourselves in future. Akkla, Parug, Bullflay, hoist them up by their tails and give them twenty lashes apiece, sluice them with salt water, let them hang there until sunset, then cut them down. The rest of you will witness the floggings as a reminder never to steal whilst aboard the red ship!'

Vurg and Beau perched on their raft, well hidden by the overhang of the high carved stern. They could not avoid hearing the screams and wails of the miscreants as they were subjected to the whipping. Neither had any pity for Sea Rogues.

'Makin' more noise than a school of confounded bottle-noses, wot. That'll teach 'em honesty's the best policy!'

'Aye, there's only one thing worse'n a thief, Beau.'

'Indeed, an' what is that, pray?'

'Two thieves!'

'Haw haw, rather good that, Vurg.'

'We'll 'ave t'be more careful of a night from now on, mate. They'll be watchin' for us, y'know.'

'Of course they jolly well will, so you do the stealin' an' I'll keep 'em diverted in me Sea Bogle costume, eh?'

Vurg chuckled. 'Sea Bogle, wot a load of ole nonsense!'

Beau fixed two horns he had made from dried bladder-wrack to his ears. He waggled them and scowled fiercely. 'Talk not like that of ye Sea Bogle, old lad, or I'll put a spell from the dark murky deeps upon thee!'

Vurg closed his eyes, enjoying the warm noon sun. 'Pity you can't put a spell on yore stummick, stop it needin' so much food, y'great fat fraud!'

'Steady on there, m'good mouse, us Sea Bogles need nourishment if we're to perform properly. No self-respectin' Sea Rogue'd be scared of a half-starved skinny Bogle. Er, any more of that skilly'n'duff left?'

'There's some in the bowl. Help yoreself, I imagine

you'll spirit it away without too much trouble. What are you writin' there? The ship's log of our raft, the *Floatin' Fender*? Put me down as mouse mate, an' you c'n be cap'n Bogle.'

Beau was scraping away with a charcoal stick on a strip of canvas, his tongue sticking out at the side of his mouth. 'Actually it's a poem I'm composin' about Bogles. Some of those ignorant vermin may be unaware of the tale, so I'm doin' a bit of publicity for meself, doncha know.'

Vurg winced as they heard the splash of water, followed by more agonised wailing from the upper decks. 'Ooh! Must sting somethin' awful, bein' flogged an' gettin' salt water chucked on the cuts.'

The hare was unmoved as he continued writing. 'Prob'ly the only decent wash they've had since their dear old mothers used to scrub 'em in the tub when they were babes. There's a thought, can you imagine a filthy beastly little pirate babe bein' scrubbed in a tub? I'll wager his language would frazzle his auntie's slippers, wot?'

In the crew's accommodation that night the vermin who had been released sat nursing their hurts, whilst others swaggered about, displaying the treasured gear they had thought lost. The rest huddled around the mess table, playing an old searat game with shells and fruit pips. The entire crew jumped with fright as the cabin door slammed open. Parug staggered in as if his paws were made of jelly, grasping a long strip of sailcloth.

The searat Willag helped him to a seat at the table. 'Wot's the matter, bosun? Y'look as if y've seen a ghost.'

Somebeast passed him a tankard of barnacle grog. He drank the fiery liquor in one long swallow, and it was dribbling down his chin as he stared wildly about.

' 'Twas the Sea Bogle, mates. I saw the Sea Bogle wid me own two eyes, on me affydavit I did!'

A chilled silence fell over the crew. Parug was quite a stolid rat, not given to silly imaginings. The tankard was refilled and Parug took a deep swig before continuing, 'I jus' came out to patrol the deck, searchin' for a sign of any thieves. Before I could blink a glim it 'ad me by the throat. Long long arms it 'ad, like steel, I couldn't move! I tell ye, shipmates, I'll never be the same agin after seein' the Bogle. It 'ad great big horns, three eyes, an' a face that was all lit up, glowin'! Covered it was, wid 'orrible flowin' weeds from the bed o' the seas, all wet an' drippin'. Ugh! 'Twas too terrifyin' to describe!'

Willag took a gulp from the tankard Parug had put down. 'Why didn't yer run an' tell the cap'n?'

Parug shot him a haunted glance, whispering dementedly, 'Cap'n won't 'ear of it, 'e don't believe in Bogles. I couldn't tell 'im, mate, 'e would've slayed me!'

Foulscale temporarily forgot his stinging back. 'Did the Bogle speak to ye, Parug? Wot did it say?'

The bosun held up the canvas strip. 'It never said nothin', jus' growled an' gave an awful squeak, like a bottlenose dolphin. Then it pressed this sailcloth inter me paw, let go of me neck an' stood there.'

Foulscale shook his head in amazement. 'So wot did you do?'

'Do? Wotjer think I did? I ran off, fast as I could!'

'Is it still out there, d'ye think?'

'I don't know. Go an' look fer yoreself!'

'Wot? Lissen, mate, I ain't movin' out o' this cabin 'til it's daylight an' the sun's shinin', so there!'

The crew nodded their heads vigorously in agreement.

Willag picked the sailcloth from Parug's shaking paws. 'See, there's writin' on it. Wot does it say, Parug?'

'I don't know, I can't read letters or words.'

Grigg the searat beckoned to Willag. 'Give it 'ere. I can read. Let's see wot it sez.'

Grigg read it out in halting tones. He could read, but only just. His voice echoed out in the awed silence.

'From the dark and icy deeps,
Where the dreaded Bogle sleeps,
He'll rise one night and climb aboard your ship,
Bringing fear and deathlike doom,
To your very cabin room,
Beware the Bogle's clammy vicelike grip!

Aye, woe betide that crew,
Sailing on the main so blue,
And to those who don't believe me double grief,
When the Bogle takes a meal,
You will hear a dreadful squeal,
He strikes when night time falls, just like a thief!

Aye, who of you can tell,
Give him gifts and feed him well,
Then the Bogle may slide back into the sea,
But if gifts and food be few,
Hearken now, for it is true,
The Bogle may eat you, or even me!

Crack some ribs or crush a skull,
Stuff down hearts 'til he is full,
Rip paws and tails off any poor seabeast,
Lock your cabin doors this night,
Shake with terror, quake with fright,
For the Bogle may invite you to his feast!'

Grigg was quaking so badly when he finished the
poem that he dropped the canvas. Willag was the first to
move. He dashed to the cabin door and locked it, calling
down the long smoky cabin to his mates, 'Bar those
skylights, batten 'em down tight! Trim the lamps an'
clean 'em, we need it good'n'bright in 'ere!'

Fleabitt and the ferret Ringpatch were on duty in the
Death Pit. The slaves were sleeping, draped across their

oars. Ringpatch, who generally worked on top deck of the trireme, took a quick glance around.

'Hoi, Fleabitt, this lot won't be no trouble fer the rest o' the night. Come on, mate. Let's go up to top deck, it stinks down 'ere. Walloper an' Ching from middle deck'll be up there, my mate Flanjear too. Top deck ain't like this pest'ole – we got a liddle oven up there. Bet they're makin' skilly'n'duff an' suppin' grog.'

Fleabitt coiled his whip over one narrow shoulder. 'Skilly'n'duff! Why didn't yer say, matey? Lead on, I'm right be'ind yer. Nothin' like a bowl o' the ole skilly'n'duff!'

The moment they were gone, Luke and Ranguvar sat up. All through the bottom deck, oarslaves became alert. Luke's orders were relayed from one to another.

'Those closest to the steps, keep watch. Give the warning if y'hear anybeast comin'!'

'Dulam, Denno, look to your oarports. Vurg will be along with food soon.'

'Ranguvar, how's that big staple coming along, nearly out?'

The black squirrel looked up from her labours. ''Tis a big 'un, set deep an' well rusted, but I've got it on the move, Luke.'

'Good, but be careful you don't splinter the wood too much. Bullflay usually stands near there, an' we don't want him to spot anything suspicious.'

Norgle the otter tossed something across to Ranguvar. 'All taken care of, matey. I'm mixin' tallow with dirt from the deck, that'll disguise it good.'

Luke nodded his approval. 'Great stuff, matey. See if y'can get more o' that tallow, we'll need it for the oar-chains.'

As Luke talked he was busy with his own oarshackles, filing a deep groove into a link close to his paw. 'Gricca, have you got those weapons stowed safe?'

An old female hedgehog several rows back answered,

'Aye, Luke, all safe'n'sound, they're jammed in slits I cut on the undersides of these benches. Here, you have this'n, 'tis a fancy liddle toy that Beau found. Duck yore nut, mate, comin' over!'

Luke bent his head as something whizzed by and stuck in the upraised oarshaft. It was a fine curved silver dagger with a bone handle. He plucked it from the oar. 'Well, this is a fine sharp gizzard slitter!'

Ranguvar sniffed the air, shaking her head in disbelief. 'I can smell hot scones dipped in honey.'

Denno confirmed the squirrel's statement. 'So you can, friend. Vurg's here!'

'Ahoy, Vurg, where'd you get these?'

'Ooh, they're still hot from the oven!'

'Pass that bag along, mates, share 'em out!'

Shaking with laughter, Vurg passed another flourbag loaded with hot scones through the oarport. 'Go easy, mates, don't crush 'em. Pass the empty bags back an' I'll fill 'em agin. Luke, how's it goin' down here?'

'Fine, Vurg, just fine. Where did all these scones come from? They're delicious. I didn't know vermin could bake as good as this. Did you'n'Beau steal all these? How in the name o' seasons did you get away with 'em?'

Vurg managed to poke his head partly through the oarport. He was grinning from ear to ear. 'We never stole 'em, Luke, we baked the scones ourselves. Ole Beau the Bogle has the crew frightened out o' their wits, an' they battened themselves up tight in the crew's accommodation, terrified. So, seein' there wasn't anybeast on deckwatch, we found the galley empty, stoked up the ovens an' went to work. Beau sends his compliments!'

The entire deck of oarslaves, conscious of the need for silence, shook with suppressed mirth until tears popped from their eyes and ribs began to ache. There was a scrabbling from the bulkhead and Beau appeared at the opposite oarport, still in Bogle garb, but with his face covered in flour and honey.

'What ho, chaps, Beau the Bogle baker here. I say, I hope you oarslave types aren't laughin' at my cookin', wot?'

A young vole, closest to the oarport, took Beau's paw and shook it heartily. 'No sir, even my ole mum couldn't cook a scone like you do, they're the best anybeast ever tasted. If we're laughin' 'tis because you've taught us how to. Some of us have been down 'ere for long seasons, treated harsh too, with no reason t'smile. We're 'appy 'cos you've given us back a reason t'live, with yore bravery an' kindness, both you an' mister Vurg, may fortune bless yer both!'

The young vole was so overcome that his tears of merriment turned to real tears, which flowed on to the hare's paw. Beau the Bogle tried to make light of things, though his long ear dipped to wipe moisture from his own eye.

'There there, young feller m'bucko, 'twas the least we could do, wot? Though if you want more scones I suggest you release my jolly old paw, you've washed it quite clean thank you, but all that oar pullin' has given you a rather powerful grip, an' you seem t'be crushin' me paw t'pulp!'

Ranguvar Foeseeker began to tremble with rage. Her voice shook as it echoed round the deck known as the Death Pit. 'All the prisoners aboard this red ship have strong paws through pulling long oars across heavy seas. But those same paws won't always be pulling oars. One day soon they'll be shaking off their chains an' taking up arms against Vilu Daskar and his Sea Rogues. Then we will take vengeance for ourselves, our families and friends and all the lost seasons of our lives. I give you my word!'

Beau took one look at the black squirrel's eyes, and said, 'I don't doubt it, marm, not one word!'

33

The *Goreleech* ploughed the seas, hours became days and days turned to weeks, the waters grew more tempestuous and the weather changed as the red ship sailed into wintry latitudes. Swathed in a soft cloak of light green wool, head protected by a purple silk turban, Vilu Daskar rested a paw on the scimitar thrust into his waist sash. Bracing himself against the for'ard rail, he gazed north over the grey spume-topped waves, narrowing his eyes against a keening wind. Akkla the ferret stood to one side, awaiting orders from his captain.

It had not been a good trip. Despite the whippings and beatings given to the crew, thievery on a grand scale had prevailed. Both Vilu and Akkla hoped it was not the Sea Rogues who were responsible, but the red ship's vermin were growing sullen, muttering among themselves about the floggings and the shortage of food. The pirate stoat knew that discipline and order had to be retained aboard ship, if he were to stay master, so he had enforced his will. Still superstitious murmurings continued, dark tales of a Sea Bogle haunting the *Goreleech*. Even though he threatened, ranted and reasoned, Vilu knew he was helpless against the ignorant beliefs held by seagoing vermin. However, with the scent of treasure in his nostrils, he was not about to give up. One idea he pounded into the thick skulls of his crew was that they would follow orders or die. Knowing they were on a ship at sea, with nowhere to run, that and the fear of their murderous captain kept the crew in line.

Vilu spoke to Akkla without looking at him. 'I'm going to my cabin. Have the mouse Warrior Luke brought there, then return here and let me know the moment you sight land. Oh, and tell Parug to keep the crew busy. I want the mess deck, galley and accommodation scrubbed and cleaned from bulkheads to deckheads.'

Willag dipped a chunk of pumice stone into a wooden pail of cold seawater and began scrubbing half-heartedly at the mess tabletop, complaining, 'Huh, clean the mess deck agin. I've wore me paws t'the bone scrubbin' at this stupid table, must've scoured it more'n ten times o'er the past few days!'

Foulscale was on all fours, toiling away at the mess deck flooring, slopping icy seawater everywhere. 'Aye, an' it ain't as if there's any vittles t'put on that table, mate. Those scummy slaves look better fed than us!'

Ringpatch the ferret, who had been rubbing the brasswork shiny with a mixture of ashes and fine sand, put down his rag and wiped a filthy paw across his brow thoughtfully. 'Yore right there, bucko. D'you think 'tis the slaves who've been swipin' our grub?'

Parug the bosun swung a length of rope, knotted at one end and stiff with pitch and resin. 'Oh aye, it has t'be the slaves,' he sneered scornfully. 'I can just see 'em, cookin' up pans o' skilly'n'duff in the galley, carryin' their oars over their shoulders o' course, wid their footpaws chained to large chunks of deck. You great blitherin' nit! 'Ow could slaves manage that? 'Ave yew got mud fer brains? Now get on wid shinin' those brasses, I wants ter see me face in 'em, or I'll feed yer a taste o' this rope's end!'

*

Luke's paws were bound behind him, and he had a rope halter round his neck. Vilu Daskar sat on the edge of his cabin table, questioning the prisoner. 'So, my friend, do you know where we are?'

The Warrior met his captor's eyes fearlessly. 'I'm not your friend, but I do know where we are, in the northland seas.'

'Oh indeed? I know that too, but where precisely in the northland seas are we?'

Luke shrugged. 'Your guess is as good as mine. One wave looks the same as another out there.'

Daskar shook his head, a thin humourless smile on his lips. 'Still the Warrior, eh? Listen well, mouse, I did not bring you here to play games with me. How soon will I know exactly where we are? Tell me or I will stop all oarslaves' water rations. That would be easy – there's little enough left for me and my crew. So tell me.'

As if ignoring the stoat, Luke shuffled past him and looked out of the cabin window at the icy heaving seas. 'Take a course east until you sight land, then steer north again. No doubt you will remember a rocky headland – that's where you massacred my tribe. Once you see that headland send for me. I will steer your ship from then on, because only I know the route.'

The bone-handled scimitar flashed skilfully, grazing Luke's ear. There was no mistaking the menace in Vilu's voice. 'Sure enough, you will steer the *Goreleech*, chained to the wheel, with this blade at your throat!'

Luke's smile was wintry as the weather outside. 'I'll look forward to it, but don't make it too easy for me, will you?'

Vilu's teeth ground audibly as he snarled to the guards, 'Get this defiant fool out of my sight!'

As he was hustled from the cabin, Luke managed to put a chuckle in his voice. 'Defiant yes, but a fool . . . never!'

When they had chained Luke back to his oar, Ranguvar

murmured out of the side of her mouth, 'When do we make our move? Everything's ready. I got word that the top deck cut their last chain whilst you were gone.'

Luke pondered the question before replying. 'Sometime tomorrow, maybe evenin', I've a feeling we may sight the headland by my old home. I'll be up on deck with Daskar probably. If my tribe see the red ship they'll be ready for trouble, so we can count on help from them.'

Ranguvar had to wait whilst Bullflay walked past down the aisle, towards the oarslaves at the stern end.

'So, if yore on deck, how will we know, Luke?'

'Hmm, good question, mate. I know, we'll have Beau or Vurg make their way up near the prow. If they hear me shout "Dead ahead" that'll be the signal to take over the ship. But if I shout "Veer north" you must do nothing. I'll be chained to the ship's wheel by then. Sit tight an' wait until I get word to you.'

Ranguvar paused as Fleabitt strode sternward.

'Got it. If Vurg or Beau tells us "Dead ahead", the attack is on, but if the message is "Veer north", we wait!'

The two messengers in question were undergoing severe hardships. Beau and Vurg were freezing and soaking from the cold weather and pounding seas. Huddled together beneath layers of stolen blanket and sail canvas, they clung grimly to the raft, which was lashed to the *Goreleech*'s lower stern. The hare poked his head out of the wet jumble, catching the backlash of a big wave. He retreated back down, wiping his face on the damp blankets.

'By the bally cringe, old lad, can't last much longer in these inclement latitudes, wot?'

Vurg closed his eyes and tried to sleep, but Beau persisted.

'My jolly old auntie'd say it's cold enough to whip the whiskers off a mole an' wet enough t'drown a lobster.

Cold'n'wet wouldn't be so blinkin' bad if I wasn't flippin' well starvin' t'death. What would you sooner do, Vurg, freeze t'death, drown t'death, or starve t'death?'

The mouse opened one eye and murmured, 'You didn't say wot wot.'

'Wot wot? Why the deuce should I say wot wot?'

Vurg smiled sleepily. ' 'Cos you always say wot wot!'

Beau's ears stood rigid with indignation. 'I beg your very pardon, sir, I do not. Wot wot? I was merely speculatin' on our demise. I said, would you rather freeze t'death, or drown t'd—'

Vurg interrupted him rudely. 'I heard what you said first time. Hmph! Freezin' drownin' or starvin' wouldn't be so bad if I wasn't already bein' nattered t'death. Don't you ever stop natterin', mate?'

Beau's indignation switched to injured innocence. 'Well, chop off m'tongue, pull out m'teeth an' sew up m'lips. I'll put a cork right in it an' quit assaultin' your dainty shell-like lugholes, old bean. Far be it from me to try an' make companionly conversation with a friend facin' adversity. Not another word, m'lips are sealed!'

Vurg immediately felt sorry for his garrulous companion. 'Take no notice of me, Beau, I'm just feelin' sorry for myself. You carry on, wot wot!'

The hare chuckled and ruffled his friend's ears. 'Well of course you are, old mouseymate, that's why fate threw us t'gether like this, so I could jolly you up whenever y'feel down in the dumps. My dear old auntie taught me a song about such situations. I say, shall I sing it for you? Cheer you up no end, wot?'

Vurg turned his head aside and pulled a wry face. 'Oh well, seein' as I can't escape the sound of yore voice I s'pose I'll have to listen. At least it'll scare any sharks away if they're hangin' about. Sing on, Beau.'

Needing no second bidding, Beau launched into his auntie's song, ears clasped in traditional hare manner.

'When you're feelin' down an' glum,
Don't just sit round lookin' dumb,
Sing tickety boo a fig for you, wot ho fol lah!
'Cos there's time for all that gloom,
When you're dead an' in the tomb,
Sing tickety boo a fig for you, wot ho fol lah!
When 'tis rainin' all the day,
An' the skies are dirty grey,
An' you've ate the last plum pudden off the shelf,
Jig an' caper in the wet,
You'll be better off I bet,
Than pullin' faces, feelin' sorry for yourself.
Oh tickety boo a fig for you, wot ho fol lah!
These few words will cheer you up an' take you far,
Not like that old frumpy duck,
Or a frog who's out of luck,
Or the little maggot who has lost his ma, ah ah ah ah
   aaaah!
If you laugh there'll be no rain,
An' the sun'll shine again,
Then your dear old aunt will bake you apple pie,
So when hedgehogs learn to fly,
Fish will quack an' wonder why?
Tickety boo a fig for you, never say die aye aye,
Aye aye, aye aye, aye aaaaaaaaaaaaaye!'

Vurg threw himself on Beau, stifling his efforts. 'What are you tryin' to do, attract the attention of the entire ship's crew?'

That put Beau into a sulk. He wrenched himself away from Vurg, working himself into a huff and muttering, 'Huh, bouncin' on a chap just as he's reachin' top note, jolly dangerous thing t'do, wot? An unexploded phrase might've backfired down m'neck an' fractured me warbler. Little you'd care, though. An' I still had another three verses t'sing. There was the line in the second verse about a toad losin' his trousers up a tree, very movin' an' profound part o' the ditty. But I ain't goin' to sing it now. What's the use of one chap singin' to cheer another chap up, if the other chap keeps jumpin' on the first chap's head? Bad form I'd say, ungrateful wretch!'

All that evening and throughout the night, the slaves were forced to row, though only at quarter speed in the wild northern seas, whose tides, rocks and currents had sent many a vessel to its doom. Fleabitt pounded his drum slowly, with a monotonous regular cadence, and Bullflay dozed fitfully, only striding the aisle when he felt the need to stretch his paws. Luke pulled the heavy oar alone, spray whipping through the oarport at odd intervals to wet his face. Sleep was the farthest thing from his mind, now that he was near to his old home.

Thoughts of his son Martin raced through the Warrior's imagination. He would be tall now, quick and strong, with the blood of a leader and a fighter flowing in his veins. Martin would know what to do, the moment the *Goreleech* was sighted. He would get the old and feeble, together with those too young to do battle, together. Having hidden them safely, Luke's son would do as he had been taught by his father: gather together the strong ones, arm them and come to his father's aid, wielding the very sword Luke had passed on to him. As the slaves broke loose and fought to gain control of the red ship, Luke would run her into the coastal shallows, causing the vessel to heel over. He would hail his son from the ship's wheel. Once Martin heard the voice of his father, he would come hurtling through the shallows at the head of his fighters to board the *Goreleech*. Then Vilu Daskar and his murderers would pay dearly for their monstrous crimes.

Ranguvar Foeseeker's whisper reached Luke, and he looked across at the fierce creature.

'Are we close to the place where you left your son?'

'Not too far now,' Luke murmured as he pulled at the oar, 'I feel it in my bones, friend.'

Grigg the searat gripped the edge of the crow's nest. Leaning forward, he peered into the leaden rainswept dawn at a rocky point in the blurred distance. With all the agility of a searat he clambered down from the rigging to the deck.

Vilu Daskar was slumbering on a window seat, a charcoal brazier glowing nearby to warm the cabin. Parug the bosun gave a perfunctory rap at the door and entered. 'Headland's been sighted, cap'n, dead ahead!'

Daskar leaped from the seat. Grabbing his wool cloak and scimitar he dashed from the cabin, with Parug at his heels, bellowing to rouse the crew.

'Land ho, all paws on deck!'

Daskar raced for'ard, wind whipping the cloak straight out behind him, calling to Parug as he went, 'Get Luke up on deck here, quick!'

Wind thrummed the rigging ropes like harp strings. Daskar perched high in the bows, his eyes shielded by a paw as he noted the headland's position. Jumping down, he gathered his cloak around him and hurried to the stern. Luke was standing by the wheel, bound and surrounded by six vermin. The pirate stoat smiled triumphantly at his oarslave.

'So, 'twas as you said, the point lies dead ahead. A wise decision, mouse, for if you had played me false, then your head would be on the deck for sure! Bind him to the wheel, make sure the ropes are tight!'

Rough paws dragged Luke to the big steering wheel. He was tied to it securely by both paws and a rope halter was placed about his neck. Vilu held the other end.

'Right, sing out, Luke, give us the course!'

, Knowing it was too early to give the signal, the Warrior murmured, keeping his voice low, 'Steady as she goes.'

Swinging on ropes, just below the stern gallery, Beau and Vurg strained their ears.

'Wot wot, did y'hear what he said, Vurg?'

'No, mate, but I'm sure he didn't shout "Dead ahead"!'

Groaning, the hare slid down his rope. 'Oh fiddlesticks, that means the attack ain't on yet. I'll go an' let Ranguvar an' the others know.'

Vilu tugged viciously at Luke's halter. 'Looks as if you're sailing her close in to land. Why?'

Moving the wheel a touch north, Luke kept his eyes ahead. 'Got to get my bearings. I'm not quite sure that's the right headland. Don't worry, Daskar, your ship's safe. I'm not going to try anything with all those poor slaves chained below. Give the order to ship oars and take her to half sail. We'll go forward nice an' easy if you're afraid.'

Vilu gave the halter another savage jerk. 'I'm not afraid, mouse, just cautious. I've sailed northern seas before – they can be treacherous.'

Luke smiled fearlessly. 'As treacherous as you?'

Vilu Daskar returned the smile. 'Not quite.'

At midday the rain cleared, though the skies still remained dull and wintry. Luke was close enough to see the shore plainly now. His heart sank, as if a great boulder was forcing it down, causing a heavy ache in his chest. Before him the shoreline lay deserted, only seagrass and some tattered rags fluttering in the wind. Charred wood and broken implements, hoes and rakes, were half buried in the shifting sand. The caves, where once he had settled his tribe, had had the protective shields of driftwood and vegetation ripped from their fronts. They stood empty, like the eyeless sockets of a corpse staring out to sea. Martin his son, Windred and the rest of the tribe were gone from the place.

Sick with grief, he slumped across the wheel. Vilu Daskar was grinning slyly as he brought his face close to Luke's.

'What a shame, my friend. Has your plan gone wrong? What sort of fool did you think you were playing me for? I would have been stupid to let you sail my ship inshore where the creatures of your tribe could have helped you.' Luke stared dully as his enemy laughed in his face. 'Fool! I am captain of the greatest ship that ever sailed the seas. How do you think I did it? I learned to read the minds of others, to out-think those who thought they were smarter than me. I knew all along that you yearned for vengeance after the slaying of your tribe. All you have lived for is a chance to kill me!'

Luke nodded. 'Then you must know there is no treasure?' He felt hot rage sweep through him as Vilu patted his cheek, almost fondly. The stoat's voice was wheedling.

'The old double bluff, eh, Luke. Don't try to pull the wool over my eyes. I know that every tribe, no matter how poor and lowly, has some kind of treasure. Right?'

Luke bit his lip, lowering his head as if defeated. 'What beast could hide anything from you. But I hold you to your promise. If I show you the way to my tribe's treasure, you must set me and my two friends free.'

Vilu leaned upon Luke's shoulder, happily surveying the empty shore. 'But of course, I am a creature of my word, all three of you will have your freedom. Now set a true course.'

Awkwardly the Warrior mouse manoeuvred the wheel round. 'It's further north up the coast. The cross-currents shouldn't give us much trouble if you pile all sail on and put the oars to a steady half pace.'

Ranguvar waited until Bullflay lumbered by before turning to the oarport. Vurg popped his head into view, spray dashing at his face.

'Luke's not given the word yet, friend. But I'd stay ready tonight if I were you. That's when we should be further upcoast, amid the high rocks and deep water!'

34

Ringpatch the ferret came in from watch and slumped down on a pile of old rope and sailcloth, glad to be back in the big smoky crew's cabin, mopping water from his fur.

'Bad night out there, mates, weather's rough as a toad's back an' cold as a cap'n's 'eart. Any vittles left?'

Foulscale pointed to the empty pan on the table. 'Take a look in there, mate. If'n there's anythin' left then save 'arf fer me. Why'n the name o' fishguts aren't we down south somewheres in the warm sun, pickin' ripe fruit offa trees an' plunderin' birds' nests? Wot's to be 'ad up 'ere, apart from yer death o' cold an' starvation, that's wot I'd like ter know?'

Akkla snuggled up to the smoking stove, shaking his head. 'Did the ice git down yore ears, Foulscale? We're in the northern waters fer treasure, or 'aven't yew 'eard?'

'Treasure?' Ringpatch crawled over to sit by the stove.

Akkla tossed some old rope into the stove and watched it burn bright as flames licked round the tarry strands. 'Aye, treasure. Y'know that Warrior mouse Luke? Well 'e's steerin' the ship up t'where he stowed 'is tribe's booty. Vilu 'ad a word with 'im, promised t'set Luke an' his two mates free if'n they let the cap'n git 'is paws on the treasure they 'id.'

Foulscale showed his blackened teeth in a knowing grin. 'Set 'em free, eh? Remember the last lot Vilu Daskar set free, those four 'edge'ogs, d'yer recall that, Willag?'

The searat chuckled with wicked glee. 'Oh, I remember it awright. They were 'oldin' back a supply of grain they'd 'arvested. Ole Vilu promises t'set 'em free once he's got 'is claws on the stuff. So they showed 'im where they'd 'idden it. Hawhawhaw!'

One rat had not been a crew member at the time, so he had to ask. 'An' did Daskar set 'em free?'

Akkla looked about for more rope to feed the stove. 'Course the cap'n did. He 'ad 'em sewed up in the grain sacks with some good 'eavy rocks an' dropped over-board. Vilu's last words to the 'edge'ogs were, "You leave my ship alive, free t'go where ye will"!'

The Sea Rogues pounded each other's backs and laughed aloud.

'Never tole a lie in 'is life 'as our cap'n. Hohoho!'

'Wonder wot 'e'll think up fer this mouse Luke an' 'is mates?'

'Heehee, bet 'e'll take 'em up ter some clifftop an' set 'em free as birds. Heeheehee!'

'Or introduce 'em t'some new friends, the sharks. Hahahaha!'

'Wotever it is, the cap'n's shore t'give us all a good laugh, mates. Then we can sail south'ard t'the sun an' prime vittles fer a while. Widout Luke an' 'is two mateys though.'

Parug the bosun gestured to Foulscale with his knotted rope. 'Oi yew, stir yer stumps there, 'tis yore turn t'relieve Ringpatch on watch. Never mind sittin' round 'ere laughin' an' jokin', git out on deck wid yer, go on!'

Foulscale shot the bosun a hateful glance. Wrapping a piece of sailcloth around him he lumbered reluctantly out. Akkla called after him, 'Don't let the Sea Bogle git yer!'

Foulscale spat out of the cabin door, and it blew back in his face. 'Tchah! Sea Bogle, that'n soon deserted ship as soon as there wasn't enough grub left t'feed a fly. Sea Bogle only brought bad luck ter this ship, just's well 'tis gone.'

He ducked as Parug flung an old seaboot at him, calling, 'It won't be Sea Bogles you'll 'ave ter worry about if'n yew stands wid that door open much longer, freezin' us all into our graves. Gerrout on watch, yew idle lump, an' shut that door after yer!'

Beau and Vurg had climbed aboard the red ship, being unable to endure further cold and hardship hanging on to the raft at the stern. Gripping any protrusions available they made their way along the outside of the *Goreleech*, avoiding being seen from the after peak, where Luke was tied to the wheel, guarded by ten crew and Vilu Daskar, who had a canvas awning to protect them and a brazier to warm their paws upon. The two friends made it to the foredeck and hid behind a sail-draped hatch cover. From their hideout they could see the shoreline: white sand backed by sheer cliffs which reared into the night.

Beau snuggled down. 'Well, it ain't much, Vurgy, but as my old auntie used t'say, somethin's better'n nothin' when y've got nothin', wot?'

Vurg threw an affectionate paw about his comrade. 'Shall I tell you wot my ole auntie used t'say, Beau? Well, she always said t'me, if yore hidin' under a hatch cover with a sailcloth over it, an' there's a hare with you, then don't let the hare talk about how 'ungry he is an' don't let 'im sing. There, that's wot my ole auntie used t'say!'

Beau was still in a fine old huff with Vurg. 'Food? Who said I was goin' to talk about food, eh, wot? Far too hungry to talk about food. An' I ain't goin' to sing to you no more, after you jumped on my head an' damaged me warbler. Savage mousewretch, that's what y'are. Oh, great seasons of stones, take a look up ahead, Vurg!'

The mouse poked his head from the sailcloth, his gaze following the bowsprit to judge the ship's course.

' 'Tis the tall rocks, Beau, we're headed straight for the tall rocks!'

Rearing like prehistoric giants to the stormy night skies, hundreds of the monolithic stone pinnacles stood out from the coast for leagues. Waves crashed into white foam at their bases, sending white spume flying high into the air. A peculiar effect, like screaming tortured animals, assaulted their ears, as the gale force winds tore between the awesome columns, whose tops seemed to touch the tempest-driven clouds.

For the first time in his life Beauclair Fethringsol Cosfortingham was robbed of the power of speech. He sat there with his mouth hanging open.

Vurg was the first to recover and do something. 'Luke's goin' to smash this ship into the tall rocks! Quick, Beau, climb down to Ranguvar. I think Luke will give the signal very soon now. I'll go astern an' listen out for it. The moment I hear Luke's voice I'll make my way along the ship's side an' yell at the top of my voice. Go now!'

Vilu Daskar was also feeling something for the first time in his life. Fear! He had seen the tall rocks, once many seasons back when he was younger. However, he had not sailed remotely near them and had vowed never to do so. But now he was in the midst of a storm, his vaunted *Goreleech* headed straight for the tall rocks, relying only on the skill of a mouse oarslave, bound to the steering wheel. Daskar stood dry-mouthed, sweating despite the cold, paws atremble and stomach churning. Tugging hard on the rope halter about Luke's neck he yelled shrilly, 'Watch what you're doing, go careful with my ship, pull her away from those rocks. Away I say!'

Luke kept his head bent, resisting the rope's tug.

'How does it feel, murderer, to have death starin' you in the face?' he gritted out from between clenched teeth. 'Think of all the innocent creatures you've sent to their deaths. Go on, tell me how it feels?'

Vilu reached past Luke and managed to get a paw on the wheel. The Warrior mouse sank his teeth into the paw, and with a yelp the pirate stoat withdrew. Vilu's guards drew their weapons. Luke shouted at them without turning his head.

'One move from you, murderer, or any of your scum, and I spin this wheel and send her side on to the rocks!'

Vilu's big mistake had been in binding Luke to the wheel. He was fully in control of steering the ship. The stoat signalled his crew to stay clear. Luke decided then to make his move. Throwing back his head he roared at the top of his lungs, loud and long, 'Dead ahead! Dead ahead! Dead aheeeeaaaaadddd!'

Slipping half in half out of the lashing churning sea, Vurg scrabbled and clawed his way along the port side until he was amidships. Ahead of him he could see Beau, balancing perilously on Ranguvar's oarshaft as it stuck out from the bowside, waiting for the signal. Vurg clambered up on to the rail, shouting, 'Dead ahead! Free the slaves, take the ship!'

In his excitement he had forgotten all else. Next instant Parug and Akkla came rushing from the crew's quarters.

'What's happenin', who's takin' the ship?'

'Somebeast's tryin' to free the slaves! Call to arms! All paws on deck!'

Slaves began pouring from the companionways of the three oardecks, some armed with what they could find, lengths of chain, pieces of timber and pitifully few daggers. Unsure how to proceed, they milled about on the deck, some weeping openly, not knowing what to do with their new-found freedom. These slaves, all from the upper and middle decks, soon found themselves set upon by masses of heavily armed Sea Rogues, veterans in the business of bloodshed. Vurg and Beau rushed to their aid. Laying two searats low with savage kicks from his long hindlegs, the hare grabbed the vermin's cutlasses and tossed one to Vurg, bellowing, 'Rally to us, you chaps, don't sit round blubberin'. Fight!'

Several of the younger and bolder spirits obeyed, but there were others, too weak and frightened, who were thoroughly intimidated by the fierce horde of the *Goreleech*'s crew. These wretched creatures ran and hid, and a lot of them tried to push their way back down to the oardecks, to the benches and chains where they had lived for long seasons.

Then Ranguvar Foeseeker arrived upon the scene.

Battering slaves aside like ninepins, Bullflay came screaming out of the companionway, terror stamped upon his ugly features. Behind him, like the shadow of death, was Ranguvar. Laying into the slavemaster with his own whip, the black squirrel was a sight to strike fear into the heart of anybeast now that she was on the loose. The long whip cracked around Bullflay's ears as Ranguvar Foeseeker went after him, the stormy night echoing to her battle cries.

'Yayalaho! I am the Foeseeker, born in moondark to the crash of thunder! Sing your deathsongs! Yayalahooooo!'

In his panic Bullflay fled straight up the rigging, with Ranguvar hard on his heels, her eyes red with blood-wrath, laughing madly as she closed on her hated foe.

Vilu Daskar felt himself gripped by the icy claws of panic. Never in his wildest imaginings had he dreamt this could happen aboard his red ship.

'Akkla! Parug! Bring the crew astern! Gather to me!'

As the Sea Rogues crowded round, Luke called to his enemy above the din of storm and battle, 'What are you goin' to do now, coward? Yore slaves are free and fightin', the *Goreleech* is bein' driven to the rocks. 'Twas a bad day for you when you murdered my wife!'

As if to emphasise the dilemma, Bullflay's body, choked by his own whiplash, came flying down from aloft and crashed through the afterdeck stairs, taking with it two vermin who were making their way aft.

Ranguvar Foeseeker climbed halfway down the rigging, then, with a bloodcurdling yell, hurled herself on a group of Sea Rogues who were hacking at helpless slaves on the main deck.

The pirate stoat turned on Luke, his voice a venomous hiss as he slashed at the bound Warrior with his sword.

'You were the cause of all this, but I will end it here!'

Luke could not protect himself from the wild, vicious onslaught, even though the swinging blade chopped the ropes free from one of his paws. Dulam and Denno were battling their way to the afterdeck when they saw Luke being attacked. Beau and Vurg saw it too, and fought their way to the shattered stairs, Vurg crying out, 'Luke! No! Hang on, mate, we're comin'!'

But Luke was not finished. Fighting his way up through waves of pain, he put all his strength into a single blow. His paw chopped down on that of Vilu Daskar, sending the bone-handled scimitar skimming off into the sea. Then Luke had Daskar in a death grip, crushing him tight against the ship's wheel. Sea Rogues hurled themselves upon the Warrior, trying to free their captain, who was screeching with fright. Pounding willy-nilly at the Warrior, they were about to break the awful grip he had on Vilu Daskar when suddenly Ranguvar Foeseeker was in their midst, armed with two swords. The black squirrel was like a berserk tornado, dealing out death and fearsome wounds, laughing madly into the stricken faces of her foes.

'Yaylaho! 'Tis a fine night to die! Yaylahooooo! Take a deep breath, buckoes, it'll be yore last! I'll hold 'em off, Luke, you hold Daskar tight! Yayalahoooooo!'

Looming up to the red ship was a towering rock, ten times the girth of any craft, with waves riding high up its sides and smashing in foamy cascades. Luke had Daskar's paws twined through the wheel spokes like a captive upon a rack, and the pirate stoat, his back pressed hard against the wheel, began begging and pleading hoarsely for his life as the *Goreleech* rode side on towards the monstrous column of wave-lashed stone.

'Spare me, Luke. You can have the treasure and freedom for all the slaves. Take the red ship too, but let me go. I speak truly, my word is my bond. Spare my life!'

Luke the Warrior pressed his face close to that of his mortal enemy, crushing him tighter and whispering, 'Cowards die a thousand times, a warrior dies only once. The spirits of all you have slain are watching you, Vilu Daskar, and they will rest in peace now that your time has come. You must die as you have lived, a coward to the last!'

When the red ship struck the rock it reverberated from stem to stern. There was a noise like an overhead peal of thunder, then it was shorn in two halves upon the mighty pinnacle of stone. The *Goreleech* hung there for one awful moment, then the whole stern, from afterdeck to midships, fell. With a huge creaking of sundered timbers it hit the water and sank instantly. Far far below the seas, never to be seen again.

BOOK THREE

A Warrior's Legacy

35

Sunlight lanced through into the cabin of the *Arfship*, dustmotes swirled lazily about the still lit lanterns. Denno took the rock crystal glasses from his nose end and placed them on the closed book in front of him. Yawning and rubbing his eyes gently, he leaned back and stared up at the noon sky.

'So now you know everythin', Martin of Redwall, that's the whole story, as best as we could remember.'

All eyes were on the stonefaced warrior, awaiting his reaction. After what seemed an interminable silence, he spoke.

'Am I to understand then that my father wrecked the *Goreleech* on the big column, knowing that he would die?'

Beau wiped a paw across his eyes and sniffed.

'Aye, that's what he did, old lad, wounded almost t'death, with Ranguvar Foeseeker holdin' off almost an entire vermin crew so Luke an' her could have their revenge on Vilu Daskar, the red ship, an' all that had caused 'em to lose their loved ones. By the fur, blood, tooth an' sword! Two braver warriors never lived!'

Vurg grasped the Warrior mouse's paw tightly. 'They did it for you – for all of us, Martin. Everybeast who'd ever suffered by the wickedness of Daskar an' his red ship. Luke was past carin' about what happened to himself – Ranguvar too. Between them their final sacrifice was to rid the land an' seas of a great evil!'

Martin's eyes were like chips of ice.

'I would have done exactly the same in my father's place!'

Dulam felt the hairs rise on his nape as he watched Martin. 'I believe you would've, too. That sounded just like yore dad talkin' then. We all would, but for the fact we were at the for'ard end when the ship broke in two.'

Martin stared keenly from one to the other.

'Is there anything else I should know? Vurg, you knew him better than most. Tell me.'

The old mouse shook his head wistfully. 'He gave you all he could, vengeance for your mother an' our tribe, freedom from a terror that the coastlands an' seas lived in fear of. But I remember that day we sailed off from the northlands, he gave you his sword. That blade had never left his paw, or that of his father an' his father before him. It was the most precious thing Luke ever owned! But there was something else, Martin, not from your father alone. When you discovered me in the old cave back there, I had found something buried in the sand. Here!'

Vurg passed the beaded linen bag to Martin. It was the sort of container a mother would use to keep her baby's things in, together with the small possessions she held dear. Martin's paw traced the beautiful pattern of tiny threaded beads worked on to the linen. He eased himself slowly away from the table and left the cabin.

Gonff called after him, 'You all right, matey? Need any help or company?' There was no answer from the Warrior. Gonff settled back against a bulkhead. 'Best leave him alone awhile. Get some shuteye, mates. I've a feelin' that when he comes back through yon door we'll be leavin' this place. You an' yore pals better pack, Vurg, we ain't leavin' you stranded up in these rocks on a broken ship. You'll have t'keep pinchin' yoreselves to make sure yore not dreamin' when you see Redwall Abbey, mates!'

Martin climbed down the front of the huge main column and sat on a ledge, with the sea almost lapping his footpaws, gazing down into the fathomless deeps. Somewhere far below lay the stern of the *Goreleech*, with his father, Luke the Warrior, pinning Vilu Daskar against the steering wheel, holding his enemy in an eternal embrace. Around them would be strewn the pirate stoat's vermin guard, and Luke's berserk friend Ranguvar Foeseeker. Pride surged through Martin. His father and the black squirrel had kept their vows, they were the bravest of the brave, true warriors.

Martin sat there a long time, staring at the spot where sunlight ended in seagreen haze. From that beaded bag he took a stone, a rounded, medium-sized pebble, banded with various colours. The sort his father might have picked up from the beach, long ago, and brought back to the cave for his wife or little son. Martin held it awhile, until the stone took on warmth from his paws. Then he dropped it gently into the sea, watching it sink rapidly from sight into the depths.

'This is for you, my father, from Sayna, the wife you lost, and Martin, the son you strove to return to. But I have made good your promise, I returned to find you. Ranguvar Foeseeker, I know not if you had any family, but you have two friends for ever. Luke the Warrior and Martin of Redwall. I will carry your memories in my heart.'

Martin left the tall rock then, with the seas still booming in his ears as they broke against it. In all his life he never went back to that place. On the next ebb tide the skiff *Honeysuckle* sailed away from Tall Rocks, bound south for Redwall.

Skipper of Otters craned his head back, staring up into the pale blue summer morn. Bella the Badgermother of

Redwall waited patiently, already knowing what her burly friend's question would be.

'Of course I can tell the squirrels to set up more scaffoldin' at the south end, marm, but why, pray?'

Bella spread her paws wide, as if the answer were obvious. 'Because summer is nearly done and autumn will soon be here.'

Sitting back on his powerful tail, the big otter shrugged. 'Huh, 'fraid you've lost me, marm. What difference will that make? Autumn always follered summer, 'tis the way o' the seasons. What's that got t'do with scaffoldin'?'

Bella sat beside him, fiddling with the strings of her apron. 'Mayhap 'tis just a foolish fancy of mine, Skip, but I'd like to see the south gable built right up as far as it will reach. According to Abbess Germaine and Martin's plans, that's where the weather vane will be, at the highest point.'

Columbine approached them and sat down, unfolding a clean white linen cloth to reveal a scone still warm from the window ledge where it had lain to cool. 'Taste that and tell me what you think?'

Breaking it in two, she gave them a piece each. Bella inspected the pastry, sniffing it appreciatively.

'Smells wonderful. I can see chopped nuts and bits of crystallised honey in there, but tell me, why is the scone pink?'

'Because it's a Redwall Abbeyscone,' the pretty mouse-wife explained. 'I used wild cherry juice in the mix, to give it the colour of our walls. I plan on making them in the shape of the sandstone blocks we've used to build our Abbey with. D'you like them, Skip?'

The otter had bolted his piece in one great mouthful, and now he picked crumbs from his whiskers and nibbled them.

'Very tasty, Columbine marm, exceedin' nice! But yore goin' t'need a big oven to bake 'em big as sandstone blocks.'

Columbine gave Skipper a playful shove. 'Oh, you

great puddenheaded riverdog, they'll only be little scones, baked in the shape of the big stones!'

The otter Chieftain scratched his head. 'Aye, marm, seems I can't get a thing right t'day. D'you know why autumn follows summer, an' that's why the squirrels must build more scaffoldin', so that we can build the south gable end up to its peak with a weather vane atop? 'Cos I'm blowed if'n I do, ole pudden'ead that I am!'

Columbine hugged Bella's huge paw. 'Oh, what a lovely, wonderful idea! Our south gable built high, with a weather vane sticking up on it. When my Gonff comes marching down the path with Martin and Dinny and Trimp, why, they'll be able to see it from a great distance. How nice!'

A slow smile spread across Skipper's face as the reason for Bella's request dawned upon him.

'Haharr, so that's it! Swoggle me rudder, why didn't I think o' that?'

He fell backward as Bella and Columbine tugged his footpaws, chuckling aloud as they chorused together, ''Cos you're a great puddenheaded old riverdog!'

Bella made the announcement right after breakfast. It was wholeheartedly supported by all the creatures of Redwall.

Lady Amber added to the excitement. 'An excellent idea. I'll get my squirrels to work straight away on the scaffolding. Though 'twill take most of the day erecting it up on the south end, so here's what I suggest. Friends, you've worked hard and long all summer, why not have a day's rest? Perhaps a picnic by the pond can be arranged for early evening. We'll have finished the scaffolding by then, so we'll be able to join you. First thing tomorrow everybeast can pitch in and we'll really go to work and top off that south gable. How's that?' Rousing cheers greeted the Squirrelqueen's scheme.

*

Ferdy and Coggs, the hedgehog Cellarkeepers, trundled barrels, kegs and casks out of the main Abbey door on to the lawn. Baby Gonflet was waiting with his gang of Dibbuns, all armed with wedge stones and prodding sticks. Coggs narrowed his eyes. 'Wot are you up to, Gonflet, ye liddle wretch?'

Gonflet waved his barrel-prodding stick dismissively. 'You'n'Ferd go now, Cogg, us take these barrels down to a pond. Not wurry, us good barrel rollers!'

Coggs exchanged glances with his twin brother. 'Wot d'ye reckon, Ferdy, shall we let 'em?'

Ferdy smiled at the Dibbuns, who were dancing about and waving their sticks eagerly.

'Aye, they got to learn sometime, I s'pose. But roll that big barrel o' strawberry fizz slow now, Gonflet, an' go easy with those firkins o' elderberry wine. An' the rest of ye, stay be'ind the barrels all the way, don't go runnin' in front. We don't want yore mammas after our blood 'cos you've been run down by some keg or cask!'

Bella walked by, followed by a group of Redwallers carrying canvas and poles.

'We'll make a good leanto,' the Badgermother was saying, 'it'll provide shade for the food and the elders can rest there. Mayberry, will you and Catkin get a trolley, line it with blankets and fetch Abbess Germaine down to the pond? Go easy with her, please – remember, she's very old and frail.'

Mayberry and Catkin, the two ottermaids, bobbed curtsies to Bella and trotted off, feeling very important.

Columbine supervised the kitchens, bringing order and calm to the bustle of cooks and helpers. 'Clear those window ledges of scones now, we need room for the turnip and parsley flans to cool. Miz Woodspike, would you like to top those blackberry tarts off with meadow-cream? I don't know anybeast who does it as neat as you do. Mister Pitclaw, could you help me to get the oatloaves out of the ovens, please? Oh, and tell your moles we need more charcoal to heat that back oven for cheese and mushroom flans. No, don't worry about your deeper'n ever pie, I'll watch it whilst you are gone. Now, let me see, strawberry shortcake, rhubarb crumble, leek and onion turnovers, deep apple pie, is that everything? Oh dearie me, I've forgotten the salad!'

A fat bewhiskered bankvole broke in on Columbine's musings. 'Never fret, missus, I been choppin' salad an' mixin' it since hard after brekkist, 'tis just about made. Gurbee, did we remember to pick some fennel?'

A jolly-looking mole dug both claws into his apron pocket, rocking back and forth as he announced, 'Hurr, you'm may 'ave furgitted ee fennyel, zurr, but oi bain't, oi gurtly loiks moi salad well fennyelled. Burr aye!' Beamingly he pointed to a sizeable pile of fennel.

Lady Amber stood high up on the south gable, heading the line of squirrels passing up thick yew scaffolding poles to others, with knives held in their teeth and lengths of stout cord draped over their shoulders. They chatted away nonchalantly, clinging by tails and paws from their perilous positions. Below them the lawns of Redwall Abbey looked like a series of green kerchiefs.

'Chuck me that big 'un with the forked top, Barko, aye, that's the one. Ashtwig, grab this end while I tie it off to the main platform. Pass more cords up, will ye!'

Swift and sure they toiled away, with a clear blue sky above and a breathtaking void beneath them.

'Looks nice'n'cool down by that pond, they're puttin' a leanto up, see.'

'Aye, an' lookit, there's miz Columbine an' the others, carryin' trays o' vittles from the Abbey. What's that noise?'

'My tummy, mate. Mmmm, I can almost smell cheese'n'mushroom flans from up here. Hope they don't start afore we get down.'

'If you don't cut the gab an' tie off that pole we'll be up here come this time t'morrow. Shape yoreself, matey!'

Mayberry and Catkin delivered Abbess Germaine to Bella, who was waiting beneath the canvas awning. Both the young ottermaids bobbed another curtsy together.

'Here she is, safe'n'sound, miz Bell!'

'Snug as a bug in a rug with all those cushions an' blankets, miz Bell. We was very very careful with 'er, marm.'

Twinkle-eyed, the ancient Abbess peered out of the trolley. 'Mm, mm, if they'd pushed me any slower we would've stopped. Two snails passed us on the way, would y'believe!'

Both ottermaids' lower lips began to tremble. Abbess Germaine chuckled, nodding fondly at them. 'Mmm, mm, now don't fret, little maids, I was jesting. An old fogey like me couldn't ask for more gentle or better care than you two showed to me. Cheer up now!'

Bella ruffled the ears of both affectionately. 'That's why I sent them. Mayberry and Catkin are my two best and most trusted helpers. Run along now, you two.'

Smiling and curtsying, they prepared to skip off.

'Thankee, miz Bell, nice t'be of service to ye!'

'An' you too, Mother Abbess, just call if'n you needs us!'

Germaine was a bit warm. She shrugged off the blankets as she watched the two ottermaids looking for others to assist.

'Such good little things, Bella, a credit to Redwall, eh?'

'I'll say they are. They're both Skipper's grand-daughters, y'know. I was only saying to him the other day— Yaaaah! Look out! Everybeast out of the waaaaaay!'

Amid squeaks of dismay and a great bumping and rumbling, Bella seized both Abbess and trolley. Heaving them up in her strong paws, she dashed from the leanto, not a moment too soon. Gonflet and his Dibbuns had let Coggs and Ferdy's cellar stock get away from them. Down the slope a thundering stampede of kegs, barrels, firkins and casks leaped, bounced and spun. In their wake came Gonflet and his gang of little Abbey creatures, hallooing and whooping wildly.

Bella ducked, covering the Abbess with her body as a keg of pennycloud cordial bounced and whizzed by overhead, missing the badger's ears by a whisker. In a trice the leanto was levelled, flattened to the ground. In a resounding boom of splashes the picnic drinks in their oaken containers hit the pond's surface, drenching everybeast within range in a cascade of pondwater.

Dripping from ears to tail, Bella turned to the saturated gang of Dibbuns. Gonflet grinned from ear to ear, pointing with his stick at the array of floating barrels bobbing about in the pond.

'All go'd too fast t'stop, miz Bell. But pond keep d'drinks nice an' cool, I fink!'

Bella could not be angry in the face of the little fellow's irresistible charm, though she hid a smile and tried to sound stern.

'I knew a young mouse one time who was just like you, a scamp, a rascal and a complete pickle!'

Gonflet pawed water from his eye, wrinkling his nose as he stared up at the big Badgermother. 'Wot was him name, miz Bell?'

The huge striped muzzle lowered, until it was level with Gonflet's face. 'If I recall rightly, his name was Gonff!'

This sent the tiny mouse off into tucks of laughter. Waving his stick he raced off with his Dibbun gang, shouting, 'Heeheehee! Jus' wait I tell my daddy. You a scamp! Raskill! Pickler! That wot miz Bell call you. Heeheehee!'

Creakily Abbess Germaine emerged from the swathe of blankets and cushions in her trolley. She began sorting out poles from the pile of collapsed canvas.

'Hmm, mmm, 'tis some long seasons since I built a leanto. Lend a paw here, Bella, come on!'

The Badgermother sighed as she dragged the canvas

aside. 'Gonflet was right, though, the pond will keep those barrels nice and cool on a day like this, Mother Abbess!'

That evening the picnic was a huge success. Lady Amber and her squirrels skipped nimbly down the scaffolding, navigating the sheer walls as if they were on level ground, singing as they descended.

'The dull old ground is not for me,
I can't stand it somehow,
Leave me in a good stout tree,
Upon a knotty bough!

'Tis hey ho and up we go,
Above the ground we dwell,
Where every leaf'n'twig we know,
And every branch right well!

A squirrel a squirrel so nimble,
Can climb most anywhere,
A tail in a tree is a symbol,
That I'm at home up there!

So ash oak rowan or pine,
Stately elm or beech,
They're all fine, they're all mine,
They're all within my reach!'

Whilst the Redwallers made merry, otters fished the barrels of drink from the pond. Gonflet and his Dibbun gang had everybeast roaring with laughter as they performed a dramatic re-enactment of the barrel incident. Skipper held his sides to stop them aching, tears of helpless merriment streaming from his eyes, as a small mole, acting a barrel of dandelion and burdock cordial, tumbled downhill into the pond. Columbine hauled him out and attempted to give the tiny creature a strict lecture, but was unable to do so because she collapsed laughing.

Lanterns were lit at the pond's edge when evening shadows deepened, the still water reflecting their glow. Mayberry and Catkin performed a graceful dance to the accompaniment of Ferdy and Coggs on drum and fiddle, playing a time-honoured favourite called 'Bide in the Rushes'. Columbine left off serving drinks, and sat eating pensively. Abbess Germaine watched her closely.

'An acorn for your thoughts, my dear.'

Columbine recovered herself as Gonflet hurled himself into her lap. 'What? Oh, er, sorry, Mother Abbess, I was in a bit of a daze. I was just thinking how much I miss Gonff – Martin and Dinny too, of course. I wish autumn would hurry and they'd return to Redwall.'

Gonflet yawned and looked up at his mother. 'I want my daddy. When it be h'autumn, mamma?'

The dancing had stopped, and all eyes turned on Columbine. Gonflet's lids began drooping as she stroked his head and softly recited an old poem.

'Round the seasons slowly turning,
Faithful as the stars and moon,
Summer fades, the earth is yearning,
Softly whisp'ring, autumn soon.

Drape the woods in mist one morning,
Now small birds have learned to fly,
Mother Nature's gentle warning,
See green leaves turn brown, and die.

In old orchards on the bough,
Fruit hangs russet, red and gold,
Purple scarlet berries now,
All the rambling hedgerows hold.

Hazel, beech and chestnut too,
Each displays its burden fair,
They will shed them, all for you,
Ere winter lays their branches bare.

Fields of ripened grain and corn,
Swaying to a murm'ring breeze,
Shaking off the dew of dawn,
When the eye sees signs like these.

Summer's long hot days are ended,
Harvest moons o'er stream and mere,
Tell the tale, as 'twas intended,
Autumn's peaceful dream is here.'

Columbine shifted slightly, trying not to disturb her sleeping babe. 'Ooh, this fellow's getting heavy these days.'

Bella relieved her friend of the burden, scooping Gonflet neatly up in one huge paw. She nodded knowingly. 'Little wonder. See, the pockets of his smock are full of wedgestones to use on the barrels. Pity the scamp never bothered to use 'em!'

Abbess Germaine could not help remarking, 'Think of the fun we'd have missed if he did. That one'll grow up a bigger rascal than his father. But you're right, Columbine, Redwall isn't the same without Martin, Dinny and your Gonff. Let's hope they'll make it back safely.'

Skipper paused, a cheese and mushroom flan halfway to his mouth. 'Only beasts I'd be worried about, beggin' yore pardon, marm, are those foolish enough to try an' stop 'em returnin' to our Abbey. Huh, I'd sure enough feel sorry for those!'

Columbine topped the otter's beaker up with October Ale. 'I suppose you're right, Skip, but my Gonff attracts trouble no matter where he is. I think he enjoys it.'

Abbess Germaine patted the mousewife's paw. 'That's

why he has two good friends – Martin, who has never been defeated by anybeast, and Dinny, full of caution and sensible mole logic. Don't fret yourself over those three, my dear, they could overcome anything!'

Bella winked at Skipper, to lighten the evening's end and take Columbine's mind off worries about Gonff and his friends.

'Getting late, Skip. Come on, you haven't sung tonight. Send us all off to our beds with one of your funny ditties.'

The burly otter was only too willing to oblige.

'Good night, sleep tight!
Don't forget t'close the door,
Good night, sleep tight!
Use the bed an' not the floor,
Good night, sleep tight!
Now don't let me hear you snore,
Good night, sleep tight!
An' don't sleepwalk any more.
Blow out the candle,
Turn down the bed,
Stop yore yawnin' sleepyhead.

Good night, sleep tight!
Up the wooden stairs y'creep,
Good night, sleep tight!
Put on yore nightie go t'sleep,
Good night, sleep tight!
Stop that talkin' in yore dreams,
Good night, sleep tight!
Don't rip y'sheets to smithereens,
If a nightmare starts t'show,
An' you wake me up, oho,
Out the window you will go . . . good night!'

Leaving the pondside they trooped slowly back to the Abbey, Bella in the lead carrying the sleeping Gonflet,

Columbine linking paws with the ottermaids, Ferdy and Coggs pulling the trolley in which the Abbess slumbered, followed by all the other beasts. Skipper brought up the rear of the procession, singing as quietly as his big gruff voice would allow. Everybeast joined in, keeping their voices low, the catchy melody acting as a gentle march, echoing softly over moonlit Abbey lawns.

As they entered the main Abbey door a vagrant breeze ruffled Bella's fur. She shuddered lightly and whispered to Columbine, 'Bit of a chill in the air just then.'

Gonflet, who was supposed to be fast asleep, opened one eye and grinned cheekily.

'Soon be's h'autumn now, miz Bell!'

36

The *Honeysuckle* skimmed southward like a playful swallow, Log a Log Furmo proudly showing off her prowess as a skiff to the four creatures from the *Arfship*. Martin sat in the prow, enjoying the sun, seaspray and breeze, with his faithful friend Gonff alongside him. Together they listened to Trimp attempting to chide Chugger for his lack of respect to the elders.

'I'll not tell you again, Chugg, please stop calling our friends old granpas, 'tis not very good manners!'

'Tchah! You don't know noffink, they good ole granpas for Chugg. We makin' lorra skillyduffs for 'em!'

Folgrim and Dinny had been appointed assistant cooks, helping Chugger to cook skilly and duff. They were on his side.

'Maister Chugg bain't doin' no 'arm, missie, bain't that so, zurr Fol?'

'Aye, let the liddle tyke be, miss, he ain't never 'ad a granpa. Haharr, now he's got four of 'em!'

Trimp appealed to Vurg and his friends. 'Please forgive Chugger. I hope he hasn't offended you.'

'There there, don't fret, young gel, wot! He can call us blather-faced bloaters as long as he keeps feedin' us. Jolly little rip, ain't he, Vurg?'

'Aye, an' seein' as we've got no families of our own, 'tis nice t'be chosen as grandsires by him. Ahoy there, cap'n Chugg, is our skilly'n'duff ready yet?'

The small squirrel gave his concoction a final stir and licked the ladle. Nodding brusquely he issued orders.

'Skillyduff cookered now. Mista Fol, Mista Din, give ole granpas some first. Miz Trimp, you serve a rest o' my crew!'

Martin and Gonff had difficulty keeping straight faces as they accepted their bowls from Trimp. The hedgehog maid was quietly seething. 'Bushtailed little villain, who does he think he is? Issuing orders to me as if I were some sort of lackey!'

Martin blew upon his spoon as he tasted the food. 'Mmm, he does make great skilly'n'duff, though. What d'you think, Gonff?'

'Never tasted better, matey. D'you reckon Chugg'd adopt us as ole granpas?'

'No, we're a bit young for that. Why don't we apply to be uncles, like Folgrim and Dinny.'

Trimp stamped off to serve the Guosim shrews, muttering, 'I don't know, everybeast aboard this boat has got that cheeky-faced villain spoiled rotten!'

Chugger's latest order interrupted her rebellious musing.

'Find more bowls for the sh'ews, miz Trimp!'

Trimp turned on Chugger, paws akimbo, shouting shrilly, 'Yes sir no sir, three bags full sir! Perhaps you'd like me to scrub the decks and polish the oars!'

Chugger's reply left her speechless. 'No no, do that later, jus' stop shoutin' for now, my ole granpas're gonna take naps. Hush y'noise now!'

It was some days later, and the weather was getting noticeably warmer. Furmo steered the *Honeysuckle* closer inshore, hallooing the creatures standing paw deep in the shallows.

'Dunespike, old mate, how are ye?'

Splashing about joyfully, the fat old Dunehog Chieftain hailed the boat. 'Sure an' I'm all the better for yore askin', Furmo. Come ashore now an' rest yer ould fur!'

Willing paws helped haul the *Honeysuckle* above the tideline. Murfo and a gang of young male hedgehogs fell over each other assisting Trimp ashore.

'Faith an' fortunes, missie, but yore lookin' grand, grand. Prettier'n ever, though I says so meself!'

Trimp grabbed an oar and vaulted over them on to the sand. 'Aye, and still well able to take care of myself, thank ye!'

Martin seized Dunespike's paw and pumped it heartily. 'Greetings, Chief, you're looking very well!'

'True, true, I'm gettin' younger by the day, plump as a pear an' brisk as a bumblebee. Well now, c'mon up t'the dwellin' an' loosen off yore belt. We've been watchin' out each day for a glimpse of y'grand little boat. Sure an' the cooks are roastin' the paws off themselves to make ye a grand ould supper. I think we'll even be able to fill Gonff's belly tonight. How are ye doodlin' there, Mousethief?'

Gonff fell into the Dunehogs' speech mode. 'Sure an' if'n I look half as grand as yerself, then I'm twice the mouse I used to be, sir!'

Linking paws and chattering away happily, crew and Dunehogs made their way into the sandhills and entered the cunningly disguised dwelling house. Beau and his friends were quite impressed by it all, and the hare expressed his admiration to all the young hedgehogs, whilst shielding Trimp from them.

'I say, what a super wheeze, a jolly great place like this inside a sand dune, wot! Well done, you chaps, top marks!'

One of the young males was winking slyly at Trimp. 'Sure an' I'd forgotten how pretty ye are. A hog'd travel ten rough country leagues an' not see the likes o' ye. I'll wager y'could charm the stars out o' the skies with just a flutter of those eyelashes!'

Beau pretended to think the Dunehog was talking to him. He tweaked the creature's ear sharply.

'Mind y'manners, sir, we haven't even been introduced, wot. Though you seem jolly perceptive for a hedgehog. Mind you, I do strike quite a handsome impression on most creatures.'

The *Honeysuckle's* crew found that the Dunehog hospitality was not lacking. For supper they dined on a fine leek and potato soup, followed by mushroom, radish and seafood stew, with an enormous fruit trifle for dessert. After that they sat about drinking cordials and Seafoam Ale whilst they were entertained to a Spinetussling exhibition, some lively Dunehog reels and jigs, and various poems, recitations and ballads. Trimp sat with a group of hogmaids and they all flirted outrageously with the young males, who danced and Spinetussled to vie for their attention. Martin sat with Dunespike and Furmo, watching them with amusement.

Furmo gestured towards them with his tankard. 'Don't you wish y'were their age again, Chief?'

Dunespike shook his great head until the spikes rattled. 'Away with ye, indeed I do not, they're completely mad, all of 'em! I'd sooner have vittles'n'drink any day!'

Martin gave Dunespike a friendly shove. 'You old fogey, look at them, they're young and happy, with not a care on earth. Good luck to them I say, eh, Furmo?'

The Guosim Chieftain nodded his agreement. 'They don't have our problems, mate. We've got to figure how t'get a boat of the *Honeysuckle's* size up a waterfall and past a pine wood full o' painted savages. Aye, an' even when we get by that lot we'll still be battlin' upstream, against the current. 'Tis goin' t'be difficult t'say the least!'

Dunespike poured himself some cordial. 'Then why d'ye not find another route?'

'Huh, easy said, Chief, but is there another route?'

'Hmm, let me think. Ah now! What about Northfork!'

Furmo stared over the rim of his tankard at Dunespike.

'Northfork? Does it run up this far?'

'Sure it does an' all, two days of a good pawslog from here.'

Furmo called across to Folgrim. 'Ahoy, mate, d'you know the Northfork stream?'

The scarred otter left off contending for the remains of the trifle with Beau.

'Aye, I know Northfork stream right enough, though I never travelled right up it. I was reared at the southern end of that stream, 'tis where my holt is at.'

Furmo thumped the rush mat they were seated on. 'Of course! It joins up to the stream we sailed here on, about three days down from my tribe's summer camp. Just one thing, though. How're we goin' to get the *Honeysuckle* overland to the Northfork stream?'

Dunespike shrugged his powerful shoulders. 'An' how else but to carry it? Sure, me an' the Dunehogs will lend a paw t'do the job. A fine lot we'd be if'n we couldn't help out. That's what friends are for!'

Martin clasped paws with the good old Hogchief. 'And you surely are a great friend to us, sir!'

Dunespike's huge frame shook with merriment. 'Sure an' I wouldn't risk bein' anythin' else to a warrior who can wield a sword like you, Martin of Redwall!'

By first light next morning they were all down on the beach. Dunespike had slept on the idea and awakened with a brilliant solution. Martin and the crew stood on one side, watching as the hedgehog Chieftain put his scheme into action. Two sets of wheels on axles were trundled out from somewhere in the dunes. Dunespike called out orders.

'Here now, Murfo, you an' the lads attend to them wheels. Martin, get that grand ould crew o' yores on the starboard side, an' I'll take the portside with my crowd.'

Paddles and stout poles were thrust beneath the skiff's flat bottom to emerge the other side. Everybeast took firm hold of them. Dunespike roared out, 'Are y'fit now. Lift!'

The *Honeysuckle* rose clear of the sand as they lifted. Murfo and the young ones rolled the wheels in for'ard and aft.

'Ah that's grand, let her down now, easy!'

Two Dunehogs with big staples and mallets fixed the axles in position beneath the boat. Dinny whispered to Trimp, 'Hurr hurr, ee boat wot doan't sail on ee seas, oi loiks et. Yon Dunespiker be a gurtly h'intelligent 'og, burr aye!'

There was some minor trouble getting the wheeled vessel through the dunes and off the soft sand. However, once they hauled her up through a low gap in the clifftop, the going was good. It was fairly flat scrubland, grass and hardpacked earth, and there was no call to use the pulling ropes. With her sail up, the *Honeysuckle* caught the wind and rolled along unaided. Beau and the other three elders were aboard her, with Dunespike, Trimp and Chugger. The rest trotted alongside, sometimes even having to tug on the towropes to slow the *Honeysuckle*'s progress.

Gonff laughed. 'Just think, if'n there was no woodlands 'twixt here an' Redwall, we could've sailed home by land!'

Later in the afternoon the land began a mild uphill slope and the breeze died completely. They split into two parties, one for'ard, pulling on the towropes, the rest at the stern, pushing. But the skiff still ran fairly smooth on its wheels, so it would have been no great effort were it not for Chugger. The little squirrel had attached a gull feather to a pole, and he dashed back and forth, tickling the pullers and pushers mercilessly and haranguing them.

'Cummon! Cummon! Run, make 'er go plenny faster, or cap'n Chugg tickle you tails off!'

Trimp decided she had put up with enough. Looping a line about the tormentor, she relieved him of the pole and tied him to the mast. Chugger set up an immediate clamour.

'I a cap'n, lemme go! 'Elp me, ole granpas, mista Din, mista Fol, 'elp Chugg!'

But no help was forthcoming. Quite the opposite, in fact. Beau took hold of the feathered pole and began tickling his adopted grandsquirrel.

'See how you like it, sah, wot! Silence now, or I'll jolly well tickle the tip of y'nose an' make you sneeze all season. Now, what d'ye say t'that, cap'n Chugg?'

'Choppa you tail off, Beau, an' Chugg not make you any no more skillyduff!'

Beau slumped down beside Vurg, nodding sadly. 'No skilly'n'duff eh wot. Ah well, such is the fate of a blinkin' mutineer, old chap!'

That night they set up camp in the lee of a wide stone outcrop at the base of a hill. Log a Log Furmo sat looking at the *Honeysuckle* speculatively.

'Y'know, Gonff, I think I'll leave those wheels on 'er. Won't do no 'arm to a flat-bottomed craft like the *Honeysuckle*. Hah, wait'll my missus sees our new boat, she'll be proud as a toad with a top hat!'

Folgrim had been to the top of the hill, to see what the going would be like next day. On his return, the otter called Martin and Dunespike to one side.

'I think I just spotted trouble the other side o' this hill.'

The Warrior mouse became instantly alert. 'What sort of trouble, Folgrim?'

'Bunch o' ragtag vermin, foxes, stoats an' the like.'

Martin was away uphill swiftly, sword in paw. 'Let's go and take a look!'

Bellying down, the three friends crawled over the hilltop. Below them on the gorse-strewn plain, several small fires were burning. There was little need to investigate further, for by the light of a half-moon they could estimate the numbers of foebeast below. Dunespike had seen the same band before.

'They were sniffin' round in our dunes last winter, but we covered our tracks well an' got the young 'uns safe inside the ould dwellin'. Sure, meself an' some others put on our sheets and stilts an' scared the blaggards off. What d'ye think we should do about 'em, Martin?'

Without hesitation the Warrior answered, 'We could defeat them in a fight, but there's no sense in that. I want everybeast to reach their homes safe. Listen now, I think I've got a solution to the problem.'

Skipper perched high up on the south gable, his footpaws firmly lodged in a roofbeam gap. From where he stood, the otter Chieftain could see out over the countless acres of Mossflower Wood to the east. He turned slowly, looking across the vast plain to the west.

'Rap me rudder, wot a sight! Now I know why birds are singin' happily. Everythin' looks so different from up 'ere.' He shut his eyes momentarily as he caught sight of Lady Amber walking along the topmost scaffold pole as if it were a broad roadway. 'Marm, I beg ye, would y'mind not doin' that 'til I'm back on the ground. Somethin' inside me just did a somersault.'

The Squirrelqueen leaped lightly down beside him. 'Sorry, Skip, I forgot there was a land dweller up here. Is the weather vane ready yet?'

'Nearly. Ole Ferdy'n'Coggs are doin' as fine a job of smithyin' as I ever saw, marm. Though miz Columbine says there won't be a scrap o' charcoal left in the kitchens t'cook with. They're usin' the open hearth fire to heat the iron an' beatin' it out on the stone floor. I came up 'ere 'cos I couldn't abide the noise. Ding! Bang! Ding! Bang! Me pore ole head's still ringin' inside.'

Lady Amber's manner was more practical than sympathetic. 'Don't tell me, Skip, you can't abide noise? Hah, 'tis usually you who creates most of the noise round here with your big foghorn voice. As for heights, if you haven't got a head for them I don't advise hanging round up here, you'll only make yourself ill. Why not pop down to the orchard and help the carpenters, that's far more peaceful.'

Skipper tugged on the pulley rope of the hoist. 'Good idea, marm, the orchard it is!'

The hoist was merely a system of counterweights. Skipper stepped aboard a small platform and it descended slowly. On the way down he was passed by the other platform, on which stood a squirrel with two blocks of sandstone going up. They waved to each other as the platforms passed.

'Where are ye bound, Skip?'

'Down to the orchard, matey, t'lend a paw with the beams.'

'Tell Gurdle to load mortar on that platform when y'get down. I'll leave one o' these blocks on as a counter-weight.'

A mole and four mice were waiting at the bottom, and they locked off the platform against a log protruding from the wall. The mole touched his snout in greeting. 'They'm needin' more blocks oop thurr, Skip?'

The otter stepped from the platform. 'Not at present, Gurdle, 'tis mortar they want.'

Gurdle and the mice began shovelling a mixture of sand, crushed limestone and water on to the platform. It would enable the builders to cement the heavy sandstone blocks firmly into place.

At the far corner of Redwall's orchard the carpenters had set up shop. A pit had been dug so that they could cut planking with long double-pawed saws, and there was a bench with vice, chisels and mallets, as well as a fire with augers and pokers resting in it. These would be used to bore holes, so the wood could be jointed with pegs. Seasoned trunks of elm, oak, beech, pine and sycamore were stacked against the wall in piles. Skipper loved the fragrant smells of fresh wood and heaps of bark shavings. A fat whiskery old bankvole with a charcoal stick behind one ear and a long canvas apron glanced up from a pine log he was working on and nodded at the otter Chieftain.

'Afternoon, Skip. D'ye fancy helpin' me strip the bark

off'n this timber? It'll make good skirtin' boards for the upper dormitories. I like pine, got a fragrance all of its own.'

Skipper found a spokeshave and began working on the other side of the log. Long pine slivers ran curling from his sharp blade, and Skipper sniffed fondly.

'Yore right, Migglo, 'tis a clean fresh smell. I can feel it clearin' me head up nicely.'

A dormouse popped her head up from the sawpit. 'Hello, Skip. How's it goin' on the south gable? I spotted you up there earlier. Huh, y'wouldn't get me anywhere that high, not for all the nuts in Mossflower, matey!'

Skipper blew off a shaving that had stuck to his nose. 'Aye, leave that to the squirrels an' a gang of crazy mice'n'hedgehogs who likes that sort o' thing. Well, I tell ye, marm, I was surprised 'ow far they'd gotten along. Lady Amber says another couple o' days should bring it to a peak. Then they can set up the weather vane.'

Migglo chuckled gruffly through his bushy whiskers. 'Amber's squirrels ain't settin' up no weather vane, 'tis Ferdy'n'Coggs who'll be doin' that job. Hohoho! Wait'll ye see those two bulky ole Cellar'ogs wobblin' about up there. They ain't lookin' forward to it, I can tell ye!'

Skipper smiled at the thought of Redwall's twin Cellar-hogs high on the south gable. 'No, nor would I fancy it!'

Carrying a big earthenware jug and beakers on a tray between them, Mayberry and Catkin the ottermaids awkwardly bobbed curtsies to all the workers.

'Miz Bella said to bring you a cool drink, mint leaf an' rosehip cordial from the cellars.'

'She said it'd wash the sawdust down, sir.'

Migglo swigged off a full beaker in one go. 'Just the stuff, colder'n ice an' very refreshin'. Thank ye.'

Skipper sipped his drink slowly, relishing it. The ottermaids topped up his beaker.

'We didn't know you were a carpenter, grandpa?'

He winked at them. 'Just shows yer, me pretties, you

don't know half the things yore ole grandpa can do.'

'Oh yes we do, we know lots of things you can do.'

'Do you now? Like wot?'

'We know you can hide underwater in the pond when 'tis your turn to wash pots'n'dishes.'

'Yes, an' we know you can wake everybeast when you talk in your sleep with your big loud voice.'

'And we know you can sup more hotroot soup than anybeast, and drink more October Ale and scoff more damson pudden . . .'

The otter Chieftain squinted fiercely at his two young granddaughters as he advanced on them. 'Haharr, me pretties, an' did ye know that I can clip the noses of liddle ottermaids with me spokeshave?'

They fled squealing and giggling from the orchard.

That evening it went cool suddenly. Standing on the outer wall ramparts of the Abbey, Bella and Columbine watched the enchanting sight of summer's last evening. Streaked to the west with slim dark cloud tails, the sunset was awesome. In the final moments the skies turned deep scarlet on the horizon, ranging up through crimson and rose to a delicate pink. Above this it faded to a broad band of buttery amber with soft dark blue pierced by the faint twinkle of early stars. Columbine let her breath out in a long wistful sigh.

'I hope my Gonff can see all of this beauty.'

Bella placed a paw gently on her friend's shoulder. 'I'm sure he can. I know he'll be thinking of you and the little one here at Redwall, awaiting his return.'

A random thought caused the mousewife to cover her mouth, stifling a chuckle. 'Unless there's food to be had, of course. Gonff would sooner gaze at a fruit puddin' than a sunset!'

Bella joined in her laughter. 'Then I suggest we post a daily lookout on this wall from now on. No doubt we can accommodate his sense of beauty with a big apple pie.'

37

A lively breeze stopped autumn's first day starting with a gentle mist. The *Honeysuckle* was positioned just below the brow of the hill, armed with slings and oars, and the crew and their Dunehog allies stood waiting.

Furmo tested the wind direction with a damp paw. 'Couldn't ask for a fairer breeze, Martin!'

The Warrior signalled to Folgrim. 'Off you go, mate, and don't forget to raise a shout at the right moment.'

The smallest of the Guosim shrews was bent double, wearing a cape which Trimp had made for Chugger. He grasped Folgrim's paw and toddled off over the hilltop, with the scarred otter adopting his old hunched hunting pose. Together they looked like a grandsire and his grandchild.

A stringy-looking weasel was arguing with a ferret, disputing over a wooden skewer festooned with insect and moth carcasses, which had been spiked there to roast over the fire. A motley collection of rats and assorted vermin watched them, knowing a fight was inevitable. As the weasel reached for the skewer, the ferret kicked him.

'Getcher dirty paws offa me vittles, longnose!'

The weasel was knocked forward, scorching his paw in the flames. He turned snarling at his tormentor.

'Half o' them are mine. Lift yer paw t'me agin an' I'll chop it off, greedyguts!'

Like a flash, a broad evil-looking blade appeared in the ferret's paw. He aimed another kick at the weasel.

'Yew couldn't chop yer way outta a daisy patch. Back off from those vittles, they're mine!'

The weasel shrugged, as if admitting defeat. Picking up the sharpened skewer, whose end was on fire, he turned to the ferret.

'Ah, wot's a pile o' squashed bugs t'me. You 'ave 'em!'

Bounding forward, he thrust the skewer hard into the ferret's gut. A shriek of agony rang out, and the ferret fell backward dying, stabbed through his stomach.

Callous laughter and coarse remarks greeted the cruel act.

'Haw haw haw! Somethin' upset 'is stummick!'

'Heeheehee! Ole Brango looks jus' like a bug on that skewer, lookit 'im wriggle!'

A fox who had lost interest in the gruesome spectacle happened to turn and look uphill. He caught sight of the two pitiful figures hobbling side by side.

'Oh lucky day, look wot's comin' this way, mates!'

Paws grasped blades as most of the vermin began inching towards the two unfortunate creatures, calling mockingly, 'Come an' join us fer dinner, friends.'

'Aye, don't be scared, you'll 'ave nought t'be worried about soon, ain't that right, mates?'

The two creatures halted, as if noticing the evil crew for the first time. Slowly they backed off uphill, crying piteously, 'Please don't hurt us, we're only poor travellers!'

Speeding up their advance, the vermin began to spread in an arc, trying to cut their quarry off. The poor travellers cut and run then, scampering uphill and yelling aloud, 'Help! Oh, help us somebeast! Help!'

Pulling a rusty axe from his belt the fox ran after them. 'I saw 'em first!'

The skinny weasel dashed past him, snarling. 'First there first served, brushtail!'

As Folgrim and the Guosim shrew reached the ridge-crest they were yanked aboard the *Honeysuckle*. Down the hill she thundered, the breeze billowing her sail full out. War cries rang round the hillside.

'Eulaliaaaaa! Redwaaaaaalll! Gorramahoggorraaaaa!'

The vermin were taken completely by surprise. Dinny whacked out with an oar, laying the skinny weasel out cold. Hard round slingstones cracked against skulls, ribs, paws and tails, filling the air like angry hornets in swarm. Heedless of the stupidity of their retreat, the vermin fled off downhill, with the *Honeysuckle* skimming behind them. Vurg caught the fox by his tail and dragged him along, whilst Beau hung over the side belabouring him with an oar. 'You thoroughly' Whack! 'despicable' Thwack whack! 'cad!'

A rat who was tripped by one of the for'ard oars leaped smartly up, only to be felled by Furmo, who from his position at the stern walloped him over the head. Onward plunged the vermin in their rout, hotly pursued by a skiff on wheels, leaving in its wake a trail of wounded and senseless creatures.

Finally the remnants of the ragtag vermin band broke, running off in separate directions, but not before Dunespike lassoed one. The terrified ferret was dragged aboard. He lay quivering on the deck of the still travelling craft, staring up into the fearsome scarred face of Folgrim.

Resting his axeblade between the ferret's eyes, the otter growled in a menacing voice, 'I see I've got yore attention, scumbrain, so lissen hard. We'll be sailin' these regions for the next couple o' seasons, huntin' down vermin an' cleanin' up the land. Yore lot are the first, ain't you the lucky ones. We're lettin' you live, so you an' yore cronies can spread the word round that we've arrived. Y'see that warrior with the nice sharp sword? He's our leader. Name o' Martin of Redwall, a very fair beast. He believes in givin' vermin a sportin' chance ... then slayin' 'em!'

Martin prodded the ferret with his bladetip. 'Up on your paws, bully, come on!'

Trembling uncontrollably the ferret rose. The *Honeysuckle* had slowed down minimally, breasting another rise, then she picked up speed, skimming downhill. Martin swung his sword up high. 'Jump or die?'

'Eeyaaaaagh!'

With a pitiful wail the ferret flung himself overboard. They watched him bounce and spin as he rolled downhill until a rock halted his progress with a juicy thud.

The breeze made a hissing sound as it ran through Dunespike's stickles, and he clapped his paws happily.

'An' isn't this the grand ould way t'be travellin'. Sure I've not had this much fun since I caught a jellyfish on me spikes. Cap'n Chugg sir, do we throw out the anchor at lunchtime, or does eatin' on the move sound like a grand ould idea to ye?'

Chugger gave Dunespike his captain's scowl. 'Wot a jellyfish is?'

The hedgehog Chieftain caught him and tickled Chugger until he broke down laughing.

'Yore a jellyfish, ye liddle omadorm, a fat wee jellyfish!'

Chugger rolled about, unable to escape. 'Heeheehee 'elp me, mista Fol! Heeheehee, I norra jellyfish, I on'y a likkle Chugg. Heeheehee, 'elp 'elp!'

The *Honeysuckle* did not stop for lunch; they kept on whilst the breezes favoured progress. During the afternoon the wind deserted the sails, and the skiff rolled to an easy halt, at the fringe of a copse.

Guosim cooks discovered a small spring among the trees, where the water was cool and sweet. Apples, pears and wild berries were plentiful. Lounging in the tree shade, the crew ate and drank their fill.

Dunespike looked about admiringly. 'Murfo, me son, does this place not look grand t'ye?'

'Aye, grand, da, grand 'tis!'

'An' a whole lot better'n livin' midst ould sand dunes?'

'Aye, 'twould be, da, 'twould be so!'

'Sure we've got fruit t'pick from the bough an' berries t'gather as we please. What would y'say to livin' here?'

'Oh, grand t'be sure, da. We'd want for nothin'!'

Dunespike cuffed his son's ear fondly. 'Well spoken. Take ten o' the lads an' start diggin' a good ould cave beneath these trees. I'll send the rest back t'the dunes for the babbies an' the elders. Would that be all right with you, Martin of Redwall?'

Martin was looking up at the sky, and replied absently, 'Yes, of course it will, Chief, providing you show us where Northfork stream lies.'

'Sure of course I will. What're ye starin' up at the sky for? Don't worry, it won't fall, it's been up there a long time.'

Martin spoke to Dunespike, though he was looking at Gonff. 'Birds are starting to fly south, the autumn has come.'

The Mousethief watched until the birds were out of sight. 'We must remember our word, mate. Time for us to fly home.'

Following breakfast in the Great Hall of Redwall Abbey, all the creatures sat awaiting the allotment of daily chores. Bella, whose duty it was to apportion the work, was deep in conversation with Abbess Germaine. Eager eyes watched the Badgermother as Redwallers speculated on which way the roster would go for them.

'Hope I'm helpin' Ferdy'n'Coggs in the cellars again!'

'Cellars are closed today, they've got to raise the weather vane on south gable. I'm not goin' up there!'

'Hurr, you'm wuddent be h'allowed oop thurr, zurr, on'y ee squirr'ls be on sou' gable to 'elp with ee vane.'

'Hope I don't get picked as cook's helper again. Huh, they had me scrubbin' pots all day last time.'

All talk ceased instantly when Bella rapped the table. 'Lady Amber and her squirrels will be assisting Ferdy and Coggs to raise the weather vane on the top of south gable.'

'Thurr see, jus' loik oi tole ee!'

Bella paused, looking in the direction of the interruption. There was a muffled giggle, followed by respectful silence. She waited a moment before continuing.

'All other building work today will be suspended. Migglo, Mayberry and Catkin, you are today's duty cooks.'

The whiskery old bankvole winked at both ottermaids, who wriggled and tittered excitedly, before realising the importance of their position and sitting up primly.

Bella nodded to the three Redwallers. 'Forget any cooking or baking for today, there's enough bread, scones and pastry been readied overnight. Concentrate on a cold buffet, salads, fruitcups and such. Skipper will take watch on the battlements for signs of our returning travellers. Without exception, every otherbeast within our walls is to go to the storerooms for sacks and baskets. Columbine, will you and Gurdle see that ladders and sticks are available, please?'

Some of the elders began smiling and nudging one another, but the younger element looked puzzled. Abbess Germaine allowed Bella to help her up on to the table, then she waved her paws in the air and called out in a reedy quaver, 'Then 'tis all to the orchard for fruit harvest!'

Gleeful cheers greeted this announcement, followed by chaos. Redwallers dashed to the storerooms, where Columbine was issuing sacks and baskets as fast as she could.

'Form a line there, don't push, there's plenty for all. Gonflet, take that sack off your head! Gurdle, will you see that all Dibbuns are given berry trugs, thank you!'

Passing out the small baskets to the little ones, the mole

chuckled at their antics. 'They'm be barskets, not sandals, take 'em off'n ee futtpaws.

Columbine was settling Abbess Germaine down in a wheelbarrow full of soft moss, beneath the shade of a spreading horse chestnut tree. Both of them broke down laughing at the sight of Bella leading the band of pickers in a harvest dance, singing as she went. Clutching Columbine's paw, the ancient Abbess chuckled. 'Oh dearie me an' preserve m'paws! It's like seeing a great boulder roll down a mountainside watching our Bella dance! Heeheehee!'

Columbine skipped aside as Bella hurtled by. 'Hahahaha! Maybe so, but there's those not even half Bella's age who can't keep up with her!'

Winding its way through trees and around bushes, the merry dance went on, with everybeast singing their hearts out.

'Now go good son and daughter,
Haste to our orchard fair,
And gather in the harvest,
Which lies a-waiting there.
Ripe apples, ripe apples, are falling to the ground,
As pears so sweet and juicy are lying all around!

Keep singing pretty daughter,
Until the work is done,
So you don't eat the berries,
And leave your mother none.
Blackberries, ripe cherries, don't bruise or break
    them miss,
For sweetness can be lost like a faithless lover's kiss!

The gooseberry and greengage,
Are bittersweet my son,
And damson has a heart stone,

You'll find before you're done.
Enchanting, enticing, like wild grape on the vine,
The maidens want to help you, to let their paws
    entwine!

So pick a berry, sing so merry,
Harvest time is here,
Go skipping round our orchard,
My son and daughter dear!'

Bella stood tall. Reaching a high branch she pulled it down to her face and sniffed deep. 'Aaahhh! Nought so sweet as the smell of a good russet apple on the bough. Mmmmm! I could sniff 'em all day!'

Beneath her a hogwife stood tapping her footpaw, sack held wide open and waiting. 'Beg pardon, miz Bell, but could y'leave off sniffin' an' start shakin' afore it goes dark?'

'Oops, silly old me. Sorry!'

The badger gave the bough a mighty shake, releasing ripe russets in a shower. When she looked down, the hogwife was still tapping her footpaws, two apples impaled on her headspikes, another two on her back.

'Tch tch! Miz Bell marm, 'twould be a help if'n you shook 'em into the sack!'

Columbine and Germaine were picking redcurrants, the Abbess keeping a curious eye on Gonflet.

'My dear, what is that little son of yours up to? He's supposed to be gathering raspberries, isn't he?'

Columbine could not help smiling as she watched the little mouse. He would fill both his smock pants with fruit, take a furtive glance left and right, then scurry off to empty his load into a trug hidden beneath the berry hedge.

'Hmm, just like his father, a real mousethief. He's not happy unless he thinks he's stealing something, Mother Abbess. I'll have to turn him upside down and shake him

351

before he goes to bed tonight. Otherwise there'll be raspberries squashed around the dormitory for the rest of the season. Little pickle. He's a good worker though!'

The harvesting was going well, moles trundling off to the storerooms with laden trollies as the fruit was picked and basketed or bagged up. At midday the cooks borrowed three trollies, to bring lunch for the pickers. Mayberry and Catkin repulsed any advances on the food with frosty glances and severe words.

'Not a single bite until you've washed at the pond!'

'Gracious me, look at those sticky paws. Away with you!'

Migglo gave them a whiskery grin. 'That's the stuff, missies, you tell 'em, go on, yore the cooks, 'tis up to you!'

Emboldened, the ottermaids spared nobeast from censure.

'Miz Bella, have you been pickin' apples with yore nose? You can just go an' wash y'face, this instant!'

'Hmph, shame on you, Mother Abbess, 'tis up t'you to set an example. Look at yourself, redcurrant juice from tail to ears. Gurdle, help her to get washed, please!'

Columbine's giggles were cut short as they turned their attentions upon her.

''Tis no laughin' matter, miz Columbine, shame on you!'

'Aye, woe 'pon you if'n mister Gonff was to see y'now. We'll inspect those paws after you've washed 'em!'

It was a simple and satisfying lunch which had been prepared for the harvesters. Sliced apples, cheese and fresh crusty bread, with new cider or cold mint tea to sip and strawberries with meadowcream for dessert. Columbine sat beneath the chestnut tree with her friends, still shaking her head and smiling over the bossy cooks.

'Honestly, I felt just like a naughty Dibbun, the way those two young snips ordered me off to the pond!'

The Abbess sandwiched a wedge of cheese with bread. 'Me too, bless their hearts. They meant well, though.'

Bella snorted. 'Meant well? The little tyrants, they sent me back to the pond twice, to wash my snout properly!'

Migglo had been eavesdropping, and he called across to them, 'Aye, but they're a credit to ole Skipper, that they are!'

Suddenly, everybeast started with fright as a loud cry rent the air.

'Redwaaaaaaaaaalll!'

Bella was on her paws in a flash, pointing upward. 'Look! They've raised the weather vane on south gable!'

Everybeast in the orchard raised their paws and returned the shout to the tiny figures high up on the Abbey building.

'Redwaaaaaaaaaallll!'

Cheering broke out as the Squirrelqueen, Lady Amber, stood out, balancing on the crosspieces of the iron vane, swaying as a light breeze turned its metal arrow topspike. Ferdy and Coggs clung to the North and South struts, waving jubilantly to their friends below. As Columbine gazed up at the completed south wall, she hugged the Abbess. 'Oh, they've done it, Mother Abbess. Isn't it beautiful!'

Germaine looked for as long as she could, then shut her eyes tight to stem the tears.

'At last! My Redwall Abbey. I never thought I'd live to see the dream become reality!'

Bella picked the Abbess up as though she weighed nothing, sitting the ancient mouse upon her shoulder to allow her a better view. Whilst Germaine was up there, Bella took advantage of her robe hem to wipe her own eyes.

'Three cheers for Redwall Abbey. May it stand as long as seasons change and the sun rises, my friends!'

Never were three cheers raised so joyously.

'Hurrah! Hurrah! Hurrah!'

38

On a rare boisterous autumn morn, two otters stood waist deep in the waters where Northfork stream merged with the main flow seaward. It was here in the swirl of currents that the finest watershrimp were to be found. Unstaking a long tubular reed net, they hauled it carefully to the bank. The elder of the pair, a sleek tough otterwife, instructed her half-grown son in the rudiments of his tribe's fishing tradition.

'Always haul the net in slow'n'easy, Jiddy. I seen silly beasts lose all their catch many a time, from rushin' things. There now, lookit our net, son, bulgin' with the liddle beauties. Tie the end off good'n'tight, that's it!'

Grinning from ear to ear, Jiddy patted the well-packed net. 'Haharr, wait'll Chief Tungro claps eyes on this lot! I bet by next season he'll let me come 'ere alone—'

The young otter had no time for further conversation. His mother knocked him flat into the cover of hanging willow fronds. Stifling his mouth with a swift paw, she lay beside him, peering upstream at the strange craft in the distance.

'Strike me rudder, will y'look at that thing. I ain't never seen nothin' like it in these waters. Wait! I'd know that beast standin' in the bows if'n he was the last otter on earth. C'mon, Jid, let's get the bad news back to Tungro!'

They hurried off southward along the bank, toting the loaded net between them, with Jiddy, like most youngsters, besieging his mother with questions.

'It was an otter on that boat, I saw 'im too. But why's it bad news for Tungro? Does he know the otter?'

'Hah, know 'im? I'll say he does. That's Folgrim, his mad brother. I thought we'd seen the last o' that 'un.'

'Mad? Why's he mad? What did he do?'

'Well he used t'go huntin' vermin, an' when he caught up with 'em he'd, er, he'd . . . Never you mind what he did. Now keep up, an' don't drop that net or 'twill burst!'

The day was rather overcast, though the sun showed at intervals, between masses of grey-white cloud, which the playful wind chased to the south-east. The *Honeysuckle* rode at half sail, Furmo steering her into the bank, which was crowded with otters. Trimp stood alongside Folgrim, watching him closely.

'My goodness, Fol, they've all turned out to welcome you home. See, there's your brother Tungro!'

Chugger launched himself from the mast on to his friend Folgrim's shoulders. 'Tchah! Otters not welcome you, mista Fol, nobeast laugh or shout 'ello t'you, big long faces on 'em.'

Folgrim settled the little squirrel on his strong shoulders. 'They got good cause not t'be cheery, mate. My tribe fears me. I was nought but a load o' trouble to 'em.'

Chugger growled. 'Gurrr! You not t'ubble, mista Fol, you my matey. I choppa they tails off for ya!'

Folgrim slid over the side, still carrying Chugger. 'You sit up there an' be'ave yoreself now. Leave this t'me.'

Otters parted ranks, fearing to be near the returning warrior. But Tungro waded swiftly forward. Clasping Folgrim's paws tightly he smiled into the heavily scarred face with great fondness.

'My brother, welcome back to the holt! Come on, matey, bring y'liddle friend, bring all yore friends. Rest and eat!'

The holt was an enlarged bank cave, old and very comfortable, filled with beautifully carved furniture, which was the speciality of Tungro's tribe, who were master craftsbeasts, proud of their carpentry skills. Most of the tribe were still wary of Folgrim, so he kept to the company of the *Honeysuckle*'s crew. They sat on elaborately carved benches by the fire, dining on fresh hotroot and watershrimp soup, oatfarls and a riverbank salad.

Martin and Gonff sat at a highly polished table with Tungro, who poured steaming blackberry and sage cordial for them whilst the cooks served their food.

'You and your friends have worked wonders with my brother. He is not the same savage beast, thanks to you, Martin.'

The Warrior sipped his cordial gratefully. 'Don't give me the credit, friend. It was young Trimp and little Chugger who wrought the change in Folgrim.'

Turning to Gonff, the otter enquired, 'Why do you keep staring at me, Mousethief?'

The irrepressible Gonff shrugged. 'The more I look at you, the stronger you remind me of somebeast. Martin, would you say Tungro resembles Skipper?'

'Aye, mate, now you come to mention it, he does, very much!'

Tungro sat up at the mention of the name. 'Skipper? Is he an otter about old enough to be my father?'

Gonff slapped the table. 'I knew it, yore related to him!'

A faraway look entered Tungro's eyes as he unfolded the tale.

'My grandmother gave birth to three sons on the same day, Bargud, my father, and his two brothers, Riverwyte and Warthorn. Riverwyte was much like my brother Folgrim, a great fighter and slayer of vermin. Everybeast thought him sick in the head because of his love for battle.

He left our holt to go roving, and they say his tail was severed by foebeasts. An otter without a rudder, as you know, is like a fish without water. Riverwyte became a woodland dweller, a master of disguises, and he called himself Mask because of this. Travellers told my father that he had been slain, though where, when an' how it all happened we never got t'know. The other brother, Warthorn, was the biggest an' strongest of all three. He left the holt when he was scarce half grown, because he couldn't ever buckle down to my grandfather's strict rule. Warthorn was such a natural leader that nobeast used his given name, they nicknamed him Skipper, which is a title we give to otter Chieftains. Anyhow, he went off to found his own tribe an' hasn't been heard of since. When Bargud my father was alive, he'd look at me an' say that I was the image of his lost brother Skipper. Then he'd turn to Folgrim an' say that he was the double of Riverwyte, his other brother.'

Martin leaned across the table and held Tungro's paw. 'Would you like to meet your uncle Warthorn?'

Tungro nodded wistfully. 'I'd love to, I've heard so many tales about him, but he'd left this holt long afore I was born. Do y'think I ever could meet Warthorn?'

'Certainly, my friend. Journey to Redwall with us, and you will.'

A few days later, Log a Log Furmo's large fierce wife, Honeysuckle, was coping with her brood on the stream-bank of their summer camp. Energetically she scrubbed at the wriggling body of her eldest.

'Be still, you liddle worm. I'll teach ye to roll about in that midden of a water margin, filthy shrew!' Flicking out with a wet rag she caught another young one a stinging slap across the tail. 'Git yore paws away from those scones, or I'll chop y'tail off an' bake ye in a pie. Go on, be off with you!'

Four tiny shrewmaids came dashing along the bank,

squeaking, 'Mamma mamma, daddy's comin' in a big boat wiv a sail!'

Honeysuckle grabbed the nearest one. 'Just lookit the bankmud on that smock, an' it was clean on this very morn. Go an' git a fresh one off'n yore granma, not one of those off the rock ledge, they ain't dry yet. So, the great rovin' Log a Log's decided to come home again, has he?'

Furmo's deep rich voice hailed her from upriver. 'Honeysuckle me precious, I'm back, O dew of me life!'

She scowled at Furmo, standing heroically in the prow of the skiff as it sailed inshore. Twirling the corner of a face cloth she wiggled it down the ear of the little shrew she was attempting to clean up. 'Back at the end o' summer, my darlin', I'll return on the first autumn mist, O jewel o' the woodlands. What time d'ye call this t'be gettin' back, you great useless lump o' Guosimfur, eh?'

Gonff sprinted ashore, with two shrews in his wake, carrying a carved otter footstool and several strings of Dunehog quills and beads in various gaudy colours. He pointed to the name plate on the skiff's bow, planting a genteel kiss on the shrew wife's sud-covered paw.

'O beauteous beast, yore spouse brings ye gifts from afar, an' all borne on a fine vessel that carries yore own fair name. He has done nought but pine f'you night'n'day!'

Honeysuckle melted immediately in the face of Gonff's gallantry. Fluttering her eyelids, she gave him a playful shove, which sent him sprawling in the shallows.

'Oh, mister Gonff, you ole flatterer, fancy callin' that luvly ship after me. Wotever gave you the idea?'

The Prince of Mousethieves stood up, shaking water from his rear end, still spouting eloquently. ''Twas all your good Furmo's idea, m'lady. We wanted to call the boat *Gullywacker*, but he wouldn't hear of it. No no, sez he, we must call it *Honeysuckle* after my beloved!'

Furmo gasped as Honeysuckle grabbed him from the prow and squeezed the air from his lungs in a mighty embrace.

'Ow ow, I wronged you, me dear one, forgive me. All these wunnerful things you brought back for yore wife. Ow ow, I could cut out me tongue for wot I said about you!'

Furmo managed to gasp out in a stifled mutter, 'Cut yore tongue out? No such luck, more's the pity!'

She dropped him in the shallows. 'Wot was that you said?'

Furmo scrambled up, thinking quickly. 'I said, cut yore tongue out? No no, my duck, yore far too pretty!'

Vurg and his friends were greatly taken with the shrewbabes, but none more so than Beau. The gluttonous hare allowed the tiny creatures to feed him vast amounts of food at the noontide meal.

'Can you eat more plum pudden, sir?'

'Just try me, laddie. Shove it this way, wot!'

'My mamma maked this salad, sir, d'you like it?'

'Rather! What a clever lady your mamma is. Fill m'bowl up again, there's a good little tyke!'

'D'you like apple'n'pear turnover, sir?'

'Like it? Steer it in my direction, y'young tailwagger, an' I'll show you whether I like it!'

Honeysuckle perched gingerly on the footstool, which she thought was a small chair, casting a jaundiced eye in Beau's direction.

'I'd hate t'be standin' next to that long-eared rabbit in a famine season. Where does he put it all? No thanks to you, Gonff, you fetched 'im 'ere, an' that tribe o' starvin' otters too. We'll soon be eaten out o' house'n'home!'

Gonff tweaked the shrew wife's cheek slyly.

'Well, me beauty, you don't want vittles goin' stale in the larder. Not whilst yore away on the nice trip that Furmo's planned for you!'

'Trip? Furmo never told me about no trip?'

'Aha, that's 'cos he wants to surprise you, pretty one. How d'you fancy a nice boat trip to Redwall Abbey?'

'Ow ow, bless 'is good 'eart, is there nothin' Furmo

wouldn't do fer me? Wot a wunnerful thoughtful beast 'e is!'

Furmo waggled a paw in his numbed ear. 'Oh, give yore wailin' a rest an' pass the beer.'

'Wot was that you said, Furmo Log a Log?'

'I said, my love's unfailin', nothin' but the best for you, my dear!'

Squeaks of fright from the little ones caused Martin to leap up, sword in paw. A dark shadow circled overhead, suddenly dropping like a stone into their midst. The great goshawk, Krar Woodwatcher, folded his wings and bowed courteously.

'Oh joyous day, thou hast returned to my fiefdom, Prince of Mousethieves, and thou too, Martin Warrior of Redwall.'

Gonff nodded formally, with appropriate regal disdain. 'Lackaday, sirrah, have thou a care, landing in such manner 'mongst the babes of Furmo, our faithful vassal!'

Krar lowered his beak to the ground in the face of such royal displeasure from the Prince of Mousethieves.

'Alas, 'twas not my intention to affright the babes thus, Prince. My hasty landing was prompted by a desire to be in company with thee an' thy noblebeasts once more.'

Martin allowed his footpaw to touch the lethal beak. Krar did not see him exchange a wink with Gonff.

'I pray you, Prince Gonff, be not wrathful with our friend Woodwatcher. For we know him to be a good an' honest bird. Tarry with us, Krar, there are victuals aplenty here.'

The huge fierce goshawk awaited Gonff's decision. Sensing he had pushed his luck far enough with the dangerous bird, Gonff smiled magnanimously, patting the ground at his side.

'I spoke in haste. Come, sit thee beside me, my faithful friend. It comes to my mind that one who battled with a swan in our defence must surely be worthy of our hospitality!'

Honeysuckle nudged Furmo, almost knocking him over. 'D'ye hear that? Why don't you learn to speak like Gonff an' Martin? Proper gentlebeasts they are!'

Beau sat watching in open-mouthed admiration as food vanished down Krar's beak at an alarming rate.

'Great seasons o' starvation, d'you suppose that chap'll be able to fly when he's finished scoffin', wot wot?'

Trimp could not help teasing the hare with a wry comment. 'I wonder if the Redwall Abbey kitchens will have enough food to keep up with the both of you?'

Dinny shook his head at the hedgehog maid's observation. 'Burr aye, miz, oi 'adn't thought o' that. They'm two'll keep ee cooks gurtly busy, oi'm surrting o' that!'

Travelling upstream was not difficult as they traced back their original path. Tungro's tribe were strong swimmers, and they weaved in and out of the growing flotilla of shrew logboats surrounding the *Honeysuckle*, lending strong paws wherever they were needed. On a lazy golden afternoon, Gonff lay stretched out beneath the stern awning, tossing hazelnut pieces in the air and catching them in his mouth. Martin was napping nearby, whiskers gently twitching against a curious midge, bent on investigating his face. A fragment of nut, which Gonff had missed, bounced off Martin's nose, and he opened one eye slowly.

'D'you mind not disturbing me? It's not often I get the chance of an odd snooze.'

Gonff aimed another piece of nut at his companion. 'Snooze? How can you talk about snoozin', mate, we're nearly home! I'll be seein' my Columbine soon, haha, an' that Gonflet o' mine. Wonder if he's grown at all?'

Martin stared up at the changing leaf patterns, blinking as the sun traced through, blurring the edges.

'Oh, I imagine Gonflet will be tall enough to cause us more trouble, young scamp! Hope the work on our

Abbey has progressed without too much bother. I bet Bella's missed us, though the kitchen crew will probably be glad you're gone. Pies can lie cooling on windowsills in safety.'

'Hah! Not with my Gonflet runnin' loose they won't!'

In one smooth motion, Tungro slid aboard the skiff. He whispered urgently to Martin, 'We're due to run into trouble, I think!'

The Warrior lay still, though his paw was seeking his blade. 'What makes you think that, friend?'

'Well I can 'ear a waterfall somewheres up ahead, but that ain't really it. Somebeasts are followin' us. I saw movement in the trees, ripples in our wake, an' I think they're up ahead of us too!'

Immediately Martin arose, sword in paw. 'Sounds like they've got us surrounded, eh, Gonff?'

'You two stop here. I'll go an' take a peek.'

Gonff crawled out on deck and took stock of the situation. Tungro's otters were in the water, guarding the shrew logboats, which Furmo had grouped around the *Honeysuckle*. Only the streamsounds and the distant waterfall broke the ominous silence. Suddenly the soft autumn noontide had grown dangerous. Krar perched upon the *Honeysuckle*'s prow, watching keenly. Folgrim had his axe out, and was standing in the stern of the back logboat. Furmo and his Guosim crouched, rapiers drawn. Gonff held up his paws, signalling everybeast to wait. His eye caught a movement in a tree-shaded shallow.

Then the Mousethief relaxed, waving his paws for the crew to stand down. He shouted then, his voice cutting the stillness. 'Haharr, I'll bite y'tail off an' stuff it down yore ear!'

A gruff voice responded from the shallows. 'Surrender, mousey, yer surrounded, mate!'

Gonff gave a broad wink to the Guosim shrews. 'Surrounded? Y'great lard barrel, stay there, I'm comin' to surround you, ye forty-faced frogflusher!'

Hurling himself from the deck, Gonff hit the water with a loud splash and threw himself on to the creature which sped out from the bank. Streamwater boiled in chaos as the pair met, roaring and bellowing.

'Garraway Bullow, ye bangtailed riverdog, I knowed it was you all along. Take that!'

'Whupperyhoo, Gonffo, don't try t'fool me. You was scared out o'yore mousey wits, admit it!'

'Scared? I been scareder of dead logs floatin' in the water. Only thing I'm scared of is that you won't 'ave supper ready, ye whiskery waterwet puddenwalloper!'

Yelling with delight, Folgrim and Tungro dived into the water. 'Auntie Garraway, 'tis us, yore nephews!'

'Oh no, lock the larders, it's Bargud's brats. Lookit the size of 'em. My pore sister must've starved t'death tryin' to feed 'em. Gonffo, get 'em off me!'

Otters of Garraway's tribe began popping up everywhere, shouting to the otters from Tungro's crew, who yelled back at them. Trimp looked to Martin, who was chuckling and shaking his head at their antics.

'It looks like the two tribes are related. We're surrounded by aunts, uncles, nieces and nephews. Yugggh!'

A large pawful of soggy bankmud caught Martin full on the nose. Both groups of otters were so happy to see each other that they had started a mud fight. The remainder of the *Honeysuckle*'s crew and Furmo's shrews did not hesitate. Laughing madly they leaped into the water, joining in the fun. Right along the bank they fought, slinging heaps of sludgy brown mud at one another, slipping, sliding and splashing as they pelted away furiously. Mud was everywhere! Swiftly aimed globs of the sticky goo splattered, sticking to fur, spikes, muzzles, paws and tails. A practically unrecognisable hedgehog maid stumbled into what appeared to be a small moving mud mound.

'Heehee, is dat you, miz Trimp?'

'Hahaha, of course it is, who're·you?'

'On'y a likkle Chugg, take dat!'

'Yutch! You filthy imp, don't chuck mud at me. Throw it at those otters, they started it!'

'Heehee, I frow muds at everybeast, here some more f'you!'

Whizz! Splat! Splotch! Whopp!

Only Krar remained aloof, perched on the skiff's prow, shaking his head in disgust at the undignified spectacle.

'Zounds, 'tis surely a day of fools' delight. These riverdogs are a mad species methinks. Yawch!'

A mud-covered Beau stooped to gather more. 'Oh, well hit, Fethringsol. Maybe that'll spoil the great pompous featherbag's appetite, wot!'

Evening had fallen by the time both sides had wearied of mud throwing and washed themselves off in the stream. Queen Garraway Bullow took a last chance to grab her nephews and duck them soundly.

Gonff waded over. 'Ahoy, what's goin' on here? Tryin' to drown off yore kin?'

'That's right, Gonffo. Disrespectful rascals, I'll teach 'em to address me as Yore Majesty, not auntie Garraway. Well, friend, we'd best rest up awhile, then I'll have my crew rig blocks'n'tackles to pull yore pretty boat over the waterfall. 'Tis the least I can do for such fighters!'

Folgrim broke the surface, blowing water. 'Aye, 'cos if you don't yore name'll be mud for ever!'

39

Milk-white mist covered the land up to the height of a tall elm tree. Early dawn silence lay over Redwall Abbey, disturbed only by muted birdsong from afar. It was an hour after dawn. Skipper and Bella leaned on the north battlements, with Gonflet between them. Keeping a paw behind the little mouse, Bella cautioned him, 'Stay away from the battlement edge. Your mum'll have a word or two to say if I let you fall.'

Gonflet stamped his paws in frustration, peering into the blanket of mist. 'When'll my daddy be's comin' back, Skip?'

Skipper sat the tiny fellow on his shoulder, out of harm.

'Oh, don't you fret, mate, he'll come back soon now. Maybe later on, when the mist lifts.'

Gonflet tugged the otter's ear. 'Phwaw! You say that alla time, every day, Skip!'

Columbine's voice sounded from the lawn below. 'Hello, Bella, Skip, where are you?'

'Up 'ere, marm, west corner o' north wall!'

Columbine came up the wallsteps, carrying a tray, which she placed on the wall.

'Gracious, you three are up here early today. Surely there's not much point yet, with all this autumn mist about. Gonflet, shouldn't you still be in your bed?'

'No no, it my turn to watch for daddy. Miz Bell an' Skip 'elpin' me. My daddy come soon, you see!'

Columbine stroked her son's head fondly. 'Yes, I'm sure he will. Oh, look, the mist is turning gold! Come and have some breakfast now. The sun will burn all this mist away before long.'

Columbine stayed on the ramparts with them. Still surrounded by the cocoon of golden autumnal mist, they ate bowls of hot oatmeal with fresh berries and honey.

With otters hauling and shrews pushing, the skiff *Honeysuckle* slid over the ditch and out of west Mossflower's trees on to the path. It was the same spot where Trimp had met Ferdy and Coggs a season before.

Gonff called through the mist to Martin, 'Hoist the sail, matey!'

Furmo shook his head at the Mousethief. 'Wot d'you want the sail spread for, matey? We're in a fog, there ain't a feather o' breeze nowheres to stir her sail.'

Taking a brightly coloured Guosim headband, Gonff bound it about his brow. He climbed to the prow and struck a pose. 'You an' the breeze can do what you like, Log a Log, but if I'm comin' home then I'm goin' to arrive in style, eh, Martin?'

His friend joined him on the prow, drawing his sword and pointing forward in an equally heroic pose. 'Right, mate. Let's go home!'

Furmo nodded admiringly at the pair. 'That's the way, crewmates. Come on, everybeast, we'll grease the wheels, comb our whiskers, haul the ropes an' sing our friends home every bit o' the way. You all know "Journey's End". Trimp, you take the top harmony, I'll do the baritone, an' Garraway the bass. One two three . . .'

Away the *Honeysuckle* rolled down the path, with her crew pulling the headropes, two tribes of otters and a tribe of Guosim crowding round to push, Martin, Gonff,

Dinny and Trimp, the original four who had set out from the Abbey, all standing in the prow. Krar perched on the masthead, keeping a firm grip on Chugger, who still considered himself captain.

Now the sun was beginning to thin the mist, they could see through it. As they rounded a bend by a grove of oaks the singing suddenly died, and the *Honeysuckle* rolled to a halt. Everybeast looked up and saw Redwall.

Floating above the golden mist like a vision from some wondrous dream, south gable reared to the soft blue skies, with the weather vane standing proud atop the dusty rose-coloured sandstone buttresses. It was a magical, breathtaking sight. For one awestruck moment they all stood, gazing dumbly, then a mighty cheer broke out. Dinny chuckled proudly, through tears he was unable to check, 'Yonder be moi 'ome!'

Gonflet sprang from Skipper's shoulders on to the north-west corner battlement, which was higher than the rest. Skipper held out his paws for the little mouse to jump back down again.

'Come offa there, matey, you can't see anythin' yet in this mist.'

Columbine sensed something. She looked up at her son. 'Gonflet, what is it?'

'I 'ear 'em, mamma! Lissen! Daddy comes 'ome! Lissen!'

Faintly at first, but growing in volume, the sound of manybeasts singing reached the walltops. Bella scrambled up on to the battlement, and laughed aloud with joy.

'There's a ship coming down the path! A ship! Would you believe it, friends, I see them! I see them!'

High into the sunny morning the song rang out.

'Marching home! Marching home!
Jolly friend! Jolly friend!

Trav'lling on, until our journey's end,
So away with all your fears,
Smile with me forget those tears,
Though the road was long an' dusty we survived.
And arrived!
Tramp tramp tramp tramp,
Lay your head down where you camp,
It ain't your home or fireside.
Tramp tramp tramp tramp,
Moorlands dry or forests damp,
Sharing together side by side.

Marching home! Marching home!
Jolly friend! Jolly friend!
O'er each highland, around each river's bend,
Keep your chin up in the rain,
Soon we'll be back home again,
Though my paws are worn an' weary never fear.
Oh my dear!
Left right left right,
Onward mate by day or night,
Lean on my shoulder now old friend,
Left right left right,
Grey the day or sunlight bright,
Until we reach our journey's end.
Marching home! Marching home!'

Bella's shouts boomed like thunder over the lawns.

'Rouse yourselves, Redwallers, they're back! Turn out
the cooks! Open the gates! They've come back home!'

As Ferdy and Coggs flung the outer gates wide,
Columbine allowed Gonflet to dash off and meet the ship.
He was swept aboard and lifted on to his father's
shoulders. Ferdy and Coggs, still in their nightshirts, held
the outer wall gates wide open. With all the creatures of
Redwall pushing it, the skiff *Honeysuckle* sailed regally
inside, halting in the centre of the main lawn. Gonff

leaped down with Gonflet still on his shoulders, swept Columbine up and hugged her tight. 'Yore Prince o' Mousethieves is returned, milady!'

Chaotic greetings broke out everywhere.

'Oh, Dinny, our faithful Foremole, how we missed you, my friend. Welcome home, welcome home!'

'Hurr, thankee, miz Bell, oi missed ee too, aye, so gurtly that oi be lostened furr wurds, marm!'

'Uncle Warthorn, it is you, ain't it?'

'Well rip me rudder, so 'tis. Don't tell me yore Bargud's sons? Lookit the size o' you both. Wot were ye fed on, boulders'n'logs? Fergit Warthorn, call me Skip. 'Ere, come an' meet Mayberry an' Catkin. I thinks they're yore cousins, but I'll let ye know when I works it out!'

'Ferdy, Coggs, hello there, 'tis me!'

'Why so 'tis, miz Trimp, y'look taller, I think!'

'Aye, an' pretty as ever. Good to 'ave ye back, me dear!'

'H'i name Chugg, only a likkle squiggle, but lotsa t'ubble!'

'Me called Gonflet, I lotsa t'ubble too, Chugg!'

'Ahoy there, Skip, whupperyhoo to ye. Let go o' those two bullies an' shake yore otterkin's paw, ye ole rascal!'

'Haharr, Garraway Bullow, me ole heart's delight. C'mere, me second cousin twice removed an' longtailed on yore granma's side!'

Amid the shouting and laughing as old friends were reunited and new ones made, a small stooped figure, leaning on a blackthorn stick, shuffled across the lawn. Everybeast made way for Abbess Germaine. Mayberry and Catkin hurried forward, assisting her to the *Honeysuckle*'s prow, where Martin stood waiting to meet her. Drawing his sword he knelt, laying it at the old mouse's footpaws. She smiled.

'Martin of Redwall, you have returned to us, my friend.'

'Aye, Mother Abbess. It was a good journey, a long and eventful summer. I am happy to be back at Redwall.'

The Abbess Germaine waved her stick at the strange craft standing in the middle of the lawn, with a great goshawk perched on its prow.

'An eventful summer indeed, Martin. What is all this?'

'That is Log a Log Furmo's skiff *Honeysuckle*, named after his goodwife, marm. Yonder noble bird is Krar Woodwatcher, a valiant fighter and a great friend to us. These shrews are Guosim, and we have with us two tribes of otters, the tribes of Queen Garraway Bullow and the brothers Folgrim and Tungro.'

Abbess Germaine silenced Martin by raising her paw.

'Enough. You will confuse my old mind if you carry on further, Martin. Welcome, welcome to you all, peace be with you, may you find happiness and joy within Redwall Abbey. If there is anything you need from me or my Redwallers, please do not hesitate to ask for it.'

In the brief silence which followed this announcement, the old hare confronted the Abbess with a courteous, though slightly creaky, bow.

'Beauclair Fethringsol Cosfortingham at y'service, marm. I was, er, wonderin', wot, er, if perchance, you maybe had, er, a slight, hmmmmm, beggin' y'pardon of course, er, er . . .'

Germaine nodded. She understood him completely. 'I take it you are hungry, mister Cosfortingham?'

Beau nodded eagerly, still stammering. 'Quite, er ah, thank ye, marm, I am mayhap a little, er, shall we say, er, peckish?'

Smiling broadly, the old Abbess took his paw. 'I never knew a hare who was not hungry, sir. We have been preparing since the back end of summer for such an event, and we have plenty enough for everybeast including you, sir. Is everything ready, Bella?'

The Badgermother nodded, pointing towards the orchard. 'By the time the mist has risen completely. Cooks, servers, cellarhogs, helpers, to your stations for the feast!'

A mighty cheer arose into the autumn morn as the Redwall helpers hurried off to the kitchens for their trolleys. Paw in paw all the guests strolled off behind them, chatting animatedly at the prospect of Redwall hospitality.

'A feast eh wot, hope there's enough for all this lot, wot?'

'Burr, zurr, you'm bain't never been to ee Redwall feast. Thurr be enuff gudd vittles to keep twice this yurr number a-goin' furr ee full season. Hurr aye!'

'Ahoy, Ferdy, wait'll you see ole Krar take to the vittles. That bird could make you look like a Dibbun at table!'

'We'll see about that, Gonff. What about yon hare?'

'Hoho, don't even ask, matey. His name should've been Famine, not Fethringsol. Don't sit next to him!'

'I sit by you, Gonflet, we eats everyfink all up, eh?'

'Ho yiss, but later, Chugg, come wiv me, we pincha pies off the windowsills, they still coolin'. Heehee!'

'Looks like you've got double trouble there, miz Columbine.'

'You could be right, Skip, treble trouble if you count Gonff. But better the trouble that we know, and at least they're home safe and sound!'

'Gurr, 'ome, marm, bain't et a wunnerful word!'

Epilogue

Extract from the journal of Germaine, Mother Abbess of Redwall Abbey.

'It is winter now, a time for sitting round the fire in Cavern Hole and storytelling on long dark evenings. By the time next winter arrives our Abbey will be completely built. Never have we had so many welcome and useful guests. This beautiful desk I am sitting at was made by the tribe of Tungro, as is all our furniture – what wonderfully skilled craftsbeasts those otters are. His brother Folgrim is to stay here and live with us; he and Skipper have become inseparable. Many of our guests will stay permanently. It gives me great joy, they are good hardworking creatures. Trimp and Chugger are now part of Gonff's family. How could they not be happy with two such as our Prince of Mousethieves and his lovely wife Columbine. Everybeast here says that I still have many seasons in front of me. I hope so, Redwall is such a joyous place to be. I look forward each morning to breakfast with my close companions, Vurg and Beau. I wish I could have gone sea roving with them in my younger seasons. What adventures they have had!

Martin seems to have regained his old zest for life. He is not the troubled Warrior any more. It was a wondrous tale he had to tell, both of himself and his brave father Luke. It was also very sad at times, but does not sadness mingle with joy, to make us grow fully into the creatures we are? Strangest of all, though, he showed me something from a beaded linen bag, which belonged to his poor mother. It was a woven tapestry of his grandsire, who was also called Martin. The picture is of a mouse in armour, bearing a great sword. I was amazed, it looked like Martin himself, to the very life. Though he said to me that it reminded him greatly of Luke, his father. Columbine has had a lovely idea: she thinks that the picture might form a centrepiece for a big tapestry, which would someday hang in Great Hall. When I look at the picture I know it is our Martin. I think that he and his ancestors have always been warriors, champions, whose spirit exists to inspire good honest creatures.

Martin has also done a remarkable thing. He has decided to give up his sword and live a life of peace. He has done so much to help found our Abbey that no creature could deny him the right to do this. The goshawk, Krar Woodwatcher, has hidden the sword where Martin directed him to put it. The only hint he gave of the great sword's location was to me and no other. These are his words.

Above where autumn's mists do rise,
Where I beheld with mine own eyes,
My dream, my vision, hov'ring there,
One morn upon old Mossflower's air.

Then he said a strange thing to me which I will tell to you.

I stand here in this world alone,

No kin of mine to take the sword,
No son or daughter of my own,
A bitter and a sad reward,
But Redwall in its hour of need,
Will bring forth one to follow me,
To that one, valiant in deed,
I leave a Warrior's legacy.

Then he would talk no more of such matters. Now i
I want to find him, I have only to follow the sound o
our Abbey babes, the Dibbuns, laughing and playing
Martin will be there, joining in with them; Gonff too
They are both enjoying a new-found happiness, though
I doubt that our Prince of Mousethieves ever really
grew up. Perhaps Martin is making up for the los
seasons of his youth, who knows? It does every
Redwaller's heart good to see him thus.

Well, my friends, I am tired now, that is the privilege
of an old Abbess, burdened with so many long seasons.
I will go down to Cavern Hole and sit in my big chair
by the fire, with a blanket on my lap. There I can listen
to the songs and the stories, watch the young ones
dance and play, drink some hot cordial and drift off
into a warm sleep, whilst winter reigns outside in the
night. I won't say goodbye to you, because one evening
you may drop by to share this good life with us. You
know you are always welcome at Redwall Abbey. All
you need to bring with you is a ready smile and an
open heart.

Germaine, Abbess of Redwall.